Holliday

Matthew Di Paoli

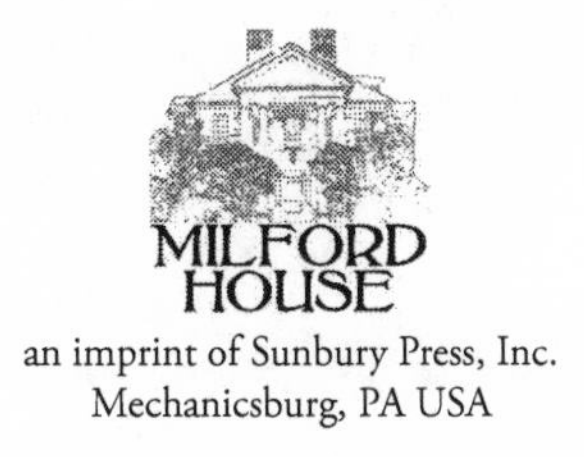

an imprint of Sunbury Press, Inc.
Mechanicsburg, PA USA

an imprint of Sunbury Press, Inc.
Mechanicsburg, PA USA

For information about special discounts for bulk purchases, please contact Sunbury Press Orders Dept. at (855) 338-8359 or orders@sunburypress.com.

To request one of our authors for speaking engagements or book signings, please contact Sunbury Press Publicity Dept. at publicity@sunburypress.com.

FIRST MILFORD HOUSE PRESS EDITION: June 2023

Set in Adobe Garamond Pro | Interior design by Crystal Devine | Cover by Lawrence Knorr | Edited by Jennifer Cappello.

Publisher's Cataloging-in-Publication Data
Names: Di Paoli, Matthew, author.
Title: Holliday / Matthew Di Paoli.
Description: First trade paperback edition. | Mechanicsburg, PA : Milford House Press, 2023.
Summary: Western legend Doc Holliday seeks the Fountain of Youth to cure him from his tuberculosis. He is helped and hindered by a cast of familiar characters.
Identifiers: ISBN : 978-1-62006-959-2 (paperback) | 979-8-88819-047-0 (ePub).
Subjects: FICTION / Westerns | FICTION / Biographical | FICTION / Historical / Civil War Era.

Product of the United States of America
0 1 1 2 3 5 8 13 21 34 55

Continue the Enlightenment!

To Mom

Contents

Author's Note

Each chapter was written alongside and inspired by a song. For an extrasensory experience, use this playlist as a reading companion.

1 Every Day Is Exactly the Same / Nine Inch Nails
2 Burning of the Midnight Lamp / Jimi Hendrix
3 Man in the Box / Alice in Chains
4 Black Hole Sun / Soundgarden
5 Hard Sun / Eddie Vedder
6 Working Class Hero / John Lennon
7 Satin in a Coffin / Modest Mouse
8 Opium / Marcy Playground
9 When You Were Young / The Killers
10 Shelter from the Storm / Bob Dylan
11 Paint It Black / The Rolling Stones
12 Tomorrow Goes Away / Delta Spirit
13 [If] You Want Trouble / Nick Waterhouse
14 Somebody That I Used to Know / Gotye
15 Pale Horse / Smashing Pumpkins
16 Where Did You Sleep Last Night / Leadbelly
17 Fake Empire / The National
18 Lonely Boy / The Black Keys
19 Hunting Bears / Radiohead
20 Short Change Hero / The Heavy
21 Alabama Song / The Doors
22 Man on Fire / Edward Sharpe and the Magnetic Zeroes
23 Like the Wheel / Tallest Man on Earth
24 Son of a Preacher Man / Dusty Springfield
25 Stubborn Love / The Lumineers
26 I Have Nothing / Noah and the Whale
27 Fool / Neutral Milk Hotel
28 Banking on a Myth / Andrew Bird

CHAPTER 1

Every Day Is Exactly the Same

Dallas, 1874

The saloon was a long, narrow room. The bartender stood behind the pine on the right, doling out booze to morning drunkards and, in the back, a loud faro game carried over from the night before. The beleaguered dealer seemed relieved to see Doc, who sat down at a table fit for one but with two chairs. He ordered three shots, an antelope steak, and buckwheat cakes, which he ate with an acute awareness of his mustache.

He cut his steak into cubes and ate each one a half-minute apart, enjoying the dry sting of the whiskey between bites. A tall man with a crusted scar above his lip and his holster showing walked over from the faro table and sat down across from Doc.

"Why, Harrison," said Doc, recognizing the man from a game earlier in the week. "I don't think I have enough for the both of us." His chalky Southern accent still contained a boyish lilt.

"That's okay. I take it bloody anyways." Harrison grabbed one of Doc's drinks and chugged it down. "You owe me from the other night, Holliday."

"That's funny," Doc placed a cube of antelope on his tongue, "I remember winning the other night."

"You cheated."

"So did you. It appears I'm simply better at it than you are. Replace my whiskey. It helps my condition."

"I don't take orders from no lungers." Harrison clenched his thick, hairy fingers on the table.

"Now, why would you say something hateful?"

All the eyes in the saloon fell on Doc. He felt rock quiet. He remembered the sound of chimes in Georgia and how one night when there was no wind, they stopped. He imagined his rounds as freedom—the wheeze and squeal of the chamber. He smelled the powder and burnt flesh. They followed him like a prayer.

"I heard you was a dentist anyway. What's a dentist doing getting himself into card playing and trouble like this, Doc?" said Harrison.

"My friends call me Doc. We ain't friends." Doc swigged down his last whiskey and motioned for another. The bartender remained frozen. "The service is just terrible here."

"Just gimme my money 'fore I end you, John Henry Holliday."

"You know, Harrison, it seems to me that you haven't given enough thought to what that end means, really. You're a misfit, God's regret. Or maybe you don't believe in anything more than the soil they scatter on you. Are you godless, Harrison?"

Harrison reached down and gripped his gun in his holster. He peered back at the faro table and then straight into Doc. "You don't ever question a man's God, lunger. I'm right square with God at this moment. I'ma better man than you."

Doc smiled. His mustache curled up like horns. He flicked his pistol from under the table and buried two shots square in Harrison's scruffy neck. "I'm convinced."

Harrison strained and thrashed to cover the holes as blood spurted onto the table; Doc lifted his buckwheat cakes away from the mess. After a few seconds of gurgling, Harrison's head dropped to the table, and his hat rolled off and down toward the bar.

"What'd you go and do that for, Doc?" said the barkeep, still teetering behind the bar. "You're not gonna be welcome here."

"Self-defense. Clear as day." Doc had made a few friends in this town, and as he searched the room, he didn't see any of them. "I'll return the plate," he added, walking out with his meal and his gun.

Doc's face simmered with new blood as he walked the streets of Dallas. He always felt less human after he'd killed someone. Like the little bit of himself that he still kept from home bled out as they did. His mother had taught him to calculate risk, anticipate every outcome, and he always did, as if it preserved her in some way; but there remained that primal moment just before the draw when he could let it all scatter to the floor. He felt nothing but the sugary drip of death in the back of his throat.

The only reason he'd headed out west in the first place was that he'd heard rumors of a wellness spring that could cure him of his consumption. Every cow town he went to though, they always said it was in the next one. But they'd all heard of it. Linwood he'd heard it called, but it wasn't on any map. He always got closer, but never close enough to smell the hot salt or taste it in his aching throat. The only thing he tasted in the Dallas streets was shit.

The spring went by many names, as it had throughout history, and much greater men had followed the path and grown old and died before ever reaching their destination. Some claimed south, in the land of the Ethiopians, or in the Caribbean, but Doc knew that his salvation lay due west. His mother taught him about this spring. The Age of Exploration, she called it. But John Henry believed wholly in his own exploration. Its restorative powers fascinated him as a child, and he actively read about Ponce de Leon, the writings of Herodotus, and Alexander the Great. However, none of them understood that this spring, this "fountain of youth," as they'd called it, would only accept desperation. Only a man at the last twist of his knot could unearth it.

Doc remembered when he first found out, the winter of 1873. It had started out as a nagging cough, and he'd lost some weight. By the summer, the cough hadn't subsided, and John Henry took time off from dentistry to tend to his health. His uncle, Dr. John Holliday, had retired from medical practice, but Doc had always trusted his steady hands. Uncle John felt around with his stethoscope and bronchoscope. Suddenly, he paused and said, "You tended to your mother's ills, didn't you?"

"Much as I could," said John Henry.

"You've got the same she had. Pulmonary tuberculosis they call it."

John Henry didn't need its name. He knew exactly what it was and what it did. His mother had died from it not all that long back. He briefly mourned his future.

"Anything to be done?"

"Medicine is improving all the time now. My recommendation is that you head out and find some warm, dry air. Eat nutritiously like Alice taught you and drink a moderate amount of wine as you feel the cough coming on. Should soothe you. I expect you'll return here fit as a daisy within six months." Then he paused as if he'd been holding something back all along. He ran his hands over his round belly, and they trembled a little. "If things don't improve in that time, there's a spring out west. It's well-known over there. Seek it out. Supposed to work wonders for consumption. Supposed to work wonders for just about anything if you can find it. If you get there, you mightn't have any other choice."

A year had come and gone since that day.

Doc thought of his uncle's fat, cherry face as he walked down Main. He was a long way from Atlanta where everything seemed to flower. Here, everything turned to dust. The town stunk of rot and manure and the ripe stench of sweat on leather. It hung in the air like fog. Sometimes, so much dirt dusted up that it was hard to see beyond five feet, and sometimes you could look out toward the mountains and witness the hand of God at work in the clouds and the sound of the sky at night.

The people of Dallas grew film on them like unwashed teeth. They yellowed and hollowed. Even the ones who'd found wealth wore it like a mask, unsure how to behave other than as the glistening animals they were. Silvered, buttressed, their canes supporting their crooked backs. Walking down Main Street, Doc always noticed a pony that no one bothered to bathe. She never grew old, only stank like burnt apples as she thrashed her clumsy tail against a ceaseless onslaught of flies. Doc felt sorry for her small body and her upbringing in a world where all the color had been drained, destined to be ridden to her death.

The storefronts did not fit the rest of the town, each one lopsided, uniquely misshapen, and bright as June. Doc always got dirt in his mouth when he turned a corner. He tipped his hat to the old coffin smith, a strange codger dealing in the sordid specificity of death; one part deranged, one part godly, and one part sage like a purgatorial cocktail.

Unable to play cards, Doc decided he might as well go to work. He took a left at the dance hall and headed for his office. His dusty glass door read:

John Henry Holliday D.D.S.

A few disgruntled patients, fidgeting with pain, waited in his cramped lobby. His associate had bought two wicker chairs for the room. They'd already sprung holes, but they were sturdy enough, figured Doc. He scrutinized a bald man whose teeth seemed too big for his mouth. They jutted out in opposing directions.

"Hope that blood ain't from a patient of yours," said the bald man. There was blood in the cracks of his teeth, and it trickled out as he spoke. It dried brown on his lips like silt.

"There's blood to be found all over this town," said Doc, smiling. Next to the bald man sat a young lady he'd seen before. Sadie Marcus. "Won't you come in?"

"I got here first, Holliday," said the bald man.

"You'll have to excuse my patient's manners, Mrs. Marcus," said Doc. "A hot tooth can make anyone less of a gentleman."

The bald man nodded in Mrs. Marcus's direction. "'Scuse me, ma'am."

She followed the good dentist into the adjoining examination room.

Doc spread out his tools carefully and with a steady hand. A glaring gas lamp hung down like a pool cue from the middle of the room. The dentist's chair was little more than a wooden armchair with a headrest, slightly reclined. Doc sat next to it on a cushioned stool. Several modern paintings that he'd acquired through debts and travel hung on the walls. The Thomas Colville that particularly moved him—a desert scene at dusk. A tired wagon, its owner trying to spark a fire before the ash clouds disappeared into moon and mountainside. It calmed him as he operated.

Mrs. Marcus had very deliberate features, a mole under her jaw, suited to an actress. Her figure appeared like a peep-show silhouette under her tight dress. She was busty but lithe like a dragonfly, and her lace sleeves gleamed like iridescent wings.

"Why, Sadie, this is the third time this month. You must have the filthiest mouth in Dallas."

Mrs. Marcus sat in the chair and hiked up her dress so that it bunched up around her garters. "I highly doubt you're suddenly interested in my teeth, Doc," she said.

He tore open her corset and ran his lips over her chest so that his mustache tickled her. She liked that, he knew.

"I'm leaving on tour tomorrow, so make it memorable."

Doc recalled all the times they'd been together in the bright lights of his office, her husband just outside. Something excited her about it, and there was the added depravity of his being paid afterward. Usually, for Doc, it was the other way around. He wheezed as he thrust into her, and his bowie knife skidded cool along his back. "You know—now that you mention it, I don't think I've ever seen the inside of your mouth."

She looked at him sideways.

"Professionally, I mean."

They went at it for a good while, and Doc dripped salty sweat when they stopped, sunken into the dentist's chair and gasping for air. Mrs. Marcus got up to straighten out her dress. Doc leaned back into the wet leather; sweat matted his mustache, beading up along his brow and sallow cheeks. A moist, gray stain spread on the leather. He coughed phlegm, motioning to Sadie for his flask.

Reluctantly, she handed it to him. "You ought to lay off the bottle, Doc."

"Doctor's orders."

He walked her out, grabbing his black cane because he felt weak. He knew his uncle had told him wine and not whiskey, but there was nothing to be gained in wine, and a dentist certainly couldn't practice in good faith with teeth the color of priests' robes. He felt closer to his end every moment, but he would endeavor onward. He'd keep looking for this miracle hot spring deep in the uncharted territories of the feral West. He'd search until he was bone.

Mrs. Marcus's husband waited impatiently for her in the lobby. "You okay, honey? I ain't never heard you scream like that. Was worried."

She nodded. "I know. And I doubt you will. Mr. Holliday here really went to work today."

"She's all set then?" asked Mr. Marcus.

"Good as new," said Doc, his cheeks flush, still covered in salty white perspiration. "Won't need to see her for a while."

She turned back to look at him, a bit sad, as if he'd given her away. But she didn't belong to him. Nobody did.

Mr. Marcus handed Doc a ten and tipped his hat as he left.

CHAPTER 2

Burning of the Midnight Lamp

The next morning, Doc smoked lazily at the Dallas hotel window. The weather had turned drizzly and gray. But he didn't need the sun to tell him he'd slept past noon again and hadn't made any of his appointments. Sometimes he thought about giving up the practice altogether. But dentistry and draws were the only times he felt calm. He was a dentist with the hands of a gunman, or maybe it was the other way.

Doc grabbed his long gray overcoat from the foot of his bed and slipped it over his nightshirt because he felt cold and because his whiskey was in the front pocket. His bowie knife hung from his neck like a pendant. He liked to sleep with it rather than his pearl-handled .38, which he kept close. He downed half the pint quickly, and even though it burned a little, it felt warm in his chest and nothing else made him feel warm that way. His cure—or at least a way to put off what consumed him.

He shivered and coughed but finished his cigarette and tossed it out into the rain. Below, townsfolk floated languidly by the road like specters. Doc watched as their camel and coal bowlers passed under his window, disappearing into the saloon. He should have gone to the office, but he decided to play some faro instead. Besides, he was nearly out of booze.

Doc was a precise dresser. He took his time to button his blue shirt and straighten his tie around his neck because he figured he could be hanging from it any time now. Sweeping the knife around carefully, he trimmed his ash-blond mustache so that it didn't curl too far over his lips, and he combed his hair straight back but a little to the right because Mattie had said she liked it that way when they were back in Atlanta. He kept her last letter, from over a month ago, in his pocket next to his flask. He placed a five-inch sheath knife in his breast pocket, buttoned his coat, and headed out.

The walk from his hotel to the saloon was short, shorter than to his office, but it didn't lack distractions. Dens of sin, prostitution, and religion lined Main Street, which was forever mired in horse dung and stained black and yellow by cigarette tar and piss. The church basement doubled as a bordello at night, and since there was no place to pray, many of the religious types gathered in insurance offices and bought fire coverage while reciting the rosary. A few carriages clinked by, loaded with tinctures and salves glowing violet from within their thick glass bottles. It was a Tuesday, and the rain made a hollow sound when it hit Doc's boots.

He turned onto Elm because he enjoyed the smell of cotton and buffalo hide. That's what they sold there, stalls all the way down the street. Hundreds of mustachioed men sniffed and poked and fingered the hide. Sometimes Doc wondered what they did with that hide when they got home with it. A man and his skin and his secrets. There was a blonde woman, mid-thirties, who would go from vendor to vendor, many of them horse-drawn carriages moving from town to town. She would take the cotton in her hands, lick her lips, and then throw it in the vendor's face. She never bought anything. That morning, Doc decided to approach her.

"Morning."

She looked around as if incredulous. Perhaps no one had ever spoken to her during her morning ventures. Doc spotted a wedding ring on her hand. She had a home to go back to. She was almost pretty in a useless sort of way—like a sparrow, unaware it could fly.

"Why is it that you never buy any of this cotton? Every morning you come here and don't buy cotton from these men."

"I hate the feel of cotton. It makes my belly turn inside out," she said and walked away. That was the last time Doc saw her on Elm Street.

Dallas was laid out in a grid, clustered in the center and then sparse with bald cypress and houses on the outskirts with a great big hunk of iron rail splitting it in two. Alongside the roads lay mulch fields, newly plucked and brown, surrounded by long, spider-legged grass that gave the countryside a little color where there were no trees.

In Dallas, it was either real quiet or the huff and clank of the railroad swelled in the air. The girls, all trussed up from the dance halls, called out to Doc. They were plump and smoked with their white petticoats showing under their red dresses. So much rouge. He loved them, their breasts bursting out of their corsets. Doc revered impropriety in women, so long as they were not his women. They even wore their hats lewdly so that he just wanted to rip them off and tamp them into the ground and tousle their long hair. Doc liked prostitutes because they were unafraid. He liked the way they all smelled like apples and how he could see their stockings even during the day.

"This your first time, honey?" one called from the porch of Louise's dance hall, not recognizing Doc hunched over with a pain in his belly. The consumption ate at him from the inside, contorted him into something unrecognizable. He'd come to manage it though; he pushed up on his cane and straightened out so she could see his eyes. "Oh hey, Doc. Sorry 'bout that. Y'all come see me later. The ladies miss you already."

Doc tipped his hat.

The dance halls weren't full-time brothels yet. But there were those, too. And people knew where to find them, so the girls didn't bother making a fuss. They waited. Some of them knew him, whispered about how he'd killed Harrison and some other Cowboys and thugs in the towns before Dallas. Each one considered him a prize because he was a real man and a gentleman, and he told them stories of what it was like to impart death.

With a fresh ten, Doc headed for Austin's Saloon; it was one of the last places he was still welcome. It wasn't a spacious place, especially around the narrow bar. Various sporting pictures hung on the walls, mostly of strongmen and white-clad boxers about to engage in fisticuffs. A few regulars lingered with warm, foamy beers at the pine bar watching themselves intoxicate through the triplet of mirrors looming over the bartender's shoulders. The room Doc frequented, of course, was the faro and poker room. It was larger by a good boxcar length, and the smoke was not as thick, trapped against the thin bar walls in the other room. A couple of chintzy chandeliers lit the place orange. The room reeked of lamp gas.

Only one other man sat at the faro table, a stoic-looking young sport. His mustache was thicker than Doc's, and he'd crumpled his sun-drawn face into his hands, elbows on the table, signaling he'd met a cold streak. He wasn't wearing a hat, so his bushy black hair was on full display. His long duster hung down over his stool, nothing too fancy. It actually had a couple of holes singed into it. He looked like he was heeled. Doc liked him almost immediately.

"You a regular player?" Doc asked the man. He motioned to one of the prostitutes by the bar and she came rushing over.

"A glass, Doc?" she asked.

"Don't be ridiculous, Kate. We've got company." He gestured to the stranger.

"Bottle then. Make hay while the sun shines."

Kate was a well-known soiled dove. She'd come over from Hungary some years back and spoke three languages but had learned long ago that men wanted to feel smarter than she was, and to feel at home, so she acquired an affinity for folksy American sayings to obscure her accent. She made good money at

Austin's selling her body for coin. She wore her red hair with flair and spark, and Doc always figured she really could've *been* something in a different world. But flesh would always sell, and she'd always be trading it. She had light gray eyes and sharp features. There was something in the way she moved that made her feline. She wasn't all that busty but made up for it with a bustier and long legs that she liked to show off.

"Not much of a drinker no more." The man's eyes didn't leave the game. The dealer flipped a jack.

"Neither am I," said Doc cheerfully. "We'll just have one bottle." He paused to introduce himself. "Name's John Henry Holliday." He was feeling especially affable with money in his pocket, but a fit of coughing suddenly took over. He hawked up a drop of blood that settled onto the felt and quickly wiped it away with his handkerchief. "You'll have to excuse my malady."

"Wyatt Earp," said the man, extending his hand as his eyes followed the thin trail of blood to Doc's pallid lips.

"That's a strong name. My friends call me Doc. And my enemies, I guess. Is there anyone who doesn't call me Doc, darlin'?" he asked Kate. She rushed over and playfully jumped onto his lap. It pinched his scrawny legs, but he liked when she was light and spontaneous because no one else ever was around him. She had a real liveliness about her, and she'd grown real fond of him over his time in Dallas. Doc didn't even mind too much that she was a prostitute. He looked forward to the days when he would see her, which were most, lately.

"You sent all of them to the bone orchard," she said, grinning.

"She's prone to hyperbole." He licked his cracked lips, anticipating the liquor. "You a gambling man, Mr. Earp?"

"Depends on the stakes," said Wyatt.

"Here ya go, Big Nose," said the bartender.

Kate leaped up, scurrying to and from the bar with an auburn bottle and three glasses. *They oughtn't to have called her that*, thought Doc. It wasn't even that much bigger than most, but in small towns, nicknames have a way of sticking. She wore a sheer pink shawl over her frilly corset. She had the face of a girl unused to being treated kindly, with a mole painted onto her left cheek like a wannabe actress. Her lipstick, like always, was satin red to attract customers, but usually she gave her services to Doc for free. He treated her more like a lady than the others.

"Come. Sit," he said to her, downing the first shot and filling up again. She sat back down on Doc's lap, where she was completely content. He wrapped his thin arm around her waist. "See, this game is pure," he said to Wyatt.

"That's why I like it. It's a rare quality around here." Faro felt instinctual to him now. "You have a loser the first card, a winner the second, and then the neck—the final three cards of the shoe. You can bet on those."

The felt was worn, caked with bourbon, ash, and spit. Each card was represented in a crescent along the table. Doc placed two dollars on the deuce and Wyatt put his on the queen.

"Loser, four. Winner deuce," said the dealer.

Doc smiled so that his mustache parted up toward his newborn blue eyes. "Some men get all the luck." He downed another shot but immediately after was again reduced to a fit of coughing as Kate caressed his back. He squeezed her hand lightly but then released her to tend to his cards.

"Sounds like you ain't got all of it," said Wyatt.

"Maybe so." Doc poured a shot for Wyatt, who just eyed it there next to his dirty knuckles and his chips.

"That is why we're here, after all," Kate chimed in.

Wyatt scrunched his face in confusion and licked the bottom of his mustache.

"The fountain. It will have Doc right as rain."

"Nothin' that good in Dallas, missy," said Wyatt.

"Maybe so, but we'll search the whole West until Doc's in apple-pie order," said Kate with blind conviction. "Isn't that right?" she kissed Doc's forehead.

He offered a fleeting smile. "With our boots on," said Doc holding up his glass, his Southern drawl exaggerated from the whiskey. It was a phrase he'd always liked and seemed more fitting every day. The soldiers would say it: 'Better to get shot with your boots on than die in a sick bed just waiting for it to come.' That's how he figured it, anyway.

Wyatt wrapped his fingers around his glass and raised it neck-high to Doc. They drank it down. Doc hardly made an expression anymore as it ignited his throat.

That night, Doc slept in sweaty alcoholic tremors with Kate by his side. They hadn't accomplished much when they got up to his room. Kate stroked him for a while as he drifted off. He didn't mind too much falling asleep next to her. He never trusted other women enough to share his bed.

Sometime before dawn, a knock came. Kate peeked over at Doc, who was asleep in a shadow of perspiration. Wanting to let him rest, she slipped on a shawl and cracked open the thick pine door. It was Mr. Marcus. He held a knife in his large, hairy palm.

CHAPTER 3

Man in the Box

They met eye to eye. Before she could shut it, Mr. Marcus slipped his fat hand inside, knocked open the door, and backhanded Kate clean across the face. The strike sent her careening into the dresser; blood percolated from the back of her head. Marcus crept up to the bed, observing Doc's slight figure with disgust.

"Get up, you piece of shit. You defiled my wife. Now I'm gonna take out your heart." He pulled a Wragg knife from his waistband, shaking Doc out of slumber with his free hand.

Doc rose hazily, still drunk. "Why, Mr. Marcus, what a pleasant surprise. Is everything all right with your wife's fillings?" he slurred.

In wild, jealous fury, Mr. Marcus leaped on top of the bed and began stabbing at Doc, catching his shoulder before he squirmed away onto the floor. Dazed, Doc reached back for his bowie hanging around his neck. Marcus was already above him and ready to strike him down when two shots rang off in succession. Marcus's chest puffed out pink, and he crumpled onto the oyster bed sheets. The blood rippled out of him in dark rings and filled the bed. He was still alive, and his eyes were open. He made a strange whistling sound in his throat as if the air were being let out of a balloon, and then he suddenly went silent, though his nose hairs continued to vibrate for a short time after.

Kate shook in the corner of the room by the door, a wild look in her eyes—holding a .41 caliber double Derringer.

From the floor, Doc asked, "That your first time?"

Kate slid down the wall, still staring at Mr. Marcus bleeding out on the bed, and the gun clattered softly to the wooden floor.

Moved by her protectiveness of him, Doc pushed himself up using the box spring and his uninjured arm and dragged a clean sheet over to Kate to calm her. He eased down next to her, put his arms around her, and held her to his chest. *A woman who's just killed for the first time is bound to be in some sort of nasty shock,* he thought.

Kate trembled with heat.

"Talk to me. It'll ease your worry, darlin'."

"There was—" she was having trouble getting the words out, flashing between sweat and chill. "A man back in Hungary. I was twelve. He had his hands around my throat. He'd paid extra for it. His fingers smelled like ash and pork. I couldn't breathe. I saw sparks in front of me; a headless angel, and it handed me the pistol. I shot him in the foot. He was off me all of a sudden, rolling on the hardwood floor, wrapping his trousers around the hole. The smoke obscured the blood."

They both looked down at the gun next to her pretty little hand, and the answer was yes; it was her first time, and they'd had it together.

Blood from his arm and her head leaked onto the sheet, mingling with the spatter from Mr. Marcus. Doc's heart was pounding. "Well, darlin', looks like you and I are cut from the same cloth. I guess you'll be leaving with me after all." He attempted to camouflage his fear. He knew his actions had cost an honest man his life. Everything around him ended in seared flesh, and he couldn't protect Kate. He couldn't lose her either. There wasn't any room left for it.

Kate nodded absently.

"I'll round us up a couple horses. Maybe we'll find that spring we're after. Every town needs a dentist, right?" He tried to distract her from the body, but it was useless. He couldn't even distract himself. "Clean yourself up and meet me in back of the hotel in fifteen minutes. And never answer the door with anything but a bullet. I got no friends other than you."

"Are we friends?" asked Kate. "I haven't got friends either."

Doc knelt down and kissed her.

She wasn't sure of anything in that moment but kissing him back. It was the only thing that made any sense to either of them.

"I'll never be your friend, darlin'. That's what's so great about us." Doc rubbed her head like a child who'd just fallen, grabbed his cane, his gun, and his flask and left.

In the dark of night, Doc visited a few acquaintances who owed him various debts. He procured whatever cash he could and bartered his way into two horses by morning. Doc held about as much belief in lawyers as he did in priests. It wasn't worth waiting around for a trial. They were as likely to string her up as they were to call her a hero. The last woman hanged was Frances Kidder in '68.

She'd drowned her stepdaughter in a ditch. Doc knew this because Kate told him once. She was terrified of the lawlessness inside her.

The ride shouldn't be very long, he figured, but he'd never had the best sense of direction other than being able to point himself due west, apparently. Kate met him as he'd asked, at the hotel. He'd packed up whatever dentistry tools he could manage along with most of his wardrobe and his pistols, of course. She carried a small bag, which seemed too heavy for her. Doc loaded it onto the horse. She saddled up like a man, her dress ruffling against the horse's sides, legs spread apart. It was almost erotic to Doc, thinking about her garters pressing against its hair. He wondered how the ride felt on her.

"Do you always ride like that?"

She was still shaken but seemed to have regained some of her sass. "Do you?"

By sunrise, the two of them were off to find sanctuary. Doc felt weak and leaned deep into his horse as they rode toward Fort Worth. It'd be a while, and there wasn't much to speak of. Kate wasn't chatty like usual.

Doc knew how she was feeling. She wasn't hopeful or scared or alive—she was numb.

About an hour into the ride, they came across a man who'd been hanged. He hung from a tall, spiny tree with stumps for branches, which seemed out of place alone by the trailside. He wasn't old or young, but as the sun hit him, they saw his face was contorted from the shock of it.

Doc recalled his first kill. They were both so young, he and his corpse. He imagined Kate felt the same way.

Death made Doc recollect things he'd kept hidden away. He remembered being only fourteen at his mother's bedside when she could hardly speak anymore. He wondered if that's when he'd caught it, nestling up to her, trying to get any warmth she had left for him. It wasn't much, but as she slept, he'd keep his head close to hers so he could feel her breath. It was just about the only time she wasn't coughing or spitting up. Her face was so white that sometimes she looked like she'd already been dead for weeks, withered up in that bed, that blue quilt pulled up to her breasts.

During the day, he didn't see her much because she insisted on his schooling: Latin, French, and the histories. It was only at night, when she could muster the energy, that they could talk a little. Her voice was burnt out from the ulcers in her throat.

"Was Pa a hero in the war?" John Henry asked.

"He had to resign, boy," she whispered.

"What for?"

"He had the runs all the time. I don't think you'll be reading about Major Holliday in any of your texts." She had a little smirk on her face as she said it.

"What about you?" John Henry curled up into her frail arms.

"What about me? I'm as big a hero as there ever was. I raised you, didn't I? Never saw a boy get into more trouble than hours in the day." She squeezed him as hard as she could, straining to kiss his cheek, but she was too frail. She sighed and eased back into the down pillow, closing her eyes. John Henry slept there that night. They both dreamt of places they might never live to see.

CHAPTER 4

Black Hole Sun

Fort Worth, Texas
1877

In the desert the lightning is silent. The sky bends and shakes and the clouds contort until they succumb to the will of God; when it rains, it hits the earth like silver coins; and when you sleep, you feel the cold through the earth. You feel it in your gut and in your bones.

Doc and Kate felt fear in the desert. Their horses felt thirst and the prickly pears, lacebark pines, and fishhook barrels underfoot as they rode over the dry, beige land. It was only the cobalt mountains etched straight into the future that gave them any hope they'd ever find Fort Worth. Kate obsessively glanced back, assuming that eventually there would be a rifle aimed at her and she'd pay for her crime, but there never was.

They sweated and told stories of what it was like before they met and how lonely you could be with someone else. Kate told the story of a Mexican teen who'd fallen in love with her and spent all his money on sex. He was thrown in prison as a debtor. She visited him once out of guilt. He said it was all worth it. Every bit. He died two months later from an infection. She thought that was the saddest, most romantic thing anyone had ever said. Doc agreed. In a way, he and Kate found each other in that desert, surrounded by the brush and darkness.

It was only a thirty-five-mile ride, and though he kept the mountains in sight, by the middle of the second day, Doc worried he'd lost the way. He didn't mention it to Kate. All they had to do was head west with a slight tilt south. It seemed simple, but without a compass, Doc feared they might never leave the desert.

"This is taking longer than making ice in June," said Kate.

Doc smiled. He could see her little Hungarian cogs pulling out American phrases like weeds. He found it adorable. "Just a little longer. I can see the city lights from here."

"I can't see a thing."

"If you were a little taller, you'd see all types of things," Doc lied. "Just keep riding."

On the second night, when they were nearly about to quit and turn back (not that they knew where to turn back to), they spotted a bonfire a half-mile off.

"We must be getting close," said Doc.

"I pray every second." Kate heeled the horse in its belly, and it trotted faster. As they approached, they saw trees and came to a small stream. Three travelers sat on logs around the fire. They aimed their rifles straight at Doc as his figure appeared in the darkness.

"Easy now, my fellow saddle bugs. My name is John Henry Holliday, and this is Kate Elder. We're traveling to Fort Worth," Doc called out. He dangled his hand by his holster. Their eyes glowed in the firelight like dogs.

They were smoking some meat, and next to the flame lay a doe with its stomach carved out. Around its legs, a vein of blood formed in a thick, syrupy vine that ran off toward the stream. Next to it lay a bear trap, some furs, a couple more rifles, and some leather goods that were harder to make out in the dim orange light.

"Still a ways to go," said one of the men. Of the three, two were white men, one clean-shaven with a gray hat, one a bit older, shaggier, and the other was a Native whose hands were shackled. The Indian had a sash over his chest, but he wore regular chaps like the other two. His feet were uncovered and pale with fungus on their soles.

"Would it be possible to camp with you until daybreak? We don't want anything but rest. If you could spare venison it'd be welcome too."

"We're decent folk," added Kate.

"No need to lie now, dear," Doc whispered.

Kate shot him a look. She and Doc neared with their horses. The three travelers kept silent. They just watched Doc and Kate and kept their rifles up. Doc stopped the horse once they got close enough and dismounted.

"I like your Indian," said Doc, lying through his smiling teeth. "Very exotic." *What a piss-poor way to treat a man of this earth,* he hought. *We grab his land, shoot his food for sport, and drag him around like a trophy. These men ought to be dragged around sometime.* But today wasn't that day.

"There's rewards for 'em in town," said the shaggy man. He had a long, fresh gash under his left eye.

Kate dismounted too.

"Would you mind putting down your rifles? It's been a long trip from Dallas," said Doc.

"Travelin' with women always slows it down," said the clean-shaven man. "Dallas ain't far neither. Name is Billy. This here's my brother Ike. We're the Clanton boys. You probably heard a us. Ain't that right?" Billy pulled on the Indian's long black hair. He yanked it so hard the Indian slipped backward, knocking his head hard against the dirt.

The trees around them didn't move. The leaves didn't move. The air didn't move. Only the fire crackled a little, and the Indian moaned and bled from his temple.

"Not so fucking hard!" said Ike. He smacked his brother's hat off. "Worth more alive."

Kate cringed at their cruelty. Doc tied the horses to a tree and brought her into his arms. He kept his right side free in case he needed to draw.

"Goddamn fucking Indians bleed so easy," said Billy, feeling around for his hat in the dark. The firelight only stretched up to their foreheads, so their features became lost in the night if they leaned back any. "Can't tell their faces from blood anyhow."

"So, is it all right if we stay?" said Doc. "She needs rest, and the horses too."

"An' you?" Ike leaned in far enough for Doc to smell his rank hair and beard. "You don't need no rest?"

"I'm a creature of the night. I survive on blood, tobacco, and bourbon."

Ike spat toward the Indian and righted him on the log again. "Yeah, sure. Ya can stay long as you respect our rules."

"What are your rules?" asked Doc. He ushered Kate down onto a log, marking their territory for the night.

"Well," Ike pushed his brother. "Tell him our rules."

"What rules?"

Ike smacked Billy. This time, Billy had secured his hat better. "Don't steal our Indian, and when we say it's time to go, you get." Ike finally lowered the rifle.

"Sounds peachy," said Doc.

"Where you from anyways?" asked Ike.

"I'm from Georgia. Kate here is a woman of the world."

"Yeah, she look it," said Billy.

Doc thought about shooting him dead right there, but he was a guest, and a guest should never kill his host. Doc maintained a strict moral code of propriety common to any Southern gentleman such as himself.

So, he sat with the two savages and the Native and drank the last of his bourbon supply, smoking tobacco until the sun dripped through the trees. Doc laid out his coat, and Kate slept on it. He wondered what dreams she might have and if they would be of him.

Ike and Billy pointed them in the direction of Fort Worth when morning came. In the distance, the Trinity River appeared, and it was clear that they would not die in the desert. A steamship bobbed along it, churning the river as white as the ship. The land grew fertile at the riverbanks, and tall willows and lush shrubs leaned toward the water's mouth. A freshness came off it.

Kate let out an audible sigh. "Hot damn. I've never been so happy to see a Podunk cow town such as this one. Sure does look spread out." Beyond the river grew trees, and their green trunks along with the church steeple in the background were a welcome sight.

When they finally reached Fort Worth, Kate teared up—Doc had never seen her do that except sometimes when he was drunk and too rough with her in bed, in which case he'd stop and apologize and then pick up again a little softer. She must've thought they'd die out there in the desert. Maybe they would have. Doc's only thought was to keep riding; deserts end, he figured. It was sweet to know that someone still wanted to live that much. It made him want to live too.

There was a little wooden sign that read "Where the West Begins" at the entrance. Doc didn't find it particularly true, but it had a certain hyperbolic quality that he liked. Fort Worth was a lot like some of the other towns that had sprung up out west. Doc had looked into its history one afternoon after getting kicked out of a Dallas saloon. He didn't have anywhere else to go, so he went to the library and studied up on the next place he'd get kicked out of.

The railroad had gotten in a few years earlier, and the town seemed to be booming. It was funny how each town mirrored another. He'd just left a Main Street, and now he was entering another one. The first building was the courthouse. It was a red brick building; *quite beautiful*, thought Doc. At its pinnacle, a clock tower, and great, imposing stairs led to its gates. On the side, smaller wings sprung out like broad shoulders. It gave the appearance of law and order. But Doc knew that nothing kept order anymore. Not guns, not money, certainly not the law. All the sheriffs cared about was their own town and if they could run you out rather than bloody themselves. As such, Doc didn't fear for Kate. Main Street was wide with deep tracks in its orange dirt from the various wagons bouncing up and down. Telegraph poles and lines ran parallel to Main—a sign of modernity.

Kate spotted a cheap hotel and pointed at it. She sturdied herself, squaring up to Doc, taking a tone he'd never known she possessed. "I'm not interested in getting hanged like that poor shack in the desert. We have to be smart for a spell. Don't you be addle-headed about this. Promise me." She was spooked, and her accent came out more with fear.

Doc took her tiny, flushed cheeks in his palms. They needed baths, and she hadn't put on any makeup in days, but he found her talking to him like an equal to be quite an attractive thing. It excited him. "Sure, darlin'. I'll be good."

"All that matters now is that we ditch the spotlight and find you that fountain."

"I think it's more like a spring."

"God in heaven, Doc—as long as it makes you well you can call it a traveling circus."

And so it went. He and Kate laid low for a while. He found a gig dealing faro and let everything subside over time. He tried to not even use his name, but it'd come out when drinking. He wasn't very good with an alias; he was just, always, Doc.

In a very quiet manner, completely antithetical to Doc, two months passed, and the Harrison and Marcus shootings seemed to have blown over. There was too much else to worry about. In the afternoons, Doc would deal at the Beehive Saloon. It was autumn now. A bit cooler, the trees turned rhubarb and marmalade, and even the wind smelled fresher.

He hadn't had a drink yet today, and his throat was dry and scratchy. His hands shook a little as he hustled toward the bar. Behind him, a man in a bowler carrying a large camera and tripod sweated, trying to catch up.

"Mr. Holliday! Doc," he called out.

Doc spun back, drawing his gun in a motion so natural it looked as if he'd been aiming it all along.

The man dropped his camera and threw his hands straight up in the air. The cap popped off and circled around in the dirt before falling flat. "I assure you, I'm eternally unarmed."

Doc looked over his slight, literary figure and holstered his weapon. The pink under his eyes showed in the thick noon sun, and it seemed that all the color in his face had scabbed away. "What is it? Teeth wait for no man."

"I was under the impression that you hadn't practiced dentistry in almost three months."

Doc thought for a moment. "And just who the hell are you telling me about myself when I don't recall knowing you?" He turned and proceeded on his intended path.

The man fumbled to pick up his dislodged camera and chased after Doc. "I'm a reporter. Wentworth." He made an awkward motion to swing his hand around Doc's front for a shake, but Doc ignored him. "It true that you've only got a few months left to live? That why you left Georgia in such a hurry?"

Doc began to roll a cigarette as he walked. "You're seriously causing me to reconsider putting my steel away."

"That is the furthest thing from my intention. I'm aiming to write a feature on you. You've made quite a name for yourself, despite your malady."

Doc licked the cigarette into a fine, girthy cylinder. "Everything you see, everything you heard about is posthumous. I died in Georgia. Don't let anyone confuse that."

Wentworth kept pace for a while, but it was clear Doc had nothing more to say. Doc stared down at some correspondence in his hands; cigarette ash flaked onto the paper, but he paid it no mind as if he'd already committed it to memory.

"I fear you've fallen from the path of rectitude, John Henry," Mattie wrote in her latest letter.

Doc thought back to the warm Georgia evenings he'd spent with her. Things weren't so cloudy then.

They sat under an old weeping willow, its veiny branches drooping over their light bodies, hiding them from sight. John Henry leaned in and kissed her, and she kissed him back a little before pulling away.

"You don't want me anyhow," she said, a bit frightened.

"You're a goddamn fool if you think that," said young John Henry.

"Taking the Lord's name in vain. You ought to catch a beating."

"I'm sure I'll catch one this way or that." His eyes shined blue. A hint of adolescent fuzz had begun to grow on his face, reddish in the daylight.

"Everything we do is a sin whether we mean to or not, John."

John Henry placed his hand on her thigh. She had a long dress on, but it was still exciting. He could feel her shape, feel what it might be like, and she let him. He knew she was referring to the fact that they were cousins, but he never cared much for propriety.

"I'll make you mine one day, I swear it."

Mattie smiled sadly. "You'd best leave me where you found me."

After his run-in with Wentworth, Doc decided to forego gambling for the day and mire himself in drink. He downed one whiskey after another at the

Beehive Bar. Patrons vomited so often that the barkeeps covered the floor with sawdust to save time. It was dim inside, but the bar itself had a certain elegance in a feral sort of way.

Hours passed. Just Doc and the bottle and a fingerprinted glass. He couldn't stand the sight of that empty glass. It poked holes in him; it made him shake. He took no joy in it, drinking alone, mechanical in his resolve to drown the day. After fourteen drinks, he was sagging. His lips were white, and he was smoking just to keep his cough down. He looked like he'd been caught in the rain, but it had been dry for weeks. The bartender, Champagne Charlie, snatched the bottle away.

"You're lookin' a bit ripe, Holliday. You been bendin' that elbow since noon."

Doc was covered in perspiration, and his head lolled back and forth. He and Champagne had a couple run-ins before, but Doc had honored his promise to Kate that they'd keep quiet for a while. Now, it was all bottled up inside him. "I'd return that whiskey to my possession, bartender—if that is your real name."

"I'm tired a seeing your dead carcass in here—you ain't good fer nothing but gettin' drunk and mouthing off."

Doc slowly lifted his eyes from his whiskey glass and set his hat gently on the bar. "You left out my knack for shooting the eyes outta mouthy saloon birds." He drew and uncorked a shot wide of Champagne Charlie, shattering the mirror behind the alcohol.

"Jesus Christ!" screamed the barkeep, losing his bravado.

The glass rained down on the bartender, gashing Charlie's neck as he reached for his pistol under the bar and let off two shots wildly. The other patrons scattered behind their tables but looked on, trying to catch a glimpse of Doc, who was already becoming a name around those parts. Doc stumbled toward the exit, firing two more shots, falling backward through the swinging doors, and passing out in the street.

He woke up in a four-by-four county cell. There was light streaming in through a little window. He looked down and saw he'd pissed himself. A familiar stranger sat outside the bars. Earp. He smelled like pussy and liquor, which wasn't altogether unpleasant, thought Doc. He appeared irritated, but maybe that was just his look.

Earp spat in a pile of sawdust underneath the cell's keyhole. From the depth of the pool of spit, he'd been there at least an hour. Nearby, a mealy-mouthed guard sat in a wicker chair, peering back at Earp every once in a while. He had the look of a man wishing he were somewhere else. Though, in Fort Worth, just about everyone had that look. A shotgun lay tilted over the guard's bunched-up trousers.

"You can find all sorts of things in prison," said Doc, clearing some of the dirt on the floor.

Wyatt raked his knuckles over the metal bars as Doc rubbed the night out of his eyes.

"You look like you're about ready to expire."

"Never a better day." Doc patted the back of his head and found his ashy blonde hair matted with dried blood. "Any conclusions as to why I'm here?"

"Believe you shot up the Beehive fixin' to kill Champagne, only you were too drunk to hit nothing but a mirror and some bourbon."

"I shall mourn the bourbon accordingly." He placed his hat over his heart. Doc's gravelly voice gave way to a dry heave.

"I never seen a man more square to die besides myself. You're headed for a reckoning one way or other."

"There's some kind of freedom to know that you've lived past your expiration."

Wyatt spat into the pile and watched it roll off like a tributary. "Good to have someone around like you, I suppose. I posted yer bail. Don't go galloping off just yet or I'll have to track you myself. I've got pretty good at it." Wyatt pushed off his chair and stood up. He was tall and broad.

Doc licked his lips. They were bone dry. "What about you? Why's your foot in the grave?"

Wyatt had the look of a man who didn't want to speak but would do it anyway. It was clear from the glassy look in his eyes that he was remembering something best left buried.

Wyatt recalled his wife, Urilla, sitting with their child. How small it was. Newborn. He was afraid to touch it. Urilla was humming something to the child, maybe a lullaby her mother had sung. But the child wouldn't sleep. He dry heaved like there was nothing inside. He wouldn't eat or cry; he just lay there with a look of helplessness. And so did Wyatt.

Wyatt sat on the bed and watched his wife cradling the baby, rocking him rhythmically. He wondered how someone could heap so much care on a lost soul. "Boy doesn't have much left in him."

"You're a cold sonofabitch," said Urilla, feeling the boy's forehead. She'd never spoken to him that way.

"You need to rest. I'll fetch the doctor," said Wyatt.

"Every time I see a doctor someone dies."

"I think there's relation there." Wyatt closed the door behind him. He walked the long path into town, leaving their small brown house as far behind view as he could. He stopped under a tree to smoke because it was drizzling, and he wondered if he and Urilla could ever get back to marriage after the baby was gone. If they could see past it.

That evening, the doctor declared that the boy had typhoid, and there was nothing more to do than pray. So, they did. They stayed up all night taking care of the boy, keeping up the fire, Hail Marys, rubbing ointment on his chest. Urilla began to show sickness, too. She refused to sleep. She sweated with fever, still rocking the child in her arms.

The boy died on a Tuesday. Urilla wept herself into a frenzy. The doctor said she'd caught it. He advised Wyatt to leave, but he stayed and tended to her until she passed in their bed two weeks later. He watched her last breath and the next day sold the house to the highest bidder and took off westward.

"I was a lawman then, got myself arrested, thrown in jail, escaped; now I'm nothing more than a pimp—a goddamn whorehouse bouncer."

"You're in good company," said Doc. "A couple of hard cases hunting refuge."

"Figured as much. Working in a house of ill repute does have its advantages—you might stop by when the trial's over. I suspect you'll walk on account you didn't kill no one." He placed Doc's engraved flask inside the cell and walked out. It read JHH in silver lettering. The guard sighted Wyatt with his shotgun barrel as he meandered down the road.

Doc shakily grabbed the flask and put it to his lips. "Apparently, you're an angel."

The trial lasted only two days, and Doc was fined five dollars in the end for disorderly conduct. Afterward, he lay in his hotel room awake, only slightly intoxicated in the heavy, wet darkness. It was one of those nights when it always felt like a cough was coming on, and he knew something barbed loomed on the horizon. These were the nights he needed Kate the most. He also knew they were the ones she would never wait around to see.

Great fluorescent plumes of lightning wriggled in the heated sky like boiling snakes. The thunder hadn't begun yet, but it lurked. There was something disconcerting about witnessing God's fury in incompletion.

He drew his thin frame up to the window and watched as the powder-packed dirt began to swell with rain; the stench of horseshit, tobacco spit, and gunpowder rose up in the thick air, and for a moment, Doc felt cleansed. A hollow rumble echoed off the mountains in the distance. Doc thought about what Earp had said—a reckoning one way or other. He hung his head out and let the rain wash over his hair and eyes. The salt ran over his lips. Morning didn't come quick that night. The dark festered around his fading body, and the hollow cracks of gunshots and thunder intermingled so it was impossible to tell the divine from destitute.

The following night, Doc decided to take Earp up on his offer and visited Lucille's, a brothel in the old style where Wyatt stood just inside the entrance. He was an imposing figure, Doc noted, as Wyatt tipped his hat to him. His work as a bouncer came as no surprise to Doc. Wyatt's odd jobs had included city policeman in Illinois, constable (in place of his father), soybean farmer, teamster, buffalo hunter with Bat Masterson, saloon-keeper, and boxing referee, as well as a decent amateur boxer himself.

"How's the dentistry business doing you?" asked Earp. He looked resigned, smoking in the brothel's narrow doorway.

"You know, I don't even know what the point of teeth is anymore, Wyatt."

Wyatt plucked the cigar from his mouth, leaned in, and took a whiff of Doc. "Jesus, yer half seas over. You drunk all day?"

Doc pulled down his hat. "I'll have you know I drank last night as well."

Wyatt just shook his head and chuckled. "Anyways, I got an offer."

"I'll double it!" Doc slurred, poking Wyatt in the chest.

"Shut up fer a second. I'm taking off. Headed out to Dodge, Kansas. They need some law up there, an' it's decent wages. Work in the day, mostly."

"Cowboy capital. Rough element." Doc winced with a shiver that ran through his chest and legs.

"And what's that make you?"

"I am refined. I speak three languages including the Lord's, am a doctor of dentistry, and read music. Now, if you'll excuse me, I'd like to have sex with several of your filthiest prostitutes."

Wyatt steadied Doc. "Think about getting out of this cow town. Ain't but quiet death here."

"Well I had always imagined my own to be appropriately audible," said Doc.

From behind the purple front curtain, one of the women emerged and placed her right hand on Wyatt's back. "Bunch of animals today. Always a grim lot in the daytime, buncha incontinent drunks."

She seemed a bit tipsy, thought Doc, but wasn't drunk. She wore a checkered dress, and her hair was black, straight, and didn't quite make it to her shoulders. She had a stern face like she didn't feel she belonged. It was ridged and angular and Doc didn't trust her from that moment on. She reminded him of a schoolmarm. Even drunk, Doc detected something between them beyond Wyatt's official job of separating the trash from the talent.

"Speaking of incontinent drunks," said Wyatt, sliding his arm around her petite shoulders, "Celia Ann, this is my friend, Doc Holliday."

"Well, aren't you a daisy, Wyatt." Doc removed his hat.

"Oh, I've heard of you. Ain't you a criminal?" she asked.

"Beautiful *and* charming, Wyatt. How *do* you find them?" Doc rolled his eyes, brushing past Celia Ann and through the velvet curtain.

"You have a good night now, Doc. Try not to get sick in the linens."

"I make no such assurances," he called over his shoulder.

Another man stood in his way beyond the curtain, better dressed, and held a book up to Doc's nose. "Signature, please."

"What for?"

"We like to keep a record of our clientele." The man was slight, effeminate even. It was hard to tell in the dim lighting. Doc didn't take a liking to his small nose, either. He glanced back at Wyatt through a split in the curtain, but Wyatt just shrugged. Doc signed the book as Tom McKey. It was his uncle's name, but his uncle was dead, so he figured he wouldn't mind the borrow.

Inside, three young, plump women greeted him. It was almost comical how luscious they were against his lanky body. They extended their gloved hands, stroking him. The velvet tickled his arm hair.

Behind them was a dark enclosure draped in silk, lit red by a lamp that someone had covered with a scarf. Four women wearing gray stockings and white corsets sat around one redhead. She reminded Doc of Kate a little, but he tried to keep things separate in a cathouse.

A girl with straight brown hair with a tulip in it had her hand to the redhead's cheek. An older woman supervised as they applied makeup to the redhead lounging on the sofa. She looked like someone had given her a sock to the face. Long lines showed under her eyes like she'd been up all night. She wasn't the youngest of the bunch, thirty maybe. For some reason she looked over at him, smudging the red lipstick the brunette sloppily applied over her cut. Her lips glowed pouty and bright. Her angular nose pointed down to her garters, somewhat obscured by the prettier girls huddled around and over her as if enveloping her in lace.

"What'll it be, Red?" asked Doc, holding back a cough.

"She's not exactly in working order, mister," said the curly blonde hovering above her on the couch. She had serpentine metal bracelets around her forearms like he'd seen in old Roman paintings in school.

"She looks right as rain. Nothing a little whiskey won't fix. Right, darlin'?"

The redhead nodded and waved off her companions. They scattered as she rose and got in tight to Doc. "My name's Pearl on account a' my skin."

"Well, Pearl, I'm Tom McKey. On account of—lack of imagination, I guess."

She giggled. *That's her job,* he thought.

She led him up a winding staircase to the third wooden door in a row of five. She peeked inside to make sure it wasn't in use and then pushed it open gently. The room was simple and smelled of pine. A few windows looked out onto the street, but the shutters were drawn, and the bed was a wooden box with four poles jutting from each corner. There was nothing else. *It's strange*, he thought, *to see a bedroom where no one slept.* Without looking back to see if he was following, she crept up onto the bed and got on all fours, her molten hair over her neck and shoulders.

Doc eyed the blue bruise under her eyelashes and the cut that leaked from her already red lips. He tweezed his flask from his jacket and took a couple swigs. He got closer and held it out to her. She took a swallow but winced, the booze burning the cut on her mouth.

Doc didn't feel right penetrating her like that, cut up and damaged, without knowing a little more about it. "You know the man who did this to you?" Doc ran his clammy hand over her cheek and held it there.

"Yeah, he's a regular, so the higher-ups told Wyatt to just throw him out, told him to sober up. He's a real curly wolf, they says to me. Wouldn't go trifling with him on account of an abandon like myself."

Doc lay down next to her and patted her bottom so she'd relax and lay with him.

"Don't you wanna get down to it?" she asked, insulted.

"You ever enjoy it?" asked Doc.

"Sure I do," she said immediately, "'specially if it's with you." It was something she must have said a hundred times to a hundred hairy, sweaty, tobacco-stained men who hadn't bathed any more than their horses had.

He thought of Kate and where she was just then and if she was saying the same thing to someone else. It made him sick. He tried to stave off any ideas of ownership. As far as he was concerned, the only things he'd ever claim to be truly his own were his .38 and his flask. He drank more. "What's your real name, Red?"

"I told you, it's Pearl, mister."

"My name is Doc. That's what you should call me."

"You trying to be like that Holliday fella from the papers?" She giggled and grabbed at the flask. She took down another swig and settled into his chest, realizing he was a talker.

"What papers?"

"Wait, are you telling me—I've got a real-life man of the West in my midst?" She looked him deep in the eyes as if searching for his legend. "Well, I'll have to treat you extra fine."

"You mean to tell me there are stories about me?" It was the first time Doc felt truly recognized. It was comforting, in a way, to know that his actions would live on.

"Sure there are. True that you cut the head off a man named Bud Ryan in Denver?"

The truth was that Bud Ryan was still alive, but he'd have an inch-wide scar along his neck to remember Doc by. "You ever wonder if there's a future in what we do, Pearl?" Doc leaned on his side and coughed violently, then collapsed back into the bed, grabbing his flask. He took a long, fat gulp and then another.

"You sure can drink, Doc."

"That's what they'll say about me. He could drink, and he could kill. But could he fuck?"

"Well, we'll just have to find that out, won't we?" She began to unbuckle his pants. He was ripe under there, he figured, but that's what she got paid for.

"Anyway, your man's about due. I'll have to pay him a visit. No sense in what men do these days." Doc ran his hand along the inseam of her thigh, over the lace garters, right to the point where most women would have slapped him. She eased onto him as she grabbed him, slipping his fingers under her panties. He liked that he'd made her damp. *It's not always easy to excite a whore—not really, anyway.* For a moment, he forgot who it was and felt Kate's lips on him. He shook it off. "I suppose we might as well get down to it for whatever I'm worth." He tipped back the bottle and let the whiskey slide down his throat until it was empty, then tossed it, clanking along the floor. "What's he go by?"

"Ed Bailey," she moaned, arching her head back.

"Well, darlin', I'm afraid he might not be able to apologize to you, so you'll have to accept mine," he said, pulling her hair back rough and thrusting into her.

When Doc woke, Pearl was gone. The bright new sun dimpled the room in thin circles through moth bites in the curtains. His mouth tasted chalky, and he eyed the flask on the floor. He figured he'd paid her. He couldn't remember much of what they'd done, but images of her pale breasts and rusty locks occupied his mind.

He ran his hand through his own thick hair and wheezed a little as he righted himself. Gun, knife, not much to speak of in terms of cash, but it was all there, more or less. The bed was turned sideways, and the sheets lay tangled on the floor. Either they'd had a good romp or she'd made it look that way to spare his feelings. *Often, whores are more considerate than proper women,* he thought.

He looked around for Wyatt as he gathered his things and left, but it was nearly ten, and he must've taken off because there was a portly gentleman by the door who looked fresh as a hotel pillow. Doc hated when strangers smiled at him in the morning, and this one had deep dimples in his fat, blushed face. It made Doc feel alone.

He thought about the springs, recalled the stories. He didn't want to become young again. He didn't need to live forever, just a little longer. Something drew him to it. *It's funny,* he thought, *when a man's destiny gets mixed up in legend and hope gets crossed with folly.* If nothing else, he was a true believer. He imagined the fountain glistening, gilded in holy tears, and he remembered his first confession, how much he could never confess.

He thought about Mattie and about Kate. He could never tell one about the other because neither would understand. Now he had a reporter to think about too. In a way, he wanted to be known, but notoriety for a man like him could also be a death sentence. Outside, the sky was devoid of clouds, and the only respites from the sun were the long, jagged shadows of buzzards circling overhead. He stunk like death. Maybe they sensed it on him.

Doc felt hollow from the inside. He could taste it on his tongue, bubbling with bile. He needed some whiskey and some sleep. The heat bore down on him so that it felt like his lips were percolating. Who knew what sores would show up? He was disgusted with himself. He felt dirtied by his disease. He felt dead; but if that were true, he couldn't have felt the pain, and he felt it sharp in his throat and gut.

As Doc inspected his surroundings, he noticed, for the first time, how sparse the town really was. Empty lots, fresh lumber. It was a grid, and the church was the tallest building by far, its black cross eternally visible over the spread-out blue and gold shop signs and rooftops. Doc searched south where the Trinity River flowed. A cloud of gnats created a haze in the distance that dissipated depending on the strength of the wind. It still felt rural because a few blocks down lay Lee Thomas's ranch where he bred cows and chickens. The ranch provided much of the meat for Fort Worth, as well as much of the street noise, along with hammering from new construction and the occasional broken glass from a saloon brawl.

The sun burned Doc's sweaty, feverish skin. He closed his eyes, breathed in deep, and held his arms out at his sides, taking in the pain. He remembered his mother telling him it all felt like dipping into the lake—first your feet and your waist, then your chest and your neck goes in, and that's when you know it's almost over, and you're relieved. And by the time you can't breathe anymore, you've already stopped trying.

The light hit his eyes funny then, almost in a flash, creasing the oily air. He opened up and realized there was a camera pointed straight at him and a man behind it under a cape. Wentworth. He was underneath his blanketed tripod, snapping candid photos of Doc. Doc got in close and yanked the reporter out by his backside. "And just what the hell do you think you're doing?"

"Getting a shot of the infamous Doc Holliday, of course. Everyone's asking for it."

"Now, why is it that I can't just be famous?"

"Lawmen are famous. Actors are famous. You're something different."

Doc's ruddy cheeks reddened even more in the beating sun, and he coughed chunky particles skyward. "Well, here I am." He stepped back and posed, straightening his hat. "There's no redemption left in me, so I hope y'all are square for a villain."

Wentworth loaded the flash and readied the camera again. It took almost three minutes before he was ready for another shot. Doc stood and waited, flagging in the breeze. He wasn't quite sure why he waited; just felt that maybe things wouldn't get any better than this. That he'd somehow missed his prime. He stared straight into his own contorted reflection in the box lens. He'd never considered himself desired until that moment, captured in immortality as whatever they believed him to be.

As the powder puffed into the air and his image forged into silver, he felt lighter, as if something of him had escaped. Wentworth was so young. He wore a black shirt with white stripes. He didn't ascribe to the fashion of the times: no jacket, no hat, his hair was short, and he was clean-shaven, which made him almost seem naked, vulnerable. The giant, torso-sized camera was broader and stronger than he was—almost lewd in its length and girth. Doc patted Wentworth on the back as he passed by. "Always with my boots on, friend. That's the rule."

CHAPTER 5

Hard Sun

It was almost morning, and the rosy daylight filtered in through the White Elephant Saloon's doors. Doc had been at it all night in a poker game against Ed Bailey, a local leatherworker. Bailey's body stunk of old sweat and tanner. He wore a Russian-looking hat atop his oval head. It was fluffy, made of beaver or bear, and his mustache almost matched, a scraggly thing that barely covered his top lip. It looked as if it had been sewn on.

Bailey sat to Doc's right, and a couple of other young sports stared at Doc across the table. One was Clay Murray, a cheap, glass-eyed gambler who'd cut the fingers off three men he suspected of stealing from him back east. The other was Carson Nevada, who got his name because regardless of what you asked him during a game he'd say "Nevada." He believed saying anything else was bad luck. Both tended to stay clear whenever Doc was in heavy.

Doc's face ran pink with fatigue, and he could barely lift the tin cup of whiskey beside him, though he continued to do so. Kate had already gone to bed, having watched a few hours of back and forth between the boys. There was a band that was still playing for some reason, in the corner of the room. No one had listened to them for hours, and one of the band members had gotten up and never come back twenty minutes before. They were down to a pianist and a man playing the accordion. It seemed that the two weren't sure how to proceed without the other man, but it didn't stop their cacophonous bleating. The room was decorated with wooden carvings of elephants and old, ornate headboards behind the bar adorned with ivory and lit by candle.

They were playing five-card draw, and Bailey kept fidgeting around with the discards. The room was dim, but Doc knew the trick well. He'd found plenty of wandering aces in his day.

"Play poker now, Ed," said Doc. It was a gentleman's phrase. No one liked to be called a cheat outright.

Ed raised his head slowly and licked his mustache hair. "Whatchu think I'm doing, Holliday?"

For a round, Bailey reformed. A couple of small pots.

"Pope's sick," said Bailey, glancing up at Doc as he began to deal.

Doc never took his blue eyes off the cards. "He'll die. Bet you a hundred lira the next pope dies too." Doc drew eights and fives, and Bailey drew three cards. Bailey's hand drifted over to the deadwood, lifting a card. Doc pulled down the pot himself—an acknowledgment of cheating.

"Just what the fuck you think yer doin', Holliday?" Bailey shoved back in his chair and whipped out his Schofield. He stood over Doc and cocked his revolver. "Maybe that coffin varnish's got to you, you goddamn lunger," said Bailey, eyeing Doc's whiskey. "You put that pot back square middle or I'll fucking kill you."

Clay Murray finally chimed in, "Calm down, Ed. We can work something out."

"Nothin' to be worked," said Bailey.

Doc eased out of his chair, exhausted, weak. He wheezed a little as he rose, leaning on the table to stand. "Now, Ed, you're not going to shoot me in front of all these people, are you?"

Bailey shook a little as he pressed the gun against Doc's papery forehead. Doc leaned into it. It felt like the only thing keeping him upright. The steel felt like it could slice his forehead open without ever pulling the trigger. It was thin and sharp and cold.

"You put that money back where it was or I'll hollow you out. You ain't got ten days left in you anyhow."

Just then, the Fort Worth marshal and two constables burst into the saloon. "Nobody's dying today. Although someone may get ditched if you don't put down that firearm, Bailey." *If they know, the whole town must know by now*, thought Doc. Word of showdowns spread quick. Law was always the last to know. Beyond the saloon doors, pairs of eyes began to appear. It was a spectacle, the theatre of the flesh.

Bailey twitched. He was nearly on the verge of tears. *Maybe it's the fatigue*, thought Doc.

"It's mine. I need it," said Bailey.

Doc looked down the barrel and met Bailey dead in the eyes. He loosened his necktie and unbuttoned his collar. "It's hotter than a whorehouse on nickel night." *It's even chances that he pulls the trigger,* thought Doc. Bailey had those glassy eyes that meant something else had taken over. He'd lost control. Doc wished he could feel something other than the booze. He thought of Mattie's hands, of Kate's slim thighs. He whiffed Bailey's gin sweat. From beneath his shirt, Doc jerked out his bowie and sliced Bailey deep below his belly. Doc tore through his flesh. It gave resistance as he sawed his way from rib to rib, spilling Ed Bailey's guts all over the table and the cash. His organs and blood poured out in grim succession, his intestines unraveling on the felt, and he collapsed immediately, banging his forehead violently across the table and convulsing on the floor.

"Jesus, Doc," said Nevada. It was the only thing other than "Nevada" he'd said all night.

Doc stood there breathing hard with the bloodied bowie in his fist. He had the look of a wild animal. Like he hardly knew where he was. He saw red, started to get sick. That body on the floor, cut open like a melon. It was talking a minute ago. He felt distinctly like it was someone else's future he'd crawled into.

After a stunned pause, the marshal ran up on Doc and attempted to disarm him. At first, Doc clenched the knife hard as if it were a part of him. Then, slowly, he released it, the blade clanging to the floor, and he exhaled, becoming himself again. The marshal's deputy declared Bailey dead a few moments later. A mob began to form outside the saloon, and the marshal rushed to get Doc out. With Doc in tow, they pushed through the crowd, still unsure as to what had happened, just trying to get a glimpse of the infamous outlaw.

Amid the confusion, the marshal and his deputy managed to stuff Doc into the local jail and lock him up. But word spread quickly that the Georgian, Doc Holliday, had murdered the local tanner in cold blood, and no one was saying otherwise.

His cell bars were rectangular, about five inches apart and twice that lengthwise. There were two bunked box springs inside attached by chain and ladder but no mattresses. The walls were sturdy red cedar, but because of the stench, the marshal had emptied bags of sawdust on the floor, so it was impossible to tell what was under it, except that it was moist. Two iron-barred windows looked out onto the streets where an angry mob gathered around the jail. They clamored for a lynching. They couldn't see him in the corner of the cell. "Give us his lungs, he don't use 'em anyway," one man called out, and the crowd cheered. In a cow town like this one, it was sometimes more prudent to hand over the prisoner than take on a riot, he knew.

Their guttural chants swelled in the hazy air until it was dense with spit and flame. They growled for his head, his eyes, and liver. He belonged to them now—he would be torn at the limbs, devoured as a sacrifice. Each would taste legend. Flashbulbs burst outside the jail like ground-spawned lightning veining the room with luster and fading back in wrinkled echoes.

Doc could see the public salivating for a glimpse of him. He clasped the window bars and pulled himself up to the light—flashes burst, and Doc addressed his crowd. "I am the god of whiskey and lightning. Have at me!"

They squished and squeezed flesh against his fingers, their plump cheeks and ankles, some pulling at each other's hair and scratching just to get a look into the window of the basement cell. Maybe a last look. Some of the onlookers gasped at his sacrilege, some fell in love. But it was undeniable that something happened in that instant that was undomesticated. It was a moment of transformation, and whether they wanted to tear his limbs off, fuck him, or cure him, they all wanted a taste.

"Shut up," the marshal knocked his pistol butt against the bars. "Yer roostered."

Doc got dizzy and let go of the bars, falling back into the sawdust pit that was his cell. "That's a perpetual state," answered Doc. Really, he was more delirious from the lack of sleep, but he was drunk too. There was always a melancholy high after he'd killed someone. The fading of adrenaline and onset of what a priest might call contrition.

The marshal chewed on a peach pit as he faced down the crowd. His deputy appeared shaken; *probably his first lynch mob*, thought Doc. The deputy was young, younger than the marshal. He wore a white scarf that hung loose around his neck and red suspenders. It seemed like he hadn't grown into his hat yet. A new beige Palm Leaf. His face was clean like a baby's, like someone back home took care of him. You could go weeks without seeing someone clean in Fort Worth.

Doc crawled back to the corner of his cell. His lungs ached. It was hard to breathe in the dust and feces caking the floor. He lay down on the wet sawdust, allowing it to engulf him as it puffed up in the air. It reminded him of a Georgia dirt storm. He remembered wanting to be straight in the middle of it, wondering what it'd be like to be devoured.

It came thick on the horizon. There was something mystical about the way the soil obscured the South. And, soon, there wasn't any sun to speak of. Dirt became the leaves, the cotton; it replaced the birds and the wind with a hollow hum.

The Fort Worth deputies searched the windows nervously. Something wicked stirred outside. Doc shut his eyes, recalling the moment his mother did not pass but was consumed. It didn't come like the preacher had told him—she died in fear. She died in terror of what lay beneath the dust.

Something brewed just beyond the bars.

Kate, unwilling to see another man pulled violently out of her life, had, on a moment's notice, concocted a plan. First, she gathered up the remaining bottles of whiskey Doc had left in his room, along with a few of his most necessary possessions, including his comb, his dentistry kit, and a couple of his colorful shirts. Everything else of import they had in holding at the jail. He'd given Kate a key to his room in case she ever wanted to stop in late at night after she'd been working. She found this to be the sweetest, most lewd declaration of love anyone had ever made to her.

Once she'd packed his tangibles in her carry-along, she stuffed in a few dresses and an extra pair of heels. She also wedged her tiny .41 Derringer in her cleavage, where there was ample room for another as well. She took a few moments to make sure this was what she wanted. There wasn't any going back afterward. She thought of Doc all alone in that cell and convinced herself she was in the right.

Next, she paid a visit to a client of hers, a man named Baldwin, who owned a stable and had once asked Kate to become his mistress. He was a rich man, but he was no Doc Holliday. She would have fucked him one last time for the favor, but there was no time. The mob could be at Doc any second. Baldwin would have the horses down in the willows by the Flats by nightfall, he said. She thanked him with a kiss on the mouth, shaking her bustle as she left.

Kate stashed all their things by the willows, except for the whiskey and her Derringer, and made her way toward the prison. It was quite a scene. Something out of a monster novel: pitchforks and lanterns, angry villagers anticipating nightfall. Fort Worth was a simple town. The more modern half was adorned with an oversized, faded American flag overhead, with most of the greengrocers selling fresh mulberries and figs, sweetshops, stationers—with pencils and notebooks for the schoolchildren, and the school, all built with fresh, unfretted wood. Eggshell whites and lobster green. That was all up on the hill.

Below it lay the Flat; the old fort stood in the center of it. Stone and empty. To its right, the church and then the myriad succession of saloons; the butcher's, filled with the skinned bodies of lambs and cow thighs; and the jail, cathouses, and dance halls. It was not uncommon to hear six or seven gunshots a night.

Between them lay the trickle of a ravine and willows that shook in the breeze, sparing the middle-class residents up on the hill from witnessing the destitution of the Flats.

Kate had thought to just march into the jail but then realized she hadn't thought at all. The crowd was enormous. Her man had made quite a reputation for himself. She circled around toward the back of the prison. Most of the shops had shut because of the mob. Their proprietors were probably out in the streets trying to sneak a gander themselves. Around the corner, the street lay barren. Kate lit a cigarette and took a deep drag.

"Well, shit," she said aloud. The bordello where she'd worked lay directly in front of her. It wasn't much to look at, just a blue residence with no signage. A ribbed balcony hung overhead. She remembered looking out there some nights, pretending she was somewhere lost in the stars. It helped with the soreness. "Sorry, Doc." She chucked one of the whiskey bottles through the window. The glass shattered, and she ducked behind a bush in case anyone heard her, but no one did. The crowd around the corner was boisterous and only getting louder. She poured the other bottle out on the wood porch. She waited for a second in case anyone was still inside. No one made a peep, so she took another drag of her cigarette and flicked it into the whiskey trail.

At first, it smoldered and smoked a little. Kate started to worry, but then a kindling flame picked up in the breeze, and it spread. It spread so fast, in fact, that Kate had to lift up the hem of her black-and-navy silk dress and run because the mob had already caught wind of the smoke and started for the cathouse.

Inside his cell, Doc smelled burnt wood, Kate's lavender perfume, and his favorite White Dog corn whiskey. He'd always had a strong sense of smell. Once, when he was little, his mother told the story that he smelled his father coming home from the war. His throat scratched, and he opened his eyes. "A whiskey and water would do me well, Marshal. In that order."

Outside, the mob had scattered in panicked disorganization. Kate walked right in the front door of the jail, all 116 pounds of her. The marshal and his deputy studied her as if she were a lost circus ape. She reached into her cleavage, and they leaned in, anticipating a wonderful surprise.

"This yer idea, Marshal?" asked the deputy with a mischievous grin.

From beneath her corset, she whipped out the Derringer and cocked it. "Against the wall," she whispered because she could not find her breath.

They both sat there, stupefied.

Doc still had his eyes shut, his head resting lazily on the box spring. "Marshal?"

"Against the motherfucking wall!"

Neither officer even attempted to draw on her. They were so shocked at the turn of events that they simply left their weapons at their chair sides and did as they were told.

As Doc opened his tired eyes, he found the marshal and his deputy with their arms splayed against wood, away from the windows. Smoke drifted in and out of the bars like breath.

Doc crawled to the front of the cell to see better. The young, clean one shook. It was the first time he'd experienced true fear. Not the manufactured kind, not the kind in spirit stories or in school, but the fear that breaks a man. The fear that alters him. Doc had felt it, too, but each time it became more and more part of him until it seemed like he always had a barrel pressed to his neck.

Kate's lithe figure appeared to him, clutching her trusty Derringer. She was gripping it so hard it looked like it might crack under her fingernails. There was something carnal about her fortitude though, thought Doc. It was an outright act of love. In that moment, he ceased to see her as anything but his girl. There would be no more money exchanged; they had each other's trust now.

The marshal tossed the key over. Kate unlocked the gate with her free hand as the pistol shook in her right. Doc struggled off the floor. "You're a good one, bumblebee." He'd started calling her that after she'd refused to let him kill a hornet in their hotel room one day, and he got stung instead.

Kate smiled wide.

Doc grabbed the Derringer, and any thoughts of overtaking Kate must have vanished from the marshal's mind because he slumped down, defeated. "You think you can escape what's coming to you, Holliday?"

"Well, yes, to be perfectly frank," said Doc. "What do you think, darlin'?"

Kate nodded.

"Kate thinks so too." He kissed her sweaty cheek.

Doc picked up the officers' pistols and lifted his pearl-handled Colt from the marshal's desk along with his flask and hat. He backed out the door with Kate and stuffed the officer's pistols in the back of his pants to sell later. The stench of cinder grew heavy outside. Smoke veined sinewy along the streets. Horned flames shot through the east side of Fort Worth, spreading quickly from the blue apartment where the blaze had begun. The air was scented of oil and dung—trapped horses flailed wildly, their nostrils flaring in the heat, breaking loose from their burning leather ties, smashing into the bodies, crushing steel on bone. Doc could hear their legs cracking. Pained cries echoed into the streets, and panic set in as waitresses and faro dealers carelessly tossed bathwater at the flames.

Doc and Kate ducked into the willows without being seen. No one was paying attention to anything but the fire. The horses were already there, tied to a tree, with canteens and clothes.

"You did this?" asked Doc.

Kate nodded. "Wouldn't say you have no friends at all."

"You may be the sweetest, most diabolical woman I've ever met." He kissed her hard.

They waited, and when night fell, they mounted the brown horses. Black, billowing smoke plumed behind them as they rode deeper into the West.

CHAPTER 6

Working-Class Hero

Dodge City, 1878

Doc was right. The law didn't find him. Maybe they weren't looking hard. It seemed all he had to do was start over and all was forgotten. The good thing about cow towns like these was that marshals usually didn't fret over crimes once you were out of their hair. It was someone else's problem until it went national, and then there was no escaping.

Doc and Kate resurfaced in Dodge City, Kansas. Wyatt had believed opportunity lay ahead there, and now he'd become the deputy marshal. Doc found it bitterly ironic that his only friend was a lawman. He'd figured Wyatt had been the one to help Kate, but he never asked. It didn't matter, really.

It was May, and the world turned gold. Butterfly milkweed grew all over the state. It was flat and dry and warm. Sometimes it was hard to tell the clouds from the dust winding off the fields. Hunks of the land had cleaved apart from drought and sun—it cracked, faded cobalt blue like bloodless veins for miles where rivers used to flow, and nothing seemed to lie within the crevices except for darkness.

The town itself was only seven years old when Doc arrived. It began as a buffalo camp and had become something of an unadulterated looking glass into the psyche of the West: ferocity, bloodshed, bordellos, and drink. It all thrived in Dodge, and Doc was drawn to it like a drunken moth. Still, it had come a long way.

Doc hadn't slept well, as usual, and he'd lost some weight in the cheeks since Dallas. He mostly kept up on drink now, and once in a while he'd eat eggs or bread if he'd won enough the night before to afford it, along with a fresh bottle.

Doc observed himself in the Dodge House hotel mirror. He ran his hand through his thick, wavy hair. His eyes didn't seem as blue anymore. He fastened his baby blue cravat with a diamond stickpin in his white shirt and delicately slipped into his long gray overcoat. It nearly reached his ankles. He fixed his front-pinch hat on his head. The brim rolled a little more on the left than the right. He grabbed his Colt and his cane because he felt weak lately without either. Kate tossed restlessly in the bed. She'd gotten in later than he did.

He wrote a short letter to Mattie:

Dear Lovely,

I've found myself in Dodge City, Kansas. It's a brutal place, which fits me fine. The air is dry, and my condition has not worsened considerably in some time now. Perhaps the drink and the climate are sustaining me. I find myself thinking about you often and the way things seemed lighter back in Atlanta. I hope you are well and safe, and I hope you think of me from time to time.

Yours always,

John Henry

Kate sleepily pushed herself upright on the ash headboard. "You're writing her again?"

Doc set down his fountain pen and sighed. "She's my cousin. She worries."

"Doesn't seem like she writes you back much. Not half as much as you pen her."

Doc turned and faced Kate. She was an awful mess, her hair in tangles, and she looked a little greenish. Doc tried not to imagine whose handprints had reddened her backside. Or where she got new clothes when he was too hard up to buy them for her.

"You're ugly when you're jealous."

"You never get jealous. You don't care if I live or fuck or die or anything." She clutched the sheets to her breasts. Her face reddened and clenched.

Doc kept an unordinary calm. "We're all going to live and die and fuck, so might as well get it over with," he said. He walked over to the bed and took her hand. She wouldn't let go of the sheet, so he just held her balled fist.

"You don't write her like she's your cousin. You act sweeter to her than to me," she said.

Doc just nodded. He envisioned Mattie's porcelain face. "I'll be home extremely late tonight, so just go about your business."

"You keep treating me like a whore and that's all I'll be." Kate pushed him off the bed.

Doc ignored her.

"Who will you murder? Whose blood do you want now?" She said it very dramatically, as if reading a theatre script.

Doc tried to clear his phlegmy throat. "Whoever's willing to give it." He stuffed the letter in his coat pocket and walked out.

He made his way down Front Street. The warm spring wind felt good on his chest. It was dry and sunny, and the grass had come in thick. Dodge hinged on this single street for most of its business purposes: dry goods and clothing, hardware, drugstore, C. Zimmerman's Lumber, G. M. Hoover Cigars, liquor, a tonsorial parlor, gunsmith, and, of course, the Long Branch Saloon, all in a row. Each storefront flat, ash, and connected at the hip.

Doc's office was located on a side street, but he was the only licensed dentist in Dodge, so people went anyway. He made most of his money from the tables, but it was important to keep a professional exterior, he felt. His mother had always valued such things. He thought of back home and the time just after his mother had passed.

The major called John Henry out onto the porch. It was an unseasonably warm December, even for Atlanta, and the winds weaved easily through the wooden deck posts. Doc remembered a tight feeling in his stomach—the same way it got before seeing Mattie. A wispy girl, a few years his senior, reclined in his mother's pine chair.

His mother had died only three months back, on September sixteenth. That was a cold day for September, he recalled. She was so small near the end as if, eventually, she would become nothing.

"Boy," said the major, "this is your new ma." He pointed to the girl on the chair.

"I'm Rachel," she said, straightening up. She didn't have any weight to her, like she'd been raised out in the wild. Her mouth was pretty, but her eyes didn't convey any knowledge of the world. It seemed to John Henry that she knew far less than he did. That she hadn't yet seen death or love or the true color of peaches, not in the way he had anyway.

John Henry backed away. He looked out to the brown grass and the dim clouds that lined the fields. The shutters rattled softly against the old house.

"Say something to 'er," said the major.

All John Henry could think about was the way his mother used to lay out his clothes before school. It was so meticulous, not one item out of place. "Pop, why aren't you in the Army no more?" He heard his mother's voice correcting his grammar. "Anymore," he whispered.

The major scratched his wooly brown beard and glanced furtively at his fiancée. "Go inside and play with your cousin. Yer bothering Rachel."

John Henry imagined his father commanding troops with a steaming load of shit in his trousers. How long had this girl been waiting for his mother to die? Watching her, stealing his father's attention? He felt something like fire boil up in his chest. He belonged to no one.

It was a Monday, and after a few hours of pulling teeth, Doc decided to move on to a less bloody setting. Three days a week, Doc dealt faro in a large room at the Long Branch Saloon. The gaming space held several other tables, but they were empty, save for a couple of lethargic dealers shuffling cards. There were three heads on Doc's table, all bucking the tiger since noon. It was an honor to play with a name like Doc Holliday, even if he won most of the time. The people of Dodge found him dangerous and charismatic, and that was just about all anyone knew about him except for Kate, Wyatt, and Mattie. In the corner of the room, several men from the Dodge City *Daily Globe* jotted down even his most mundane movements in an effort to decipher the burgeoning legend:

"He has the delicate fingers of a watchmaker and a body to match. There is not much of him to see behind the gentlemanly attire and his thin sandy-hued mustache. The only part of him that does not seem to shake intermittently is his hands. He often drinks with his left hand, presumably to shoot with his right if need be. Although sometimes bitter, he seems to make his acquaintances laugh from time to time and he is very knowledgeable of the world and of fine culture. There is something to be deeply respected in his brooding nature and something equally to be feared."

His silver timepiece hung just below his heart. Each man at the table sported a mustache and a large-brimmed round hat, but Doc was more elegant than the others. His clothing was crisper.

A doorway to a larger bar area connected the rooms. Every so often, profanities or broken glass would break the gamblers' tension.

And on and off someone played current sheet music; forgettable, comfortable tunes—"Oh, Better Far to Live and Die," "When a Felon's Not Engaged," and "Emmett's Lullaby."

Smoke drifted over the cards, and Doc's face drained of any color it had left. He dripped with sweat. It soaked through under his jacket, but he refused to roll up his sleeves. He wondered if Kate was still in bed and whose bed it was. Doc drank his whiskey down and flipped an ace. Since they'd landed in Dodge, she seemed to be more of a figure passing through his life than his lover. He tried not to think about it when he was gambling, and the whiskey helped erase his apprehensions.

Then, through the doorway, he made out a familiar silhouette. Even through the smoke, he recognized that bushy mustache.

"At two in the afternoon, if I was lookin' for most men I'd scout their place a business," said Wyatt.

"And here you find me—in my place of business," said Doc, swatting smoke away from his nose.

John LeBarron, a nomadic miner, jerked his head up from his cards. "Wyatt Earp?"

Wyatt stared him down.

"It's all right, Wyatt," said Doc. "He's innocuous."

"I'll take that to mean somethin' good," said LeBarron. "True you stood down twenty-odd men in Wichita? You buffaloed Ed Morrison in the face with the butt of your double barrel?"

Wyatt lit a cigar and held it out at arm's length. He took a puff and exhaled slowly, taking in the room. There were peanut shells on the floor, and horseflies smacked their wings against the green light fixtures that hung low off the ceiling. "Sounds familiar," he said finally.

"Well, we've got a hero in our midst, gentlemen," said Doc. "Drinks for me!" He took a swig out of the bottle next to his glass and then smashed it on the floor, motioning to the bartender.

"A real live lawman. How's that refined woman of yours?"

"Celia Ann's my wife now," said Wyatt.

Doc was taken aback. He sat stupefied for a moment. "Well, she certainly is—strong-willed." Doc forced a smile, eyeing Wyatt's badge. It was just a thick iron rectangle, but it was a powerful symbol in any cow town.

The bartender brought over a fresh, full glass of whiskey. "This one's on the house, Doc," he said then grabbed a broom and swept the glass shards on the floor.

"If I remember anything of tonight," said Doc, "I won't forget that."

CHAPTER 7

Satin in a Coffin

Doc and Wyatt stood at the entrance of the Comique Theatre while Eddie Foy, a local actor, performed *A Night in Town*, a light musical comedy. The theatre was very grand inside with ornately whittled ceilings telling the stories of Greek gods like Dionysus and Athena. The red velvet curtains billowed fresh along the sides of the stage and glowed with chandelier lights hanging down from the rafters. The seating shifted slightly up so you could see just above everyone's head in front of you if you were all patrons of the same height, but it did not account for the many bulbous hats worn by theatergoers.

Doc had invited Kate, but she said she'd be in playing bridge with Celia Ann, something Doc decided not to tell Wyatt about. It was a strange friendship they'd formed based on a mutual disgust for each other's man—and affection for opium. It was a foul partnership, and Doc hoped that Celia Ann had gotten Kate on the laudanum and not the other way around, though he doubted it. The Comique marquee read:

High Class
Continuous Performance
1:30 PM to 10:30 PM
Stay As Long As You Like
5cents to 10cents

It was in stark, bold lettering, and there were two wide open doors on either side of the theatre. The music slunk along the streets and the crowd, and there was something electric about the smoke and dust and laughter all mixing together. It was June. The playhouse filled with humidity and perspiration. Doc could feel the crowd's hot, stale breath on his back and neck. Each theatergoer seemed to have a different tic that irritated Doc. One man kept inching his finger closer and closer to his nostril, and a couple, bloated from money, touched the tips of their fat rolls together between the seats.

It was the premiere. There was press for the show, but most of them had their eyes and ears trained on Doc and Wyatt. On Wyatt's left stood Sheriff Bat Masterson—the man who'd given Wyatt the job. He was slightly taller than Wyatt with a narrow face and gray eyes like a dove. The two deputies wore white shirts and long black jackets with their badges. Masterson's mustache was the pointiest out of the three.

"You two look like the unhappiest couple ever to attend a comedy," said Doc, swigging whiskey from his silver flask. The whiskey was warm from his pocket and burned.

Masterson shot him a disapproving look but quickly returned his gaze to the stage. Even an accomplished lawman like Masterson knew not to provoke Doc Holliday. They didn't care much for one another, so Wyatt usually kept them apart. Foy's acrobatics and high voice on stage made for a light atmosphere. He had a very fluid way about his dancing, and Doc watched as he took control of the stage, filling every part of it. The crowd laughed in unison like trained beasts that had once been wild. These were not refined men. These were thieves, smugglers, killers, and taxidermists. As they hooted, Doc wondered if they knew what he knew—if they'd seen anything like he had. They all seemed so happy engulfed in distraction.

Outside, a few Cowboys, or their like, drunkenly hollered. It was too loud inside to make out what they were yelling about. It wasn't out of the ordinary. The clack and snort of horses drew closer to the theatre until it was right outside, the shouting mostly drowned out by the theatre's booming acoustics.

Bat removed a tin from his pocket and opened it. He scooped a greasy fingerful of murky jelly, lifted his waistband, and rubbed it around his groin.

"The hell you got there?" whispered Wyatt.

"New balm. I got a mean case of the itches." The shiny tin read 'Vaseline.'

The trotting outside slowed. Bat, perturbed, leaned his head out of the theatre door. There was a shrill whistle in the wind. The smell of horseflesh permeated the space. It grew coffin quiet outside. Just then, a round of shots blasted into the theatre, shattering the wooden frames around the doors and hurtling splintered steel into the crowd. Wyatt and Doc hit the ground immediately, but Bat just stood there like some tin soldier unafraid of being pierced. The show immediately halted, and a handful of patrons fled for the exits. Their hats fluttered to the ground, and they pushed up over one another, fingers clawing into eye sockets and heels on thighs. Many of the patrons remained seated out of shock or propriety. There was no protocol for gunshots in Dodge except not to get hit.

The bullets shattered one of the chandeliers at the side of the theatre, and crystal flaked down. No one screamed. It was all perfectly silent, as if the panic had rendered them mute, and all that could be heard were the sounds of their boots slapping the floor toward the exits. When it was clear, Wyatt got up, pistol in hand. He looked around for anyone wounded, but no one had been shot, just bruises from the small exodus. He ambled outside. Doc remained splayed out on the floor next to the entrance.

Bat still stood there, untouched, staring out into the starry Kansas night as if nothing had happened. "Y'all got down right quick," he said, finally.

"You either get down or draw," said Doc from the theatre floor. "Nobody told me to draw, and I've certainly got no badge."

Bat licked his lips. "God help us you ever did." He walked out to confer with Wyatt and started to pack a cigarette. The theatre buzzed with anxiety.

Foy got up from behind a giant moose head on stage. "Well, hope you're enjoying the production value," he quickly joked.

About half the audience remained. The others dragged crystal on their heels all the way home. Those who were left stood uncomfortably. Foy cued the piano player, who had been hiding behind the Steinway, and picked up more or less where he left off. There were considerably fewer patrons than when he started, but the show was a success nonetheless because the press was thrilled. Wentworth and some of his compatriots patted each other on the back and wrote furiously, hoping to have the tale in the morning paper. They seemed to revel in the fact that they, themselves, preceded the story. They survived it.

The experience brought a feeling of closeness for Wentworth. He felt he finally understood Doc Holliday, if only a little.

Doc picked himself up off the ground. He felt worn down. He figured he could buck the tiger with what he had left or head home. It was getting late, and he figured Celia Ann would have headed back already. He decided it was time to see Kate. He missed her. They'd been fighting too much, he knew. On his way back up Main Street, he picked a few flowers from the side of the road. Little yellow ones he didn't know the name of. He had so much mucus in his throat and nose he couldn't smell them, but he figured they'd make her smile.

The last vestiges of the Kansas sun lit the petals on his hand, and the night came on calm and sudden. It was dark before he knew it, and the air cooled a little. Doc tried to clear his throat before he entered the house but couldn't. His voice grew thin and raspy. He opened the door, offering the flowers first, but as he pushed in, he saw she wasn't there. He lay down on the bed and removed the knife from around his neck. The steel singed against his wet skin. He wondered if it smelled like her in the room. He spread his arms, and the flowers flitted onto the ground. On the bedside table was a note:

Gone get happy
—K.

Doc shook his head. He'd been trying to teach her how to write since they got to Dodge. Sometimes she left out the prepositions. He could only think of one place she might mean. The Chinese section. The opium pits. All he wanted to do was close his eyes. To dream for once. Not just serrated alcoholic flashes. He'd have to find her though. That's the way it worked with her. That's what was expected.

CHAPTER 8

Opium

Doc raised himself off the bed and hobbled back outside. The air was cooling down, and it was peaceful out, just the resonance of wolves in the distance and tangled chimes from the General Store.

The opium pits were a particular kind of degradation. They had their own code, but not like the one Doc knew; no honor there. The Chinese part of town was tucked in the south of Dodge, and even though he still couldn't smell, the air tasted thicker. Three orange cats began to follow him, licking his boots as he walked. He tried to shoo them with his cane. He gripped the silver handle in his raw palm. He passed wheelbarrows of vegetables and rotten squirrel meat covered in maggots. Skinned dogs and chickens dangled in the store windows. From a few blocks away, he could make it out in the moonlight.

It was a shack somewhat detached from the sprawl of the city, made of moldy, planked ashen wood, narrow and long. Three windows asymmetrically orbited the swinging door. Two of them were boarded up, but one glowed dim with candlelight, and lazy white smoke drifted into the navy Kansas midnight.

Doc pushed through the doors and walked up a rickety staircase to the room above. There wasn't much space. A bunk bed, a table, some pipes, and not much else. Four Chinese men surrounded Kate. She sat with her legs intertwined with another woman's, both smoking from a rosewood opium pipe. It was a long and flat with a bronze pipe and a jade mouthpiece. Two of the men looked to be passed out or overdosed. The other two just stared down Doc.

"You're coming home now, Kate."

Kate turned her head languidly, so her auburn hair dripped off her shoulder. The other girl turned too. It was Wyatt's wife.

"Devils leading devils," said Doc.

"I knew you'd come," said Kate. She started to tear up.

"Are you all right?"

The two men in the corner started speaking Chinese. They stood.

"I want to go now," said Kate.

"Well come on then," demanded Doc.

One of the men put his hand on Kate's shoulder and pushed her down. He shook his head.

Doc's insides bubbled up. His heart overflowed with blood. He was sick and incensed at the thought of Kate being in danger. The man kept his hand on Kate's shoulder. His fingernails pried at her white skin, and Doc was just about to burst.

"If you would kindly let my wife go," said Doc in his calmest possible voice. One of the other two men in the pit started to rouse. Doc twitched his fingers.

"You pay," said one of the men.

"Darlin', pay the man," said Doc.

"All gone," she said and lowered her head.

He tried not to think about how she would've paid otherwise. How he'd called her his wife even though her body was for sale. He was disgusted in love. He reached into his pocket, but one of the men jerked out a knife and held it to Kate's throat. The blade was brown, like he'd stuck someone and never cleaned it.

"No!" yelled Doc. "I'm paying you." He held out the money, all his winnings. He gingerly walked over and handed the man three dollars and sixty cents. "Get up, ladies."

The man retracted his dirty knife. He spat onto the wall. It oozed and slunk, disappearing into a dark crevice. The two women picked up their frilly dresses and hurried behind Doc as fast as they could.

"I know you," said the man with the knife.

"Then I'm impressed you still took my money," said Doc.

"Nothing left to fear down here."

Doc nodded. "Pleasure, gentlemen." He backed out, slowly turned, and followed the women outside.

He returned Celia Ann to Wyatt's house, expecting there would be a confrontation between them, but Wyatt wasn't even home. He must have gone out to buck the tiger. Doc would never mention it. Some things were better left buried.

CHAPTER 9

When You Were Young

Summer 1878

There was a growing legend forming around the Cowboy boss Curly Bill and his dead-eyed hound dog, Ringo. One thing had become clear after the Comique shooting—it was the Cowboys against the law. The Cowboys were cow and horse wranglers, thieving their way from state to state and shooting anyone who didn't play along. They weren't going to be trifled with anymore, and they were making a point of it all over the territories. Shootings in the street, bar stabbings, train robberies. Most marshals got killed or paid. Doc didn't care much for their brand, but he certainly wasn't law either; he steered clear of trouble so long as they didn't come looking for it.

He sat at the Monte table in the back room of the Comique bar in his tenth hour of play. Doc had been on a losing streak and was attempting to break even before the night was through. He smoked a long cigarette, gripping it in his clenched teeth.

Doc picked up his dangling silver timepiece. It was nearly ten, and he didn't have much left in him. He could feel it in his bones. He was used up. His lungs felt like paper as he ached to suppress his constant coughing. It embarrassed him. He disgusted himself, hocking thick, dark-green mucus streaked with yellow into his handkerchief. His fever had run out of control some hours ago, so he was sitting there, sweating profusely but freezing cold.

He jiggled his throat, pretending to fix his collar, and wobbled in his chair as the voices in the adjacent barroom rose in volume. The few gamblers in the parlor turned their heads. Someone tossed a chair across the wood floor in the path of the connecting blue door. The smoke was thick and black and tasted like old figs from what Doc could remember. His throat clicked dry.

He hadn't come prepared for trouble. It was a Sunday, and he had no gun, only his knife, and he was beat, so he'd leave the spilled blood to someone else, he figured. In the other room, several thick figures encircled one, shifting in and out of view from the doorway. Whoever it was was in for a hurt.

In the other room, Wyatt Earp had run into an old foe. It was Ed Morrison. They'd traded blows back when Wyatt was making a living bounty hunting with Bat Masterson. Wyatt had embarrassed Morrison, buffaloing him over the head and going about his business with Ed unconscious at his feet. Morrison had come looking for him with some of his Cowboy buddies. Four of them had Wyatt surrounded.

Morrison slapped Wyatt across the face. "I got you now, you motherfucker. I come to kill you."

"Funny hearin' you talk. Only way I remember you is with your ear on the ground and blood pouring out your dome," said Wyatt. He thought about drawing, but it was a death sentence. He wondered what getting shot felt like. Hadn't happened yet, not for lack of trying.

Even in the other room, Doc recognized Wyatt's husky voice immediately. "Gimme your pistol," Doc said to the dealer, holding out his clammy palm.

"You sure, Doc? You look right balmy," said the dealer.

"It's either that or I go in there swinging my cock and cane."

He handed Doc the long-barreled Colt .45 every dealer was required to strap under the table. "Wouldn't want that," said the dealer.

Doc checked the chamber, snapped it back, and cocked it. He headed toward the blue doorway. Through the smoke, he saw Ed Morrison and Tony Driskell with two of their Cowboy cronies, the same band that Wyatt had stood down in Wichita. Back for revenge or something of the like, Doc figured. Ed Morrison had the face of a raven. It was long and pincered. His features were shallow, and he talked funny because his front tooth had been knocked loose. Driskell had the face of an older man, though he was young. He was beginning to bald under the brim of his hat, and Doc could smell the stink of him from the doorway—unwashed, unloved, semen in his pants, and twelve quarters in his pocket that he'd probably looted off a corpse.

"You been tellin' stories," said Morrison. "You'll bleed." His beaked face pecked at Wyatt as he spoke. Spittle misted from his dislodged tooth.

Wyatt remained stoic. His hand rested by his Smith & Wesson, but he didn't draw. All four had the drop on him. Even a sport like Earp couldn't swing that. Sweat spread in the pits of his shirt. *They must have surprised him*, Doc figured, since his duster dangled on the chair next to him. He rarely took that ratty thing off.

Morrison spat in his face. "Draw, you fuck."

Wyatt wiped the spit off with his sleeve.

Doc crept up closer to the doorway without being seen. Behind Wyatt, Tony Driskell reached for his holster, hoping to end things himself.

"Look out, Wyatt!" Doc shouted as he fired. The shot landed in the middle of Driskell's spine. He whimpered a little as he crumpled limply to his bony knees. Wyatt drew and cracked Morrison in the face with his gun butt. His forehead split easy like pear skin, and his neck slammed sideways against the ground—the second time Wyatt had buffaloed Driskell in their short history. It would almost have been humorous except for the deadly gravity of the situation. Nevertheless, Doc smiled a little, noting the strange ways they'd all be remembered. The circumstances of a man's life and how he passed coldly into the next so unceremoniously. The other two Cowboys stood and stared, about ready to fight, when Doc fixed his Colt on them. "When you get to killin', three's true as one."

For a minute, they just eyed Driskell, crying on the ground from the hole in his back and belly. He could not writhe or move or feel because the body was no longer his. It belonged to the bullet now. It belonged to Doc. Doc thought of the fountain, deep in the woods, due west—how when they found it, he and Kate would make love in the frothing mixture, and everything that made them ancient, their magnetic fear, would scab off like an old wound. They would be free.

One of the Cowboys unbuckled his holster. The other dropped his belt and gun to the wood. They walked out, just like that. Wyatt nodded to Doc, relieved. He was breathing heavy, the adrenaline still coursing through him. Doc took a long drag of his cigarette, still gritted between his teeth despite the showdown. The murmurs of a crowd began to build outside. He figured it was another mob vying for his neck.

"What's a day without a lynch mob?" he said to Wyatt.

How did they hear about these things so fast, he wondered. He trained his gun on the saloon doors, but a new caste of assailant was after Doc. Seven men in round hats with cameras and notepads stormed into the Comique bar, shoving Wyatt aside and propping Doc on the bar like an empty beer bottle.

Behind them, adoring fans pushed at their backs, spreading the cluster of press like a pig's belly and screaming Doc's name. Doc was in no condition to resist. He just sat there atop the bar as they positioned their tripods. Making the best of it, he pinched a bottle of liquor from behind him and gulped some down. It was something minty and he hated it, but he drank more. They fired questions at him as the flashbulbs shattered into the dead nicotine air. He felt disoriented, dripping with flop sweat and feverish with blood.

How does it feel?

"Like I'm two feet in."

Is this your greatest kill?

"Certainly is my most recent."

Would you say you saved Marshal Earp's life?

"I'll have to read about that in the papers."

People are saying you're making consumption fashionable. Any comment?

"Tell them I've got a set of lungs to trade. They'll be the talk of the town."

Two loose women, trussed up in short purple dresses, pushed to the front of the crowd. "Do you want us to kiss over his body? We followed you from Dallas!" they screamed.

Doc stretched his neck to find Driskell on the saloon floor through the crowd, but he couldn't see or hear through the commotion. "Ladies, I'm not quite sure he's dead yet."

They giggled as Driskell gurgled helplessly, blood trailing from his gut. Doc could hardly breathe in the hot exhalation. The women kissed his cheeks and posed for pictures.

"Doc's double-time," said one reporter, jotting the phrase in his notepad.

"Don't write that," said Doc. *Kate won't like that at all*, he knew, feebly attempting to escape the photograph. But they pinned him down. He searched for his cane in the smoke and dust. His vision blurred so that the hot ash and glass and their blotchy red faces all blended into a single gray thing. He collapsed in a frenzy of hacking.

By the time he could right himself, everyone had cleared out. Wyatt stood in the corner of the room, smoking a cigar by Driskell's corpse.

"You about spent with all that?" Wyatt walked over and helped Doc to his feet, handing him his cane from the gaming room.

"They're taking the little I got left," said Doc.

"I know it. Might try not bein' so charming."

"Finally, something you can teach me," said Doc, smiling, as he swigged from the bottle.

Wyatt laughed audibly, which was almost off-putting to Doc. Maybe he was still rattled from the fight.

Just then, a coffin maker nonchalantly pushed through the saloon doors and began measuring Driskell. He only had a few white hairs left on his head and a thin, crooked nose.

Doc got disoriented. He thought of a place less foreign. "Sure do work fast here. We used to have great processions for the fallen back home."

"Ain't fallen," said the coffin maker. "Raped a twelve-year-old girl a town over and made her father watch it. Y'all deserve praise for this killin'."

Doc wondered if one death was really better than another. He wobbled on his feet. Wyatt rushed over to support him.

"Enough for tonight," said Wyatt.

The two of them stepped out into the blue moonlight, their figures merging into one. Wyatt dragged Doc's frail, limp body back down the road.

About halfway home, Wyatt suddenly swung around—Doc in one arm, his drawn Schofield in the other—and whispered through gritted teeth, "This sonofabitch has been shadowing us since the bar."

"Mind if I take over?" the man called out from fifty paces.

Doc twisted his neck toward the familiar voice. "Wentworth? That you?"

"Wouldn't miss a Doc Holliday gunfight," said Wentworth.

"You fermilier with this twig?" asked Wyatt.

Wyatt set Doc down on the gunsmith's porch nearby in case he had to shoot. The darkness had cooled the air, but the stink of the day lingered, and the paper-yellow moon left a thin haze over everything like silt.

"It's all right," said Doc.

Wyatt licked the bottom of his mustache straight and turned Doc around so he could see Wentworth.

"How much you see?" asked Doc, hunched over his knees.

"The aftermath along with everybody else. I'd best keep a better eye on you or I might miss a dozen showdowns between now and sunrise."

Doc exhaled, scratching the grain of the wood beneath him with his fingernails. "No one keeps eyes on me anymore. Except death. He's got me square."

Wyatt sort of cleared his throat as he lit a girthy cigar in the chilly night.

"You feel something when you take the breath out of a man? Wentworth had a pad and pencil in his hands.

Wyatt chimed in, "This man saved my life."

Wentworth nodded and jotted it down.

Doc inhaled deeply, flaring his nostrils. "Depends on what kind of man he was, I reckon."

Wentworth sat down next to Doc on the damp porch. "And Driskell?"

"It's a lot like pulling out a tooth. When you're gripping it and tearing it from his bloody gums and he's screaming, you see the worst of a man. You sympathize. But when it's over, no one feels a thing. Get about it quick. Got no room left for fear or remorse or any of those words you'd like to print."

Wentworth helped Doc to his feet. "And what about your fans?"

"That's a funny thing, isn't it? I suppose once I'm dead they'll find some other miscreant to trail." Doc lit a cigarette and let out a phlegmy cough in anticipation.

"That means a bad man," Doc explained to Wyatt.

"How 'bout you go and fuck yerself," said Wyatt.

Doc burst out in choking laughter.

Wentworth leaned in closer to Doc, trying to make out his silhouette in the darkness. "I dunno. You might just be the greatest ne'er-do-well to ever live. Though there is word that there's a better gunman than you: Johnny Ringo. It's said he killed Louis Hancock for ordering a beer when Ringo told him to order whiskey."

"Seems a bit severe. If I see him, I'll be sure to test his title."

Wyatt smirked.

"I'll quote you on that." Wentworth's figure was nearly as slight as Doc's. He looked as if he might disappear at any moment compared to Wyatt.

"You go right on ahead." Doc patted Wentworth on the shoulder as he eased up onto his feet and nestled under Wyatt's thick arms again. He was about to bid Wentworth farewell when he squinted and saw the young reporter, without his camera for once, scrawling away at a sketch of the outlaw and the lawman. He shook his head at the strength of youthful eyes in the starless darkness, then he hobbled off down the road with Wyatt, their figures blurring into the hazy Kansas midnight.

Doc played faro, Kate smoked opium, and Wyatt kept the peace. Soon, winter approached. The city council passed an ordinance against gambling and prostitution as if to send a signal directly to its most famous couple that the town was going straight. Doc still found ways around it, but even *he* wasn't immune to fines. Kate took it as a sign to put her profession behind her and concentrate on Doc, at least for the time being.

In December, it snowed. It was only the fourth time Doc had ever seen snowfall, and there was something sinister about it. *There is something ominous about everything in Dodge*, thought Doc.

Wyatt said he wanted to talk about something, so Doc walked to the edge of town, where the bare trees moaned and cracked from the ice and, in the distance, a wild black mare trotted across the gray plain in search of food. There was none to be had, Doc knew. He imagined its gaunt ribcage heaving against the fresh drift and wished he could save it. Every shallow breath of cold air burned his lungs.

The sky was bright enough to see the murky clouds contort and mingle. The long fields dusted up with powder and Doc didn't feel a thing. He sensed a presence behind him but didn't turn.

"Don't startle. It's me," said Wyatt from a few paces. "Been looking for you."

"Snow makes it all so quiet."

Wyatt spat tobacco into a fresh pile. "Reckon there ain't no birds and none to brave it."

Doc nodded. "Can't have good news if you hauled all ways out here," he said, taking a swig of whiskey. He offered some to Wyatt, who waved it off. Doc's hand shook as he placed the flask back in his breast pocket.

"You been accused a robbing Jacob Collar's store."

"By who?"

"Robert Wright."

"Man near created this town from dust," said Doc. "My word's no good against his."

"Nope. Biggest toad in the puddle 'round Dodge."

"So what then?"

"I done all I could to defend yer name. He won't budge. Friend a Driskell's 'parently. I reckon it'd be a real mess to bed him down, 'specially since I'd more than likely have to arrest you myself."

The snow started to fall harder, thick flakes pelting the flat earth.

Doc turned toward Wyatt. The snow collected in his hair and mustache. "Heard Las Vegas might be a little friendlier to a man such as myself."

"Keep it to yerself. I'll seek you out when I'm done here." He held out his hand and Doc took it. Wyatt wiped his nose with his coat sleeve and headed back to town. Doc lingered there as the snow built up around him like ash, and the wind bit through his coat until he couldn't feel his lungs and chest or taste the blood on his tongue.

CHAPTER 10

Shelter from the Storm

Trinidad, Colorado
Winter 1878

The next morning, after some heated discussion, Doc and Kate caught the first train out of Dodge. Kate wasn't happy with leaving Celia Ann behind, but she understood the consequences of staying, and more than that, she knew in order to find the fountain they'd have to keep moving. It was within the third hour of the train ride that Doc began to feel the effects of the cold. It was suddenly hard for him to keep his eyes open. His tongue turned chalky white and great black rings formed under his lashes. He rested his hand on Kate's leg. That's when she began to really worry.

"You look like just about a barber's cat," she said, pressing the back of her hand against his forehead.

He closed his eyes and lay back deep against the brown train cushion. Outside, the land passed by in white stills; it seemed like nothing survived the snow. All over the countryside, wiry trees bent over the drifts like sickles. The diving black crows chewing the remains of frozen antelope and their icicled red bellies provided the only color. There was one lake that glistened solid like a mirror and reflected the evergreens in endless patterns so that it seemed like the forest might stretch forever, and maybe it did.

"Maybe we should stop somewhere an' get you a doctor."

"I am a doctor, darlin'," he whispered. He could hardly get the words out without coughing. It was nice to have her care for him. He hadn't felt that in a while.

"I mean a real one."

"I think the only thing that might help me is a Bible sharp."

"Don't you say that. No preacher's carrying you off. You ain't gone coon yet. You got plenty of years you still gotta make me happy."

Doc opened his eyes. Kate cradled his head in her arms. "Aren't you happy?"

"Not right at this moment, no."

Doc suddenly thrust himself into a coughing fit and hocked blood all over the seat in front of him before convulsing onto the train carpet.

"Goddamn you, Doc."

Doc's condition forced them to lay up in Trinidad for over a week, delaying their Las Vegas arrival. Doc didn't have much life in him, so Kate tended to him with iced towels and read him articles about himself in the papers, mispronouncing the big words. His fevers had become more frequent and severe. He shook his head deliriously as Kate tried to force stewed fruit down his swollen throat.

"It's all they got," she said, prying his mouth open with the spoon.

"Don't want anything stewed. Just about slave food," whispered Doc, grimacing at the food like it was a bloody rag. Whispering was about all he could do. He'd almost lost his voice completely. Doc looked down at the dried brown spots on his pillow, trying to wipe them away, embarrassed in front of Kate.

"Stop being infantilized! You haven't eaten solid things in two days," scolded Kate. There was a hopeless concern in her voice that made it waver. "They've got stewed liver, too." She hadn't brushed her hair and it was tangled and scraggly. Her skin glowed oily. But Doc loved her very much in that moment. He'd been reduced to nothing. She was his pulse.

He drifted in and out of consciousness. She sat by his side for hours, stroking his sweaty, pallid face, singing little nightingale tunes she'd learned growing up in brothels. The older ladies sang them to keep up morale. They were sweet lullabies, and Doc envisioned them as icy, dark petals drifting over his burning cheeks.

He found it hard to keep his lids open and grasped onto Kate's waist because sometimes it felt like he was falling. As if there were a sinkhole right in the middle of his chest and the rest of him was slipping down and down. His coughing cracked the ulcers in his throat. He wondered if maybe he deserved this. If he was suffering all the blood and pain and death he'd ever dealt.

"Bosh! Don't you say that," said Kate.

Doc opened his eyes. "Say what?" He tried to swallow, but it burned too much.

"You're not leaving yet. We've got lots more fun to have. Lots more sex and drink and cards. You haven't even seen Vegas yet. Nobody knows you like I do." She tried to feed him stale bread, but he squirmed away like a mouse. "You rest now and I'll be here."

And he did. His dreams felt like drowning.

After ten days in the sick bed, half gone, with Kate always by his side, Doc's symptoms began to fade. He started feeling like his usual self. Not back to his Georgia days, but nearly. His raspy voice returned. The sleep and care did him good, and he was able to eat again, now and then, between whiskies.

One day, out of nowhere, he got out of the bed and peered at himself in the mirror. He saw Kate watching him in the reflection as he did this. He stripped off his robe and stood stark naked in front of her. The color had returned to his face, but his mustache had grown wild and bushy and his hair was too long. He was thinner, too, so that all his ribs stuck out of his papery skin. For the first time, he could feel the curvature of his hips. He strutted back to Kate on the bed, looming over her.

She slid down, hiking up her dress. She looked at his crotch. "Well, that's a welcome vision. I was beginning to think you didn't want me like that."

Doc pulled her blouse down and kissed her breasts. He kissed her mouth, felt her heartbeat as they made love, much faster, much stronger than his own. He loved how soft her thighs were. He didn't think of anything but her eyes as he climaxed for the first time in weeks.

He held her for a while afterward.

"I'm sorry," she said, burying her face in his sweaty chest.

"What for?" He stroked her long red hair.

"All the things I haven't told you."

"You don't answer to me, bumblebee. Answer to the Maker if you want. You and I are more than square."

"Have you thought about marrying your little bee in the eyes of the lord?" Kate's boney fingers glided across Doc's crotch. She grabbed ahold of him.

"I think he turned his eyes away years ago. But, if it would make a difference to you. I suppose."

She bit her lip hard so she wouldn't cry and swung her tiny arms around his neck. She kissed his dry lips and snagged his flask. "I've had enough of being holed up in this goddamn, shitkicker hotel!" She said the last few words ecstatically as if she'd overheard them somewhere and she'd been waiting for just the right moment to use them.

"You and I are of the same mind, darlin'." Doc took his time getting ready. He made sure to bring his .38 and put on his finest clothes. Kate wore the garters he liked under her dress for later. Then, they headed out into Trinidad for the first time.

In his state, Doc hadn't really noticed the town when he arrived. He found it very beautiful. It smelled of burnt wood, which reminded him of winters back in Georgia. Rivulets ran down from the looming mountains in the distance so that there was a constant stream flowing by the edges of Trinidad. If the boisterous city died down, you could hear it even in the town center.

It was a colorful place with red and pink rooftops, its lush greenery dissipating into the mountainside. They were flat mountaintops, brown and white and jagged—snowcapped like the houses and stores. It was clear that the town had spread outward from the church. Builders hammered and sawed at the new storefronts rising at the town's periphery. Horses and foreigners and young sports flooded the streets. Trinidad was booming.

Doc finally felt hungry again, so he and Kate decided to patronize the Columbian Hotel bar. It was a dusty place with a fine crystal chandelier that seemed like it didn't belong. It was funny how each bar smelled different. This one smelled like must and cinnamon. Doc liked how the cool air drifted inside. He could feel the winter in his bones.

The bar was busy with miners and hard cases, but Doc wasn't paying attention. He was just happy to be out with Kate, and he felt like playing the piano. There wasn't one by the bar, but as he waited for the barman, he played Tchaikovsky in his head and watched the notes fall from the ceiling like rain.

Kate observed him. She enjoyed these times of levity, when it almost seemed like they were a normal couple with normal problems. She hugged him and he hugged her back as he broke from his musical reverie.

When they drank, it felt normal again, and as the night passed by, Doc realized how much he wanted to live. How much he desperately wanted Kate by his side for decades more that he was being cheated out of. The room stunk of dried bourbon and charcoal, and he inhaled every bit of it because it meant he could still breathe.

CHAPTER 11

Paint It Black

Las Vegas, New Mexico

They'd asked around, and there were no signs that the fountain was nearby. Just far away stories, always a few towns over, where people had heard of a way to be healed. Doc held on to the hope that he could still live to see such a place. He hadn't realized how much living meant to him until he nearly went away. He knew he should hurry, but he wasn't sure where he was hurrying to.

Doc and Kate set off the next morning for Las Vegas, New Mexico. It was a long shot for the fountain to be in a den of incandescent sin—and word had it that it was more filled with bunko artists and scoundrels than Dodge—but it was worth a try and the gambling was good.

Doc peered out the dirt-encrusted windows at the buffalo. Every once in a while someone shot out of the train. A plume of smoke would glide along the cars as one of the herd crumpled in a brown heap. The others would scatter, but not all that far. They'd let up and go on about their business until another bored passenger took his turn.

Soon, Doc knew, the maggots and the wolves would tear away the meat, festering in the noon sun, and it would go forgotten.

The rumble from the train settled Doc in a rhythmic comfort. It was only in these unimportant moments that he could recall Georgia with any clarity. Recall the way it was, and not how he'd wanted it to be.

He remembered his mother back when she was well and the major was still in the war. She was energetic, always busying herself with cleaning the house, but mostly just moving furniture around and stacking fire logs. She wasn't fond of housework, but she did it out of obligation. Even as a boy, John Henry could tell she much preferred to read him a chapter from one of her books than cook a meal.

When she first got sick, there was a moment when she was stirring a pot in the kitchen and her skin suddenly looked used up. She coughed off to the side and told John Henry to come closer.

"Your mama still looks pretty, doesn't she?"

It was such a human reaction. Something John Henry didn't understand at the time. To fixate on her vanity as she died of tuberculosis, wanting to be beautiful even when there was no one around to see her.

Even as she faded to dirt, he saw it living inside her. He saw the disease would outgrow her frail body someday, and that it was already bigger than he was. John Henry nodded and asked to taste the soup. He was hungry. Things were simple then: Yes. No. Soup. When that beauty had faded altogether, the major took up with Rachel at night while Alice Holliday tossed in fevered dreams.

Hundreds of snow geese gathered by ice-topped watering holes, and snow pattered the train windows. The rolling fog tumbled along the mountains that appeared layered in centuries of black and white rock. The snow turned into sleet and back into snow until the trails mixed with the tracks, and it was impossible to tell where anything began or ended except for the slick orange sky.

Six trains came through Las Vegas every day, but Doc's was the first that morning. He and Kate brought their small bags off the train. Doc extended his hand and helped Kate down. She looked spent from the trip, her hair splaying off in different directions. Doc's back was drenched in sweat so that his white shirt stuck to his shoulder blades. He inspected the town. A big real estate sign stood out, and he could make out a drugstore and some carriages passing through Center Street.

The town wasn't too busy so early in the morning. As Kate got down the last train step, a couple of young sports made their way over. One of them, the one who seemed to be in charge, had tiny eyes like a newt. His body was shaped like a long bean, and his mustache was ragged and bushy. His beige shirt was buttoned all the way up, but his collar stuck up on the left side like he hadn't looked in a mirror all day. He extended his hand to Doc, and the other young man followed close behind. They weren't afraid to show they were heeled either, their pistols prominently holstered alongside their crotches. *Mustn't be any gun laws here,* thought Doc. *Useful information.*

Doc shook the man's hand.

"Mayor Hoodoo Brown. I'm also justice a the peace and coroner. This is my associate, Marshal John Joshua Webb."

Webb stepped in and shook Doc's hand. "Hell, J.J.'s simpler," he said. Marshal Webb was more put together than his counterpart. He wore a brown hide overcoat with only the collar buttoned so that it settled down into an upside-down V, allowing access to his weapon, and a straight-brimmed black hat. He was not a man of trends, it seemed. It was something old that he'd wear a hole into before he replaced it.

"Justice, coroner, and mayor? The triumvirate of figurehead positions. Now why would a busy man like you bother with a couple out of towners?" Doc asked.

"We like to meet all the new arrivals," replied Hoodoo, hardly taking note of the other passengers leaving the train.

"They call me Tom McKey," Doc lied, still searching Brown's beady eyes.

Kate picked up the bottom of her red and black day gown. Lace stitching ran down the middle, and the top flourished in a ribbon at her neck. It was her mother's and one of the only pieces of Hungary that remained. This was the dress she liked to wear when arriving somewhere new. She pushed Doc aside momentarily. "Don't go lying to the mayor now." She took both of their hands forcefully and shook them, surprising the two locals with her impertinence. "Kate Elder. They called me Big Nose Kate sometimes. We're hitching, so I'll be Kate Holliday soon enough, and then no one will have to confuse themselves."

Doc was taken aback by her boldness. Perhaps she saw the two as equals since she'd saved his life twice now. Maybe she was right, but he still didn't like feeling uncovered by a woman. He'd have a talk with her later.

The two men reevaluated the newcomer. Doc sighed and stole three deep swigs from his flask. He clinked the side, and it made a hollow sound. He was near dry.

Hoodoo Brown grinned deliriously. "Well God fuckin' damn. I knew there was something special 'bout you. Didn't I say it? I heard about you from Earp."

Doc's eyes lit up. "You know Wyatt?"

"We was lawmen together for some bits. Keep order here now. He still back there in Dodge?"

"Last I heard he was headed out to Tombstone. Fortunes to be made there," said J.J.

"Arizona?" Doc was about to say something else, but his cough took hold, and he bent over hacking into the dirt until blood dribbled down his chin.

"You ought to check yourself into the springs," J.J. added.

As Kate was rubbing Doc's back, her ears perked up. "There are springs here?"

"Sure there is, right outside town," said J.J. "As our guest, let me take you there, Doc. Kate, you'll wanna check into the Plaza Hotel. Best we got."

Doc righted himself and wiped his lips. He placed his hand on Kate's shoulder. "What do you think, darlin'? Do we trust them?"

Kate blushed. "If we can't trust the mayor, who can we? Springs, you hear that, Doc? All our prayers."

There didn't seem to be anything malicious in J.J., but this man Hoodoo—there was something Doc couldn't quite understand about him yet, and Doc prided himself on figuring out just about everyone. He didn't like the idea of leaving Kate in the hands of strangers. Still, Doc figured if he was friends with Wyatt they'd be safe. Besides, he knew Kate could take care of herself. Lately, he'd been the one needing tending.

Still, consequences had to be established. "She may not be my wife yet, but I treat her like that, so if anyone in this town touches her, I'll come through it like the Devil. I'll tear it down with my teeth." Doc looked straight at Hoodoo as he said this.

"Isn't he just the sweetest romancer you've ever seen?" Kate kissed him on the cheek. "Go and play with your friends, Doc. I'm feeling fire-new."

Hoodoo tipped his hat. "This young—" he hesitated around the word, "maiden has nothing to fear, Mr. Holliday. As mayor, I guarantee it." He smiled like a seasoned politician, showing nearly all his teeth.

"Now, you go with Mr. Webb to that fountain, er, springs. You'll brisk up in two shakes. This is what we've awaited." She kissed his sweaty cheek again in her excitement.

Doc poured the remainder of his flask down his dry throat and let J.J. lead the way as Kate and all their possessions headed toward the Plaza Hotel along with Fast Hoodoo Brown.

As he and J.J. rode toward the springs, Doc got a feeling in his belly like two squirrels fighting over jam. He was taut and charged. What if this was it? What if he'd stumbled upon something of legend? No one had told him to come out to New Mexico. And certainly no one had told him to go to a spring miles outside of the known limits.

The mountains in the distance glistened emerald, and the sky lit up with promise. J.J.'s jaunty brown horse bumped along a red road of clay and stone.

When they got to the entrance, an hour's ride outside the city, J.J. stopped the carriage.

"Hope you find what you're after."

Doc got out. He gave J.J. a look as if he might take a shot at him. "You're just leaving me here?"

"Too much to wrangle back in town," said J.J. as he whipped the horse around. "Be back for you in three days."

"Wait a minute!"

J.J. rode off fast, kicking up powder. "You'll be fine!" he yelled back over the ass of the carriage.

The wilderness suddenly pressed in on Doc. Sweat dried on his back, and the stagnant wind made him cold. The sign at the mouth of the springs read:

Many are the afflictions of the righteous, but the Lord delivers him out of them all.

The sulfurous steam bubbled up like shit as he approached. Gazing around the water, he found seven other consumptives, drunks, and madmen on the edge of death, wading like rotting lily pads. A few priests bumbled around with unguents and rags, anointing the sick and reading scripture.

The sky glowed copper as the mountains filtered the sun. A single bare tree held hundreds of tiny rock wrens, and a few cranes heated their stalky legs in the water. The branches contorted and cracked like fingers in the viscous steam. Black stones surrounded the spring, and the priests who oversaw the operation walked around with candles and incense that they wafted over the rotting bodies of their emaciated patients. It smelled like a child's funeral. Doc still held a dry hope inside him that the fountain lay here in front of him between the bones of nonbelievers, but a great fear overtook his trembling body.

"Do I just walk in?" he asked as one of the priests passed by him. He felt like a boy asking permission to play sabers. He'd whittle a stick down to a sharp point and fight his cousin in the bluegrass fields in front of the house. One day, John Henry got stabbed in the neck, and he made Mattie stitch him up so his mother wouldn't find out. He wore turtlenecks for three weeks after that, and it was still springtime.

Doc stripped down and eased into the hot spring. He realized how small he'd gotten now that there were no clothes in the way. His arms looked like a couple of draught-riddled squashes. The blond hair around his crotch seemed to overtake his thighs. He covered himself with his dirty palms.

The water was boiling, and a thin film of skin bubbled to the top as he entered. It was white and gray, and it was hard to believe it had come from him, like some snakeskin he'd been wearing all that time. He let the heat and the dry New Mexico light sink into him, staring, all along, at the wood cabin next to the springs where he figured he'd be holing up.

These other men appeared so sick, so close to the next world, or to nothing. He wondered how long he'd been lying to himself. He felt his cheeks, how shallow they were. He used to have a little fat on him, he remembered. He used to eat like a man. The distance seemed infinite. He thought of Kate and Mattie and what his body felt like before the sickness. It was hard to recall being strong anymore. The evergreens and mountains turned the color of silver, and he felt a lightness inside him. He wondered if the water was already altering him, turning away cough, making him young.

He closed his eyes. He wanted to catch God in his chest, lifting out the blood and mucus. He wanted to inhale the world. The sulfurous fumes tightened in his throat. It reeked of boiled eggs. His skin turned pink from the heat. He wondered if the cure meant boiling alive. Maybe he had to die before he could be reborn. He sank down to his neck. Sharp pebbles pinched his bare buttocks.

Doc felt the ripples in the water and opened his eyes to one of the other consumptives paddling toward him. He was hoping not to have to converse. It felt, somehow, sacrilegious.

"You came in search a something, you came wrong," said the man. His ribs protruded like wheel spokes. His beard was full of holes, and he was bald. His breath smelled like old apples, and his skin was thin like dandelion petals. Around them, the priests flittered like lightning bugs, candles in hand, checking bodies for sores.

"I'm not looking for anything but some respite and some warmth in my lungs," Doc lied. He leaned his head back to the setting sun. His fingertips wrinkled.

"You came lookin' for the springs though. The real ones."

Doc nodded begrudgingly. "I reckon."

"I tell you this 'cause I recanize you. There's an Apache in the desert. Not even all that far out. He can tell you things that you might want to hear." The man's breath coated Doc.

"The desert? Trying to make buzzard bait out of me?"

"No, sir." The man paddled back to his spot near the black rocks. "Not for old Doc Holliday. Never'd do that. I know of him 'cause I deal in gold when I can. When the sickness ain't at me."

"So, you're telling me this is all a sham?" Doc could make out the man's hairless thighs through the white water. He felt like a fool for thinking this place was anything but a hole in the desert. He'd wanted it to be so much more, and he hoped Kate was all right back in town.

"It's as good a place as any to die if you're into that sorta thing." The man's eyes and teeth glowed yellow, reflecting the candlelight. The sky turned brown. "The priests are real nice, and they got a place to sleep, but I'm flying the coop soon as I get my legs back under me."

"Any liquor around here?"

"There's a whole storeroom a gut warmer in the cabin. Just steer clear a the Converter inside. He don't shut up. You get me a glass and I'll tell you how to find the Indian."

"This place is growing on me," said Doc, pushing clear out of the water and heading inside, his warm member bouncing back and forth. "Some preacher tries to get between me and whiskey, he better hope he really has found God."

CHAPTER 12

Tomorrow Goes Away

After a few days, Doc was feeling about as well as he was going to, and J.J. picked him up from the springs in a wagon as he said he would. They didn't talk for a while, just smoked in silence. Doc tapped his fingertips on the wood to the rhythm of a Schumann piano concerto that he'd learned by ear. Otherwise, the sound of the road seemed enough for them—chalky and dry like stale bread between fingers.

"Heard of an Apache in the desert?" asked Doc about a half hour in.

J.J. didn't take his eyes off the trail; he just nodded and spat toward the horse.

"Does he know anything?" asked Doc.

"He knows lotsa things, I guess, but you oughtn't bother with him. We got acres to discuss."

"How's Kate settling in?"

"Just fine. Listen, you're a man who has particular skills that we could use more of."

Doc noticed a lizard with only three legs on the side of the road. It was dragging its body slowly against the dirt and sand. A rickety yellow windmill churned against the breeze, creaking from years of neglect. "If you need a lawman, I'm not your man."

"It's not like that all. I'm discussin' business. You're a man who likes fine things, and clearly your wife does."

"We're not married."

"Point is, I want to buy a bar, but I need a partner. I need someone I can trust, and Earp vouches for you. I talked it over with Hoodoo too."

Doc licked his lips. He thought about his expensive habits. "I haven't got much to put in. Only some faro winnings, but a lot of that went to travel and . . . medicine."

"I think you don't comprehend. I'm the money. You're the muscle. Sixty-forty."

"I don't think I have a muscle left in this sack."

J.J. looked over Doc's withered body. He chuckled. "Long as you can lift that pistol, that's all the assurances I require."

The roadside was flat and dry with burnt, honey-yellow reeds covering the land. In the distance, dull mountains cut into the gray sky. Dust kicked up into Doc's throat and nostrils. He tried to hold his breath. *I might as well be sand inside anyway*, he thought. There were hundreds of hoofprints in the dirt, and Doc wondered how many consumptives had taken the trip out to the springs—and how many had taken the trip back. He was looking forward to seeing Kate. He finally had some energy to give her what she wanted. She was a voraciously sexual being, something for which he felt both great veneration and shame.

In the distance, Doc could make out the town through the wavy desert air.

"What we talked about—keep that dry. Don't need no one comin' in late on the land," said J.J.

Doc grinned as the horse defecated in front of him in small patties, swishing its tail. "I'm a veritable jewelry box of secrets."

"Right, well let's get us some nose paint. I'll show you the locale."

"It's about time. I was beginning to think you were sober," said Doc.

"I wouldn't survive nary a minute in this town without some pop skull and a painted lady."

Doc enjoyed J.J.'s colorful language. He was a like mind. Whiskey and women always did him right. He began to think of Mattie and what she'd say if she knew what he'd gotten into. His girl was faithless, his lungs full of blood and liquor. He would write her when he got back. Just to say hello. Just to remember what being ordinary felt like.

When they got back to town, J.J. and Doc went to inspect the saloon. It sat at the end of Center Street, a bit removed, and it was basically a plain white front and a hitching post with a single horse latched to it. Four wooden columns supported the balcony where Doc imagined wild intimacies might happen under his perverted supervision. Inside, there wasn't much improvement. The parlor reeked of stale beer, and three buck heads hung above the dimly lit wood bar. It was narrow, filthy, and the only customer was so still that he could have been deceased. The only thing it did have was bourbon, lots and lots of bourbon. Probably because no one ever came in to drink it. The other saloons were too popular. The bartender was old and withered and didn't even notice when they walked in. The mosquitoes scattered sideways into the walls, their bodies swollen with blood.

Doc wiped his sweaty forehead with his handkerchief. "Is it always this parched here?" he asked.

The barkeep slowly turned around. "Most of the business stays farther up the street." He picked up a brown, opaque bottle of booze.

"Two of those," said J.J., turning his attention to Doc. "So?"

"I think it is the most vile, inconsequential, vacant space I've ever laid my eyes on." Doc rested his hat on the dusty bar and wiped more sweat off his skull, but it poured down into his eyes. He grew feverish.

"Don't think many patrons will scatter the chance to meet a legend in person."

"And this is the part where you offer me fifty percent."

"Yer ace-high, Holliday, you know that?"

Doc cleared his throat. He inhaled the moldy air and threw back his drink, cringing as it singed its way down. "Well, you've got your legend. And, apparently, I've got a bar."

By the time Doc arrived at the Plaza it was sundown, and he was drunk. Kate wasn't in the room, so he sat and started writing a letter to Mattie:

Dear Sweet Mattie,

I have not heard from you in some time. I am at the Plaza Hotel in Las Vegas, New Mexico and the nearby springs have replenished me for the time being. I have done things that I know will never allow you to be mine and I will die before I ever am able to return to Georgia to explain, unless by some miracle I find the fountain, so please remember me in the way that I was. What they say about me in the papers is mostly lies. I wouldn't even have had time to shoot that many men and the drink, as you know, is my only relief from the cough. Please let me know you are safe and well and that I am not alone in all of this.

With love,

John Henry

Doc looked around for an envelope, but there was none. His head lolled back, and he began to drift off. Flies covered the ceiling, their hairy black bodies scratching against one another. *The nicest hotel in town*, he recalled.

When Kate walked in, Doc wrenched open his eyes. He tried not to appear relieved to see her. He tried not to show his love because it weakened him, and he couldn't afford any more weakening. "I think I'm cured, darlin'." His voice was raspy with drink.

"Hmmf, you sound it."

"Good to see you've been thriving in my absence." Doc noticed a new necklace draped around her neck. He was almost sure Hoodoo had given it to her. "I'm endeavoring to buy a bar with J.J. Webb."

"Is that prudent?"

Doc rose from his chair and wrapped his arms around Kate's corseted waist.

"Now where did you go and learn a big word like that? Have you been reading behind my back?"

"For God sakes. I wish I could once come home and not find you soused on corn juice." She peeled his arms away, standing in front of the bedside mirror, watching Doc behind her, his eyes circled in dark rings.

"I saw a three-legged lizard."

"Well, I think it's fine that you'll be pulling in steady money again. You always seemed happier when you was working on teeth." She faced Doc and ran her hands over his shoulders. She lowered her fingers to his crotch, but the slightest touch tipped him onto the bed. He fell effortlessly and closed his eyes. "You used to want to romp when you were drunk." Kate straightened out her corset, a bit deflated. She took his guns and placed them on the bedside table, took off his boots and socks too. "I'll be dinnering on my own then? Maybe I'll find someone to keep me company."

"Have fun now, bumblebee." Doc moaned a little and rubbed his bare feet together.

Kate didn't bother to shut the door as she left.

The next morning, Doc picked the crust out of his eyes. Kate never came home. He decided if there was no one keeping him that he'd find out what the Apache knew, so he took his guns, his flask, a stale piece of bread, a compass, and the note with the directions and headed toward the desert. The man at the springs had drawn a very detailed map with all sorts of markers along the way. Trees that looked like ears and lynching poles and that sort of thing. Doc trusted him enough to try it. He figured as long as he turned around before dark he'd be all right even if there was nothing out there.

The ground was the color of creamed coffee. Patches of brittle grass interrupted the dirt. In the distance, where Doc was headed, a large mountain jutted up from the ground as if everything around it had eroded from the wind. The sun was heavy and the sky too blue to look up at. Doc perspired under his hat, and the horse that Hoodoo had lent him pushed on through the day.

It took three hours: zigzagging into the sun, southeast, checking the map, the ink on the paper running with his sweat. It was just like the man had said. There was a house where there shouldn't be one. There wasn't even a well that he could make out. The heat blurred the ground in front of him.

Doc was relieved to find something. Any little bit that got him closer to the fountain held him together. Doc didn't want to face death in the same way he didn't want to face Kate, so he just ignored them both and kept his focus on the fountain. He was dried up from the ride. His horse needed water, and he needed whiskey. He hitched his horse on a wobbly post outside the Apache's house. It was just a shack next to a tall, thorny tree. A shovel and a club sat next to the door, which was painted turquoise but was chipped and flaking from the wind and heat. There was no glass in the windows, and Doc could see the Apache sitting inside, sweating.

The Apache's hair was long and greasy. He wore a band on his forehead, and he'd stuck two turkey vulture feathers over his left ear. He wasn't wearing much more than a brown sheet over his dark body. His face had seen too much sun and was dry and leathery. His eyes were deep brown with green speckles that seemed almost painted in; Doc thought maybe they weren't always that way, and he'd seen something that changed him.

Doc didn't bother knocking; he just pushed open the door and stood before the wrinkled man. The Apache got up and poured him a cup of coffee as if they already knew each other. He placed it on a small table next to the entrance and asked Doc to sit, which he did. The Apache remained standing.

"How did you hear about me?"

He didn't have an accent like other Indians. He'd been educated somewhere, or he'd spent enough time with Whites that he was comfortable with the language.

"A man at the springs told me," said Doc. He pulled out some tobacco, placed it in his lap, and grabbed some rolling papers from his jacket pocket.

"William Leonard," said the Apache.

Doc glanced up from the tobacco. “Never did get his name.”

“His name is William Leonard.” The Apache stared straight into Doc until Doc finally felt uncomfortable and returned to his rolling.

“He’s a lunger jeweler like you’re a lunger dentist. You fill a blanket like a woman by the way.” The Apache pointed to his thin cigarette and laughed. “Dainty fingers.”

Doc tweezed the end of the rolling paper and licked it closed. “So, you heard I was coming?”

“You know, last September, Leonard shot a man dead right in front of Ilfeld’s General Store. His name was Jose Mares.”

“Well, no wonder he and I got along,” said Doc with a big grin that dissipated as he thought of Ed Bailey’s sawed-off belly. He stuck the cigarette in his mouth and lit up. Almost immediately, the coughing began. It was a full minute before he could pull himself out of it, and the Apache just sipped coffee and watched him.

“Mares’s friends almost beat Leonard to death. That’s why he’s hiding out where you must’ve met him.” The Apache tinked his fingernail against the coffee mug. “You really should try.”

“You know where the real springs are? The fountain. That’s why I’m here.”

“Have some Arbuckle’s. Relax.” The Apache motioned toward the coffee cooling next to Doc.

Doc continued to sweat. He recognized his bootprints on the dusty floor. “It’s about a hundred degrees in here. Why in the hell would I want coffee?” Doc felt the frustration of all his failures bubbling up within him. Was this another dead end?

“Coffee is sacred to Apaches. It is a great insult to refuse when an Apache offers you coffee.”

“Really?” Doc glanced down at the mug as if it were a sacred relic. The steam rose into his eyes and made him tear up. He placed his palms around the tin cup. It burned his hands, but he raised it to his achingly chapped lips and took a sip. He waited a moment. “That is really excellent coffee.”

“The best.”

“I didn’t know your people were so tied to the coffee bean.”

“Huh? Oh, no I just said that to make you drink it.” The Apache smiled and took another sip of his coffee.

Doc felt lightheaded and leaned back into the chair. He was no longer sure where he was. Dark, gelatinous water pooled at his feet. It began to rise, and he could feel the water creep up on his ankles, then his knees. It forced him to the ground, but he wasn't afraid to drown in it. The Apache was gone, and all he saw was a sign that said 'Glenwood.' His fingers turned to sand, and Mattie knelt in front of him. Her hands massaged his crotch. She wore a nun's habit.

"You're on your own," she said.

Doc woke with a gasp. He searched around the room. Everything was the same as before. His feet weren't wet. He touched his fingertips together.

"You all right there?" said the Apache.

"What did you put in my coffee?"

"Nothing out of the ordinary."

"What is Glenwood?" asked Doc.

"Where'd you hear that name?"

"I'm not really sure."

"You want to know if there are springs out there that can cure what you've got? Make you young like a fawn. Make your joints stop aching and your shit smell fresher and your lungs pump again." The Apache took a long breath as if searching for a glimmer of the future. "Shit, I dunno."

Doc grimaced. "You know, I thought you would be more of a holy man or the sort."

"Sorry, I'm just a regular ol' Apache man. Nothing special with me. But the coffee is real good, right?"

Doc nodded and got up. "Have you got any water? It was a long trip."

The Apache filled a tin cup with water out of a large ceramic jug and handed it to Doc. "For what it's worth, Glenwood might mean the Glenwood Springs in Colorado. Not sure if that's the one of legend, but it might be worth a look-see. I've never been, but I hear it's real nice there. Not on any maps though. They have to choose you. Bring you in. I hear people never leave once they find it. Maybe it's what you're after."

"Funny, was just in Colorado. That's a daisy of a parting gift," said Doc, tipping his hat. He pushed open the door and returned to his borrowed horse. It was busy shooing flies away with its ratty tail. The sun was warm and high. He held the tin cup up to the horse's lips, and it slurped down the water with its thick, filmy tongue. "You need it more than I do," he whispered, dropping the empty cup down to the ground. When the horse was done, they started toward the blue mountains, miles off. Back west.

CHAPTER 13

[If] You Want Trouble

J.J. hadn't lied. By July, the business was up and running and Doc was in charge. He saw to it that if there was any blood spilled in the bar he was the one to do it. Mostly it had become a destination to be seen with Doc Holliday, lose some money to him, and take a photograph. He was a carnival act, but the money was green, and he hadn't had to do more than touch his holster when he saw trouble. *Maybe this is the life I've been waiting for,* he thought.

J.J. and Hoodoo had completely transformed the saloon. The bucks' heads were gone, and ox horns now hung above the shiny oak bar. They brought in artisans and carpenters to finely craft the woodwork around the bar, and they only served three types of liquor: bourbon, whiskey, and beer. The bar itself didn't have any stools, but there were a few tables for patrons and a gambling space by the door. Upstairs was the balcony where you could hire out one of the local girls for the night. It wasn't very private, but the patrons they attracted didn't seem to mind.

Doc usually stood in the corner of the bar with a glass of bourbon. Two or three women, all young and pretty, tended to his every need, waiting for their opportunity to take him to the balcony, though he hadn't yet obliged them. They were all cocktail waitresses, but they would have followed Doc if he were a barber or a coroner just as easily. Doc had earned himself groupies: Sally, Ida, and Clara. Clara smoked a lot and always wore a small hat to hide the gray streak in her hair, of which she was ashamed. Around her neck, she wore a pearl that an admirer had given her before he died in the war. Sometimes when she touched Doc's shoulder she would become very flush and run off to the bathroom to pray. Ida had large nostrils and would never stop talking about how "grand" she thought Doc was. "You're so grand, Doc," she'd say and Doc would pretend to yawn and watch Sally instead. Sally was the prettiest, but she had a hard case boyfriend who came around too often and didn't like that she worked there.

It made Doc feel healthy and powerful to attract these women. He wondered how much of it was his notoriety and how much was him, but the liquor dulled his doubts. It dulled everything just neatly enough most nights.

Each evening, Doc flirted and told stories and caroused with the locals. Each night, he would come home late not knowing if Kate would be in his bed. She'd taken to another saloon to spite him. Everyone knew her there. He wondered how many other men knew her. He imagined her paper-white thighs and how they belonged to him, and how he probably touched them less than the local gunsmith.

There was a lot of waiting in those days. Waiting to see if Kate would come back one night to the next. Doc wondered if he should smack her around like the other good ol' boys did or if he could reason with her. But it wasn't something to be reasoned. He couldn't tame her any more than she could harness his destruction, and they were a match made in the sticky pits of Hell for that reason. Maybe he liked her wildness.

He wondered what she'd be like as a regular wife, a regular woman cooking him meals and fetching him at the gambling parlor when the sun set. He imagined he'd like to feel normal in that way and knew that was a fading dream. He could never be normal again. She was only what he desired at midnight, not before or after.

Doc nodded off at around two in the morning. Kate wandered in drunk a few hours later with her shoulder strap ripped, her green eye shadow raccooned from tears. She tried to sneak in but tripped over Doc's shoes.

"Goddamn, goddamn," she muttered, rubbing her toe.

Doc turned on the light. "I take it you'll need more money tomorrow. Or maybe you made some tonight."

She slipped off her stockings while trying to shield her eyes from the light. "You're home early."

"Tables went cold."

"Well, no steak for us."

"Where in the fuck were you?"

"You've got—" She searched for the word through languages. "Bull testicles asking me that. God knows you've bedded every painted cat in ten miles. Lucky we both don't have French Pox!"

"I'm going to miss you when I'm gone," said Doc. He pulled the covers up on his throat. He sweated with fever. Kate looked down at him, lifting her blue dress over her head. Her breasts were small and perky. She walked to the washroom and grabbed a wet cloth. Carefully, she climbed into bed and dabbed Doc's burning forehead. It felt cool and calm. It was the happiest he'd been all day, he realized.

"I missed you a little bit," he whispered.

"I knew you did. I'm sick as a miner's canary over it. I'll stay in tomorrow morning. We can just laze around and you can shower me with attention." She rubbed the tufts of hair on his chest.

"Sounds like every other day." He smiled, and only his teeth showed under the damp cloth.

She smacked him playfully on the arm and nestled up against his warm body. "Don't pretend one of us could exist without the other," she said.

It was the middle of July, and the town was agitated with sweat and the stink of hot horseshit foaming in the streets. People's minds began to bend from the stinging sun. An old woman died from thirst a few nights back. Hoodoo organized a small procession down Center Street for her withered body. Not many people knew her, but as it passed, Doc came out of the saloon and removed his hat. He had an affinity with the dead.

He imagined himself being paraded down Center Street in a box, rotten from heat. Who would know him, really? They could write whatever they wanted about him, fiction mixed with legend, mixed with flint and sex.

He stepped back into the bar where he found a familiar face.

"Maybe the next spot can be a bit north," said Wentworth, wiping his sweaty forehead with his sleeve.

Doc was happy to see him. "You won't have much to report here. I'm just a small business owner now." He smiled, flattening his mustache.

"You're never just one thing, Mr. Holliday." Wentworth held a lens in his hand. He breathed on it, and it fogged up. As his breath cleared, Doc saw himself in it, contorted, curved like an hourglass. Wentworth wiped it with his coat sleeve.

"I find it hard to believe that you can stay out of trouble for more than an hour at a time. I'd wager my career on it." Wentworth started to set up his tripod.

"Haven't you already?" Doc motioned to the bartender for two drinks.

"There aren't many things in this world surer than you shooting someone or someone trying to shoot you. It's hard to tell if you'd be worth more alive or dead, but I do enjoy our conversations."

"Well, then it's settled. I'll live a little longer." The bartender arrived with two whiskies and placed them in Doc's and Wentworth's sweaty palms. "With our boots on." They drank them down like old friends, but Doc was always wary of Wentworth too. *You can't trust a man who'd watch someone die just to have a good story to tell,* he thought.

"Any luck with that Indian?" asked Wentworth, but he'd already lost Doc's attention.

By the bar, Mike Gordon was drunk and arguing with his girlfriend, Sally, again. The other two waitresses tried to wedge themselves between the bickering couple, but Gordon just swatted them aside like dragonflies. Sally had these cat eyes, a little yellowish. It was hard not to stare at them, so Doc did. Gordon grabbed her arm and slapped her clear across the face. It was a loud, hollow sound that carried throughout the room, and the men nearby turned away. It was not polite to interfere with a sport and his girl. From her timid reaction it wasn't the first time he'd smacked her, but Doc had taken a liking to Sally, and he didn't much care for violence against the defenseless, whether they be women, cripples, or writers.

He patted Wentworth on the shoulder, slugged down his whiskey, and made his way over to Gordon, who was looming over Sally, crumpled on the floor. "I'm afraid you're no longer welcome, Mike. Our waitstaff needs to be in working order."

Gordon was taller than Doc with a concrete frame. He had large, rough hands.

"Think you can tell me how things is? I know how they is."

"Something tells me you were a poet before Las Vegas. Am I right?" said Doc. By now, everyone was watching. Gordon was a local, a Cowboy, former Army scout.

"Goddamn you and this pisshole lush-crib. You got no rights keeping Sally here. She belongs with me, not whoring around with some lunger," Gordon slurred.

"Now there's no need to insult the establishment, except for over-serving, perhaps." Doc shot a glance at the bartender, who was ducking behind the stacked glasses. "You'll be welcome back tomorrow when you're not loaded to the gunwales. Until then, it's best you leave Sally to her duties."

Gordon wound back as if to punch Doc, but Doc readied his hand at his holster.

Gordon tightened his knuckles but didn't swing his arm around. His face reddened with frustration. "You ain't nothing but yer equalizer."

"We have a—symbiotic relationship," said Doc, clicking his fingernails against the pistol butt.

Gordon grabbed Sally's arm and started to drag her out with him.

Doc cut him off, digging his heel into Gordon's toes. "That's not the deal, friend. I feel I'm being a real gentleman about this." Doc twisted his boot edge further into Gordon's foot until he finally released Sally, leaving four thick red lines on her forearm.

After a moment, Doc lifted his boot, and Gordon pushed past him, crashing through the swinging doors as he left. Doc watched him leave with his hand still dangling quick at his waist. After Gordon got through the doors, Doc helped Sally up, and immediately Ida and Clara came to her aid. Sally was holding back tears. Ida gave Doc a kiss on his flushed cheek.

The bar was silent. "Well, I sure could use some firewater after all that," said Doc, smiling. The tension in the room dissipated. But just as Doc took as deep a breath as possible, two shots came screaming into the bar from out front. Sally burst out into a scream. The bartender crumpled down in a heap. Doc knew what would come next. All the eyes in the bar trained on him. Wentworth furiously attempted to load his camera.

With a resignation, Doc drew his Colt from his holster and walked toward the saloon doors. From inside, he could see Gordon with his pistol up.

"You goddamn gallinipper, you motherfucker. You fucked her," screamed Gordon.

Doc pushed through the doors.

Gordon fired another shot into the bar, wide of Doc.

"Don't you come no closer," Doc said to Gordon, who had a mad look—the same as Marcus had the night Kate shot him in the back. He recalled the weight of his oily body. How he could hardly breathe. Doc walked closer. They locked eyes.

At five feet, Doc lifted his arm, aimed, and shot Mike Gordon dead in the middle of Center Street. He stood over the body, watching his syrupy blood run into the dirt. Doc tried to swallow, but his throat was too dry. He felt weak. From inside the saloon, he saw a flash go off in his periphery. Hoodoo Brown and J.J. came running up.

"Jesus," said Hoodoo, mesmerized by the hole in Gordon's chest. "What happened?"

Doc cleared his throat and holstered his pistol. "Well, clearly he died of natural causes."

CHAPTER 14

Somebody That I Used to Know

Doc, Hoodoo, and J.J. sat in Hoodoo's office just off Center Street. Behind Doc stood two tilted bookshelves with a litany of large hardcovers that Hoodoo had clearly never opened. A hose hung down from the gas light fixture in the middle of the room and trailed off under Hoodoo's desk. A spotty map of the region hung on the wall adjacent to Doc, who swished the bourbon in his cup and stared out the window as Hoodoo spoke.

"You sure stirred up some shit, Holliday. I got a buncha angry people calling for your neck. It's already bad enough covering up for J.J. and Dirty Dave and Mather, but you just killed a Cowboy in broad daylight in front of a bunch of his friends."

Doc licked his salty lips, glaring at J.J. "If they were such good friends they would have told him to stop shooting at my bar."

"Our bar," said J.J.

"Exactly right. Our bar. And what was my assigned role in our bar, pray tell?"

Hoodoo waited on J.J.'s answer, already shaking his head.

"Well, hell, you didn't have to kill 'em!"

"Look, Doc." Hoodoo came over from behind his desk and placed his hand on Doc's shoulder.

"You don't need to tell me. This town is run by criminals, and you could do with one less," snapped Doc.

J.J. laughed. "You are one hard case motherfucker. I like you, Doc."

Doc slapped Hoodoo's arm away. "Well, hell, what do you do to the men you don't like?"

"There are easier ways to get rid of you than to sit down and talk it out," said Hoodoo.

"And just what might those be?" Doc's blue eyes widened so that they nearly consumed the room.

"Hell, Doc. Not everything everybody says is a goddamn draw," said J.J.

Hoodoo placed an envelope of folded bills on the edge of his desk. "Consider it a parting gift."

Doc got up and finished his glass. He slammed it on Hoodoo's desk and grabbed the cash. "It's a real fine operation you all are running here. Glad you found use for me."

Doc put on his hat and headed out. Outside of Hoodoo's office, someone had posted a sign:

TO MURDERERS, CONFIDENCE MEN, THIEVES:

"The citizens of Las Vegas have tired of robbery, murder, and other crimes that have made this town a byword in every civilized community. They have resolved to put a stop to crime, if in attaining that end they have to forget the law and resort to a speedier justice than it will afford. All such characters are therefore, hereby, notified that they must either leave this town or conform themselves to the requirements of law, or they will be summarily dealt with. The flow of blood must and shall be stopped in this community, and the good citizens of both the old and new towns have determined to stop it, if they have to HANG by the strong arm of FORCE every violator of the law in this country."

—Vigilantes

It seemed blood followed Doc everywhere. He headed back to the Plaza to pack up and tell Kate they'd be moving on again. She wouldn't be happy, but it was better than getting lynched or shot in the back. They'd head to Tombstone, he figured. That's where J.J. said he'd heard Wyatt was headed. Wyatt could protect him there now that things had blown over. Doc felt like he'd been running ever since that watering hole, and yet he'd hardly once turned down a fight or refused a challenge. He'd killed nearly every man who'd ever drawn on him. Still, as he walked through the downy New Mexico heat he couldn't help but feel like a coward. Just as worthless as the major.

He remembered walking into the house while his father's fiancée, Rachel, was trying on her wedding dress in the major's room. She didn't hear him come in, and John Henry just stood in the doorway, watching. The veil came down to her ankles, and the top ruffled around her bust, but the corset was taut so that it pinched her waist almost to nothing. She didn't notice him at first and looked very pretty gazing into the cloudy mirror when she thought no one was watching.

It was the first time Doc had wanted to touch anyone but Mattie. He felt guilty for it. He'd never seen anything so white. Then he felt it come on. He had to cough so badly. He tried to hold it in, get back outside before she noticed him, but he couldn't, and the force dropped him onto his knees right there in the doorway. Rachel whipped around and ran over as fast as she could, her dress swishing side to side. She knelt down and rested her warm hand over his convulsing chest.

He felt something close to comfort then. "I'm sorry," he gagged.

"Nothin' to be sorry for," she said, helping him to his feet.

After a moment, he didn't need to cough anymore. He was going to say something about her dress or how pretty she looked, but the major walked in. He was heavy with whiskey, his eyes drooping. He was red and sweaty from chopping wood in the back.

"Hell, I'm not supposed to see you in that. What's he doing here?"

Rachel froze in place. She had seen the major in that state before.

John Henry was slight, his mustache thin. He walked straight up to his father and said, "You just come and go as you please. You left Ma to die. You couldn't even defend yourself because you're too busy shitting your pants."

Without hesitation, the major wound his arm back and struck John Henry with all the force in his thick, hairy body. His backhand landed like a brick, driving John Henry several feet. His face split open below the eye where the major's ring had made contact.

"Yer no longer wanted here. Best be gone before the nuptials. Best for everbody." The major wrenched his wrist as he walked away.

When he was out of sight, Rachel went over and tended to John Henry's cut, tearing a piece of her dress off and wrapping it around his gushing head.

"You don't have to do that," said John Henry. There was a smear of blood on her dress, and the bottom was tattered and uneven.

"The bottle makes him a real sonofabitch. Don't want you remembrin' him that way. Or me. You remember people how they are."

He saw something of his mother in Rachel that night. Something true. It made him even more incensed that he would never have her. That the major would toss her around and penetrate her, his thick, hairy hands roaming over her lithe body.

Blood dripped into his mouth. He got up and dusted himself off. That night, he'd pack up and be gone by morning. Off west to be free. To find some comfort before the sickness took everything. He wiped the blood from his lips. "I'm real sorry about your dress, Rachel. It looked pretty. I wanted to tell you that."

By the time Doc got back to the Plaza, he was dripping with chunky, boozy sweat. Three young women and two young men, none of whom were much beyond their teen years, were waiting in the lobby. They immediately rushed up to him with fountain pens, asking him to sign their breasts and white-brimmed hats respectively.

"How salacious," mumbled Doc as he scribbled his signature on their pale flesh and cloth. He stared down into the girls' endless cleavage. It was like a chasm, dark and cool, and he wished he could jump inside and wade his cock in their innocence. The girls kissed him on his wet cheeks and the men shook his clammy, flaccid hand.

"We've been waiting since yesterday. We heard you were here, and we had to see you ourselves. You're in all the papers," said the tallest girl. She was thin, like she didn't eat three meals a day, but her skin was sunny with youth.

"Wentworth must be doing his job," said Doc.

"Who?"

"Nobody."

The girls compared notes; they held his picture up to his face, lingering, hoping for another touch.

"Go on now, you got what you came for," said Doc.

The ladies giggled and said goodbye, and with excited grins they headed out to celebrate a small victory. They could now always say they'd met the husk of Doc Holliday. Doc wobbled in the middle of the lobby.

"You okay, Mr. Holliday?" asked the boy at the front desk. They kept a kid there in the day and a decrepit older lady at night.

"Never you mind," Doc said.

He struggled up the long, winding staircase, each step aching in his thighs. He took long, sharp breaths and held onto the banister when he felt dizzy, eventually reaching his room on the third floor. The carpets always smelled wet there. Kate wasn't inside. He crumpled onto the bed, wheezing heavily. Something was different about the room, he realized; most of her things were gone. There was a letter on his desk. He pushed himself upright. Someone had opened it.

Dear John Henry,

I shudder to think of the horrible weight those men's souls must put on you every day. I pray for you. I pray for them, too. Atlanta was a long time ago and we've both become something entirely new. I have entered the Church and have taken my vows. I suppose we can both take solace that those summers when you were so close to me, when I knew you best, is the closest I will ever come to loving anyone. I will always remember those moments, but I fear you must forget them. Save yourself, John Henry, and repent. Your path is dark with blood, and I've stopped reading the papers because they say such grisly things about you. Things you tell me are true. In a way, I believe we both died the moment you left, or maybe that's just the way I like to see it.

Goodbye with love,

Mattie

Doc feared that was the last time he'd ever hear from Mattie. God took away something that belonged to him. It was a theme now. A sick feeling grew in his belly, a mixture of hunger, solitude, and diarrhea. Kate must have found the letter and taken off. It seemed he'd pushed everyone in his life just to the brink and then over.

He rested his revolver on his chest. It was hot from the sun and smelled like hide. He sunk into his bed, his eyes open for hours—unable to look away from the brown, cloud-like stains on the ceiling and the cluster flies darting and fornicating between them. It was the only sky he knew. He could still taste Kate in the air; on the bed, her perfume. When he couldn't take it anymore, he packed up his clothes and whiskey. Downstairs, he ran into the bellboy.

"If Ms. Elder comes back you let her know I took off to Tombstone to track Wyatt Earp. Tell her she's welcome to come home whenever she sees fit. Tell her I'm sorry, I guess."

The boy nodded absently. "You mean Mrs. Holliday?"

Hearing his name as hers gave Doc pause. He wondered if it was because he wanted it that way. Maybe it was okay for a wife to act like a whore but impossible for a whore to act like a wife. Maybe he'd sought too much from her. "If that's what she's been calling herself."

Doc waited at the train station. It was quiet there. A light breeze moved the hollow reeds against the tracks, and the day was bright and clear. Couples passed him, their arms locked, the most modest women in long black dresses in July. It disgusted him. He imagined their moist bodies underneath, their suffocating genitals and lace undergarments. He saw them for who they were. He lit up a cigarette to keep from coughing. Blood soaked the paper like lipstick.

CHAPTER 15

Pale Horse

Tombstone, Arizona 1880

Time passed slowly on the train. The distance turned red; the rock of the foothills. The air scratched like paper. Crickets itched, and their bodies echoed through the chili pepper mountains into the scarlet earth. It almost seemed as if someone had carved the desert himself. Someone like God but with less at stake.

Doc was excited to see Wyatt. It was rare to find someone he could call a friend, and he wondered if Wyatt felt the same way or if it was out of debt for his life that he tolerated him. He thought of the last time he was on a train and how Kate had nursed him back to life. Wyatt had family, a wife—even if she was a whore. Certainly, Doc was no one to judge. He wondered if Wyatt's brothers had followed him to Arizona. Wyatt only talked about them when he got drunk and nostalgic, but it seemed that they had a real kinship, or anyway, thought Doc, they stuck by blood.

Outside, the terrain was flat, mostly, with conical hay bales dotting the land like sharp brown figs. The heat burned the grass so it was brittle and beige. As his eyes passed languidly over the fields, someone tapped Doc on the shoulder.

"I suppose you're in this for the duration," said Doc, unsurprised to see Wentworth.

Wentworth nodded and sat across from Doc. The train wasn't crowded, and each man occupied his own cloth-seated booth. A wooden table separated them.

"You're fortunate that the duration might only consist of a month or two," said Doc, returning his gaze to the window.

"It's really incredible that you've managed to incite another lynch mob in a new town. You've got a real talent. How's the missus?"

"None of your goddamn business." He didn't feel like talking about her. Just another woman he couldn't count on. He licked his lips and took a swig straight from a full-sized bottle of Kentucky bourbon.

"Not fooling around," said Wentworth, pointing at the bottle.

"Some sympathetic admirers brought it for me as a gift right as I was boarding the train. They didn't ask for anything in return. Isn't that strange?"

"Not really." Wentworth thought hard for a moment. "People seek you out. They find freedom in you. How you are."

"But you know better." Doc inhaled as deep as he could and tapped his fingernails on the table, wheezing the air back out of his mouth.

"I think I know you all right. I think I know that you're not unafraid, that you think about how you'll die, you think about home. About the fountain. Renewal."

"I don't think about home anymore."

"Something I should know about?"

The train rumbled. It shook the phlegm loose in Doc's chest. They were slowing down, approaching a station. "I was a good dentist, you know. I took pride in that."

The wheels squealed against the rusty track. "Nobody says you can't practice."

"They'll never leave me be. I had a business. Legitimate. You kill one man and the whole town forgets the rules."

"If it's any consolation, I wrote what I saw."

"And what did you see, Wentworth?" Doc's eyes were bloodshot. He was tired and the alcohol made his face bloated and heavy. Faint scruff grew on his cheeks. He laid his head back.

"Indulgence, devotion—recklessness. They worship or fear you, but they're simple. That's all there is for them."

"I'd describe myself as a mountain cat with the heart of a beaver," said Doc, baring his teeth.

"Couldn't have said it better myself."

They both settled into their booths. Doc smoked, and Wentworth closed his eyes, trying to sleep. The rest of the trip would be quiet, each man dreaming of comfort, ambition, and the most recent corpse. It was getting harder and harder to keep track.

There was something different in the clouds above Tombstone. The way they swirled, there was something black in them. The sun never seemed to reach the ground. In the distance, a smoky funnel twisted over the cracked earth and left Doc with a funny feeling in his belly.

Doc and Wentworth separated as they exited the train, agreeing to have lunch the next day so that Wentworth could write a story on his arrival, on the condition that he lied about Doc's reason for leaving New Mexico. The town was fairly large and growing. People dressed up—petunia, scarlet, and mint. Hulking, ruffled shoulders and long trains dragging along the dirt; bonnets like great winged doves, fluttering oriental fans, and tiny cloth umbrellas that could not impede the sun, certainly not the rain. Women in their finest during the day was unusual in places out west. *Tombstone isn't just another silver boomtown,* thought Doc. But he'd heard stories too. This was where the Cowboys set up shop. This was where they called home, and they had stakes all over Tombstone. This town was bloody too. Doc felt like he already belonged. Like he was supposed to be there.

With one hand, Doc dragged his bag down the dusty road leading to the main street. He pushed off on his cane with his other hand. He was spent from the ride. Too many moves; maybe he'd finally found a place to settle. Immediately, his mind jumped to Kate, and he wondered if it would really be settling without her. He hoped she was all right. In a way, he hated her for putting them through this business of caring. Making him wish it would all just be over and he could go back to dying on his own like he'd planned. He wondered if she even loved him. Most of the time it seemed like she despised him. When he met her she was just another whore, but she'd become someone who could salt his insides. He shook off the thought.

As Doc trudged his way into the town center, a man a little shorter than him walked out in front and stopped him. He wore a badge on his long white coat. His hair was curly from the heat, and he kept a thin mustache. He was in his early thirties, maybe. Doc figured him for the marshal.

"You know how to read them signs?" The marshal pointed past Doc, to his right.

A sign read:

ALL GUNS MUST BE CHECKED AT
SHERIFF'S OFFICE OR GRAND HOTEL

"Reading is one of my more mundane talents," said Doc.

"Look, we got laws here. Dunno where yer from—"

"Georgia."

"Yeah, well this ain't Georgia. This is Tombstone, and I'm marshal here, and you gotta check yer guns."

"I've just arrived. How could I have checked my guns already?"

The marshal spat to his side, stalling for time. "I don't need to answer yer questions."

"No, I suppose you don't. Well played." Just then, from behind the marshal, Doc saw a familiar face.

He took his time walking over on the scorching July afternoon. "Fred," Wyatt Earp said to the marshal. "This is Doc Holliday. He's harmless."

"Holliday?" said the marshal, searching his memory. "Oh. Well doesn't that cap the climax. Harmless? That's not what they says in the papers."

"Ah, so you're a literary as well!" said Doc. "We're like a couple of songbirds in June, you and I."

"How are you, Doc?" Wyatt shook Doc's hand firmly.

"Better for seeing you, Wyatt." It felt like true relief to see his friend. He felt genuine comfort in Wyatt's presence. It was one of the few times he didn't have to be what everyone expected of him. It wasn't an act with Wyatt. For a moment, he feared his friend would see him diminished, smaller than he used to be, withered. But a moment passed between them, and all was right. He was as reliable as a broke-in horse. "I usually like to be harassed on my way *out* of town."

"This here's Marshal Fred White. He's a good man. They're trying to keep this place from becoming Dodge all over again," said Wyatt.

"I had some great times in Dodge. Hell, you met your wife there." Doc paused for a moment and turned to Marshal White. "Well, if I don't have my guns how do you expect me to fight?"

"We don't 'spect fightin'," said the marshal.

Doc chuckled. "I see. This is a town of peace. So be it. I'll be sure to check my weapons as soon as I settle in."

White checked with Wyatt and Wyatt nodded. He was wearing a badge too. "I'll leave him in your hands, Earp."

Wyatt tipped his hat as White took off down the road.

Without commenting on Doc's weakened state, Wyatt lifted his bag with one arm and carried it as they sauntered into the town center. Tombstone was a pastel abomination, a multicolored eyesore of modernity, but all the wood was rotting and the prostitutes looked just as fresh. It was a hog masquerading as a mustang. The only establishments with new paint and level staircases were the gambling dens and bordellos. Doc sneered at their cleanliness, the appearance of order. He glimpsed Tombstone's future. This town would burn. Nothing drew carnage like an abundance of law. Nothing irked Doc more than hypocrisy. There would always be someone looking to get famous for killing him, and he knew it. They'd have to pry his steel out of his hands.

The buildings were taller in Tombstone, the newest of them gleaming like polished bronze. A couple of fancy hotels stood out, particularly the Cosmopolitan. As they walked, Doc was astonished to find a public library at J. Goldtree & Company's cigar store, something he planned on frequenting. Wyatt filled him in on Tombstone's goings-on, pointed out a school and reading room under construction. There was a miner's hospital, the Home Dramatic Association, the Tombstone Social Club, a functional fire department, and not one but two newspapers. *Wentworth will finally have somewhere local to publish his jabberings*, he figured.

"So, you're sticking with the law business," said Doc after a while.

Wyatt dangled the suitcase just above the dusty road. A horse and carriage rumbled by. "As decent as anything else. Virgil and Morgan bought in."

"How fraternal."

"Suppose you should meet them so they don't try and arrest you too."

Doc stopped in the road, holding his arms out like on a cross, his cane extending from his right hand. "What is it about me that everyone finds so threatening?"

"I reckon it's yer face."

Doc smiled. "But you. You've got the face of an angel." He caught up to Wyatt.

Wyatt's face had eroded with anxiety—the kind of worry born in injustice, born in the knowledge that nothing would ever feel permanent again. "No, I just have a badge," he said.

Doc coughed from the dust in the road. A little blood sprayed on the back of his hand, and he wiped it away quickly.

"I'll take you over to the Cosmopolitan. You'll be comfortable there. By the way, where's the rib?"

Doc swallowed, and the spit burned down his dry throat. He chuckled a little at Wyatt's choice of words. "Wherever she is I'm sure she's gallivanting."

"Yeah, she does that. Galli-vant." It sounded coarser coming from him.

Doc's feet throbbed. They arrived at the Cosmopolitan. It was surrounded by wooden steps, which felt strange. Long, thin white pillars held up the second level and then another set of them held up the blue roof. *They love their colors*, thought Doc.

Dangling black lanterns lined the windows and doorways. Maybe it looked better on the inside.

"Get some sleep. This town's ripe for profit," said Wyatt. "I ain't just here for lawing." He returned Doc's bag.

"I'm fresh as a daisy," Doc wheezed. Sweat dripped down the brim of his black hat.

"You look like yer just about ready to shoot the cat. You can find me at the Oriental when you're ready. There's always a scrap or two to be breakin'."

"Sounds like my type of lush-crib." Doc trudged up the stairs and into the hotel. He dropped his bag on the floor, but the bellboy just stood there and stared at him like he was naked.

The man at the desk nudged him forward.

"You're Doc Holliday, ain't you?" asked the boy.

Doc removed his moist hat. "Set me up with a pint of scamper juice in my room, and if a man named Wentworth comes looking you tell him where I am. If anyone else comes looking, you tell me where *he* is. Clear as diamond's dust, yes?"

The boy nodded and rushed to pick up Doc's bag. He started up the staircase to the second floor.

"Let's see this urban paradise."

The room was adequate. It seemed cluttered, red velvet drapes gilded by frills on top. There was a bed in the right-hand corner and various armoires with empty water pots atop them that lined the room. A wooden reading chair, a bathtub. The boy set down Doc's bags. Doc fumbled in his pockets for a coin to give the boy.

"Wait!" said the boy and ran out of the room.

Doc wasn't sure what to make of it. Not many people he'd ever run into refused money. He was usually shooting someone just to keep it.

Two minutes later, the boy returned with a pen and a torn piece of paper. "I'd much rather have this, if it's all the same."

Doc looked down at him. He took the paper and signed it. "Saves me notes. I'm happy to." He gave it back. The boy smiled big. He nodded, closed the door, and left Doc to sleep off the train ride.

CHAPTER 16

Where Did You Sleep Last Night

Doc was dozing in the hotel when he heard a commotion at the door. He grabbed his Colt from the nightstand, cocked it, and waited, stiff as a dead squirrel. He couldn't make out what was being said, but there was a man and a woman. Suddenly, the voices were all too familiar.

"You'll do nothing but get Doc bushelled. Why don't you stay clear of him?" said Kate. "We have plans. I've got to make him better, and you and all your peoples just make him worse."

"I was just coming up to check on him. You haven't been real attentive."

"Relations between my husband and I are none of your concern."

"You're married now?"

"It's just a formality! He asked and I accepted."

"Congratulations," said Wyatt.

"Fuck you."

Doc opened the door with a sleepy look on his face. He looked down at all of Kate's bags. "Well, hello, darlin'. I wasn't expecting you."

Kate immediately embraced him tightly and kissed his rosy cheeks. He hugged her lightly back.

"Wyatt. Nice of you to drop by. Sorry for our lack of hospitality."

He rolled his eyes. "Well, I'll leave you two to it then." Wyatt walked off, forsaking all pleasantries with Kate.

Kate dropped her bags inside the door and fell into Doc. She hugged him tight like she'd been through something. But Doc felt a very raw sort of resentment poke up inside him like glass. Still, he was glad she'd come back to him. He didn't have much left that was familiar.

He held her so tightly that it forced all the air out of her, and even though she was struggling to get out of his grip, he wouldn't let go. "Can't even be happy right now. I'm just relieved." Doc wanted to express something other than relief, but anything that had been inside of him was choked into a bodily sigh that she was unharmed. He couldn't remember how much he'd missed her or how he imagined her showing up one night and stripping down for him, laying her small breasts on his cold body. He couldn't remember all those nights when he sweated thinking about her and the other men entering her. The way he drank to forget her eyes. He'd only blurred them in his memory. They were impossible to erase. He only felt slightly unburdened by her presence now. Nothing more or less. And bitter that she'd put him through it. Not even a letter that she was alive.

She wriggled out of his grip and caught her breath. "My goodness, Doc. You must have really missed your little bee. For such a slight man you have a firmer grasp than a wrestling crow. Think about me?"

"I need to lie down now. It's quite a thing to lose someone and get her back. I figured you didn't think about me at all."

"But you still love me?"

"That's not something that dissipates. It just festers." Doc sighed. "Besides, wasn't my decision. Please believe that. You're the last person I wanted to love."

"That's a horrible thing to say to your girl."

Doc hobbled over to the bed and eased under the eggshell sheets. "You haven't been a girl in years, darlin'. You're all grown up. You hurt like a woman. Take pride in that."

"Aren't you the least bit interested in where I've been?"

Doc burrowed under the sheets. "This room gets cold at night. You should wear something to bed."

A couple of rocks skipped off the window. A girl yelled something from below.

"What in the hell?" Kate marched over to the window and opened it. Underneath, a small crowd had gathered. They all looked very excited and then, at once, wildly disappointed.

"Where's Doc?" a young man yelled up.

"He's sleeping. Now get the hell away before I call the marshal!" She slammed the window shut. "Can't get a moment of peace. Don't they know your condition?" She unlaced her girdle and sat on the bed next to Doc.

"God help them. They'd better learn *your* condition," said Doc.

"Stupid young girls trying to steal my man. They don't even know you. What is it they think they can offer?" She ran her hand over his clammy forehead. "I'll get you some whiskey and milk to warm up."

Doc closed his eyes and smiled. "Now I remember why I love you."

Tombstone Epitaph, October 12, 1880
"Interview with A Gambler, Carouser, Consumptive, Gunfighter, Dentist, and Most Charming Scoundrel Ever to Grace This Earth"
credit: John S. Wentworth

Doc Holliday sits with a tall glass of whiskey and a grin as if he knows everything I'm about to ask him and each answer is ricocheting around his erudite skull. He is a slight man, sickly, but his cheeks are red and his hair is kempt and polished. He is dressed well, a sharp gray outfit and silver about him. His gun protrudes slightly from his hip. He nods and takes a drink, signaling the beginning of the interview:

WENTWORTH: How many men would you say you've shot?

DOC HOLLIDAY: Not wasting time with pleasantries, I see. That depends. On the record, only the ones who had it coming to them. Fifteen or so. In self-defense, of course.

W: What would you say makes you so attractive to the youth of this nation?

DH: It must be our mutual love of philosophy.

W: Is that really your answer?

DH: I think everyone likes to identify with the villain now and then. Gives them a feeling of power because there's the sensation they're liberated, but it isn't true.

W: So you see yourself as a villain?

DH: Nothing's more colorless than a hero. There has to be some dichotomy to a man. He has to cheat the system every once and again. He has to be willing to be disliked.

W: Some people are wondering about Kate Elder, sometimes known as Big Nose Kate, and what your relationship is to her.

DH: I'm an on-again, off-again customer of Miss Elder's.

W: So there's no truth to the rumor that you two got married back in New Mexico?

DH: I believe in marriage about as much as I believe in the healing power of Jesus Christ.

W: Are you an atheist?

DH: I'm part of the Church of Smith & Wesson. I have no time for hypocrites. Too many men invoke God's name and live their lives like ungroomed weevils.

W: Speaking of living, how much longer do you expect to persist with your condition?

DH: How long is this interview?

W: Why did you leave Las Vegas?

DH: You know, I'm glad you asked me that. The rumors of my wrongdoing were wholly exaggerated, and I left of my own accord. I'd invite anyone who runs into Hoodoo Brown to take a shot at him for your old hero, John Henry Holliday. That town's flush with ne'er-do-wells.

W: What do you expect from Tombstone?

DH: What else is there? I've seen about everything I can expect from every man who draws on me. Every man who wants a footnote in a history book. I expect blood.

W: This town has come to be known as a Cowboy town, regardless of what the mayor says. Are you at peace with that faction?

DH: I've never been at peace my whole life.

W: Johnny Ringo is here.

DH: Is that a question?

W: They say he's the fastest pull in the West. Faster than you.

DH: The only man who's faster than I am is the one who cuts me down.

W: How would you describe your drinking habits?

DH: Tenacious.

W: You have consumption and you're searching for a mythical fountain, a cure-all. You're an educated man. Do you really believe such a thing exists?

DH: A lot of people out there haven't seen a light bulb yet. That doesn't make it any less bright.

W: Mr. Edison's invention aside, are you really saying you're a believer in a legend?

DH: I don't believe in much, but there's something out there that can cure me. Why is it that scholars have been seeking this out, writing about it since the age of exploration? It's reserved for the walking dead. That's me.

W: Fair enough. When asked in the underworld if he would do it all over again, Achilles said he would have been a farmer. Would you choose this life?

DH: Not sure you're pandering to your demographic here, but no one chooses to be this way. It's thrown upon us. It's our time. We're just living best we know how.

W: Finally, you seem to have a—we'll say, precarious relationship with God. Is there any chance of reconciliation?

DH: He'd have to make the first move.

CHAPTER 17

Fake Empire

Doc sat at the Oriental after a long session, with Wyatt standing nearby in case he collapsed. Marshal White was there, too, smoking a short cigar by the bar. Below the table, a young lady sucked on Doc's long, bony fingers. He didn't even seem to notice. The table was unusually full for such an odd time, mostly because Doc was still playing. Eight men in top hats and bowlers crowded around, bucking the tiger, trying to take something off of Doc so they could go back to their friends and brag. Even the dealer looked about ready to expire. Half of them were Slopers—West Coast card sharks—and half Easterners—the two sects of scoundrel gamblers flooding into burgeoning Tombstone. Their only difference was where they came from. Their thirst for disorder was the same.

The Oriental was a trendy saloon, slender and fixed with gas lamps on the walls. Next to the lights hung coats and hats, and the bar in the back was quiet for the moment. The bar itself was a quarter full, patrons leaning their dusty boots on the scuffed bronze railing running along the foot of the wood bar. In the corner sat a metal spittoon with spittle and dip drippings crusted down its side. The barkeeps wore white shirts and vests and bowties. Their greatest skill was taking all the abuse from inebriated madmen and killers and living to pour drinks another day.

Sunrise crept into the shadowy room.

"We're living in ruin, Wyatt," said Doc, inspecting his dirty fingers. He noticed the woman beneath him. "Oh, hello there." He gave her a pat on the head.

"You always did have some drama to you," said Wyatt. It was breaking dawn and there was nothing keeping Wyatt there but Doc's well-being. Doc vaguely knew Wyatt would have been to bed and up again if it were up to him.

Doc tried to clear his throat but couldn't. It made an ugly, guttural sound like a wounded elk. He drank down whatever was left in his tin cup. "They say it's a fallacy that if a man were born in a different time he'd be better off than he is now. But that's the God's honest truth. If I were a Roman under Trajan or a Frenchman under Louis Quatorze I'd be in just the right place."

"Can't say I'm familiar, Doc."

Doc whipped his head around and wobbled in his chair. "We've got to get some culture into you, Wyatt. You can't be like the rest of these thugs." The other players at the table became uneasy. "Not you all, of course; you're Oxford men. I can tell." Doc grinned.

Johnny Tyler, a Sloper from Missouri, took exception. "You mean to slight me? You saying I ain't learned?"

Doc staggered to his feet. He thought of the others he'd had to kill and how they hadn't given him a choice. Or maybe they had, and this was the way he chose to remember it. Tyler was a dirty sport and someone who ought to be dead one way or the other. He didn't like the way it felt when he downed a man, but he enjoyed the moment before. It felt like the ringing of church bells and biting into a fatty steak all at once. Doc tasted blood under his tongue. "Why don't you just draw, Sloper?" Doc grew tired of the dance.

Tyler sweated and flared his nostrils. His hat hung a dark shadow over his eyes, and the room lit up crimson behind him. His grizzled beard bled into his chest hair so that it resembled a bearskin. His pupils narrowed and he breathed heavy, staring down Doc. In an instant, Tyler twitched as if about to draw, but from behind, Marshal White wrapped his arms around him and dragged him away from the table. He took Tyler's gun and motioned to Wyatt to grab Doc's.

Doc turned around to Wyatt.

Wyatt gave him a look of resignation. "Don't make this a scene, Doc. You know what has to happen."

"My *friend*," slurred Doc. He handed over his pistol.

White pushed Tyler out of the bar and then returned after a couple minutes to place their guns behind the bar. Doc was in the exact same spot, Wyatt watching him worriedly. "You can pick it up when yer sober," he said.

"Well then I'd never see my gun again, would I?" Doc just stood there wobbling.

"Time to go home, Doc," said Wyatt, placing his hand on Doc's shoulder.

Doc smacked his hand away.

"Don't you tell me about home. You have a home as much as I do. This place is a rented grave."

Joyce, the bartender, came out from behind the oak bar. "Holliday, why don't you just do us all a favor an' die already? Not doing good for no one."

Doc smiled. "Finally, someone who speaks my language. If you'll kindly hand me my pistol from behind your ill-kept bar, I'll do some good by adding another hole to your head so you don't have to speak out the side of your mouth."

Joyce charged at Doc and picked him up by his belt, knocking Wyatt aside in the process. Doc was too weak to resist, limply struggling against the much larger Joyce. Joyce tossed him out on the street. Wyatt calmly stepped outside to gather him up. Doc was all limbs. Wyatt nearly carried him all the way back to the hotel. The two didn't speak a word, but Doc was raw about the whole scene. When Wyatt put him to bed, Kate wasn't there. Wyatt lingered in the doorway a moment as Doc's watery lungs struggled to breathe through the blood. After a bit, he shut the door and left.

The following afternoon, Doc returned to the Oriental. There was something bubbling up inside him. He hadn't slept; he looked ragged, up all night stewing with the embarrassment of being overpowered by Joyce. He felt weak. It was around two on Wednesday, and Doc wondered when the last time he drank water was.

He'd made the decision sometime during the night, in and out of consciousness. He made the decision because it didn't matter anymore and one death was just as good as another, even his own. Doc opened fire on Joyce with Kate's self-cocker that he found in one of the hotel drawers. The sound bounced around the old wood bar. "You're a real mail-order cowboy, Joyce. You're a fucking molly, sitting behind that bar with that smug look like there's something you do other than pour drinks for men who spit on your neck when your back's turned!"

Joyce hit the floor, grabbed Doc's own confiscated pistol from behind the bar, and fired three shots back, all wide of Doc. Doc got in closer, cocked Kate's pistol, and fired a shot straight through Joyce's left hand. It shattered the tiny bones inside, splattering pink flesh on the mirror behind the bar so that it looked like someone had been tossing ripe strawberries. Joyce grunted in pain but rushed at Doc and knocked him out cold with the steel butt of his own pistol. The blow left an imprint on Doc's forehead that read backward: *Property of J.H.H.*

Doc sat in a six-by-six wrought-iron cell that didn't quite reach to the ceiling. He leaned against the corner of the wall. Frenzied crowds waited outside the jail, trying to catch a glimpse of Doc from the single window that peeked into the dim room. Outside, it was a beautiful day and the sun washed over the desert and over Tombstone in radiant tangerine lights. The entire jail vibrated from the frenzied fanatics outside its walls. Doc vomited into the left-hand corner of his cell. "I could use some neck oil," he called out, clinking his flask against the bars.

His nose had been broken, and the marshal had decided to set it himself, so it was a little crooked now. A gash above his blackened eye leaked blood over his cheek and lips, and his mouth swelled. Joyce had put a good beating on him.

Marshal White leaned up against the cell. "That's the last thing you need, Holliday."

"Where's Wyatt? He'll tell you. It's for my malady." Doc belched. He tasted the corn and breadcrumbs he'd eaten the night before. It was getting harder and harder to force solids down his torn throat. He heard the crowd outside chanting his name. Except it wasn't his name. He considered who this man 'Doc' really was and how different he'd become from John Henry. John Henry loved music, his mother, and Mattie. Doc didn't love anyone but his own legend. He tried to reconcile the two personas, but the truth was that neither one was true. John Henry had all the mischief of Doc, and Doc still kept his romanticism when he could. He wasn't all bad, though sometimes he liked to pretend.

"Why don't you leave Wyatt out of your troubles? He's aiming at an honest living. Not like you."

"I'm honest as the whiskers on your ears," said Doc, dabbing his cut with his dirty sleeve.

"Sounds 'bout right. You know they say Joyce might die."

Doc wasn't certain how to feel. If he had to guess, he'd say he felt bad; but every man he killed meant less and less and added more and more to his popularity and notoriety—that had to be true, he'd decided, or else he'd be charged with unlawful murder. *That* he would regret. Besides, Joyce was just another man trying to take him down. *Still*, he thought, *he didn't deserve to die.* He wondered what Kate was doing right then. Where she was and if she kept her dress on. "What's the matter with him?" Doc licked the dripping blood off his auburn mustache.

"What's the matter? You shot him."

"In his hand."

"Well he's been bleeding all night, so I suggest you make your peace with him in case he goes. They might have to take the hand. Maybe he'll say a good word about you to the investigators."

"You mean you?" Doc chuckled, but he stopped because it burned his chest. "Haven't heard a good word about myself in some time."

"Seems like they all enjoy your brand." White motioned with his pointy chin in the direction of the chanting. Outside, the masses of fans seemed to swell by the hour, and the lines were five thick. They held up signs that read: *Nothing's More Colorless Than a Hero* and *Make The First Move, God!* His fans dressed in black dusters, gussied up like Southern sports, imitating a legend searching for a myth.

"Don't know better yet."

In the tiny window, one of the groupies squeezed her enormous breasts through the bars and jiggled them in Doc's direction.

"Suppose there's some advantage to having you here," said Marshal White. He appraised the breasts as he would a young horse. Her pale breasts bounced and squished against the iron. "No sense a propriety."

Pushing his way through the crowd, Wyatt rumbled into the jail, slamming the wood door behind him. "You see that naked one out there?"

Doc and the marshal nodded. "Hell, Doc, you're a regular Jesse James."

"Jesse James is a regular me. Kate come by?"

"No," said Wyatt. "You know, Doc, I feel like I done this before."

"There's a word for that, but it's French and I doubt you'd appreciate it," said Doc.

"Can't we build something? There's money to be had here. Can't we settle?"

"I'll die if I ever stop. I have to squeeze out every bit I got left."

Wyatt handed the marshal a few bills. "I'll see to him getting back to his lodging."

Doc got up off the floor. He stank the way fish do in the summer. The marshal opened the iron cell. It felt like climbing out of a casket. But as soon as Wyatt opened the jailhouse door, the crowd, frenzied with celebratory arousal, rushed into the building, knocking Wyatt back and encircling Doc. They smothered, licked him, covered him with garters and seaside petunias, Indian paintbrushes, and notes containing their innermost secrets:

"I made love to my holster once."

"My nipple is too big for my breast."

"I've never seen the sun rise."

Doc read them quietly and with great interest as Wyatt and the marshal beat his adoring fans back from him, flinging them into the street one by one. Wyatt and White made quick work of them until they lay bruised but sated on Tombstone's tobacco-covered Basin Street.

CHAPTER 18

Lonely Boy

In Tombstone, the leaves had all turned canary, complementing the grass, which had burnt beige. Evergreens swayed in the distance, and the mountains loomed ash and golden like the clouds. It was mid-October and the weather finally dropped below eighty. The rotten stench of politics lingered in the air as Garfield made his final push against Hancock. Doc never voted because he always felt like he lost no matter who got elected. Still, he admired Garfield's beard. It reminded him of a fashionable lady's pubis.

Having been released under Wyatt's supervision, Doc decided to pay Joyce a visit on his sickbed. He was holed up with his wife and a doctor in his house. Outside teetered a curlicue metal fence that Joyce had probably built himself. *From his craftsmanship*, thought Doc, *it wouldn't matter much if he had one hand or two*. Doc could see Joyce on the bed through the dirt-caked window, so he climbed over the knee-high fence and knocked on the glass.

When Joyce saw him, he immediately glowered. Doc knocked again. Indignantly, Joyce rose from the bed, opening the window with his good hand. The doctor had wrapped the other hand in gauze, but it soaked through with blood. When the window opened, a stench of old blood and hot saliva left the room. Doc was happy he hadn't eaten anything.

"Just what the hell you think you're doing here?" said Joyce. "And why don't you just use the front door?" He sat back on the bed as Doc poked his pale head through the window.

"I hardly think you'd want to see me," said Doc.

"I don't!"

"Well, exactly. Your wife would have just ushered me away or your doctor would've claimed that you're dying or some such." Doc eyed the room. It was an ugly pine box like the coffin he'd soon lie in.

"I am!"

"Nonsense. Do you want your tombstone to read 'died of a flesh wound'?"

"You shot straight through my hand."

"And is your hand not made of flesh? Think about your legacy, Joyce. Look at me. Look at the licks you put on me."

Joyce did look sickly. He was pallid and sweaty and in need of a bath.

"Is that why you came here? To berate my means of makin' the big jump? You bushwacked me!"

"Well, you gave me a good lacing, so we're square. All I wanted to say is that it was all a misunderstanding. Have you spoken to the marshal yet?"

"I ain't spoken to no one but the doctor and my wife."

"Well, perfect then." Doc pulled out his flask and offered it to Joyce, who hesitated but then took a swig. Doc took one too. He grimaced as the alcohol stung down his dry gullet. "All's better then. Accidents will happen—just don't go dying now."

"Go to Hell, Holliday."

"One of the few things you can count on."

After making his peace with Joyce, Doc felt confident he wouldn't be charged with murder even if the infection took hold. He rolled a cigarette pristinely, despite walking the whole time. He figured he owed Wyatt a visit. They hadn't spoken about anything but the trouble he'd been causing lately, and Doc felt a bit selfish.

Wyatt kept a tidy house. It was simple and rustic, like him. Two unsanded rocking chairs sat on the slanted porch, one smaller than the other. The house had two identical doors and windows. Lot 102. It looked like a place where a man could start a family, but Wyatt's family had died years back. Celia Ann didn't seem like the breeding type, not after what he'd seen in that opium den.

Doc rapped on the door with his cane. He puffed on his cigarette as he waited.

Wyatt answered with a scowl. "How'd you know I'd be home?"

"It's lunchtime," said Doc. In fact, Doc always kept tabs on where the town's lawmen might be at any given moment in case he had to pull a trigger sometime or another. "Why—you look like you've just swallowed a June bug."

"Nah." He sighed. "Come on in."

"Oh, now yer letting him in. I'm not done talking with you," said Celia Ann.

"Can't you see we got company?" growled Wyatt.

Celia Ann seemed to be trying to remember something unnatural to her. "Won't you sit down? Can I offer you something?"

"Bourbon, up. Or down. Whichever way you'd like to serve me bourbon is just fine, dear." Doc grinned.

"What brings you over here? You never come by before," said Wyatt.

"I imagined it to be just like this except with a room for all your spare mustaches."

"You never stop amazing me, Doc."

"Just a friendly visit, Wyatt, to check on your marital bliss. Any gossip around town regarding myself or my estranged lover?"

Celia Ann slammed down a glass of bourbon on the kitchen table. "Here."

Doc lifted the highball to his lips and nodded his head. Celia Ann made her way to the bedroom.

"How is the life, Wyatt? Is Tombstone everything you wanted?"

"Working some business plans. I got my brothers. In fact, they're meant to come over for dinner soon. You should join us. You still eat, right?"

Doc nearly coughed on his bourbon. "That's funny. I'd taken it for granted that you turned in your sense of humor when you received that badge."

Wyatt ran his thumbnail over the tin on his chest. "We're not all that way, just like not all two-bit gamblers will kill you for pocket change."

"No, not that little—" Doc was cut off by the sound of glass shattering in the other room. He and Wyatt rushed in. Broken milky shards skittered all over the floor, and Celia Ann tried to pick up the tiny pieces. Doc knelt down and read the label sinking into the liquid on the floor. Laudanum. She was still at it, doping up. It must have been what they were fighting about.

Wyatt's eyes got big like two shining pocket watches. "Go outside while I clean this up," he said, deep from his throat.

Celia Ann hung her head as she exited, her long brown hair blanketing any expression. She closed the door and sat out on the porch rocking back and forth with increasing speed. Any harder and she might have flown off into the vegetable garden.

"This is embarrassing," said Wyatt, bending down to collect the broken bottle parts.

Doc remained silent for a moment. He admired how bare the house was and realized it was Wyatt's hand and not Celia Ann's. He could tell by the details. The elk antlers on the wall. The oak chest that Wyatt must have built to hold his guns and other valuables sat in the middle of the room. Doc found it funny that a chest could be a centerpiece to him. All the things that had brought him to his point locked up neatly like treasure. A couple of chairs sat next to the window, one with a pillow on it and one hard as a rock where Wyatt sat in contemplation of the horrific ferocity of the land. A breeze fluttered the yellow curtains. Doc took a swig of the bourbon but then set it down to help out. "You know Kate once threw a mirror at me and threatened to kill me if I didn't buy her a new dress."

"That right?" Wyatt seemed to perk up. "So, what'd you resolve?"

"I bought her a new dress, and she said it was ugly. I said, 'It's ugly, huh? So shoot me!'"

Wyatt laughed despite himself in his deep baritone way. Something lightened in him. "That's a terrible joke."

Doc had always found that sharing misery was a decent way to delay it. "One day, fiction'll mix with history, and that's how they'll remember us. Not like we were—couple of lost boys."

"Maybe so." Wyatt scooped the remaining shards in his calloused palm. "You can come back in now," he yelled. But she didn't. She just stayed out there, shaking because it was getting cooler and the desert wind approached.

Doc and Wyatt drank and caught up. Eventually, Celia Ann was forced to return to the kitchen because she was cooking for the brothers Earp that evening. Morgan and Virgil walked right in without knocking. *It must be nice to have that sort of family*, thought Doc. Morgan was a good-looking slender man with a skinny bow tie and the scent of innocence that neither Wyatt nor Virgil had maintained through the years. They were all lawmen in one way or another now, but that wasn't their goal anymore. They wanted to sit back and pick the town clean from afar with investments in real estate and mining—the easy way to retirement.

Virgil was a bit thicker, a bit older. He shook hands as if he still had something to prove though—a quick, viselike grip that squeezed Doc's fingertips instead of his palm. They all parted their black hair the same way, and their mustaches were bushy, trailing off in whiskered horns at their ends. Virgil had some white in his mustache and his face had worn from time, blades, and indifference. He was the oldest, and Doc could tell it just by looking at him, the feel of his skin.

The men each removed their hats and placed them on the kitchen table. They sat and relaxed into their chairs. They all wore badges, which always made Doc uncomfortable. Virgil smoked.

"So, you all sleep in those things?" said Doc.

Morgan guffawed. "Doc fuckin' Holliday. Sure is a hoot to meet you. Brother always told me you two fretrenized, but seeing you in the flesh is really something."

"It's nice to be spoken of," said Doc.

"Sorry the wives couldn't make it, Celia Ann," Virgil called into the kitchen.

They certainly must see her as improper company, thought Doc. She had been a woman who sold her body, after all. Not exactly the kind of woman most respectable men brought home to meet the family. But Doc was used to such company. He almost preferred it.

Celia Ann glared at the whole table as if a pack of wolves had wandered into her house. She was a strange woman with habits that Doc didn't understand, but not much different than Kate, so he watched her with a sort of melancholic intrigue.

"So, what's this plot you got picked?" asked Morgan.

Virgil looked over at Doc. "Would you pardon us a tic? We got a couple of family business measures to clean up."

"I'll leave you to it." Doc swished his bourbon all the way into the other room where he could still hear the brothers. They were talking about buying a plot of land with a mine on it and how they couldn't marshal forever. It was the talk every man had with his family when he finally realized he wasn't immortal. Doc never had to have that talk with anyone. He'd put it off with Kate as long as he could. As long as the fountain would let him.

Doc meandered around the living room where a rickety bronze gas lamp hung from the center of the waterlogged ceiling. Doc almost hit his head on it. A couple of pictures hung from the ceiling, too, suspended by fishing wire. One was of Wyatt's family: his father, a bear of a man; Virgil and Morgan; James, who was a lawman somewhere else that Doc couldn't recall; and Warren, who was a schoolteacher. What a funny reunion that would be for poor Warren, the black sheep. Doc knew what that felt like.

In the left-hand corner of the room, nearest to the kitchen where Celia Ann worked on a roast, an entire shelf of photographs stood—mostly portraits of Wyatt and Celia Ann. Very official, as if the couple should always be viewed in sepia tone. There was one of Wyatt's youngest brothers, Morgan. Of the three chairs in the room, each was uniquely ornate and mismatched—a wooden rocking chair that did not mesh with the white table in the center or the Oriental-patterned couch. Doc plopped himself on the smooth cushions.

Celia Ann walked in with a spoon in her hand. She brought the smell of gravy with her. They observed one another for a moment, each in an unnatural environment. In a perverse way, they understood each other for their failings, their inability to attach to society. Smoke and the sound of grave and detailed accounting emanated from the room to their right where there was a slightly ajar door separating them.

"How's Kate?" she asked. "Haven't seen much of her lately."

"It's probably Wyatt's wish that you two don't . . . fraternize." He tried to inhale deeply. "I like the way you've made it smell in here."

"He don't own me."

"I reckon not." Doc took a long swig of bourbon to break the awkwardness. He found himself doing this more and more. It was sometimes easier to tilt the bottle than look someone in the eye. He didn't care for pleasantries anymore.

"I never thanked you proper for what you done."

Doc puckered his slimy lips. He peered through the crack in the door. "Wyatt's my friend."

"Well, just so you know, I ain't forgot." She clacked her fingernails on the wooden spoon and faded back into the kitchen.

Virgil poked his head into the study. "Doc, you can come back in now," he said, very officially.

Doc took his cue and reentered the room with the three Earps. He sat down.

"So, it must be real funny you sitting here with a bunch of law," said Morgan.

"Funny? Why?" said Doc. Smoke drifted over his pale face.

"Well, you know—" he became nervous and appealed to Wyatt.

"Shit, you said it, Morgan." Wyatt raised his eyebrows.

"Well, it's just that, you know—from the papers." Morgan's throat dried up.

"What does it say in the papers about me?" asked Doc.

"I mean it says good things too. Real good things."

Doc remained hushed, and the tense moment spread between the two men. Morgan turned red and began to sweat. With a sudden burst, Doc and Wyatt laughed simultaneously. "I like you, Morgan," said Doc, cheerfully swigging his bourbon.

Morgan exhaled. "I thought you was really mad."

"You'll get used to it," said Wyatt.

Virgil remained stoic as if watching a Greek play. "The real thing we should be bothered about is them Cowboys. They think they run this town, and the law is here to serve. Behan ain't helping none."

"Behan?" asked Doc.

"Two-bit politician running for sheriff. Goddamn figurehead piece of shit," added Wyatt.

"So we're all quite fond of this Behan. I'll make a note of it." Doc glanced toward the kitchen to see if Celia Ann needed any help.

Wyatt noticed his concern. "Leave her be. It's good for her to be doing something a lady does and tending her house."

Virgil shook his head disapprovingly toward Celia Ann. A few moments later, she emerged with a slew of cold meats and a canteen of beer. "So's y'all don't start eating the tablecloth."

No one thanked her. They just dug in. Fingers everywhere, covered in soil and grease. Doc leaned back and watched. He sipped his bourbon and thought of a time when things seemed less carnivorous.

Doc's earliest memories were those of his cousin Robert. He recalled an old tree where they would shoot their grandfather's Revolutionary War pistols under Doc's father's loose supervision. This was before the war for the Confederacy. He remembered learning the feel of barrel and flint and the buck of a horse before he could even speak properly.

John Henry's mother diligently administered speech lessons because of his impediment, his cleft pallet. He was extremely self-conscious about it, so she was the only one allowed in the room. Robert never cared though. He seemed to be the only one, along with his mother, who could understand him in those early years before he got it fixed. It was what first attracted him to dentistry. His little miracle, his mother had called it.

When John Henry got older, it was mostly Chainey, his most loyal and beloved slave girl, who'd watch over him and Robert and fix them sandwiches before his mother's tutoring lessons.

John Henry aimed at the knot in the old tree. There were spherical splintered holes in it from years of practice, but it was as big a target as ever. He closed one eye and fired off a blast. The shot nicked the tree, but John Henry went flying back from the recoil. Robert laughed and pointed at him.

"Have a' it ten!" barked John Henry in his broken tongue.

Robert cocked his pistol and fired, sending him into a tailspin so that they were soon side-by-side, screeching and giggling on the ground. The tree was hardly worse for wear. They helped each other up and began to reload their pistols with powder.

"Theys ain't playthings. Time for lunch," called Chainey. She was small with soft brown eyes, and she wore a red kerchief most days.

Inside, the men gathered in the smoke-filled study: Major Holliday, Uncle James, and some of the other cousins. John Henry so badly wanted to be part of that musty, gray, brandied room filled with grave discussions of secession and inheritance. He, of course, didn't understand the consequences of these talks until much later, but his mother taught him the words themselves. "To become sovereign." He liked that part. John Henry peered into the room as if on the other side of a dream. The pipe smoke wafted over his puerile eyes, but Robert pulled him away before he got in trouble.

"They're all stuffed anyhow. Let's eat!"

Robert was always better at being young. John Henry looked at youth as something to be overcome, like influenza or a very tall hill. He imagined a life where he could make the rules, where no one would ever dare to keep him out of a room. He practiced drinking out of a tumbler just like they did, so that a little got left on your mustache, so that you could still smell it. And he envisioned a day when he'd be stronger than his father and people would know the name John Henry Holliday.

CHAPTER 19

Hunting Bears

All Hallows' Eve approached, and the town grew more spirited than usual. There was always a darkness to it, but something had crept in that night. The Oriental was a madhouse filled with Cowboys discussing a recent cattle deal, throwing new money around. A few of the notables attended: Curly Bill, Frank Patterson, Edward Collins, Dick Lloyd, and John Ringo. It was the first time Doc had seen Ringo in the flesh, and he took an immediate liking to him despite his affiliations.

He wore a tiny, checkered bow tie and no hat. His hair was greasy and untamed. His mustache was thin and ratty, and he was spectacularly intoxicated. Doc felt that he should make up ground, so he ordered two shots of whiskey and walked over. Ringo was a bit removed from the other boisterous, lewd Cowboys grabbing at all the barmaids, even the ones not offering services, and spewing expletives into the tobacco-slung air.

"What's your pleasure?" asked Doc, choking on the haze.

Ringo turned slowly. His reactions had faded with drink. "On the dead?"

"Why not?" Doc figured he could spare a round on a new friend.

"Old Orchard then," said Ringo.

Doc signaled to the barkeep for another two whiskies. He poured a Gilbert and Parsons. Doc snickered because on the bottle it said "for medical use," and if that were true, he'd be the healthiest man in the West and so would John Ringo by the looks of him. The bartender was not Joyce, and Doc was thankful for that. Doc was due in court in two days, and he worried that Joyce might lose that hand. The new bartender, a smaller, older gentleman, slid over two more shots as Doc raised his own.

"With our boots on," said Doc, toasting with John Ringo.

"Our boots on. I like that. Your own?"

"It's what the soldiers would say in the war." He began to slur his speech, and he liked it. The liquor burned warm in his stomach, and he couldn't remember the last time he'd eaten solid food. Forgetting was his favorite time of night.

Ringo pointed his glass at some of the scantily clad prostitutes mingling with his friends. "You gonna get one a them painted cats for later?"

"I might be a bit too far along for pirooting tonight." Doc made a limp phallic gesture with his forefinger then signaled to the bartender for another round.

"That's the finest when you're mauled, and they really have to work. Get your money worth."

"So, what do you do with these upstanding gentlemen?" Doc observed Curly Bill lifting the skirt of a prostitute, howling, and then ripping her panties off and shoving them in Dick Lloyd's face.

"What I do? Play second fiddle, that's what." Ringo took a step back and vomited some green liquid then immediately mashed his boot in it.

"Are you all right?"

"As rain. I think I must've ate something green before."

"I surely hope so," said Doc.

Ringo wobbled in place.

"My journalist friend tells me you're a crack shot. A killer. A man of my breed."

"Your breed? What are you anyway?"

"John Henry Holliday."

It took Ringo a moment to place the name. "No shit? Hey, Curly!" he called out. "Hey, Curly, this here is Doc Holliday."

Curly Bill made a slow turn toward Doc. He was tall and thin with corkscrew locks and a very slight black mustache that almost looked clean-shaven. "That right? I heard a you."

"I *am* the most famous man in Tombstone," said Doc.

There was something less human about Curly Bill than any man Doc had ever seen, as if nothing lay beneath his gray eyes. He was older than Doc expected, nearly forty, if he had to guess. He wore a black vest with a shiny gold chain under his long gray overcoat. He spat on the floor like a hound marking its territory. "You here to fight?"

Doc thought about it for a moment. He took a swig of whiskey. "Not unless you are."

Curly Bill didn't even react. He just turned back to the other Cowboys and the prostitutes and went about his business.

"A lot of personality, that one," said Doc.

"They tell me I shot a man for refusing to have a drink with me back in Texas," said Ringo.

"Who tells you?"

"They." He swung his head loosely around the whole room and ended back up on Doc. "I don't remember nothing. You got family?"

"Something about this town makes me taste blood in the whiskey."

Ringo seemed to suddenly delve into a dark place. His eyes watered up and he slumped down into a barstool. "My daddy blew his brains out with a shotgun when we was in Wyoming. Mama said it was on accident. That's what the papers said too. I still keep them somewhere I can't recall."

Doc felt awkward discussing such a gruesome memory. He tried to catch the bartender as he glided by. "Nothing like some neck oil to wash away the thought."

"Went straight through his right eye. I remember burying him on the roadside and how heavy the shovel was. Then just carried on. It was on a hillside. Sometimes I wonder if anyone ever walks over his grave."

"My mother died too. Now I'm dying. Supposed to be out west for the cure."

Ringo cleared his throat. He grabbed his glass and raised it to Doc. "With our boots on."

Just then, Curly Bill and the rest whipped out their pistols and spilled out into the streets. They fired wildly into the air. Doc and Ringo followed behind just to get a look at the action. *Some gun laws they've got here*, thought Doc. They weren't firing at anyone in particular, but he'd heard stories in Texas about firing bullets straight up and someone getting killed the town over.

The night was quiet and black, save for the half-moon, so when the shots started rattling, lights switched on around Tombstone, and everyone began to poke their heads out hoping to catch some savage entertainment. It wasn't long before Marshal White showed up with his gun out, finger on the trigger.

"That'll be enough. You know the law here. Hand it over, Bill," said White in his most stolid voice. They'd had a few run-ins, but for the most part, the Cowboys respected White, and he let them be.

In the distance, Doc noticed a lone figure sprinting from what must have been the Bank Exchange Saloon about five blocks away. Doc could only see him because the moon was at his back and no one else was out in the streets. From the left, Morgan Earp and Fred Dodge looked on. Doc hadn't even seen them at the saloon.

The other Cowboys had stopped shooting, but Curly Bill continued to unload into the sky. "Marshal, I'm just at the heights a celebration. I'm the proud new owner of some cows or a ranch or some such." He laughed in an awkward way as if he'd never done it before. His voice was hoarse from bourbon.

From Curly Bill's backside, the shadowy figure approached, sprinting harder, heaving in the darkness. White pointed his pistol and got up closer to Curly Bill. "This'll all go away . . . just hand over that barking iron. Don't be a chucklehead about this all."

The shadow was only a block away now, and though Doc didn't want to turn his attention, out of the corner of his eye he saw the glint of metal on the man's chest.

CHAPTER 20

Short-Change Hero

Curly Bill salivated as he cocked his pistol, slowly lowering it farther and farther from the star-blanket sky until it was nearly at White's forehead. There was a moment when the entire crowd, the Cowboys, the Oriental patrons, midnight voyeurs, all grew flat silent as if admiring a watercolor from very far away. In that brief instant of bloodlust, Wyatt Earp leaped from the darkness; with a violent, sweeping motion, he wrenched his thick arms around Curly Bill Brocius. They struggled for a moment, Brocius trying desperately to throw him off.

White moved in closer, howling, "Now, you goddamn sonofabitch, give up that pistol!" He reached in and grabbed the barrel. As he jerked it from Curly Bill's hand, the pistol discharged, blasting straight through White's intestines and groin. He crumpled to the ground, screeching and flapping his hairy arms on the dirt in an expanding pool of blood. Curly Bill dropped his pistol immediately, and Wyatt buffaloed him over the head so that he lay unconscious next to White.

It was in that moment that the crowd awoke from its trance and the Cowboys all came to Bill's aid. Even John Ringo trudged over, and Doc saw in him a dogged loyalty. A quality he also possessed, he reckoned, though few had earned it. Wyatt pulled his gun on the Cowboys as Virgil and Morgan joined him. They'd just watched the whole thing unfold like everyone else.

There was a mist in the air that drifted lazily over the crowd. Flashbulbs burst into the haze, and the light was hard to distinguish from the moon. The Cowboys didn't immediately surrender their de facto leader. They actually looked to Ringo. Morgan, Virgil, and Wyatt now had their guns aimed his way.

"He wasn't involved," said Doc, referring to Ringo. Wyatt searched the crowd as Doc emerged with his hand on his holster. "He was with me." The buzzard blue night pinched in on Tombstone, and all the stars and all the mountains crackled with the inevitability of blood. The air got moist as if it were about to rain, except it wasn't. It hadn't rained in weeks. Doc could taste it on his tongue like a sugar cube.

"I don't need vouching," said Ringo.

Wyatt paused for a moment. "The rest of you need to come with me for disorderly and illegal possession of weapons."

"I'll pick all y'all up in the morning," said Ringo.

"An' you?" asked Lloyd.

"You heard the man. Not prisoning myself."

The Cowboys surrendered their weapons, and the Earps, with Doc's cover, dragged off Curly Bill and hauled the rest to a cell for the night. Ringo didn't even look back. He just headed straight into the Oriental and ordered another round.

CHAPTER 21

Alabama Song

The morning after the shooting, Doc was in court, and the Cowboys, save Curly Bill, were released. Marshal White had been bleeding out all night, but he gave Wyatt his final statement after receiving extreme unction.

Wyatt described the wound as grisly. It was an infected puss ring around his lower abdomen. The bullet seemed to have exited through the bottom of his groin. It was a miracle that he'd survived as long as he did, or maybe it was punishment. He was delirious, mumbling with fever. But when Wyatt asked him for his statement he just said, "He couldn'tve meant it."

There was a mythology to the Cowboys that Doc hadn't yet grasped. A certain feeling of camaraderie with the locals despite their thievery and devious nature. They had the persona of a watchdog but never protected anyone but their own.

Doc's courthouse soon became a ludicrous playpen for the absurd. His notoriety had turned the trial into an event, and people had come from far and wide to catch a glimpse of the famed Doc Holliday. It was a circus. All types of harlots, businessmen, opiate junkies, and even Chinese men followed the life and misadventures of Doc Holliday. It was as if he were already some figure of the past—a ghost whose trail could be walked, a posthumous demigod of id. Inside, it smelled of old boots and charcoal. There was carnage on their minds, and someone would take the brunt of it.

In the back of the room, Wentworth snapped flash photographs and kept trying to catch Doc's eye. *It seems he is always here when he needs to be*, thought Doc. A nuisance but a good journalist. Doc almost considered him a friend except that he'd only ever profited off Doc and all Doc got in return was fame.

The crowd had the feel of a violent orgy of miscreants. It seemed everyone in Tombstone had taken an interest in Doc's freedom, and they scaled the rafters and chanted poetry until the judge frothed at the mouth with rage. Some gaslights burned overhead, the chandeliers casting grim, spiderlike shadows over the bench. The ceilings were high, but the heat from the crowd rose and swelled in the courtroom. Each bench was packed with Doc supporters and a few religious zealots, who, at intervals of three minutes would scream, "God damns the wicked." In unison, the drunken Holliday fans would scream, "Go back to Mexico!" In the end, the judge merely fined Doc ten dollars because he "had not killed anyone particularly recently, and the integrity of the courtroom could not endure another minute of deliberation."

The courtroom guards could not stem the tide, and the liquored masses of Hollideans (as they'd come to call themselves) poured their congratulations and gratitude upon John Henry Holliday. As he attempted to exit the courtroom, they ripped his white button-down, exposing pink nipples on pale skin. They clawed at him, scratching his flesh. He bled through his tattered shirt, and they tore off his overcoat, cutting it up with small knives and divvying it out amongst themselves. They lowered themselves to the floor, sniffing his boots and lathering his ankles in dry tongues and knuckles. They'd powdered their faces to give the appearance of his pallor and carried long black canes along with an unearned air of intellectualism.

They wore holsters with no guns, sipped on flasks of root juice, and glued on mustaches made of horsehair. Some waved articles about him in the air in the hopes that he would sign them, but he was overwhelmed, bleeding from his pallid chest, and unintentional tears ran down his cheek because their hands were salty and burned his wounds.

It was astonishing to Doc that anyone would want to look like a murderous consumptive, but he took a modicum of pride in his legacy, and he appreciated the concept that something might live beyond his ebbing years.

Each pale body seemed to be clawing at him like a blurry reflection of his own cadaver. He imagined living forever and how horrible that might be. There was something liberating about living without consequence. Knowing the end waited comfortably around every coughing fit. Even if Kate still believed in the fountain, she was nowhere to be found—nothing but a bullet awaited him in Tombstone.

At that moment, his followers' bodies were suddenly thrown aside, and in their wake, he saw the pretty, mascaraed face of Kate Elder. He hadn't realized how much he'd missed her until seeing her again. She hauled him out of the bench, and the judge, who'd nearly passed out from fury, sighed with relief as she helped Doc through the crowd and out of the courthouse.

"My angel."

"You'll get yerself killed with admiring if you ain't wiser," said Kate, bearing his weight on her shoulder. He'd lost some pounds, and his bloody ribs pressed against her.

"Doesn't sound like a bad way to go."

"Well, it is. We've got to get you outta this town so you can get cured and get some meat on them bones."

Doc remembered a picture in one of the books about the fountain from when he was a boy. It was ineffably beautiful, a deep crystalline pool with pale bathing women, busty and glistening in the surroundings. From beyond the pool came the decrepit, pushed along in wheelbarrows, sagging with time and plague, but inside, the fountain rained adolescent diamonds. It was impossible not to feel redeemed. He recalled his tiny member coming alive at the thought of all those young women rinsing him in eternal waves, and he knew one day he was destined to find it, hidden by orange groves and frost-gilded mountains.

His reverie broke with the realization that couldn't remember the last time he'd eaten a good steak. He envisioned the hunk of muscle. "Are you coming back?" He realized then it hadn't even sunk in that she was gone because, in a way, she was never really there. Never really his.

"Of course I am. I always come back. You know that," said Kate.

"You make me happy, darlin'," said Doc. And in that moment, he knew it was true. The happiest he ever was wasn't with Mattie or at a faro table, but it was with Kate. Big Nose Kate, the love of his life. He wondered sometimes if he ever made it clear. Maybe it didn't matter. Maybe her words were enough.

By the time she dragged him outside he was ready to walk on his own, leaning on his cane. They meandered toward the hotel. Doc anticipated filling the drawers with her underthings. He feasted on her scent. It was familiar, but there was something new about her too. He ignored it and thought only of her porcelain skin against the sheets.

After they'd made love, Doc lay in bed smoking as Kate organized her things around the hotel room. She dusted a little, cleaned up after him. It was very comforting having her there. Her body belonged next to his. It made him stronger, but he felt lingering a strange tightness in his gut like he might lose her again. He watched her hips sway back and forth in her little red nightgown. Now that she was home, he couldn't believe he'd lived before or after her.

Doc remembered a similar feeling when his father and uncles first packed up to leave for the war. The day Carolina seceded. He was shoved into the body of a man when he'd been a boy the night before. He suddenly felt larger, like a corn snake after swallowing a possum. It was a largeness he'd always wanted, but he always imagined seizing it. *It's funny*, he thought, *that the two disparate moments seem so similar somehow.*

He was ten when his father enlisted. Henry Holliday was appointed by Jefferson Davis himself to be assistant quartermaster and would soon move on to quartermaster and finally major before he lost his battle with chronic diarrhea and was honorably discharged. John Henry didn't know any of this at the time, of course, but he knew things would be different in the South from then on. It wouldn't have the same smoothness to it. There would be lists. Lists of the dead. Lists of what the North wouldn't allow them. There was leanness to those years that resembled a constant hunger.

His father sat him down just before he went. There were clothes everywhere, and his mother was frantic trying to fit an unreasonable number of shirts into a compact carrying bag that his father would never use anyway.

"John Henry," his father called him over and groaned down to one knee. He smelled like hunting, like the outdoors. "We're a dying breed, you and I. We may be the last of 'em."

John Henry nodded even though he wasn't sure what his father meant. He liked being included anyway. Henry Holliday got up, shook his son's hand, and that was the last time they spoke before the war.

Doc now dreaded the idea that he was anything like his father. That he looked like him or fucked like him, an old, fat, abusive drunkard. Then again, the major had gentle Rachel, a house, and two air-filled lungs, and maybe that made him superior.

Doc watched Kate putting away her belongings. It seemed like he'd watched it in reverse so many times. Forward and back, coming and going. For a moment, he forgot which she was doing.

"What is it that you love about me?"

Kate stopped what she was doing and laughed uncomfortably. "What a funny question." She furrowed her brow and returned to folding her blouses. "You know, you should be more careful with all those lunatics scattered around chasing your moves. With your state."

"What state is that?" said Doc.

"The state you're in. Your state. No other way to put it."

"You feel free here with me?"

Kate placed her hands on the wood dresser and leaned hard on her small palms. "Freer than I was."

"And happy?"

"Are *you* happy? Yer the saddest bean in the sun I ever met."

Doc nodded. *Maybe she has a point*, he thought. "I've got a feeling this town is headed for a fall. You might not want to be around for that." He fumbled around the nightstand for his flask. It had about an eighth of whiskey left in it. He unscrewed the cap slowly, anticipating the bite.

"We should cut dirt. Isn't any solution for your ills here." Kate sighed. She pulled a cigarette from her cleavage, placing it between her lips.

"Got to help Wyatt. He'll need me now."

"Goddamn you. You choose that stranger over me every day. It's me who saves you."

Doc poured the remaining whiskey down his throat. He coughed and wiped the sides of his mouth with his shirt. "Could say the same to you, darlin'. Except that stranger is my friend. One and only. Who are yours? What's it like to lie next to them at night? You dream all the same?"

Kate bit down on the cigarette. She sat down on the bed next to Doc. "How 'bout now? Why don't we start fresh straight from where we are?"

He took her hand. It was still very delicate. Not a mark on it. He trembled. "We've passed the point of beginnings, my dear. I'm afraid we're at my epilogue."

"You're not dying as long as I'm with you. As long as it's out there. You don't get to die."

CHAPTER 22

Man on Fire

November 9, 1880
Seven Days After Local Election

Doc stood next to Wyatt, Virgil, and Morgan. Kate stood in front of him, though they were not touching as they had in the past. There was a boot's distance between them where the dry wind ruffled Kate's black dress. The clouds moved slowly south against the cool sky, and a crowd had formed outside Tombstone City Hall to greet the newly elected officials. Garfield would take over the presidency.

It was all empty ceremony. The only reason Doc was there was to support Wyatt, who was stepping down from the deputy sheriff's seat. Really, he was replaced. When the Democrats got elected, they handpicked John Behan to take over the position. He was more of a politician than a lawman. Wyatt was just the opposite, Doc knew. That's probably why he liked him so much—not the law part, but the killing.

The crowd was riled up about the recent shooting of Marshal White and the arrests. They waved their dirty limbs at the sun, and some burned small portraits of Curly Bill they'd found at the general store for a half dollar. It was an uneasy feeling in Tombstone. No one knew which way the public would ultimately lean, but people were starting to take sides. The Cowboys had already taken theirs, as they were clearly on the Democratic bandwagon. They seemed to take a liking to the new regime and, in turn, Behan. It all seemed too convenient for Doc, who paid little attention to the speeches as he drank and watched Kate's curly locks tumble and roll in the dry wind.

The City Hall building was barn red with white trimming. The bottom floor held three corn-shaped doors, all white, and the top floor consisted of four symmetrical rectangular windows. It was very clean. It gave an appearance of authority that the politicians could never match. Behan wore his hair flat and parted. He did not wear a hat. *Perhaps to make him seem approachable*, thought Doc. His black strands hung bushy on the sides like his thick mustache. He wore a gray overcoat and a tie. When he spoke, he seemed not to be speaking to anyone in particular, almost as if rehearsing in a mirror. He was very pleased with himself, lingering only briefly regarding his new position:

"The people of Tombstone need no longer fear the lawlessness running rampant under our old regime. We were all very sorry to hear about Marshal White. He was a good man full of bravery and valor. He will be missed.

"I also want to take the time to thank my predecessor, Wyatt Earp, a lawman of great renown. He handled the position admirably and with purpose. Let us give him a hand now."

Everyone clapped and searched for Wyatt, who wasn't hard to find given his height. Most people's eyes were already fixed on Doc, anyway. He was the only real celebrity at the event. In the back of the crowd, Wentworth made his way toward the group.

"The people love you, Wyatt. You're a regular—me," said Doc.

Morgan chuckled.

"Fuck off, Doc," said Wyatt through his teeth while tipping his hat to the crowd.

Wentworth ambled up to Doc, lugging his camera and notepad with him.

"Well, if it isn't our resident reporter," said Doc. "Well, resident wherever I am."

"How are you? It's been hard to get a moment for any quotes about what's been going on in this town," said Wentworth, breathing heavily as he set up his tripod.

"Mr. Earp, would you like to tell the people of Tombstone how you feel about the election of the Democrats and Deputy Sheriff Behan? Any truth to the rumors that you'll now run for sheriff?"

Wyatt spat lazily down at Wentworth's loafers. The spit dribbled down his chin, and he tapped his brothers on the shoulders signaling it was time to go. "You can quote that." To Doc, he said, "I dunno how you put up with this shit."

"I appreciate the ephemerality of fame," Doc said. "It suits me."

In the background, Behan had continued his speech but quickly wrapped up when he noticed Wyatt leaving. He ran off the stage after him.

"Mr. Earp. Mr. Earp!" Behan called.

Wyatt turned. "I'm not the kinda man you wanna brag to."

"Not at all, Mr. Earp. Rather, I have a job offer." He held out his delicate hand. "I don't believe we've been introduced properly."

"I know who y'are." He shook his hand dismissively. "Ever hold a gun in that little oven mitt, Deputy?"

"That's just the thing. I don't really wish to handle the more—physical aspects of the position. That's why I propose that you would take the undersheriff position. You would, of course, not be able to run for sheriff."

"I see."

"You'd handle the enforcement just as you've been, and I'll concentrate on tax collection and the more public political duties. From what I know of you, I think it suits us both well."

"And whaddaya know?" said Wyatt.

"I know you're a man who'd rather enforce the law than talk about it in an assembly hall. I'm just the opposite of that. Have we got a deal?"

Wyatt knew he was right. Doc could see it on him. Earp nodded, and the brothers went on their way.

"I'll draw up the papers," Behan said to Wyatt's backside.

"You do that," Wyatt said without turning around.

Wentworth stayed behind with Doc and Kate. More and more of the townspeople gathered nearby Doc, asking for autographed bullets and for him to cough on them for good luck. There was a rumor that a stock of DH bullets was circulating the town but that they weren't real and some Chinaman with small hands had actually signed Doc's name for 29 cents. It was starting to get claustrophobic, though many of the hardcore Hollideans were still asleep. They were more nocturnal, like him, bounding around the Oriental, trying to pick fights with locals, and sometimes dying because they were so convinced they were part of his legend and were immortal.

CHAPTER 23

Like the Wheel

When White died, they didn't put him in the ground straight away. There were larger matters to deal with—Curly Bill and the elections. White rotted in a box for weeks like a nameless stray. At the end of November, the town held a proper funeral for him. It was a somber affair. Nearly the whole town turned out, including the Earps and the Cowboys for an awkward reunion.

The trees were bare now, and their black branches traced a pulse along the cloud cover. A priest recited Latin verses at the gravesite. He did it mechanically as if he did not know their meaning. It was so quiet there. Doc kept his hands in his pockets because it was cool, and the air moved in strange patterns between the tombstones. White's widow wept into the arms of a neighbor. She was very sweet and small. Her life would be forever altered, hollowed out. Doc imagined washing her in the fresh spring waters, her life renewed, her withered feet and heart cleansed by unabashedly exposed nymphs, their ambrosial nipples gleaming in the turquoise light—or anyway, that's how Doc pictured it.

He wondered if he would one day lie in a place like this, abstracted from the world he knew. He stood with Wyatt and Celia Ann. They bowed their heads. Kate hadn't wanted to come. She said funerals were too sad and that there was no point in celebrating sad things. Maybe she was right. What was so special about something everyone got to have?

It was peculiar peering across the open grave, soil dug out, the Cowboys and Behan beside them. Behan stood with a shapely woman, her face veiled in black. There was Curly Bill, too, along with Ringo and some of the gang. Bill had been released on White's own testimony. Doc recognized a couple of fellow travelers from sometime back. It was the Clanton boys: Ike and Billy. He wondered what ever happened to that Indian of theirs—but, of course, he already knew. Beaten, dismembered for parts. They were Cowboys now. That was something new. It suited their ilk.

Once the service was over, Curly Bill, Behan, and Behan's girl walked over to the Earps. Doc took a step back and opened his coat in case he had to bed someone down.

"A friendly visit," hushed Curly Bill, noting Doc's readied fingers. The wind picked up and blew some loose dirt into the grave behind them.

"Are you two a couple now?" asked Wyatt, referring to the two men, but at that moment Behan's girl removed her veil. Doc recognized Sadie Marcus immediately. She looked radiant. Her travels and subsequent lovers must have treated her well. Doc hadn't seen her since the incident in Dallas. He felt Mr. Marcus's body on his, tasted his stale blood.

Doc turned to whisper the coincidence to Wyatt, but Wyatt was consumed. His body entered a strange, paralytic trance. He was completely taken with the young actress from first sight, like some perverted fairy tale triangle.

"Why, Sadie, what a pleasant surprise," said Doc, stepping forward. He leaned in to kiss her hand, but she didn't offer it. She was stunned to see him.

"Josephine, you know this man?" demanded Behan.

"Josephine," how formal, Doc quipped. "Have you two gotten to hand-holding yet?" Doc knew her full name was Josephine Sarah Marcus, but anyone who knew her, especially in the biblical sense, called her Sadie. This signaled to Doc that she was into Behan for his considerable wealth and station rather than his undoubtedly tiny prick.

"Mr. Holliday, how are you?" said Sadie.

"Jesus, Sadie, I thought you were supposed to be an actress!" Doc laughed in her face and slapped Wyatt on the back. Wyatt didn't seem to like the insinuation any more than Behan.

"This is outrageous, and at a funeral no less," said Behan.

"I agree wholeheartedly," Doc agreed, "but you're the one who brought her!" Doc carefully plucked his flask from his coat and took a nip. Curly Bill nearly drew at the sight. "Now, now, so jumpy, Bill. Don't want you shooting off anyone's genitals now do we?" Doc winked and offered Bill the flask.

He remained stolid, flicking some grease out of his mustache with his fingernails. They were yellow and cracked with gunpowder-black cuticles.

"For Christ sakes—"

"Doc, shut the hell up, will you?" Wyatt interrupted.

"Control your man," said Behan. "This is highly inappropriate in front of a lady. Josephine, let me properly introduce you to Assistant Sheriff Earp and his brothers who are helping him to uphold our city's integrity. Virgil and Morgan Earp. All fine Tombstone lawmen."

Sadie held out her black-laced fingertips to Wyatt. He kissed them tenderly. Doc didn't like how he was acting and neither did Celia Ann. She could sense his erection even under all that cloth and leather. She turned and snuck a bit of laudanum from her pocket. Only Doc could see it the way she angled herself. They were more and more alike, he realized. Eluding the present with no future to run to. There was already enough trouble, Doc figured, without adding a love triangle. Something was brewing.

Doc left Wyatt to fawn over his former lover, and he circled around to Ike and Billy. "You two seem well," said Doc.

Ike didn't recognize him. Doc was considerably thinner but also considerably more kempt than the last time they'd met—as vampires, their eyes iridescent in the circular morning hours when the sun and the moon live simultaneously for a brief moment and it's unclear if you're ending or beginning.

"I remember you," said Billy. "You had that lady with you. It was when we was with the Indian."

"Precisely. How fortuitous that we all end up in Tombstone."

"Yeah, maybe," said Ike, a bit apprehensive.

"What happened to yer lady?" said Billy.

"She's not a funeral sort of girl."

"An' you?"

"Oh, that's just my game," said Doc, amused with himself.

"Come on, you two," Bill called them over. "Fun's done. We got work."

They took off like lapdogs at his command. Ringo, trailing in the back of the group, tipped his hat to Doc. Booze trailed his lithe body. Doc nodded, and the Cowboys worked their way through the graveyard, trampling flowers and dirt as they left.

Doc returned to the Earps, who loomed over White's coffin, scattering prayers and ash over the wood. It was unsanded pine, nothing pretty. It suited him. The graveyard grew eerie without the priest to make sense of it, even if he was a fraud of a priest. Celia Ann was gone.

"Where's wifey?" asked Doc.

"So, you know that girl? That actress?" said Wyatt.

"My, you are all business, Wyatt."

Wyatt's brothers stepped away, not wanting to overhear infidelities. Perhaps selfishly, so it would be easier to deny later on.

"I knew her," said Doc.

"She a whore?" Wyatt asked bluntly.

"It was a nice service, wasn't it?"

"Suppose. Reckon he deserved more. Ain't no more to give."

"She wasn't that or anything else. We had relations on our own accord. I ended up having to run a lead plumb through her husband over it." Doc figured he should leave Kate out of it. One more murder on his belt didn't mean a thing.

"So, she ain't married."

"Ha-ha, you're a quick one today, my friend. Consider it a favor."

'Can you tell me anything she fancies?"

Doc took a deep breath, letting the air cool his broiling lungs. It smelled of grass; the scent brought him back to Georgia soil, and he reveled in the thought that he might go back one day, buy a farm, and live Achilles's delusion. "My dear friend, a woman like that who seeks fame and fucks for pleasure is an anomaly in this world. All I can say is that I always thought she had a sweetness about her in the moments when she wasn't so aware of herself. When she thought no one else was looking. That's when you'll find her."

"Don't know why they still got priests with you out here." Wyatt smiled and stuck a cigarette in his mouth. His breath imitated smoke.

"I can speak Latin, you know. All they have to do is ask." He made the sign of the cross over Wyatt and lit Wyatt's cigarette all in one motion. "Better than a burning bush."

The two made their way through the graves, careful not to disturb the restless souls below. Beneath them, the worms consumed everything that ever was and voided it back into the earth in brilliant dark spindles. Memory expunged, only relics and stone angels remained, their eyes molten with salt.

CHAPTER 24

Son of a Preacher Man

It seemed that Wyatt was incapable of getting Sadie off his mind. For weeks he devised ways to see her, arranging frivolous meetings with Behan when he knew she'd be around and going to every show he could at the theatre without raising too much suspicion from Celia Ann, who remained in a suspended state of doped-up animation. The laudanum made her erratically ill-tempered when it wasn't available, and disinterested when it was. Doc assumed she and Wyatt hadn't made love since they'd gotten to Tombstone, which was sad because, really, Celia Ann was an attractive girl in her truest form. But most harlots never return to their truest.

January temperatures proved mild. Seventies in the daytime and a chill at night. The winter materialized in other ways. It felt like a desolate time. It felt cold even in the light. Sometimes Doc would take walks trying to find his breath on the edge of Tombstone, a bare desert trail leading up into sleet mountains. It was actually very easy to get away from the 1,200 town residents, all trying to get rich off the barren land. They had no respect for it. Their stink and waste drew buzzards in because they would all die in Tombstone's grim, rotting corners by the hilt of the sun.

On the edges, there was a wild ivory horse that would trot along the urine-sprayed shrubs and sometimes stare back at Doc as if trying to save him. Doc imagined what it would be like to ride the mustang into the unknown desert, their backs against the salt of the sky and seven-foot cacti gashing the landscape. He could never get close. They were both wild, impossible to be near. Even from afar, he could tell the horse was a girl and named her Lottie. Sometimes he would bring her apples, but she would never eat them from his hand. He'd have to roll them like tiny green heads against the soil, and she'd sniff them with her gaping black nostrils and finally chomp in.

"Lottie, I'm sorry you and I could never be friends," he'd say. And the horse would look back at him with her brown eyes like she was sorry too. One day Doc came with a basket of apples, but Lottie wasn't there. Over the expanse of the cracked dirt, about forty yards away, he spotted a mound swarmed with flies laying their sticky eggs into hot flesh, rubbing their prickly, dry legs together like naked innkeepers trying to stay warm. Doc never got close enough to know if that mound was white. Or if it had her eyes. To know that everything he cared about rotted in this Arizona sun, and he would, too, if he didn't get out. He didn't know any of it and never would.

Meanwhile, Curly Bill's reign over Tombstone had commenced. He was emboldened every day Behan remained in office, and he'd been running his mouth all over town; Wyatt and Virgil had been told to back off since he wasn't "harming anyone." The Cowboys recruited and were growing in number. Bill fancied himself a pious man and attended Mass alongside Ike Clanton every Sunday. The church he preferred lay on the outskirts of Tombstone, not all that far from where Doc tried to find his own peace. Away from the town center and all its degradation.

The church was white adobe with three matching crosses atop its steeples. It was the only building for nearly a half-mile. A small brass bell hung in the leftmost tower, and the priest had opened its heaving doors wide to let the air in. A small light fixture swayed from the buttressed wooden ceiling that seemed to curve in on itself like the hull of a ship. A worn purple carpet separated the east from the west between the dark cedar pews, and behind the preacher the sun glared through the multi-colored rose window so that he was only a shadow in the blinding mint light. It was about half full inside, and the preacher wiped his brow as he delivered his sermon.

"Be strong and courageous. Do not be afraid or terrified because of them, for the Lord your God goes with you; he will never leave you nor forsake you. This is to say. This is to say—" the preacher paused again, as he had been all afternoon, wiping his forehead. He breathed heavily. He'd always had a stutter. The weight beneath his robes seemed to slow his speech. He was sopping wet under the folds of his belly.

Curly Bill rose from the middle pew. "Well, what the fuck is it to say?"

The churchgoers, men and women wrapped in the Holy Spirit and all its wickedness, gasped with sacrilegious mortification. All eyes fell on Bill. "This is the worst sermon I heard since the last worst sermon you gave last Sunday. An' that one was terrible! Aren't you all tired of bein' told how to feel by a halfwit?"

Ike rose, anticipating violence. His hairs pricked up, and he whipped his bulky body around toward the doors. Curly Bill picked up an old woman by her straight gray hair and held her taught in his fist. He removed his pistol from his holster and shoved the gun barrel into her soft, aged skin. It bruised her cheek like a spoon pressing against cheese.

"Tell you what, preacher. If you don't deliver the best sermon I ever heard, I'll blow this old lady's head straight off." He smiled as he said this and nudged Ike. Ike didn't seem to think one way or the other about it. He searched the congregation for any trouble. Dark colors, the dim light of afternoon, and fear.

"This is a house of God—it's deplorable. You will burn in hellfire for such an act directly under God's eyes," said the preacher. He was sweating even more now, and the perspiration mixed with warm urine running down his hairy thighs so that he stood in a puddle of sanctified salt and piss on the velveteen carpet.

"Well, now he can speak! Look what an equalizer can bring out in a man. No more stammering, just good ol' fashion religion from the mouth of a flawed mortal. An' don't you threaten me with Hell, boy. If I go, you're all beside me."

The young children in the congregation began to weep; infants and toddlers red in the face, coughing mucus from the backs of their cholic throats; and a woman near the door crept along her pew, attempting escape.

"Wouldn't do that, missy," said Ike.

"Thank you, Ike. This is Ike, everyone. He's a real ne'er-do-well." Curly Bill laughed at his own twisted humor. "Well, go on now, preacher. Save this woman's life. For once since your birth do something that you haven't memorized and jacked off to in the confessional booth."

Small tears of pain formed in the corner of the old woman's eyes, and they skittered down the wrinkles of her face in chaotic zigzags. Curly Bill could taste her weakness as he laughed; it fed him. He cocked the pistol. A cluster of dark clouds obscured the sun from outside, and as the green light receded, the preacher became visible against his dark background, sodden, broken, unhinged. He could not speak or act or think. He pinched the rosary in his trembling fingertips and asked for God's vengeance.

"Why ain't no one saving you, preacher? You devote your heart, your eyes, your useless goddamn lips to God and no one saves you when you need Him most. No one at yer side. Hell, even *I* got Ike here at least."

Ike tipped his hat.

The preacher dramatically raised his arms out as if he were Jesus on the cross and closed his eyes. "Take me instead. I will be right with the Lord when I die."

Curly Bill combed the room. He inhaled their terror. He'd engulfed them in his madness, felt the power of it in his toes and in his cock. He was rock hard as he lowered his gun. "Hell, I ain't gonna kill this ugly old lady." He released her crackling hair, and she crumpled into the wood, going unconscious. "What the hell good would that do me?" He tapped Ike on the shoulder. "I just wanted some entertainment in here for once." He and Ike tiptoed their way out of the pew. Bill pushed aside the old lady's limp body with his boot toe. The soles were worn down so you could see his toes through his left boot. "Excuse me."

The two of them made their way to the door. The sun filtered back in so that the preacher was a stone black cross in the midday rose. Bill let loose his entire chamber at the priest's dripping feet. The priest leaped up in the air, lifting his robes, squishing his shoes against the piss-soaked carpet.

"Dance, you mutherfucker," snarled Bill. The sound carried over the pews and the ceiling and ended up in the church bell, ringing it twice with gunpowder echo. Curly Bill removed his hat. "Preacher, you're one hell of a dancer. I'll see ya next week." Bill lingered for a moment, his iron smoking, diligently reloading his warm pistol. Then, without another word, the two Cowboys sauntered out and headed back toward the Oriental for drinks and a midday fuck.

It was noon the following day, and Curly Bill lay with his cock in his hand and an experienced prostitute asleep, naked in his bed. He shoved her to the floor.

"Who told you to sleep here?"

She had a shattered look in her eyes as if once, when she was a child, her father had said those exact words to her. She was forty, and her breasts did not hold the same form they had when they were young. They used to salute and now they bowed. A long white scar on her neck smiled at Bill. She'd gotten it when a drunk Cowboy wanted to see how sharp his nails were while he was sodomizing her.

"You told me to stay, Bill," she said in a familiar tone as if he was a regular, but he wasn't.

"The fuck I did. That don't sound like me."

"You had a few."

"Don't need no whore to lecture me 'bout how much I can drink." His teeth bled yellow in the light.

She lay splayed out on the floor, unashamed by her own nakedness. She reached up to the nightstand and grabbed a cigarette that Curly Bill had sloppily rolled the night before. She looked up at his bloated, rough face. The hair in his nostrils twisted up and around like weeds. "Light?"

"You old calico queens got some balls. I'll give ya that." He reached down and struck a match. He lit her cigarette, and she spread out on the carpet. His thighs were hairy and oily. "Yer boring me."

She raised her head, blowing smoke rings around his flaccid member. "Just like horseshoes."

"Suck me off before I shut yer dumb whore mouth."

"Well if you're gonna talk sweet like that maybe I'll just take my dumb whore mouth to somebody who can appreciate it." She mashed the cigarette into the carpet and got up. In the fresh light, her thighs glistened. Her green veins had begun to show through like ancient ivy.

Curly Bill laughed and became aroused nearly immediately.

"Looks like nobody talks to you like that."

He got up, grabbed her by the back of the neck, and slammed her head down onto his cock. He kept her down and down until she could hardly breathe. She gagged, and saliva pooled around her tongue and dripped down her lips onto her breasts.

"Yeah, there's reason for that." He pushed her down farther. "Good goddamn reason."

After a minute, he flung her away and pulled on his pants. They felt cool from the floor. She lay gasping for air on the carpet next to the cigarette ash, her eyes teared. The carpet crunched with toenails and semen. Curly Bill dropped some coins on her breasts as she turned over on her back, her painted nails digging into the floor. "No one's got me pinned. 'Specially not some relic pillowleech." He strapped on his pistol and buttoned his blue-striped shirt. "Enjoy the rest a your day."

Curly Bill made his way to the Oriental where Ike and Ringo played faro with Doc for several hours. They were all three sheets. "Come on," said Bill. "I'm sick a this place. Let's head to the Alhambra." The two settled up their chips and followed Bill into the coarse sunshine.

Normally, Doc wouldn't have given a second thought to a trio of hellblasted madmen heading toward a saloon around noontime. In fact, he might have given thought to joining them. But the Alhambra wasn't just a saloon, it was a theatre upstairs, too—a theatre where Sadie performed. Doc figured Wyatt might like to know if his favorite little songbird was in any sort of danger.

As Doc took off to warn Wyatt, the three Cowboys approached the slightly classier Alhambra Saloon. It was only a five-minute walk from the Oriental.

Sadie was singing by the piano. A couple of Mexican men sat drinking tequila, watching her, falling in love. She looked like a movie star only just past her run. She wore a long silk dress that was nearly sheer, but the lights kept it opaque. Just enough for men's minds to wander past their wives and up her slip.

A gentleman in a top hat sat outside the Alhambra with a lockbox and a look of resignation. Bill, Ringo, and Ike approached. They were all heeled and didn't bother concealing it. They walked straight past the ticket taker toward the door.

"That'll be seventy-five cents, gentlemen," said the taker.

Curly Bill whipped his head around. His hair never moved, a curled dome like a shrub. "What in the fuck would I pay that for?"

Ike and Ringo waited patiently by the door, holding it shut in case they had to kill him.

"For the entertainment," said the taker.

"Don't you know?" Bill cocked his head like a wolf. "We're the entertainment!" He laughed maniacally. "Don't nobody entertain like us."

The taker's body recoiled in fear. He inched back on his seat. "I—Josephine is already—"

"Tell you what," whispered Bill. "If I don't got every patron in that bar dancing within two minutes of me entering, I'll come back here and pay you double. We got a deal?" He held out his unwashed hand. It still smelled like unwashed pussy.

"I recommend you take the deal, or we shoot you. You understand," said Ringo.

"Now, Ringo, why do you always have to go an' spoil things? He don't know that! Now he's got no choice," said Bill.

The taker quickly shook Curly Bill's grimy hand.

"I like to think he woulda done it anyways. I believe in man's free will." Bill chuckled to himself as they entered. "Two minutes!" he called back. "Promise is a promise."

The three men entered the bar. The windows were clouded on the outside so onlookers couldn't steal the entertainment. The bar was a U-shape, and upstairs, next to the piano, Sadie Marcus sang. By the bar, a buffalo head hung, its massive woolly face stringy with oil. Its olive-shaped eyes had clouded with smoke over time. The bartender wore a long white coat with a black bolo. Sadie was a mediocre singer, but her bubbling cleavage made up for any missteps. Immediately, Bill keyed in on the two Mexicans enjoying the show. One of them smoked a cigar. They both wore loose white button-downs and scruffy beards. They could have been brothers, one slightly darker than the other.

"Goddamn I hate Mexicans," said Ike.

"Is that your contribution, Ike?" said Bill. "You goddamn hate everyone."

"Goddamn right. Everyone isn't us."

"Well, nuthin' to be done but get them naked," said Bill. The music soothed his burning eyes. He couldn't tell if he was awake or dreaming. He felt the gun come up from his holster like it wasn't even his idea. "I'm so tired."

"Did you say you want them naked?" asked Ike.

"*I* don't want them fucking naked. They need to *be* naked!" screamed Bill. The piano player ceased mid-key, and the two Mexicans turned in their seats. Smoke drifted up like dandelion seed.

Ringo made his way over to the bar, excusing himself. "You all get more and more perverse every time I see you." He tugged on the bartender's shirt. "Gimme a pair a overalls." The bartender poured him two whiskies. Ringo gulped each one in a mechanical fashion. He ordered another.

"Get goddamn naked!" screamed Curly Bill. He made a stripping motion with his top button, then walked straight up to one of the Mexican men and shoved the muzzle of his gun up the man's nostril. "I ain't even begun to make you dance."

"You sure you mean naked, Bill?" questioned Ike.

Curly Bill rammed his palm into the butt of his gun so that it shattered the man's septum. He clattered to the floor in a heap. The other Mexican man immediately began to strip down. Bill stopped him when he got down to his undershirt. The other Mexican slowly stripped down on the sawdusted floor. He writhed in his own bloody mucus. It mixed with the sawdust and dissipated in the air as breath.

"See, now these gentlemen understand. They don't speak English, Ike. We're welcoming them. Now, dance!"

They didn't understand. They just stood there. Ike made a swinging motion with his arms to assist them. The two undressed Mexicans swung their arms like monkeys, one with his face cloaked in red like a carnival mask.

"Ringo, would you be a dear and get the taker back in here?"

Begrudgingly, Ringo set down his newly ordered whiskey and pulled the taker in from outside. He downed his shot quickly and turned away, unable to watch their degradation. He kept his hand by his holster though. The man was speechless with embarrassment.

"Now, isn't this better? We're the entertainment!" Curly Bill laughed. The music washed over his greasy body. "We're the good guys!" There was no music.

At that moment, Curly Bill searched the room and found Sadie fidgeting anxiously by the piano player, looking for anyone to save her. "Why don't you come down now, whore?"

"I'm an actress."

Curly Bill grinned. "So you're a dishonest whore. Now come on down. Ike, go get'er."

Ike made his way past the swaying, half-naked men and up the stairs toward Sadie.

"I'm Sheriff Behan's girl," she cried out.

"Behan? That boy's more of a slommack than you. Might as well have a cock slipped in his asshole as soon as he won office. You think he'll care if I bloody you all night? You think he cares about some whore actress from California? I know you, and more, I know him. He keeps the peace, darlin', and now so do you."

Ike lazily climbed the spiraling stairs, breathing heavy.

"Goddamn, Ike, you're fat." Bill sighed.

Before Ike could reach Sadie, three shots splintered the wood at Curly Bill's feet. It was Wyatt's Smith & Wesson, and Doc stood behind him with his fingers at his pearl-handled .38.

"Don't make me bed you down, Bill. Almost did it once already," said Wyatt.

"Gonna kill me over a couple naked Mexicans?"

"Thank Christ!" shrieked the taker.

Ringo came up behind him and shoved him against the glass door. "Get the hell out."

The taker scurried off without looking back.

"What'd you have in mind for Miss Marcus?" asked Doc.

Bill placed his pistol back in his waistband and eyed Doc. "Miss Marcus? You mean Behan's girl?"

"If that's what she calls herself."

"Don't you, Miss Marcus?" Doc prompted her.

Sadie just stared straight down into Wyatt's eyes, and in that moment, she was no longer Behan's at all. She never responded to the question, but Doc knew what it meant. He had seen that look once. It was a look of ownership, a deviant stare that promised her thighs and parted lips. It was charged with something hallucinogenic and sweet.

"Doc, I thought better of you than to go and tattle on new friends," said Bill.

"That what we are now? Friends?" Doc shot a glance at Ringo, who swayed uneasily. It seemed none of them wanted to draw against Doc, but they wouldn't have backed down either.

Wyatt motioned to Sadie to come down to him. She pushed past Ike's squishy belly, down the staircase into Wyatt's broad arms. She was shaking. Her skin was hot and smooth against him.

"What exactly are you doing with those Mexican gentlemen?" asked Doc, addressing the elephant in the room.

The two naked Mexicans continued to swing their arms and shuffle their feet as if they'd been wound up. Their confused heads faced the door, not wanting to make eye contact with Bill.

"Just having a dance," said Ringo.

"Oh, well carry on then." Doc tipped his hat. He and Wyatt ducked out of the bar with Sadie. Doc shuffled backward for a bit in case anyone was following. No one was. They walked back toward Wyatt's house.

"Let's get you somewhere safe for now," said Wyatt to Sadie.

She was grateful and showed it in her light touches to his arms and how close she stood. Wyatt had a very calming presence. It was something that Doc always admired about him. Doc made people's hair stand on end; they fidgeted, they blinked excessively. Wyatt had a way of putting everyone at ease. He was a rocking chair and Doc was a splinter. Still, one came with the other.

When they arrived at Wyatt's house, Wyatt looked around for a minute, checking if Celia Ann was home.

"Celia?"

"You're married?" asked Sadie.

Wyatt didn't respond. He checked the kitchen and the bedroom. No wife in sight. Doc went straight to the bar in the living room and poured himself a whiskey. "Wyatt's situation is almost always evolving. Isn't that right, Wyatt?" Doc allowed the liquor to seep through the gaps in his teeth. It felt like acid along his bloody gums. His stomach and insides were raw. He sweated immediately.

Wyatt plopped down on his bed for a moment and removed his hat. He sighed with relief and fatigue. He looked down at his hands, still steady. Sadie entered. Wyatt knew Doc was far enough away that he couldn't really see or hear. Still, it was strange having him there since he'd already bedded Sadie.

"Prolly shouldn't be in here," said Wyatt. He flicked away one of Celia Ann's shoes with his boot toe.

"Let me get those for you." Sadie dropped to her knees in between Wyatt's legs, setting her palms on his thighs. She ran her fingernails down the length of his shins and then slipped off his left boot. The stink of the day came out. No lawman's boots were ever fresh, but she didn't seem to mind. She just went and pulled off the other boot smoothly. She rubbed his rotten feet. It felt good on his heels. "How can I thank you?"

"Ain't you Behan's girl?"

"You're married, I'm Behan's girl. Sounds like we're perfect for one another."

She rested her head in his crotch, and her black hair ran down his thigh and along her cleavage. "Behan can't protect me, but you can, can't you?"

"You ever feel like things happened that wasn't meant to?"

"None of it is."

Wyatt could feel her voice in his groin. It was sweet and small. Not like when she was on stage.

"You come see me a lot," she said.

"You're good at singing."

"No, I'm not. Even *I* know that. Acting maybe, but not singing like they have me here."

Doc sat alone in the kitchen now, listening to their conversation. It was a passive listening because the house had a sort of acoustic where you could hear something from one end to the next. It would be strange to have shared a lover with Wyatt. He wondered what would happen to Celia Ann. He wondered if he'd have the strength to move on one day, too, that is, if he were to find his cure, his fountain. He hadn't given up yet. Almost on cue, he coughed up blood onto the yellow tablecloth. His cough reverberated through the house like a roar.

Wyatt heard Doc hacking and nearly got up to check on him, but Sadie was comfortable and warm in his lap, and he liked having her there. It might never happen again. "Anyway, I like how you sing," said Wyatt after a while.

"And that's it? Nothing to do with me? Just my singing?"

"I'm not real good at this sort of thing."

Sadie opened her mouth and breathed hot onto Wyatt's groin. She ran her hands over him until he started to grow bigger and pressed against her cheek. "Doesn't seem that way to me," she said with a smile in her voice.

"Wouldn't mind seein' you again."

"Tomorrow, after my show. Let's go somewhere that doesn't remind you of what you're doing wrong." Sadie got up and straightened out her sateen dress.

"I doubt there's much future for any of us, but if there is, I wouldn't mind this one."

Sadie walked out of the bedroom. On her way out, she passed Doc in the kitchen.

He tipped his hat to her. "Sounds like you and my boy there are plotting quite the scandal."

"Do me a favor, Doc. Don't get this one killed before I can have some fun with him."

Doc watched her shiny apple bottom leave as the screen door rattled shut behind her. He recalled the last time he'd touched her and how much less he had in him now. Still, he was glad he'd had her. *There was always life in that one*, he thought, choking down the last of his glass.

CHAPTER 25

Stubborn Love

Doc knew there would soon come a time when lust, greed, and force would all combine into a single gray thing spied from rifle sights. Until then, though, he thought he and Kate ought to find the same peace that Wyatt had found in Sadie. Wyatt and Sadie stole off night after night, making love in the Alhambra changing rooms, screaming like unchained virgins. In a way, it made Doc jealous. Not that he wasn't happy for his friend; he was. But that perhaps Wyatt had found his youth. To Doc, that seemed more and more unattainable every day spent in Tombstone. It was late, but he lay awake next to Kate, who pretended to be asleep in their hotel room.

"You seen Celia Ann at all recently?" asked Doc. He bit down hard on the sides of his cheeks to make sure they were still there. Sometimes parts of him went numb, unannounced. "I know you're awake, darlin'. I can hear your throat clicking, and it only does that when you're awake." He passed her a glass of water.

For a moment, she continued to pretend, then she quickly snatched it out of his hand. "That girl's a poor mess."

"I figure. I've been getting into some prospecting and water rights with the Earps. Haven't seen her though. They seem to know what's what, and it should bring us in some coin."

"I'm restless here," said Kate.

"You're restless. Here doesn't account for it."

"I can see you cracking like a pigeon egg in hawk's claws."

"I'm as strong as ever, darlin'." Doc got up, his slight body sticky and his pale body hair matted down with sweat. He knelt down, attempting to lift the dresser, but instead, the ashtray and all the cigarettes, along with a bottle of Pointer he'd drunk half of all clattered to the floor and shattered. The glass struck his bare toes and he bled and the whiskey stung. It washed over his feet and he wanted to lick it all up. He felt sick to waste it like that, disappearing into the cracks in the wood, the rats between the boards and his downstairs neighbors enjoying his earnings.

Kate helped him back onto the bed. She wiped the blood off his foot with the sheets. "We need to leave here." She turned over onto her back. She kept her eyes shut as if dreaming her escape. "No sense in settling in, Doc. We have to find that fountain. Let's pack up and leave outright. I'll even go tonight. I'll follow you anywhere. You know it."

"You know I can't do that just yet. Not when Wyatt needs me like he does."

Kate huffed and pinched Doc's gaunt body. "Has he ever said that? He needs you as much as a porch needs termites. You need him is what it is. More than you need me. You fancy yourself some halfways hero. You're not, and he doesn't need diddly shit but that actress's snatch."

Doc ran his hand over Kate's shoulders, down her neckline, over her naked breasts, and down to her hand where he pressed her knuckles together with his. The night air from the window ate at his cuts and his throat. "One day, everything will be quiet, and you'll despise it. You'll miss the chaos just like I will." He brought her fingers up to his lips and kissed them. "Anyway, I love you."

Kate slipped out of his grip and turned back over. Her bony shoulders chattered in the draft. "I'm never sure if you're thinking of me or Wyatt Earp when you say that. Next time you feel guilty, don't bother me about it. There's a reason I pretend to sleep."

Doc, who had kept an utter calm during the whole conversation, suddenly stood up straight on the bed, looming over Kate. He jumped up and down on the mattress until Kate swung her fist into his shin.

"Quit acting like a little boy. You're too worn for all that."

A couple of pebbles tapped the window as they often did. Usually the Hollideans hoping Doc would come to the sill. Often it was Kate with a scowl and cusses if she was home.

Doc hopped down from the bed and opened the window as far as it could manage. It creaked up and the air gushed in. Kate pulled the covers tighter over herself. Doc searched around for the Hollideans. It was late, but they were loyal beings, if not a bit demented. There were two young men under the window.

"Hey, you there!" called Doc.

The boy pointed to himself incredulously.

"Yeah, you and your friend. How would you like to drink with Doc Holliday?"

"Nobody gives a goddamn who you are," groaned Kate.

"Do you care who I am?" Doc called down. He didn't wait for an answer but instead slid on his slacks and grabbed as much booze as he had left. He swigged some as he came back to the window. "Too many cunts up here!"

The two young men could hardly contain their excitement. Doc made his way down the hotel's winding stairs and met his fans in the lobby.

"What're your names?" he asked, pouring whiskey down his throat easy as sugar water.

"This here is Arthur, and I'm Clarence. We're mighty big fans of yours, Mr. Holliday." They were schoolboys, neither of fighting age.

"Please, boys, call me Mr. Doc Holliday. No need to be formal." He chuckled and killed the flask. "I'll even let you buy me drinks tonight. 'Tis a great honor, I assure you." He walked them outside and began to head east.

"Well, actually—" Clarence hesitated. His oily skin shone in the moonlight. "The reason we came, not that we hadn't before, but tonight in particular—there's a man says he knows you and would like to buy all our drinks for the night."

"Ah, a rich patron of my arts, eh? Like the Medicis."

"That a saloon?" asked Clarence.

Doc disregarded the boy's ignorance. "I wish it were a woman. Well, as long as he understands we're out for drinks. I may be illuminated, but I have boundaries, Arthur."

Arthur was too starstruck to speak.

"Chatty one, aren't you? Okay, lead the way."

Clarence and Arthur took Doc straight to the Oriental. Doc kept his pistol ready in case there was some sort of funny business. He was still angry with Kate. He could feel the bile building inside him. His shoulders and ribs ached. He was tired. He needed more whiskey.

Sitting at the bar of the Oriental was a familiar face. It was scraggly, gaunt-faced William Leonard. His hair was longer.

"Well, I didn't think I'd see you again after the Vegas springs."

Leonard rose gingerly from his barstool and shook Doc's hand. "Ever go see that Indian?"

"I did."

"Great fucking coffee."

Doc smiled. Leonard had wasted away since Doc had last seen him. He was a frail hundred and twenty pounds, if Doc had to guess. His face contained so little color it made Doc look tan by comparison. They sat down together at the bar. Leonard signaled to the bartender and gave the boys a bottle of brown.

"You're free to go now, boys. Enjoy a job well done," said Leonard.

"But, we'd like to stay," said Clarence. Arthur remained too shy to speak.

"Mr. Holliday and I have some catching up to do."

Doc removed his handkerchief and handed it to the boys. It had little brown blood spots all over it. "You go show that to the girls and see if they don't up and spread their legs."

"Thank you, Mr. Holliday! Yer just like in the papers!" The boys banged through the Oriental door and bounded out into the melting darkness.

"So, you look about ready to explode," said Leonard.

Doc signaled to the bartender and began drinking from a fresh bottle. "Fucking woman. Don't know why I keep up hope that she'll love me right."

Doc's eyes grew red. Only a couple of other patrons drank alongside them. It was a Tuesday and well after midnight. Doc tipped the bottle back and let the booze sting down his gullet. He slammed the whiskey onto the table, drew his pistol, and fired three shots into the Oriental ceiling.

Everyone scattered and dove except for Leonard. The only sound was splinters sifting to the floor. "I think I'd best take you to my place before you're staying at the crowbar hotel." He nudged Doc off the barstool, poking him in the direction of the door.

The night was quiet except for a couple of thirsty horses clacking their lips at the filthy darkness. Tombstone felt like an empty theatre at night. It smelled of manure and brimstone.

Leonard's office was north on Safford Street and Third. It was a small room with a jewelry display and a short hallway that led into a private workspace. That's where he took Doc. There was a smelting table and some bent metal tools. A mask, lots of long rods, misshapen hammers of stone and iron, an oven, and a large armoire with a safe lock. A large leaden coat hung from a hook.

"What's all this for?" asked Doc, running his fingertips over a gilded bangle.

"I melt gold down for a price."

"Why don't they just hock it?"

"Because it ain't theirs." Leonard picked up a golden crucifix and held it to the dim light bulb illuminating the space. It glowed orange from inside the dusty glass.

"Cowboys?"

"Mostly. Some others too." Leonard placed the crucifix back down on the smelting table and unlocked his armoire. He pulled out a needle and a belt. "You want?"

Doc shook his head. He was still carrying the bottle from the bar. He'd have to go back and pay tomorrow. Probably pay the court, too, for the ceiling damage. Leonard tied off, shooting a syringe full of morphine into his vein. He relaxed immediately. He placed his drug kit back into the armoire and locked it.

"When did this all start?"

"'Bout the time when I saw God."

Doc licked the whiskey off his mustache hairs. "When was that?"

"'Bout the time I started up with the morphine. It's like that ol' saying, What came first, the needle or the egg?"

Doc eased into the welding chair next to Leonard. "What do you think of Cochise County?"

Leonard's eyes fluttered shut. His muscles let go. "You know you never struck me as someone who believed in myth."

Doc picked up the golden crucifix. "That is one thing you can be sure of, William. We're all beholden to something." He thought of Kate, Mattie, Rachel, his mother, the fountain, the innumerable wonders that the Natives had hidden from the White man. It was their only means of revenge; to veil the one thing that anyone ever really wanted— to wipe away original sin, become children again in the eyes of God, regurgitate the apple and consume the serpent.

The women in his life formed the corners of a deep lake where he would one day drown. His vision blurred. Leonard was already asleep, his head hanging back over the chair, jaw agape. Doc scrutinized William's mouth like he used to when he was practicing. William's teeth were stained brown from smoke. Cavities rotted the left side of his mouth; they smelled like turned beef. He peered down into the nebulous folds of William's throat and saw the future.

CHAPTER 26

I Have Nothing

March 15, 1881

When Doc returned from William Leonard's the next morning, Kate was asleep with Celia Ann curled up next to her.

The night before, they'd snuck out to the Alhambra to take a peek at Sadie. Celia Ann heard stories about her, and she wanted to see for herself. Celia Ann had become bony; her gown hung off of her as if she were a young boy. Her breathing was labored, and she spoke with a constant slur from all the laudanum. Kate's pupils had become tiny like a bird's, but she did not suffer all the ill effects of the opium on her body the way Celia Ann did. She had Doc's tolerance for the fast life, though she'd admitted that couldn't remember the first time she and Doc had met, as if it were a fading photograph.

The two of them had sat, swaying uncontrollably, waiting for Sadie to come on, sleepy, their makeup smudged and hair askew. Kate leaped from her seat when she felt a cold hand on her back. When she turned, there was no one there. "Which one of you desert pigs put your hand on me?" The crowd looked around worriedly.

The bouncer came out from in front of the entrance. "I think you two ought to leave."

"Not till that whore shows her face," slurred Celia Ann.

Sadie waited backstage, unwilling to perform until they were gone.

"I'm going to have to call your husbands, ladies."

"Don't have one. Son of a bitch won't marry me."

Celia Ann wobbled. "Don't fetch him," she said. A thin, golden ream of light wafted in front of her eyes, and she made a face like she was very afraid. "We'll go. Don't tell him we been here. You all work for him. I know it."

When they got home, they slept like lambs. Fully clothed. An unending stream of lace flowing over their eyes and mouths. Kate wheezed in her sleep.

They were high-class junkies now, impossible to wake, dreaming up horrific opiate nightmares of goldfish heads and loose serpentine genitalia.

Doc imagined how much simpler it would be if he could stop loving Kate, but he did not feel worthy of such respite. He longed to be new again before her eyes, but only one place could reform them in that way.

The stale tang of their florid perfumes haunted the room. Doc hated that smell now. It meant abandon. For the next two months, he and Kate barely slept in the same bed. Sometimes she would come to him for comfort late at night when the darkness obscured everything. It could have been anyone, but he knew her shape too well and how she tasted at each hour of the day. During that time, Doc operated the faro bank at the Alhambra with the dual purpose of keeping an eye on Sadie for Wyatt. Wyatt was shamefully in love with her but kept up appearances with Celia Ann for the sake of his position and her honor, whatever was left of it. Doc liked the Alhambra because after the incident with the Mexicans they'd hired a guard who kept photographers and fans away. Even Wentworth hadn't gotten an interview for some time.

On the ides of March, Doc caught wind of a high-stakes poker game in Charleston, Arizona—a game that could bring in more money than he'd made in a month. The Earps' water rights claims and mining hadn't made them much more than a week's salary and proved to be more of a nuisance than anything else to Doc, who cared little for business. On the bright side for Wyatt, the Cowboys had been generally quiet, their eyes seemingly set on something bigger and their partnership with William Leonard paying dividends.

That night, Kate had stayed home, and Doc tried not to wake her as he came in from a long night of faro. He stripped down, placing his clothes on the nightstand, redressed neatly in a new button-down, and combed his hair. He did not smell like himself anymore. He smelled more like a patient, but he could still be groomed as if he were a gentleman, he thought. His mother had told him about the most important thing for a man was to be thought of as a gentleman. He thought of his father as he tied his cravat tight over his pressed, royal blue shirt and straightened the pin in it. He took his pearl-handled .38

and his rifle, which he rarely had occasion to use. He didn't trust the roads around Tombstone.

Kate opened one eye. "You never came home, now you're off again?"

"I've business. Find supper on your own tonight, darlin'."

"Different than any other?"

"Suppose not. Get some rest."

"Don't you goddamn pretend you can take care of me. Selfish. Selfish." She drifted back into sleep like a narcoleptic wasp. Doc pressed his clothes down on his body one more time. He noticed the empty spaces where his thighs had once been. He could no longer fill out his trousers.

Charleston was a tiny spot with just 350 silver miners but fifteen saloons. It was Doc's kind of town. A saloon for every man and child. It wasn't all that far from Tombstone but lacked Tombstone's modernity. There was a cow fence that ran through the town center as if the whole thing were someone's farm. There were no roads, only spots where boots had trodden down the brush, mulched it enough that it became a path, and at the end of every path lay a watering hole. It was flat, but to the north of the town rose a hill of dirt like a woman's back. Often, it blocked the sun so the only things that survived were low-water shrubs like saltbush and desert hackberry.

When the ore would run out, as it always did, the weeds would take over. First, it would overtake the stone, the land, their eyes and mouths; it would become, affectionately, a ghost town. Their souls would grind into the land and salt the earth until nothing remained but the memory of silver and the horror of the boom.

By the time Doc arrived in Charleston, it was already later than he'd hoped. He tied down his horse, left it with water, and meandered around to a few saloons until he found the Bar Room, owned by J.W. Swart, who owned most of everything there and was hosting the game. Doc walked in and ordered a twelve-and-a-half-cent bourbon.

"Where's this doozy of a poker match?" Doc asked the bartender as the bourbon relaxed his weary body. He swished it around his sore-ridden mouth.

The barkeep pointed to an empty table.

"High stakes, indeed."

"Swart lost early on and demanded that everyone else stop playing on account of it being his game and his bar. Not no one's place to argue I suppose."

"How endearing." With the game broken up, it was a lost day of revenue for Doc unless he could turn around and get back in time for the seven o'clock faro game. He patted his horse on the side of its face. "Sorry, my amicable equine. Looks like you'll have to rest when I do. I know you'll hate me for it. I've got a healthy carrot with your name on it back in the Tomb."

On the ride back, he ran into Old Man Fuller, a local water hauler, shipping a load back to Tombstone from the wells outside of town, so Doc tied his horse behind Fuller's wagon and hitched a ride. Doc thought nothing of this at the time, of course. He did not recall times because there was no reason to recall them, only if the sun was up or obscured and if his flask was full.

Doc returned to town and ate some flank steak and hard Idaho potatoes with a side of yellow mustard, happy that he could stomach anything down. He walked straight to the Alhambra, where he sat down for faro. He wasn't dealing that night. He lost most of his stack almost immediately and tried to whittle his way back over the course of the night.

After hours of up and down, about midnight, Wyatt came in and sat down with him. "Where you been?"

"Unfortunately, Charleston. Apparently, the stakes were too high for the high-stakesman," said Doc with his usual Southern lilt.

"You seen Sadie today?"

"I'm surprised you haven't."

"Her day off."

"She still keeping up with pretty boy Behan?"

Wyatt didn't respond. Maybe he didn't want to know.

Doc lost another shoe and realized he didn't have enough to buy in. He plucked his gold watch chain from his jacket. It was something he'd once treasured. His vest looked naked without it. He slid it over to the dealer. "How much in chips?"

The dealer weighed it in his hands and then held it up to the light as if he knew what he was doing. "Thirty, let's say. I mean this ain't just any watch, after all."

"Thirty it is," said Doc. It was well more than the chain was worth, but Doc knew he was expected to return the favor, and he would. That's the way things worked.

The dealer stacked thirty dollars in red, black, and green chips. He palmed the stacks over to Doc. "Better luck with these than the last."

"I rarely believe in luck. There's too much order in it."

Suddenly, the glass door to the Alhambra burst open in a chaotic fashion. It was Bob Paul, who owned the general store. "Deputy Earp!" he called, searching the smoky bar.

"What is it?"

"There's been a hold-up! Yer necessary to the process."

Wyatt ushered Paul outside, past the guard and the taker, away from prying ears. "You informed anyone else?"

Paul shook and sweated. He swallowed and caught his breath. "I trust you most, but I run into Sheriff Behan on my way to you and he noticed my demeanor and got the tale outta me."

"Tell me now."

"It was a Kinnear & Company stagecoach. One a the cushy ones from here to Benson. Bud Philpott was to drive as usual, and I rode shotgun. We made stops at Watervale, picked up two. Bat Masterson was one of them. I forget the other."

"Bat was with you?" Wyatt interrupted.

"Yessir, but he wasn't in real working condition. Looked a bit soused."

"Let's leave that out next time."

Paul's face turned red with embarrassment. "Surely. Anyways, stage was loaded so one a the boys, Roerig, I think, he had to ride up top with us. Around ten, a wash required us to slow near Drew's station past Contention. Then I heard it in the darkness. Someone yelled, 'Hold!'

"We all froze 'cause we couldn't see far past the coach lantern. But then, remembering my business, I let fire two shots out my shotgun into the brush where the voice come out of. I says, 'By God, I hold for nobody!' I remember saying such because it was bold the way you sometimes think you can be but rare have occasion. I hear one man scream. I must've hit him. Then, the men, they opened fire upon us. Philpott got hit hardest and tumbled over."

Wyatt rubbed the coarse hair on his chin. "Go on."

"He never said a word. He was closest to the light, easiest to hit. The thing was that he had them reins gripped real tight, and when he toppled, the horses went into full gallop. I couldn't quell them for nearly a mile. They loved Bud, I think it was.

"In any case, I slid into his vacated seat and applied the brake, easing them into a trot. I recovered the reins at their feet, but Bud was gone. I only found blood where he been. That poor boy, Roerig, got hit too. In the belly, and I knew he ain't got much time in him the way he was paled. I drove us fast to Benson, but he was gone. I telegraphed Tombstone at that time and learnt that someone else already had and that some men outside Drew's station had caught glimpse of some of the robbers running away, and they'd also found Philpott. Nothing needs be explained there, I suppose."

"No, nothing. Thank you, Bob. You'd best come with the posse and show us the way." Wyatt unraveled the leather to his horse and started for the sheriff's office. Outside stood the Wells Fargo agent, Marshall Williams, Morgan, Virgil, and Behan, acting sheriff as he was.

Virgil took a deep breath and mounted his horse. He nodded to Wyatt. "Let's hunt."

CHAPTER 27

Fool

For three days, they hunted. Bat Masterson joined them too. Doc stayed back with Kate. This was official business, and there was no legal way for Doc to join. Around the robbery site, the posse found fifteen shell casings, three wigs, and rope yarn. Virgil and Bat agreed that there must have been four robbers, and the dried blood on the ground meant that Paul had severely injured one of them. Three days on horseback. Three days sniffing a trail. The bits of shit in their trousers combined with the sweat and the dirt and the heat into a soupy mixture that sloshed against their thighs in the day and solidified in the cool nights. There was a redness to the land like tanned hide, and the air all tasted like someone else had used it before.

On Wyatt's hunch, they stopped by Len Redfield's ranch, a Cowboy loyalist who happened to live along the way. After casing the farm for a spell, Wyatt discovered a man milking a cow with two revolvers in his belt and a rifle alongside. He and Morgan ran up from behind and arrested him before he could draw. The man's name was Luther King. While Wyatt and Paul conferred, Behan allowed King to speak with his brother, Hank, who quickly rode off behind the barn.

When Wyatt noticed, he was irate. "And what in the fuck did I just say?"

Behan checked the time on his pocket watch. "Unfortunately, deputy, as of four o'clock today, you're not giving orders around here, are you?"

Wyatt stepped into Behan's face. "You sonofabitch. You're in the bag for them."

"You'd best watch your tone with the sheriff, Earp."

As the two of them argued, Virgil grabbed King by the throat and threw him behind a patch of scraggly bushes where no one could see. "I'll give you one chance to tell me where your brother's headed and where the rest of them boys are."

"I don't know nothing. I—" Before King could even finish his denial, Virgil whipped back his hand and cracked his gloved fist straight into King's nose. The bridge severed, and a small flick of blood shot out.

"Jesus," muttered King, his hands over his nose, collecting the blood like rainwater.

"Again?" said Virgil.

"I—"

Virgil backhanded him over his nose again.

He gurgled in pain. "I'll tell you! I swear. Please."

As he spat blood, King told Virgil where the others were headed and a shortened version of the robbery. Virgil picked him up by his wet shirt and dragged him over to Wyatt and Behan, who continued to argue. They both stopped cold when they saw King.

Virgil pushed the bloodied King into Behan's arms. "He's yours now," said Virgil. "I think we ought to ride on and catch the other three. Now that they been warned it'll be that much more a task." He shot Behan a rough look, but Behan was busy trying to rustle the prisoner. "I think, Williams, you'd best accompany. Behan's not much with his hands."

Williams, who was an honest lawman and only cared for the interest of Wells Fargo, nodded in agreement, having gained a general distrust of Behan through their time spent. So, Paul, Masterson, and the Earp brothers rode on. They were close. They found smoldering campfires but also signs that the fugitives had acquired new horses. On the ninth day of the hunt, Paul's horse got sick, and he was so upset over it that Wyatt had to shoot it in the face himself. Paul said a short prayer and was not the same for the rest of the journey. His horse's death seemed to affect him far more gravely than Bud Philpott's.

Wyatt's horse got sick, too, so they left it with a small kindly woman in a nearby town, handing the last mount to Paul. Wyatt and Bat proceeded to walk eighteen miles back to Tombstone. Virgil continued the search and reported back to Wyatt through coded telegrams in an opaque language of their childhood.

With this information, Wyatt knocked on Doc's hotel room door at nine in the morning—the only time he could be certain Doc would be home. Doc coughed hollow and spat pink on the floor before he was able to push off the covers and rouse himself out of bed.

"The hell is that?" said Kate.

Doc sniffled and cocked his .38 in his hand. He stood to the side of the door. "If you'd like to shoot, then go ahead, but I'd urge you find your God first."

"You fool. It's me," said Wyatt. "Open up."

Recognizing his surly voice, Doc unlatched the door.

"William Leonard, Jim Crane, and Harry Head," said Wyatt, walking straight in. Kate was naked with her breasts bare, the sheets down around her knees. Wyatt immediately shielded his eyes with his hat. "I'm sorry."

"It's all right. Go ahead and look," said Kate. She rose up from the bed and bared her lithe, porcelain body and her red bush. Her nipples rose from the coarse sheets.

She's striking, thought Doc, and he wondered if maybe their problem was forgetting who they really were. Whore and customer. But he could never return to that place. He saw her as his girl now, and she would never relinquish that power. "Please don't be crass in front of our guest, dear. It could suit you to step out of character every now and then." Doc appreciated his friend never peeking at her icy body. It dripped with temptation.

Doc stepped outside the door with Wyatt. It was cracked, so he knew Kate could still hear in all her nakedness. It was the first time he was able to think. Wyatt was listing the bandits. "Wait, William Leonard was part of this fiasco? The damned fool. I did not think that of him."

"What's worse is—some say you were involved." Wyatt paced anxiously outside the hotel door.

Doc heard a thud as Kate fumbled with something on the other side of the door. He knew Wyatt's words would cause her worry.

"There's talk that while the coach was stopped in Watervale, so were you. Billy Breakenridge says you tried to get Paul a drink. Claims it was drugged."

"And you?" asked Doc.

"'Course I don't believe it. Hell, I had seen you the same night."

"Good, then I'll not waste my time denying it. Besides, who in the hell is Billy Breakenridge? How would he know the drink was drugged? A bunch of schoolgirl gossip."

"Fame ain't all cunnilingus and candy canes. People enjoy it to invoke the name of Doc Holliday. 'Sides, he's pals with Joyce, and you did shoot his hand near off."

"Everyone likes a good crash and burn, is that it?" Doc patted Wyatt on the shoulder. "Go and grab some shut-eye. You look balmy, Wyatt."

"I'll clear you of this. I swear it."

Doc laughed. "Don't they have enough to talk about with all the malfeasance I committed in earnest?"

Wyatt shook his head. His eyes were red and puffy. He hadn't shaven in days and patchy stubble grew over his thick neck. "Best clear this with Kate 'fore you set things straight elsewheres."

They shook hands. Doc went back inside and closed the door. Kate stood with her suitcase, fully dressed. She had the look of someone who'd already made up her mind. Her hair was pulled back for travel, and she held a parasol since the weather was turning outside.

"Going somewhere, my dear?"

"I heard your conversing," said Kate.

"So you did. Should I pin a blue ribbon on you?"

"Why'd you need that rifle?" She was dead serious. More than that, she was accusing him.

"Roads are dangerous." He took a step closer to her.

She backed away. "Where'd you go that day?"

"How dare you, woman. How dare you interrogate me. Have I ever given you reason to distrust me?"

"Every day."

"Goddamn you. I'll give you no more explanation. Leave with your wardrobe that I bought. Take your laudanum. It's cold out there for a tramp like you."

"All I ever wanted for you was to find you well. Those Earps, this place, it's rotted you. You ain't even searching no more. You're nothin' but a shell casing. You ain't Doc no more, and you sure as hell ain't no John Henry."

Doc limped up to her and grabbed her throat. "You never knew John Henry. He never would've taken a second look at an incredulous trollop like you."

"Naw, he woulda been too busy fuckin' his own cousin's sweet peach." She pried his hand off her. It left four thin marks like a rake.

"You'll never be like her."

She pushed past him and lugged her things to the door. Her perfume whipped around him. In it, he inhaled their past. He remembered the night he'd met Wyatt. How obedient she was then. He'd spoiled her.

"Never had no mind to. That was you who did." She slammed the door behind her.

Doc crumpled on the bed with a pain in his chest. He coughed lightly, not wanting to dig deeper into his lungs. Not wanting to find what waste really lay within him.

"Tombstone has a population of six thousand—five thousand of them are bad—one thousand of them known outlaws."

—J.S. Wentworth

The next morning, the *Tombstone Evening Gossip* reported with some glee that at seven-thirty the night before, King, in the laziest escape attempt in recent history, merely stepped out the back of an open prison door, grabbing the deputy's pistol as he left, and rode out on the horse that deputy was trying to sell at the time.

Doc decided to pay his old friend a visit. With his name being sullied by the media, he knew he always had one friend there. Wentworth had used his early articles about Doc to make a shiny career for himself in Tombstone. When Doc exited the hotel, he was mobbed by a mixture of reporters and fans all bellowing questions at him.

Many of the reporters had abandoned their unwieldy tripods and switched to a sleeker wooden box camera, which could fold up for transportation into the size of a suitcase. It was a marvel of invention. Six reporters, all at once as if synchronizing their voyeurism, unhooked the front latch, and their accordion lenses popped forward. With one hand balancing the camera from beneath like a dinner platter and the other holding the flash pump attached to a cord, they were able to waddle alongside Doc as he limped toward Wentworth. It was funny not seeing him as part of the scene.

Is there any validity to the stories of your involvement?

"None whatsoever," said Doc, walking faster. His cane caught in the mud. "It's a shame you all are prone to such idle gossip like a pack of carnivorous women." He wrenched it out with his fist.

Glass flashes shattered the air.

What do you make of the robbery itself?

"I think I would be ashamed. One should certainly steal something if he claims himself to be a robber. If I had pulled that job, I would have got the $80,000. Whoever shot Philpott was a rank amateur. If he had downed a horse, he'd have the bullion. All in all, seems like a magnificent waste of good drinking time."

Sheriff Behan says that he'll personally investigate you. Any thoughts?

A drunk Hollidean poured whiskey all over Doc and himself as if to light them ablaze. Doc licked it off his stubbly chin hairs. He hadn't thought to shave. It was unlike him, but his mind was occupied. "If Behan is investigating, then by his own incompetence he will prove my innocence. That man is more a fraud than the common flea circus."

Six journalists sidestepped alongside Doc with their giant photograph machines. The Hollideans were that much more inappropriate, attempting to lick him and mimic his coughs. They had begun to appear even in daylight. The women wore firebrick and yellow like harlots, bearing their calves, their teeth, their eyes wild with the lust of celebrity. They hid under display caskets and in water troughs, trying to grab at him. Doc thought back to when Kate rode that horse like a man—the saddle between her legs. These poor girls were pubescent fodder. It excited him to think of the Bacchanalian corruption he could thrust upon them so willingly. He wondered what infatuations Kate held at their age. If she'd ever known anything but savagery.

Many call you a heathen. Is it true?

"I am a man of both rapture and worship. If God does not believe in such juxtaposition, then I truly am a heathen."

The reporters continued to bark queries at him, but he finally reached the *Evening Gossip* and nudged his way inside. They seemed to respect the sovereignty of another journal; but the Hollideans flung themselves at the glass windows like doomed sparrows, until one burst, shattering all over their forearms and hands. An old journalist was forced to pull a shotgun from under his desk and aim it at the youngest one until the stars in their eyes vanished and their makeup ran down their faces. They scattered aimlessly into midday.

From the back office, Wentworth emerged. He'd gained a little fat on his bones from success. "Well, you're not dead yet. Good for you!"

Doc patted his bones. "Isn't it amazing no one's just up and shot me in the back like Wild Bill?"

"But all you've made are friends." Wentworth laughed. They shook hands, and Wentworth invited him into his office. "So, you want me to squash this?"

"You've always been the sharpest railroad spike in the Chinamen's arsenal."

"You never fail, Holliday. So that's it, but I think this is bigger than just a refutation. You've got to catch those other three and squeeze out a confession. People are talking like they know you did this."

"And how can that be?" Doc searched his pockets for tobacco. Wentworth lit a cigarette on his own and handed it to Doc. Doc took a long drag. The smoke exited his nostrils and up into the stale office lamplight.

"People believe what sounds best on a headline. The other names here are boring. You're exciting. That's always been your problem, Doc. You're just too damn exciting."

Doc reached over to the glass lamp. It had a green glass frame and a worn gas knob. He turned it, and the office went dark. He turned it again and the light returned, this time with Doc a step closer. The smoke drowned his face, catching on his mustache. "Well, seems all my excitement's gotten you a corner office."

Wentworth smiled. "So, it has. I'll see what I can do from here, but you've got some lawmen on your side. They're your real ticket. Good luck, my friend."

They shook again. "And to you, sir." Doc turned to leave.

"Oh, and just so you know—Behan named Harry Woods undersheriff, not Earp. He can't be too pleased with that."

Doc nodded absently with his hand on the door. "No, I reckon not."

CHAPTER 28

Banking on a Myth

Even after Behan failed to keep his word about the undersheriff position, Wyatt continued on his singular mission to clear Doc's name. Any retribution for the betrayal would be secondary. Wyatt had taken on various odd jobs to pay for both his affair and Celia Ann's laudanum. He'd begun dealing at the Oriental, which suited Doc just fine. Doc often stopped by as a customer. He arranged a sit-down for Ike Clanton and Wyatt one day, as per Wyatt's request. It all looked perfectly normal since Wyatt always dealt on Saturdays, and Ike loved to gamble. Doc placed his hat and gun on the other two chairs, respectively, indicating a private match.

Wyatt turned over a three of hearts.

"Gummy! I win again!" said Ike, spitting black dip into a tin cup on the table.

Wyatt pushed a stack of chips over. "You sure have been lucky today, Ike," said Wyatt. "How'd you like that luck to continue?"

"How'd you mean?"

Doc's mouth tasted like school chalk. He twisted his head around for the bartender. It was Joyce, and he wanted nothing to do with Doc, who was ready for his second bottle of the day. "Jesus, with the service around here you'd think I'd shot the bartender or something."

Joyce didn't respond. He kept on drying glasses with a dirty rag Doc knew smelled of fungus and beer.

"Doc, stop givin' him a hard time. Milt, will ya?" asked Wyatt.

Joyce brought over a fresh bottle. "For the stage robber."

Doc snatched the bottle from Joyce's one good hand. "Not much of a grip on you anymore, eh, Joyce? How ever do you pleasure your poor old mother with that deformed hand?"

Joyce grabbed Doc by his collar with his left hand. "You'll be in jail soon enough. I'll make sure of that. I got friends. You don't know nothin' 'bout that." He released Doc, who didn't even flinch. He was only concerned with not dropping the bourbon. Doc figured he was referring to Behan. They'd become chummy of late. Common enemies and all that.

Wyatt sighed with frustration. He returned his attention to Ike. "What I mean is—getting back to it, we can help one another."

"You think Curly Bill don't slit my throat up he finds I been dealing with Johnny law 'emself?"

"Here's what I think. I capture the men who killed Philpott, there are rewards. Big ones. Thirty-six hundred altogether. It's all yours. I just need to know where they are. Nothin' more."

Doc nearly fell off his chair. "Thirty-six . . . ? Well, I might as well find them myself."

"An' assuming I'm privy to this infermation, what's in it for you?" said Ike.

"I'm eyeing that sheriff position. Figure this should put me over the top. Behan's days are numbered." Wyatt flipped over another three. "Winner three. Imagine that."

Ike nodded. "Yeah, I'm imaginin'."

Ike had inserted himself nicely as Curly Bill's left-hand man, next to Ringo. But that kind of money didn't come along every day. Greed was the one thing that always won out. Doc was smart enough to know it wasn't always money. Sometimes it was pussy. Sometimes power, a glimpse at salvation. But every man had one thing in common: desire. If you found what he truly craved, he would fold to your will. Ike was a simple man. Money was enough.

Ike searched around the gaming room for anyone who might know him. It was dead empty, save for a couple silver-faced miners by the bar in the other room. "They hidin' out by the Hasletts' ranch. Goes without saying we ain't friends, and we never talked but little—you telling me what a good faro player I am."

Wyatt grinned. He nodded to Doc and turned over another three of hearts. "Winner, three. Your lucky day, Ike."

Ike took his winnings, got up, and walked out. Doc closed his eyes and imagined the rumors lifted off him. He'd lied to those reporters. The thought of another trial made his legs heavy. He felt suddenly stagnant. He thought of Kate and how all she'd wanted was to save him. Even *she* didn't trust him anymore.

The next morning, as Wyatt and Doc prepared to ride alongside Virgil and find the remaining stagecoach robbers, Behan approached the trio outside the sheriff's office.

"Where are you three off to with such big guns?" said Behan, grabbing Doc's reins.

"Off to catch some road agents. You should try it sometime." Wyatt mounted his horse. "That is, if yer not too caught up in politickin'."

"A worthy endeavor, I'm sure. I only hope you all are not after William Leonard or Harry Head. I'm very sorry to say they were found dead today. Holes in their bellies. Over at the Hasletts', who are in our custody as we speak."

"Leonard's dead?" asked Doc. He never realized how disturbed the news would make him. He was a scoundrel, and their friendship had brought Doc's name into this mess, but there was something distinctly decent about the man. Doc choked down something that nearly came up. He suddenly felt very warm and wiped his brow with his handkerchief. He thought of William Leonard's teeth.

"I know you two were close." Behan's stiff hair remained perfectly parted, even in the breeze. He spoke with an affected Southern accent, so it was impossible to tell where he was really from. *Maybe bastards like that don't come from anywhere*, thought Doc. "Listen, now that Leonard and Head are dead, that just leaves *you* alive."

"Doc didn't have nothin' to do with this thumper," said Virgil.

Doc appreciated that it wasn't just Wyatt coming to his defense.

"You know—I truly want to believe that. Certainly we can trust our justice system to find out. I've expedited the case due to the recent departures of the other witnesses and your—notoriety. We don't want this dragging out." Behan took a deep breath. Doc couldn't take his eyes off of Behan's tiny nostrils. Feminine, like the rest of his nose. He hadn't noticed until this moment, and now he couldn't even fathom how a man could live on those dainty things.

"Gentlemen, all I really care about is a safer, more family-friendly Tombstone. I wish you the very best." He walked back into his office. His clothes were tighter than they needed to be and hugged his skinny thighs.

Wyatt hung his head. He dismounted and patted his horse on its haunches. "Goddammit. This fucks it all to hell."

From their left, Ike strode up to them, looking both ways before he spoke. His hair was a curled-up mess, and his goatee was crooked with sweat. "You knew about this too?" he said to Virgil.

"'Bout what?"

"Y'all have too-big mouths. You were suppose to find them three an' that was to be the end of it."

"You made a deal with Ike Clanton?" said Virgil.

"Oh, goddamn. You didn't know? Yes you did. To hell with all y'all. Yer in it together."

"Ike, calm yourself before you begin chasing your own tail," said Doc. His duster and necktie dangled in the warm air.

"Deals off. You think you got somethin' on me now?"

"Go home, Ike. This ain't good for nobody," said Wyatt.

"You got that certain. The Hasletts killed 'em."

"We don't know what happened yet. They're at the office answering questions," said Virgil. "Now quit wakin' snakes and move along."

"Real pleasure, you three," Ike spat and walked off, straight to the Oriental to find Curly Bill. He was gnashing his thick teeth the whole way. His fingers twitched with nerves.

Curly Bill and Ringo sat at the bar trading shots of whiskey. Ringo was already full as a tick when Ike walked in. He was signaling to the bartender. "'Nother shot of Kansas sheep dip for me an' Bill."

"You don't slow down we'll have to float you to the next gunfight," cracked Curly Bill.

"I'll take 'em all." Ringo's face was splotchy and slick with oil and sweat. He slurred fantastically. Struggling to keep his eyes open, he tried to fix his hat, but he only skewed it more to the left.

"What's the good in that hair case you don't know how to use it?" Curly Bill said, already chuckling.

Ringo leaped off his seat, throwing a winding haymaker at Bill that missed by over a foot. Bill never moved. He laughed even harder and signaled to Ike.

Ike picked up Ringo and set him back on his stool.

"You done?" said Curly Bill.

Ringo swayed precariously on the stool and held his forehead in his palm.

Ike interrupted. "Hasletts are at the sheriff's office. They killed Head and Leonard," said Ike.

Curly Bill's face altered immediately. A grave expression overtook him. "Well, somebody ain't playin' by the Cowboy rules. What are we if we ain't got rules, Johnny?"

Ringo stretched his hands all the way out on the bar. There were a few drops of liquor like a collection of tears. He tilted his head sideways, lowered his tongue to the bar, and licked them up, dragging his tongue along the length of the grain. "Nothin' but animals."

That afternoon, a crippling flash fever overtook Doc. His temperature rose so high over the next few hours that he stripped himself down in his hotel room where he sweated deep shadows into the sheets. His head swelled and cheeks flushed. He felt that the heat might overwhelm him. The cracks on the ceiling combined with the flies so that each deep black space grew wings that terrified him when he could open his eyes. His naked bones protruded through his glassy skin, and he felt death's hand like a cat's claws in his throat.

Through the waves of heat, Doc could see his mother. They'd been moving around during Reconstruction. John Henry was thirteen at the time, and he remembered these piles of Confederate money sitting in the foyer of their home. They were as worthless as tomato seeds in winter.

They'd just moved into their new home in Bemiss when his mother took ill. She spent two years dying in that house. Each day there was less of her. She couldn't eat anything the maid, Sophie, brought her, and some days John Henry would take the plate in to try. He'd walk in, careful not to knock over the coffee can of sputum resting next to her. The bed was about up to his nostrils, so he'd balance the plate on top of his mother's flat body. Usually a tiny sandwich. The room smelled of lettuce and unwashed hair. He'd rest his head on her arm, and because it was him, she'd take a bite.

It took her so long to raise her arms then. She didn't have much time left. It was moving so fast. She'd given into it, in a way. It would have been easier for the major if she just got out of the way, but she took the two years for John Henry because he wasn't ready yet. He was still a boy when she caught it, and she'd tried not to succumb till he was a man.

John Henry fell asleep on her gaunt body, her hipbone digging into his cheek. He awoke from her shaking. She always had chills but was always metal hot. He tried to speak to her, but she was away in some famished nightmare. He lifted the sandwich off her ribcage, just the one bite chewed out like a mouse had gotten to it.

Now, Doc suffocated silently. He was dying. He could feel it. He couldn't even bear the energy to cough up the liquid that built in his rotting lungs. He flung himself off the bed, crawling to the window, crawling for air. It burned. He managed to drag himself to the window and force it open with the little strength remaining in his brittle arms. He stuck his head out. No one was there. No fans, no friends. He could make out the library, the gunsmith, and the sheriff's office. He tried to spot Wyatt, but the streets were quiet. It was dinnertime, and he was either with Celia Ann or Sadie. At least he was happy half the time.

There was the strangest thing. It was Curly Bill and Ike and Ringo and Billy and the young McClaury brothers with about ten other Cowboys all converging on the sheriff's office. Doc squinted as salt burned his eyes, and he waited. It was almost choreographed, the lot of them just standing there with their Navy models drawn. Doc couldn't tell how much time passed. It could have been hours, feverish, dangling over that dusty windowsill. And then, there it was, what they were waiting for. All Doc saw was a hand push the Hasletts out of the sheriff's office.

Both Hasletts stumbled and fell because their wrists were bound, but the Cowboys never hesitated. They opened fire. They danced and howled with carnivorous pleasure at their grim destruction. Their bullets carved and twisted like practiced ballet. The carnage was elegant. Doc could feel the discord in the air, smell flesh. The prisoners had no time to scream as metal cleaved bone, and the powder of their marrow permeated the atmosphere like talcum. Their cheeks and lungs softened the soil. Ringo, Ike, and Curly Bill were jackals. Nothing remained of the Hasletts' bodies but the husks of something that had once been human. There could be no burial. They had been slaughtered and then cauterized by fury. And then, one by one, the Cowboys urinated onto their juicy remains and vanished.

The hotel door swung open. With everything he had left, Doc leaped toward the bed for his gun. He scrambled. His vision went blurry. He sweated, and mucus ran down his chin. He looked up at a dark figure in the doorway.

CHAPTER 29

Personal Jesus

Doc pressed his back against the bed and shut his eyes. Water accumulated on his lips. It was the fountain. He could see it in front of him, a black liquid chasm like oil. All he had to do was fall in. He would be reborn. No fever, no sickness, the end of bone and bullet. He felt himself slipping in, first his toes, then deeper into the water, but a voice wrenched him out. A familiar voice. Someone he loved.

"Whatcha doin' naked on the floor?"

Doc opened his pink-ringed eyes. The figure in the doorway was short with long red hair. Legs like stockinged straws. "Kate?"

She was sloppy drunk, and eyeliner ran down her face. "I done it, baby." She stumbled toward him and threw herself with all her weight on top of his moist, sticky skin. She was slurring her words like he'd never heard her. "Yer warm."

"What have you done, bumblebee?"

"I got us free. I got us clear a them Earps finally . . ." She was trailing off into sleep. "This town."

"How long have you been back?" Doc clapped his hand lightly on her chin. "What do you mean? What've you done?"

"It's okay," she raked his jaw with her long nails. "I talked to the sheriff. Everything gone be fine."

Doc extricated himself from her silk and lace. He slid out from under her. His pale member recoiled into itself. "Behan? Is that the man? You spoke to Behan in this state?"

"He said he'd fix it. Yer all mine now." Her eyes rolled back into her head. She spat up onto the hotel carpet in little orange chunks; then she slid down against the bed into deep, inebriated slumber. Doc, unable to keep his eyes open any longer, soon followed suit, heat radiating off his skin like a pig in August.

Doc woke up with drool down the crease of his lips and a prickling pain in his throat. Kate was still asleep on the floor, her hair matted in her own sick. He was naked and cold. The fever had passed. He threw a blanket around himself, shut the window, and emptied his flask onto his coated tongue.

Doc sat back down on the bed; with one foot, he nudged Kate awake. She cringed at the light through the window.

"Can't you let me be fer once?" She wiped the crust out of her lashes. Her makeup had spread over her face, and she peered at him from behind her brittle hair like a destitute raccoon.

"Get up, woman."

"I'll leave again. I will!"

"What did you tell Behan?" Doc nudged her harder with the side of his shin.

She grumbled, picking dried gobs of half-digested food out of her hair. "Who?"

"Goddamn it. Sheriff Behan. You were going on last night telling him all sorts of things I'm certain you know nothing about."

"I—" Kate wore a crooked look of confusion on her face. She sniffled. "I don't know what I said."

"Truly?"

"Honest Injin."

Doc rested his head in his palms. "Did you sign anything?"

Kate tried to clear her throat. "There was dancin', and Celia Ann was there for a brief moment. You know how I am with tequila."

"Save your empties. God knows you'll catch me my end before the cough ever does."

Kate gathered herself and flung her arms dramatically around Doc's weak legs. "Whatever I said, I don't mean none of it."

"If you've done what I fear, there's only one person left who can clear me. I've got to find Crane."

"Who's that?"

"My dear, I think it's safe to say you've lost your privileges for a spell." Doc got up and checked himself in the mirror. He combed his hair and his mustache. He buttoned up his shirt, straightened his silver chain. He missed the gold one he'd let go in faro. He went for his pistol, coat, and pants. "You certainly make life interesting, Kate. How can I die when you've given me so much to tidy up?"

Doc poured fresh bourbon into his flask. It pinged against the metal. He slipped it into his jacket and shut the hotel door behind him. The air in the hallway was much fresher than in his room. He took off immediately for the deputy's office to find Wyatt. No one waited outside for him anymore. Neither the Stetson shop owner nor Bob Paul met his gaze; they feared him. Paul remained in mourning over his horse. Doc was now a stagecoach robber in their eyes, a murderer, a liar. Even the Hollideans laid low, fearing that perhaps he had betrayed them too. Doc hoped that finding Crane could fix it all. He'd grown accustomed to his celebrity. Kate had been right about one thing: Maybe he didn't want to move on again.

When Doc got to the deputy's office, he found Earps, but none of the Wyatt variety. Morgan, Virgil, and Warren, who'd just joined his other brothers from California, sat there, discussing a land deal.

"Has anyone seen Wyatt?" Doc interjected.

"Yeah, he's elbow deep in that actress right now," said Morgan, snickering.

"Not your business," Virgil interrupted.

Morgan straightened up in his seat, filling the role of the younger brother.

"Something I can do you for?" said Virgil.

"Actually, I believe there is. You may have heard some rumors swirling around town. They are as true as a wag-tail swearing it's her first time. I would like to clear my name of them with your assistance."

"How do you suppose we go 'bout that?"

Doc lifted his watch. He felt the weight of it in his palm. It was always a few minutes slow before Leonard fixed it for him. Now it was perfect. Eleven on the button. "When I was in Will Leonard's company, we used to discuss Jim Crane from time to time. He was working with Old Man Clanton moving cattle. If he still is, we can find him. You all can be heroes—catching the last of the robbers alive, and I can clear my name."

Virgil turned to his brothers. They both nodded. He picked up his rifle. "Show us. I'll snatch Wyatt from his adulterating."

Wyatt, Virgil, Morgan, Warren, and Doc all left Tombstone that afternoon and headed toward the Mexican border, where the Arizona territory met with New Mexico. Virgil deputized Wyatt because he was in a legal gray area after Behan's political betrayal. There was no point in deputizing Doc.

They camped in the desert by firelight overnight, and by daybreak, they neared the border. The mountains glowed green with summer flora, and mist drifted over their peaks. The five riders approached a plateau, at the end of which lay a sheer drop of fifty feet into the river. The rock was brown and white there. The bright-eyed sky reflected off the water in ripples.

Across the canyon, they spotted a campsite with about twenty cattle and seven men. It was tough to tell if one of them was Crane, but there was no one else around and it would make sense if it were. Doc finally felt like he was part of something. He and the brothers. Maybe he could never be family, but Wyatt was as close as he would ever get.

"How's Sadie treating you, Wyatt?" asked Doc. "Does she still do that little trick with your neck fat where she sort of twists—"

"Would you shut up? Let's circle around to the other side. I don't think they spotted us yet," said Wyatt.

There was a point where the canyon raised enough, along the leftmost bank, that it was possible for the horses to cross to the other side. It was also far enough away not to be heard. The sun wasn't all the way flush yet, and it was possible that the campers were still asleep; it was still too far to make out their eyes. The cliffside was covered with small berry bushes, and a winding dirt path now separated them from the campsite. The posse flanked the seven men from the left as quietly as they could, but someone must have heard their horse steps.

"Who be it?" said Old Man Clanton. He cocked his shotgun, hurriedly waking the other men.

They were close enough to see each other now. Seven armed Cowboys. They were easy to spot. Old Man Clanton had the face of a billy goat. His thick white beard covered the butt of the shotgun propped against his shoulder. He was bald, wore a hide vest over his sweat-stained undershirt, and a gold crucifix hung from his breast pocket. It was the same one from Leonard's shop.

"We're looking for Jim Crane. Give him over an' go about your business," yelled Wyatt. He checked that his peacemaker was full. Virgil, Morgan, and Warren all readied their rifles. Doc pulled his .38. Blood rushed through him, into his fingertips. He felt fast. The sharp rush of the kill flooded his gut.

A shot rang out from the Cowboys, and the cattle scattered in wild zigzags. Wyatt's horse reared up. The fight was on.

CHAPTER 30

Happy Together

Wyatt and Doc dismounted and began firing into the campsite, laying down cover. The ground was muddy, and it was tough to get a good foothold in the sludge. Virgil fired a few shots screaming wide of Clanton. One of the Cowboys took off. He just started sprinting in the other direction, winding his way through the ambling cattle. They let him go in case it was Crane. Through the ashes of a smoldering fire, Old Man Clanton let loose a shotgun blast that severed Morgan's horse's front leg. The tinder sparked up and settled in his beard so that his face lit up electric crimson; small flames sparkled off the split ends of his white hair. Morgan leaped off his horse as it crumpled into the black slush, teeth first. It writhed, shaking its stump, braying and flailing helplessly. Morgan's ankle bent funny on his landing, so he couldn't risk standing. He looked away as he shot the horse in the brain, its eyes still open like two marbles.

Wyatt caught one of the Cowboys, Billy Bryers, in the arm and the belly. He bent to his knees, clutching his wrist, trying to slow the blood with his open palm. Old Man Clanton continued to tread closer, cocking his shotgun and firing another burst into the posse. The sharp Arizona sun came on harder and made it difficult to see past the orange haze. The yellow moon remained. From behind Doc and Wyatt, Warren yelped and fell from his mount. Doc kept his eyes forward, but Wyatt turned back to see that Warren's leg had been shattered by Clanton's shotgun pellet.

A cloud passed overhead. Doc's vision cleared. He planted his right boot on the ground. His mind went white with quiet. He straightened his arm, the steel aligned with his eye, in unison with the trigger. He landed two shots in Clanton's wrinkled neck. He could taste the hot blood on his tongue. It spurted out in parabolic fountains. Doc found it strange that such deranged horror could create such unified beauty. Clanton splashed to the ground, clutching his shotgun to his chest. Doc felt his presence extinguish.

Virgil, still on horseback, circled around from behind and bedded down two more Cowboys with surgical kill shots to their backsides. The bullets, at such close range, tore through them easily and with gruesome force so that when one fell forward into a bush it pushed through his ribs and stuck clear out the other side. Wyatt picked off another man with calm accuracy until there was only powder and pink dust. Ashes kicked up in the air, clinging to Doc's wet face. His heart slowed. The fight was over. Morgan, who had only turned his ankle, hobbled over to Warren. He ripped off his belt and tied a tourniquet around Warren's girthy thigh. The shin protruded through his skin like a steak bone.

Wyatt and Doc approached the carnage carefully as Virgil remained vigilant on his horse, covering them with his rifle. Doc turned over Old Man Clanton's body. It was heavy with mud but flaccid. The cross dangled off him, glinting in the dry light.

"Buzzards will fatten today," said Doc.

"Ike'll be none pleased about this." Wyatt wiped his face with the back of his hand. There were eight bodies—five Cowboys, two cows, and Morgan's horse. The sun heated the mud. Their corpses would rot, become earth once again.

Wyatt turned over the next stiff. It was Jim Crane. "Goddamn. I'm sorry, Doc." He was young. No beard. A necktie and a bullet through his right cheek that shattered his bone and caved in his face; the other side was him, as if by profile he could still be alive.

"Dirty business, this," said Doc.

Wyatt called to Morgan. "How is he?"

"He'll be okay, I think. Needs a doctor," said Morgan, his arm on Warren's knee.

Doc took a couple of tentative steps toward Warren, about to volunteer his services.

"A real one!" said Morgan.

"Take my horse," said Wyatt. "I'll ride back with Doc."

As Virgil, Wyatt, and Doc approached Tombstone on horseback, they noticed concentrated black smoke spiraling up from the center of town—the spice of dry firewood, faint screams. Tombstone was ablaze. Wyatt picked up speed, Doc right behind him. Virgil headed straight for the sheriff's office on Fremont and Seventh. As he sped off, Doc and Wyatt watched the smoke billow and build like an ebony halo over the town center. The thickest smoke was right around the Oriental. Wyatt snapped the reins and rode to the Alhambra. The blaze hadn't hit there yet, but it was in its path. Heat slunk along the streets in coils.

Wyatt steadied the horse, wrenching his neck back. "I need you to look after Sadie. Make sure she's all right. Can you do that for me?"

"Surely. Kate can take care of herself. Heading home?"

"Celia Ann is liable to be out cold. She'd never even feel herself burn with all that shit in her system. Meet you back at the Oriental in half an hour. See if we can be of use there."

Doc stepped off, and Wyatt rode off toward his house on Third Street. Doc entered the Alhambra theatre, but it was empty. Everyone must have left in a hurry because there were full drinks all over the bar. He downed one quickly, then took off, heading closer to the heart of the flames, toward the Oriental.

Panicked townspeople with inadequate water pails and loosed mounts darted through the streets. It reminded him of Fort Worth. The fire department raced to get to the town center, just a red wagon with two firemen sitting atop it on leather chairs, fitted with a few axes, a couple of lanterns, a ladder, and four bucketfuls of water. Even the horses proudly wore red reins and kerchiefs around their necks.

With all the commotion in the streets, Doc moved about as fast as the hook and ladder, even with his cane. He arrived at the Oriental to see the most surreal sight. It was, indeed, ablaze, but there were panicked cries coming from inside. The two buildings next to it had been engulfed, and the Oriental was next to become totally demolished. The firemen eventually made it through by honking their horn, and with their axes they broke down the Oriental door only to find Curly Bill and Ringo inside with a dealer, still playing poker.

It was a tense hand between them, and there was at least a hundred dollars on the green felt.

"Help! My God, these men will burn me down!" screamed the dealer to the firemen.

Curly Bill tucked his cards into his palm, pulled out his Colt Navy revolver, and pressed it to the dealer's temple. "The sooner we finish this hand the sooner you can leave. I swear, no one takes their jobs serious no more."

By now, a large crowd had gathered outside the Oriental, including Behan and Sadie. Doc wasn't sure which Wyatt would prefer her to be—caught in the fire or standing with Behan. Doc found it strange to be in such a large crowd and not be the centerpiece. The ceiling had caught flame, and the chandelier broke loose. As the roof cracked, it swung overhead. The whiskey on the bar burst, bottle by bottle, sending lines of smoldering glass searing through the wood.

"Oh dear God, the place is coming apart!" said the dealer.

"If you don't let me concentrate, none of us is making it out," said Ringo calmly. He took a small sip of whiskey, checking his cards again. "Call."

The flames crawled along the walls, and the smoke thickened like skin. The firemen backed out of the Oriental, a bit befuddled, and simply began pouring water around the poker table from as far away as possible with wooden beams splintering and crashing to the floor. Smoldering daylight poked through the roof.

Curly Bill flipped his cards. "Pair of twos."

Ringo peeked at his hand again. "There's no more betting?"

"No, you drunk fool. It's five card." Bill slid the hammer of his pistol back down and holstered it. The dealer bolted into the firemen's arms, but they threw him aside, attempting to keep the flames from Ringo and Bill as long as they could. The deer heads on the walls crackled and their antlers baked. The scent of hide and hair puffed out into the streets.

Doc turned his head away from the absurd scene to momentarily check out the surrounding damage. A block away, Virgil had organized his deputies and was fighting the spreading fire, saving lives on Fourth Street.

Ringo sighed. The chandelier cracked down to the right of the poker table, fragmenting, spewing crystal against their boots. "Well, I got nothing. I lost my place."

"Ha, yer just roostered." Curly Bill swept up as much cash as he could, and the two Cowboys nonchalantly exited the building as the inferno charred the poker felt, swallowing it whole. All that was left of the Oriental was its emaciated frame.

Doc applauded the two of them as they exited. "And they say no one has conviction anymore."

Ringo tipped his hat.

Behan, who hadn't noticed Doc standing there earlier, sauntered over, leaving Sadie alone in the street.

"Why, Sheriff, you seem to be handling this spark with great aplomb."

Behan did not retort; he simply held up a piece of paper. Behind him, the town burned. "You know what this is?"

Doc couldn't quite make it out. He got in closer. It was an affidavit, his name plastered all over it. Someone had confessed to knowing his whereabouts the night of the robbery, accusing him of the murders of Philpott and Roerig. "What fallacy is this? Who claims to know me?"

Behan pointed at the signature with his middle finger on the bottom of the page. *Kate!* She'd really turned on him this time, he thought. This was as true a betrayal as he could ever imagine.

"She was drunk. What have you done to coerce her?" Doc grabbed onto Behan's shirt collar, tugging him forward.

"Now, now, Mr. Holliday. Certainly you're in enough trouble without adding on assault of an officer."

Sadie hurried over. "What's all this about?"

Doc released Behan, and he tumbled back a step into Sadie's arms.

"Stick to Wyatt, my dear. This snake is worth no amount of gold." The smoke thickened in the street, and the crowd began to clear out. Doc flowed with them, toward Third. He hoped Wyatt was okay—and Kate, too, despite it all. In the background, all he heard was the crackle of wood and Behan saying, "Wyatt Earp? What could he mean by that, Josephine?"

In the meantime, Wyatt had nearly reached his home when Ike Clanton ran out in front of his horse. The horse reared up.

"Get the hell outta the way, Clanton. I've got to get to my wife!" said Wyatt, coaxing the horse left.

Ike wrapped his arms around the horse's neck, hanging on the beast to stand. "This fire, yer wife, that don't change nothin'. You got hell comin' to you."

"What are you on about?"

Ike's eyes drooped. He hadn't slept. The drink on his breath made it all the way up to Wyatt.

"Dear God, you're near flammable."

"I'll kill you fer my father. He was better than all of us. He was the only one who knew the words."

Wyatt pried Ike's fingers off his horse with one hand. "The words to what?"

Ike let go all at once, horsehair caught in his jagged fingernails. He muttered to himself as he stumbled away. "I ain't got any. I ain't got the words like he had."

Wyatt kept an eye on Ike as he made his way toward Third Street. In his heart, he couldn't reconcile that he'd be relieved if the fire had taken her. He justified this feeling, as best he could, with the knowledge that she'd be relieved too. He hoped, with all his being, that Sadie was safe with Doc.

CHAPTER 31

Let's Shake Some Dust

Territory of Arizona v. Doc Holliday

July 9, 1881

The Tombstone fire took all night to quell. When all was said and done, over sixty businesses burned down to the ground, but the blaze never reached Wyatt and Celia Ann on Third Street. Kate was with Celia Ann when Wyatt got there, stoned and asleep, which was fortunate because Doc's hotel had burnt halfway to hell.

In the aftermath of the fire, Wyatt sent Warren home to California to recover from his wounds with their parents. Warren was the youngest and never seemed to fit in with his brothers. He would limp the rest of his life, something Doc knew plenty about.

Due to Virgil's quick thinking and heroism, he was promoted to marshal by Behan's superiors and immediately reinstated Wyatt as a "special" with powers of arrest and keeping the peace, which basically made him law without all of the day-to-day responsibilities. For Wyatt, it was perfect.

During that time of reconstruction, Behan almost single-handedly forced Doc into court. Doc's lawyer attempted dismissals at the local level, but Behan's influence, both politically and monetarily, drove the case forward to an indictment. Doc's popularity dropped to the point where he was only a celebrity in the sense that he'd once been admired. People still recognized him, of course, but it was more a feeling like you've been somewhere before, and you're not sure why: infamy. The droves of Hollideans, cameras, and screaming fans no longer followed his every move. Since the Cosmopolitan took fire damage, he was forced to stay at Fly's Boarding House along with Kate, who he suspected secretly preferred his waning fame.

The courthouse was only half-full. A couple of fledgling reporters, Wyatt and the Earps, Behan, Bud Paul, and four steadfast groupies who'd come all the way from Indiana to see Doc's trial. Wentworth was there, too, but not in any professional capacity.

Justice Spicer had heard from Wyatt, who'd defended Doc wholeheartedly, then from Behan and Breakenridge, casting some suspicion but all in hearsay and loose evidence.

Joyce's greatest contribution to the prosecution was, "He's the same man who shot my hand. Do I think he could shoot someone dead? Yes, I do. I think it could've been me."

To which Doc replied, "Seems I should have, you falsity-driven grandstander!"

The justice gaveled as the four Hollideans cheered. It made for the most excitement of the day.

Finally, the judge called on Kate.

The courtroom was painted white with four sunlit windows and no shades. The windows were shut, and it was hot inside, but that's how Justice Spicer liked it. To the left of the judge stood a limp American flag. Above him hung portraits of Alexander Hamilton and President Rutherford B. Hayes. His tall wooden bench was imposing; below it, to the right, sat Doc and his lawyer, A.G.P. George. Adjacent to them was the Arizona District Attorney. He had a very long neck and a handsome suit that Doc admired. The audience seats only went four rows back, making for a cramped courtroom.

Kate stood up from the second row. She made her way to the stand. The bailiff swore her in.

"Ms. Elder—" the judge began.

"I'd prefer to be called Mrs. Holliday."

The judge furrowed his brow. He sifted through some paperwork in front of him. "Are you married to Mr. Holliday?"

"Not yet, but he just hasn't gotten 'round to it. He promised."

"Ms. Elder, your confession here states that you believe Mr. Holliday was responsible for the Benson stage robbery and Bud Philpott's murder. Is this your understanding?"

Behan and Joyce leaned over the front row of the courtroom on the left. Behan whispered something into Joyce's ear.

Kate took a moment to think. She breathed deeply and looked at Doc. His red cheeks, his blue eyes, the way he could smile even when no one else dared. She turned and eyed Behan. He nodded to her, his small nose bobbing up and down. Doc wondered what he'd promised her.

"I was sauced on bug juice when I said that."

Justice Spicer shook the affidavit in the air. "You directly accuse Mr. Holliday of thievery and murder in this. This is perjury, Ms. Elder. Do you understand?"

Kate nodded. "I reckon, but that man said he'd hired Mattie the Gambler to kill me and Doc and the only way he'd call her off is if I did as he asked. So he got me liquored up and got me to sign some letters and then had his way with me for three dollars and fifty cents."

Behan burst out of his seat. "This is outrageous! I am the sheriff of this town, a respectable man. Are you going to believe this harlot? She's less credible than the murderer himself."

"He's right, that's a heckuva price!" added Doc.

Justice Spicer slammed his gavel on the table. "Well, Mr. Behan, that 'incredible' witness was brought into this trial by—let's see." He squinted, reading the signature. "You."

Behan was about to speak again, but he thought better of it and sat back down.

"Mr. District Attorney, how would you like to proceed?" said the judge.

The DA scratched his brown ear hair. "Justice, I am satisfied that there is not even the slightest evidence to show the guilt of the defendant. I, therefore, ask that the complaint be withdrawn and the case dismissed."

"Let it be so," said Justice Spicer. And that was it. Kate and the Hollideans let out a collective yelp of joy, but Doc had already made his way to the courtroom exit, past Wyatt and Behan, his fans, and Wentworth.

He wanted to feel absolution as he left, but all he felt was thirst.

CHAPTER 32

Earthly Pleasure

Despite the cinder in the air and the smell of silver fumes in his hotel room, Doc was feeling healthier than he had in years. Maybe it was a mixture of the Arizona climate and relief. Doc lay on his pencil-stiff mattress at Fly's Boarding House, counting the earwigs on the wall. They were brown, hard-backed beetles with mustard legs and red-tipped horns on their rears. They clicked along the wall, three or four of them at a time, and Doc believed what was said about them—how if you fell asleep, they'd crawl into your earhole and lay eggs.

Fly's was attached to a photography studio and gallery. It probably accounted for more of their business than the room and board. To its left was the Cristini Grocery and Meats, so it wasn't unusual to mix the scent of raw steak with film developer. The boarding house itself was as simple as a log cabin, four white posts out back, four white posts out in front of the photography studio. Lanterned windows lay symmetrically adjacent to the door, and the façade was made up of horizontal wood planks they'd never bothered to paint. Up top, in tall, thin lettering it read:

Fly's Photography Gallery
C.S. FLY. PROP.

That's where Kate spent most of her time lately. She'd gotten Fly, who was an innocuous man, to fall in love and take endless portraits of her with all her clothes on, which Doc found to be preposterous. Fly was convinced they would be worth something one day, if to no one else than himself. It was the most she'd been dressed in months.

Doc listened to the incessant clanging and hammering that marked the reconstruction of Tombstone. He'd known Reconstruction. Sawdust and ash clouded the air so that at any moment you might inhale the charred bodies of the old and the weak who had not escaped the flames. The townspeople banded together in an effort to rebuild, to mourn, to carry on. All Doc saw was the smoky blur of the fire—stain, the aftertaste of skin and tooth. *They had it all wrong*, he thought; Tombstone hadn't even begun to be razed.

It was already one p.m., and Doc figured he should start his day with some cards and coffin varnish at the Alhambra. Wyatt often lunched there with his brothers, since the Oriental was burnt to a husk. He thought of Curly Bill's eyes wide and wild with sheets of fire dancing around his ankles. Doc found his imprudence remarkable. He now saw Ringo as a man of immortality. They were both brave and foolish in their own way because they didn't have a choice.

He took a gander at his cane, propped up against the nightstand to the right of the door. That's about all the room was: a bed, a nightstand, and a stand-up closet. The bathroom was around the hall. He left the cane, feeling good and damn sure he could manage without it.

The walk from Fly's to the Alhambra was short and quiet. Doc told himself he preferred it that way, that there were others more deserving of the hot limelight. He wondered if he was even worth remembering now or if he was just some lackey of the Earp clan. Perhaps he and Kate should have been off long ago searching for the fountain while he still had breath to search with.

When Doc arrived at the saloon, Wyatt was sitting with his lunch: a plate of salted rabbit, a doughnut, and a glass of milk. Morgan stood at the bar with the saloonkeeper, chatting about mounts. Ike paced back and forth, muttering under his breath behind Wyatt so that no one else could hear. Wyatt ignored him, slathering the rabbit in butter and forking it into his mouth.

Doc got in closer.

"You planned to rat me out all along. I know yer kind. You ain't worth the shit on my shoes."

Wyatt tongued the inside of his mouth, dislodging a chunk of meat. "You been shitting on your shoes again, Ike?" He chewed the newly dislodged morsel.

"Fuck you, lawman. You think cuz yer brother says you law, you law?" He'd been drinking all morning and was stuck in repetitions. "I'll kill you an' all yer worthless Earps."

Doc grabbed Ike's shoulder and spun him around. "Ike, no one cares about you enough to mention your name to anyone but a coroner, so why don't you go light your fire elsewheres."

Ike's breath was bright with whiskey. "Goddamn lunger. Yer in on this, too, almost forgot. Shoulda stabbed you and your big-nosed whore back when—puckered like a wet sheepskin before a hot fire."

"Is that a bluff, or do you mean it for play?" Doc squared to Ike, he dropped his right hand down to his soft leather holster.

"I may be soaked, but I ain't no bluffer," said Ike.

"Well, I'm just going to have to cut your suspenders, you virulent stinking piece of shit. You cowpie. You countrified Mary. You crosspatch, marrow-sucking chimp. I'll have you in a cold meat wagon before you can put a single finger on that steel!"

Wyatt, who'd continued to eat the whole time, finally got up out of his seat, realizing Doc really meant to cut down Clanton. "Is it possible to get a single meal down in this cunt of a town?"

Ike's body tensed, and he backed away toward the lunch counter like cornered prey. "I'll do it. I'll take you down, Holliday."

Doc's eyes lit with fury. "Sonofabitch Cowboy. Pull out that gun if there's any grit in you. Get to the fighting." His heart slowed and his pupils dilated. He was ready to draw. The creak of the horses by the water trough, the clink of fork against porcelain, it all receded until the only thing Doc could hear was the sweat beading against Ike's beard and the pulse in his veins.

CHAPTER 33

Pistol of Fire

Doc snapped his hand to his pearl-handle, but just before he could draw, Morgan leaped over the lunchroom bar, clamping down on Doc's trigger hand and using all his force to drive Doc out of the bar.

Wyatt exhaled, sat back down, and started on his doughnut. Ike followed closely as Doc struggled furiously against Morgan's young, muscled frame. Doc was no match for his sheer force as Morgan finally wrangled him outside, shoving him away from the door. They both sweated and caught their breath for a moment before realizing Ike was standing in the Alhambra entrance, swaying back and forth like a wet reed.

"Goddamn, don't you know when someone's doing you favors?" Morgan barked at Ike. "Now get!"

"Don't need favors. Don't need nothing but bodies." Ike had lost his hat somewhere in the bar, and his sweaty hair flapped against his forehead. The sun was bright hot and bore down on the three of them. It was nearly a hundred degrees, and not a single cloud bothered the clear sky. It stunk of dead. Flies gathered around the bloated corpses of rats that drowned in water troughs or died of thirst under Mac's General Store porch.

Morgan positioned his body between the two parties so that Doc wouldn't shoot. He kept his eyes on Ike, though with all his bluster, not one of them had ever seen him draw. Not once. Down the road, after hearing the commotion from the Occidental Saloon, Virgil's tall figure emerged, draped in black, walking toward the Alhambra. He was always the last of the brothers to lunch because he had the most responsibilities.

"Here comes another one. I'll have all of you licking my boots fer mercy 'fore I down you like beat dogs."

Morgan, weary of playing peacekeeper, gritted his teeth. "You know what, Ike—you can have all the fight you want now." Morgan made two swift steps toward Ike when Virgil stepped in.

"The heller you doing?" He swiped Morgan aside. "Goddamn hothead. Hell of a way for an officer of the law to act. You—" he motioned to Doc, "I expect it from."

"I am but a product of our time, Virgil. A vessel of original sin."

"Yeah, well, be that as it may, I'll arrest all three a ya if you don't stop this all post haste. Now get the fuck out of here, Ike!"

Virgil sent Ike toward Sixth Street, Morgan inside to Wyatt, and Doc back home to Fly's. "Cool yerselves before you resurface."

Virgil sat down next to Morgan and Wyatt at the lunch counter.

"The rabbit's real good today," said Wyatt, his head down.

"You didn't feel like maybe you oughta do something?" said Virgil.

"I think the two of you handled that real well. I would've just beat Clanton into the ground."

"Glad to see you're taking the job serious."

"If I wasn't serious I woulda told Doc to shoot that mouthy sonofabitch. Tired of him threatening this family. I'm done with you both for the moment." He pushed his seat out, leaving a buttery plate and fifty cents on the counter.

"What'd *I* do?" asked Morgan, but Wyatt was already bashing through the grated saloon doors and out into the white glare. It was time for a drink.

Wyatt sat down at the Eagle Brewery Saloon. It was actually one of the newer watering holes, but he didn't frequent it often because it had no history. It felt like someone's vision of what a saloon should look like, not what one was. It was a large joint with ten tables side by side down the long window side of the room, and a shiny bar, freshly polished and adorned with elaborate woodworking and fine, four-pronged barstools lining it. The bar behind it was fully stocked with all sorts of liquors, vodka, gin, wine, and port. A newfangled light fixture hung in the center of the room, hooked up to the gas line, but not by any wires Wyatt could see.

Wyatt ordered bourbon, neat, and sat at the bar. They didn't even provide the full bottle at Eagle Brewery. *It's only by the glass here because they're so "high class,"* thought Wyatt. Wyatt was a couple down, wishing he'd asked Doc to join him, when Ike rumbled into the bar. There were a few other men sitting at the bar with Wyatt. Dandies in bright red and teal shirts and black topcoats grinning like ignorant fools. They'd probably never watched something die. They whispered to one another and moved to a seat by the window when they saw Ike. He was disheveled and clearly had not stopped drinking since he'd left the Alhambra. It was almost impressive.

He must have found another hat, but it wasn't his because it didn't fit his rotund head. He carried his pistol in his hand.

Wyatt spied him through the bar mirror and spun around in his seat. "You intend to use that, Clanton?" Wyatt felt for his Smith & Wesson, but the bourbon made him a little slow.

Ike stopped in his place. "Where's Holliday?"

"Not here, I reckon."

"Last time I seen him I wasn't fixed just right. Tomorrow, I'll have him man-for-man. 'Bout time to fetch this all to a close." The gun teetered between aim and the floor. The two dandies in the corner braced themselves against the wood table as if the earth were about to shake.

"I won't fight no one if I can get away from it," said Wyatt.

"That a fact?" Ike smiled, his rotten, yellowed canines gleaming in the soft bar light.

"There's no money in it."

Ike sniffed and picked something out of his nose with his thumb and forefinger. He inspected it for a moment, then flung it against the saloon wall. "I'll be ready for you in the morning." He said each word as precisely as he could, trying not to slur. He holstered his pistol, turned, and left.

One of the dandies cowering by the window exhaled. "What a brutish man."

Wyatt gulped down the rest of his bourbon, motioning for another. "He's the least of them."

CHAPTER 34

No Church in The Wild

October 26, 1881

At 7:40 in the morning, Ike loaded his revolver and picked up a Winchester from some friends at the West End Corral. The Cowboys had friends at just about every corral in town. Ike had continued to drink all night without sleep, mixing moonshine, whiskey, and apple juice in a canteen once the saloons all told him to go home. The mixture had a way of bringing out what's vicious in a man, and there was plenty to be found in Ike. Wandering the streets, he ran into Ned Boyle, a bartender on his way to the breakfast shift.

"What you doin' out here with all that so early in the morning?" asked Ned. He'd seen Ike around the bar scene time and again, but rarely as soused as that.

He'd sweated through his white shirt and faded mint jacket. Dark stains expanded under his chest and armpits. "Soon as the Earps and Holliday show themselves, the ball'll start and they'll have a fight," slurred Ike, walking in tempered zigzags.

Sniffing trouble, Boyle scurried for Wyatt's house on Third Street. He knocked seven times, each a few seconds apart.

"The hell could that be?" chirped Celia Ann from the other room.

"Back to bed." Wyatt pawed the empty spot on the bed. He wished Sadie could fill it. With all the commotion of late, he'd seen less of her. Sleepily picking up his pistol, Wyatt loped to the door. "Fuck's there?" he shouted into the wood frame.

"Ned Boyle."

Wyatt kept his six-shooter pointed but opened the door. There was forty-year-old Ned Boyle. He removed his hat, revealing his friar tuck. He had a slight mustache and a wiry frame. His face was flat and squished like a bullfrog. "Saloon birds making house calls now? You'll find a better customer in Doc Holliday." Wyatt stretched his neck out the door, checked around, then finally lowered his steel.

Ned fidgeted with his hat.

"You got something to say or'd you come here to stare?"

Ned rubbed his hands together. "No—it's just that Ike Clanton is going around with a rifle threatening you and your brothers. Doc too."

"Man's too yellow to do any more but stick that rifle up his own back door. I appreciate your concern." Wyatt shut the door and went back to bed.

"Who was it?" called Celia Ann.

"A concerned citizen. Says they're worried there's not enough laudanum for the rest of town."

"Burn in Hell, Wyatt."

After being dismissed, Ned decided it was his civic duty to tell someone who would listen, so he made his way to Virgil's house farther down the street. He knocked seven times. Their houses were very similar because the brothers helped one another with construction and planning. Picket fence, a patch of yellow grass, slice of the dream.

Virgil slept with his arm around his wife. She didn't wake as he quietly slipped out of bed and grabbed his Colt .44. He snuck around to the front window that looked out onto the porch and saw little Ned Boyle standing there, hat in hand. He set the pistol on the living room couch and opened the front door. "To what do I owe the pleasure, Ned?"

"I tried your brother, but—well, Ike Clanton is out making threats against you, and he's got a couple firearms. I know it's not legal to carry out on the streets. I know people do, but it's not nearly legal the way he's at it."

Virgil wiped his leathery face. He hardly recognized his own skin anymore. He felt old, like one day soon his eyes would just stay crusted shut. "Ike, huh? Sure is a lapper. He drunk?"

"Enormously so."

"He'll tire of it and plunk out any minute. Many thanks for it."

"But—"

Virgil shut the door on little Ned Boyle and went back to bed where his wife, Allie, a deep sleeper, never woke.

Ned put his hat back on and walking away muttered, "Serves you both if you get shot today."

Meanwhile, Ike had not tired and only seemed to grow louder with each slurp of cowboy cocktail. Having heard Doc was holed up at Fly's Boarding House, Ike drank his way there. He slapped the bell at the counter. Mr. Fly, who'd been in the photography studio with Kate, hurried to the counter. He was surprised to find Ike Clanton at this hour; less surprised to find him disheveled and rank like an old alley cat.

"I'm lookin' fer Doc Holliday. You seen 'im?" Ike's hair reached in every different direction, and his breath stunk of sharp cheese and firewater.

"'Fraid he and the missus checked out last night. Not sure where they were headed," Fly lied. He quickly buckled his loose belt.

Ike didn't seem to notice. "Ha!" Ike spat from the back of his throat as he laughed. "That scared old boy. He knew I'd come." Ike pointed the rifle at Mr. Fly. It wavered in the air. "You see him. You tell him."

Fly nodded, unsure what he was meant to tell. Ike ambled out the door, back into the street. As soon as he was far enough away, Mr. Fly ran into the photo studio, but Kate was already gone. She'd headed up the stairs and straight into her and Doc's room. She rattled Doc awake.

"Clanton is after you. He came for you, loaded to the gunwales and heeled," said Kate.

Doc, only half out of sleep, licked his mustache and coughed some green mucus into his balled fist. It oozed down the cracks of his skin. He sniffled a little and tilted his head toward Kate, who wore a look of earnest concern. "If God lets me live long enough to get my clothes on, he shall see me," said Doc.

Kate fetched Doc's black fedora with its satin hatband and placed it atop his head. He pulled on his black trousers and boots; in haste, she draped one of his rattier black overcoats over his bed shirt.

"You expect me to kill a man dressed like this?"

She grabbed his gun belt from the dressing table. "Hurry along now. I'm sure no one will make note of what you wear today. Only how you shoot."

Doc's chest tightened up. He poured a shot of bourbon into the bottle cap and drank it down. "It's too early for a gunfight, darlin'." He ran his fingers over the butt of his .38.

"For once, the other man is drunker than you. It should be a cinch." She leaned in and kissed Doc on the cheek, prodding him out the door as if he was late to work. She didn't let go right away though. There was a moment when she clutched his jacket as if to pull him back inside. Then, she let go. Kate stood tall, as if summoning the strength. They both knew she had to let him be Doc Holliday or they'd never make it to the fountain in one piece.

Before he headed down the staircase, he turned back to Kate. He wondered how she'd known about Ike, and if she'd be where he left her. He wondered if a draw would feel different if it was about to be his last. He wanted to ask Kate if she was scared for him, but instead, he just peered down at his scuffed boots. "They need a shining."

"I'll shine them first thing when you're back."

He nodded, blew Kate a kiss, and left.

Doc exited Fly's and started walking down Allen Street. At the other end, he spotted Ike's stocky frame, just a shadow with the Tombstone sun behind him. It reminded Doc of the fight at the canyon; he wouldn't be able to see much. But he didn't need to. He could kill a man like Ike blind—just a hard case with too many words in his mouth to swallow them all.

Ike spotted Doc and began to move slowly toward him. They were still several blocks away, just dots on the dirt road. A couple of cactus wrens warbled along the low-rising buildings, perched precariously on telegraph wires. The two sports moved in closer, only a block away now. Doc wished he had his cane; his legs weakened. He hadn't slept enough, hadn't eaten, but most of all, he ached for a drink. He craved it in his bones. They felt brittle as porcelain plates.

Then, when they were about fifty yards out from firing range, Doc spotted a figure converging on Ike at Fourth Street between Fremont and Allen. Around them, many of the buildings stood as ashen husks, crumbling with wind and claw. Slick, charred, and shining like caskets. Doc imagined Troy, burnt and salted. He recalled Achilles, living an eternity of regret in the rank underworld. He'd be there soon, too, unless he could find the fountain first.

A hot breeze swarmed the street, and all Doc could make out through sand and slag were the Winchester and the pistol in Ike's slithery palms. From behind, the figure leaped up on Ike, snatching away Ike's rifle. They struggled for a moment. Doc caught a glint of iron on his chest. He ran up to see, fighting the cinder in the air. It was Virgil. Ike froze in the middle of the desolate street. He couldn't look Virgil in the eyes; he drew his pistol, but Virgil, using the butt of Ike's own Winchester, buffaloed him in the face, knocking him out cold.

After a minute, Ike was back on his feet, concussed but able to walk. He vomited translucent bile on his boots, mostly liquid. Virgil swiped Ike's pistol from its holster. Ike whirled around and swung his arm clumsily in a semicircle.

"You couldn't hit a hundred a me with that swing," said Virgil, pushing Ike up the road.

Doc followed close behind with his pistol drawn. "You have something in mind. I happen to know precisely where the jail is from previous experience. It is nearly opposite this."

"Tension's high enough as is. I'll take him to the courthouse. They'll fine him, hold him there for a bit. No sense in making this more than it already is."

"Ike Clanton lives a charmed life, doesn't he?" Doc felt the urge to pull the trigger and land a slug square in Ike's sweaty, slouching back. It wasn't in his nature, he resolved, no matter how much of a villain they all tried to make him. Ike stumbled along the dirt road, the sun blinding them all and beating shadows along the packed earth like raven wings.

The plan was flawed from the outset. For some reason, Judge Wallace wasn't in the courtroom. One of the bailiffs said he was tending to a personal matter, which in Tombstone usually meant he was frequenting some ladies of the line. It was the same courtroom Doc had been in for his trial, and Doc chuckled at the turn of events. *The judge was always here for my sentencing*, he thought.

As Ike began to recover his wits, Virgil stood and waited. He, the bailiff, and Doc kept their eyes on him, but they were quickly outnumbered by the droves of busybodies that soon packed the petite courtroom. Apparently, Ned hadn't just told the Earps; he'd told everyone in Tombstone. Hordes of on-lookers prepped for a fight, placing bets, pressing their greasy chins against the cloudy windows when the bailiff wouldn't let anyone else enter.

Before long, Morgan and Wyatt showed up, along with another lawman, Deputy Sheriff Campbell, a large man with crooked teeth. The hair had been singed off his arms and the backs of his hands in the fire and had not grown back properly. Burns on his neck and earlobes made him seem more serpentine than anything else. Still, he was a worthy deputy, and Doc knew Wyatt liked having him around in case of trouble. Half the Tombstone Sheriff's Office was now crammed into that congested sweatbox of a courthouse.

"Decided to make a spectacle of it, I see," said Wyatt upon entering the circus atmosphere. He pushed his way to the front with Morgan and Deputy Sheriff Campbell. Bartenders, bankers, even Mrs. Whitley from down Wyatt's block, dressed in frills and her Sunday best with a purple Easter bonnet atop her head, watched intently as Ike grew increasingly restless.

"My boys will be here soon enough."

"Hit him in his lips!" said Mrs. Whitley in a sweet voice.

"Where in hell's shit-stained pants is the judge?" Virgil exploded, finally responding to Wyatt. Virgil handed Clanton's Winchester and six-shooter to

Morgan as he went looking for the judge. "Keep him here," he said before making his way through the crowd and out the door.

"You all've treated me like a dog. Fight's my racket, and all I want is four feet of ground," snapped Ike.

Morgan pointed Ike's own rifle at him, pinning him against the judge's bench.

Ike's shirt had soaked through so that it was impossible to tell it was once white. His red, sweaty cheeks gave way to bloodshot, drooping eyes and a sunburn on his forehead. "Second later an' I would've sent Holliday and big brother to the coroner. I'll make even."

Morgan once again lost his temper, offering Ike's revolver back to him. He held it out in his palm like butterscotch. "Here, take this; you can have all the show you want right now!"

With this one violent proposition, acute panic jolted the onlookers. The crowd of schoolboys and old gossips cleared out faster than a Cowboy at the sight of a bar tab. They jammed through the open courtroom doors, shoving, trampling one another for the exit.

Doc had found some rolling papers and tobacco in his overcoat. He smiled because he thought he'd run out. During the commotion, Ike leaped for his pistol. He would have had it, too, except hulking Deputy Sheriff Campbell sprung off the wall, careening into Clanton and knocking him into the lawyer's chair. The two bodies sailed in opposite directions, but Clanton tumbled with more force.

Doc meticulously rolled a cigarette in the last row and lit it, watching the smoke stray lazily up to the ceiling as the crowd fled. Feet and flailing arms scratched by his head as the panic set in, and a young boy was slightly trampled before a white-faced Hollidean swooped in and swept up the boy in his coat on the way out. Doc had been a moment away from ending Ike's lip himself; now, he was merely a spectator. He hated the sideline of anything.

Wyatt grunted savagely, striding up to Clanton on the floor. "You cattle-thieving sonofabitch, you've threatened us enough, and you gotta fight." With that, he turned and marched out of the courtroom irately.

As he left, Doc grinned widely. He'd never seen Wyatt lose his temper so completely. "Let me know when you need me," he said, unsure if Wyatt could hear above his feverish rage.

On his way out, Wyatt sideswiped young, beardless Tom McLaury, one of Ike's compatriots there to spring him. "Fuck out of my way, Cowboy trash."

"If you wanna fight, I'll fight you right here!" McLaury fired back.

"You heeled? Right here, right now!" Earp slapped the butt of his Smith & Wesson with the flat of his palm. This time, Doc jumped up on the courtroom bench, about to draw on McLaury's backside, but it was too late—Wyatt back-handed Tom McLaury clear across the face with his left, stunning him. Then with his right, Wyatt jerked McLaury's own pistol from its holster, bashing Tom over the head in two brutal strikes. McLaury's hat tumbled off, rolling away. He crumpled to the floor, a solid dark streak of blood rivering down over his nose and open eyes.

Wyatt didn't even stop to look back. "I could kill the sonbitch," he muttered, walking straight to Hafford's Cigar Shop for a smoke.

Tom McLaury tried to clear the blood from his eyes with his shit-stained fingernails, smearing his eyelids and cheeks brown. He stabbed at his silver-banded hat in the dirt, wobbling upright. A moment later, Virgil returned with Justice Wallace to find Doc with his pistol trained on a bloodied McLaury and Ike wailing high-pitched obscenities in the center of the empty courtroom—Morgan and Deputy Campbell on either side of him.

"The hell happened here?" said Virgil.

Doc holstered his weapon in the presence of the judge and took a short puff of his cigarette. He removed it carefully from his lips. "Let us put it this way: I believe you are perhaps the only diplomat of the family."

CHAPTER 35

Bulls on Parade

The Shootout Near the O.K. Corral

It all happened quick. Around eleven in the morning. Fresh off the ruckus at the courthouse, Doc was on his way to breakfast near the Grand Hotel. He'd restored his appetite of late. Frank McLaury and Billy Clanton had just arrived back in town from a cattle run. Frank wore a scraggly goatee. A few white chin hairs crept in. His circular gray hat was caked with dried mud, and his long nose peeked out from under its brim. He was slightly older than his brother, Tom, and had ten years on nineteen-year-old Billy. They were heading to hitch their horses at the O.K. Corral. It was by coincidence that they crossed paths with Doc at all, unaware of the morning's activities.

Doc strode up to Billy Clanton, extending his hand. "How are you?"

Billy reached down from his horse and shook Doc's hand. "Fine, thanks," he said, a little confused.

"Well, I'm sure I'll see you soon." Doc continued on his path, smiling to himself. He tightened his black overcoat so no one would notice his bed shirt underneath. He hadn't had a chance to change with all the commotion. It was unseemly.

In the meantime, across the street from Spangenberg's Gun Shop sat Hafford's Cigars, where Wyatt was attempting to cool off with a Blue Label cigar. The smoke wafted up against the toasted walls, which were adorned with pelicans, ravens, gulls, and all sorts of raptor shadows that glided and sang along the ridges and cigar-stained paint. Stuffed waterfowl hung from the beams like coyote bait, and a couple of rickety ceiling fans vibrated the hot air down on Wyatt's cheeks. He was the only customer.

He reclined in a lavish velvet chair that looked as if it'd been made in England and had just put his feet up on a divan when he noticed Ike pass right in front of him. Ike, bandaged and hungover, entered Spangenberg's Gun Shop behind Brown's Hotel—to purchase some new steel, Wyatt surmised. His had been confiscated in the altercation and subsequent fine, which ended up costing him $25. Wyatt decided to wait and see what would transpire. Fifteen minutes went by, then half an hour; finally, some movement. Billy Clanton and Frank McLaury joined him inside. After a few moments, they exited, their gun belts loaded for a fight. Tom stuck a revolver in his trousers. Wyatt got up, fixing to find Virgil.

Somehow, in the way that all small towns have long ears, in no time at all, the entire population buzzed with fearful anticipation at the idea of the Earps and the Cowboys finally shedding blood. They salivated like Romans at the gate of the Coliseum, although the fight card was not nearly the one they craved with Ringo and Curly Bill out of town robbing a bank on the outskirts of Mexico.

It was at this point that Behan found out about the trouble. He was getting a shave when Ned Boyle bounded into the barbershop.

"Clantons and McLaurys are up to no good!" The man paused to catch his breath. "I ran myself from the O.K. where I saw 'em. You should go and disarm the bunch!"

With his typical showmanship, Behan threw off the barber's rag, and half-shaven proclaimed, "There'll be no trouble in Tombstone if I can help it," as if someone were quoting him. He tipped the barber a quarter and immediately set off to find Virgil. Ned puffed out his chest, convinced he'd saved Tombstone, and followed close behind Sheriff Behan.

Virgil stood in his typical black duster, carrying a double barrel ten-gauge shotgun he'd borrowed at the Wells Fargo office. Behan jogged up to them, tearing a hole in the seam of his tight pinstriped pants as he rushed.

"What's going on here?" demanded Behan, pointing to the sawed-off ten-gauge.

"Some sonsabitches been looking for a fight, and now they can have it!" boomed Virgil. His eyes blazed in a way that Wyatt, or anyone, had rarely seen. Once Virgil lost his temper, there was no stopping him.

"You had better disarm them. It is your duty as an officer," said Behan. He lifted Virgil's coat lapel, poking his badge.

"I'll give 'em their chance to make a fight."

Behan realized there was no turning back for Virgil. "I will go down to the O.K. Corral where they are. They won't hurt me. And I will get them to lay off their arms."

Virgil glanced at Wyatt. Wyatt shook his head.

"You do what you need. Things've been set in motion." He turned to Wyatt and said, "Time to round up Morgan," and the two set off for the Alhambra Saloon, leaving Behan behind, half a beard, shaving foam hanging off his cheek.

Doc and Morgan ate breakfast at the Alhambra a little later than usual. Biscuits, gravy, and eggs with coffee for Morgan; the same for Doc, except sausage instead of eggs and bourbon instead of coffee. Doc had run back to Fly's to change before meeting with Morgan. He wore a gray suit, pink button-down, a stiff collar, and a black tie. He'd changed into a slouch hat and a heavy gray overcoat that did him no favors in the mild autumn weather. He'd also fetched his silver-crowned cane. He was happy to be dressed like a proper Southern gentleman after wearing dregs out all morning. It was near noon when Virgil and Wyatt walked into the Alhambra.

"Morgan, we've need of you," said Virgil very officially.

Morgan, as if responding to his father rather than his brother, obediently forked another egg into his mouth and plucked his hat from the sticky bar top.

Doc rose from his stool, pushing himself up on his cane. "Where are you going?"

"We're going to make a fight," said Wyatt.

"A fight? All right, you've convinced me."

"This is none of your affair," said Wyatt, worriedly checking the bullets in his chamber for the second time. He snapped it back in place.

Doc took three small steps, tapping his cane loudly against the wood floor until he was square in front of Wyatt. "That is a hell of a thing for you to say to me."

"I know what you're giving up to be here," said Wyatt. In his own opaque way, he was referring to the fountain.

"I've lived my whole life for myself. Don't you dare take me for a martyr, Wyatt." Doc redirected a mucusy cough into his handkerchief.

Wyatt placed his hand on Doc's bony shoulder, squeezing it with his powerful fingers. "It's gonna be the bloody kind."

Doc faced Wyatt, his hazel-blue eyes lighting up in the gaslight. "Those are just the kind I like."

"I'm damn glad to have you," said Wyatt.

Without hesitation, Virgil exchanged the shotgun for Doc's cane. "Stash it in your overcoat. No sense in creatin' any more excitement in the streets than's already there."

Doc tucked the sawed-off shotgun in his gray overcoat. He hadn't handled shotguns much. This wouldn't have the precision of his lightning .38, but he could wield it. His mind was calm with any firearm.

The four of them started toward Fremont Street, toward the O.K. Corral where the Cowboys kept their mounts.

They walked with purpose, every boot step observed, every twitch noted. Virgil swung Doc's cane like a vicious conductor. Doc finally felt that he was part of something truly righteous. That the best thing he'd ever done was meet Wyatt and that perhaps, if he was remembered now, it wouldn't be for the robbery or for Joyce's half-hand, or Ed Bailey's split belly, not for the Hollideans, or his cough or drink or Old Man Clanton's ripped up chest—it'd be for this. It would be alongside Wyatt Earp, a man of principle, with his boots on at the gunfight at the O.K. Corral.

The entire town had turned out for the event. For the first time in a while, cameras surrounded Doc again. Reporters emerged in droves; the townspeople frothed at their mouths and pissed in the streets and drank, salivating at the orgiastic idea of true blood sport—infamous American gunfighting taking place in their no-name town. He could see the headlines. The second coming of Doc Holliday. Wentworth and a slew of other reporters buzzed alongside the foursome who walked arm to arm in a straight line down Fremont. There was no breeze, and the fire-branded town held still, its burnt and bare trees, naked gutters balancing white ash like a silent snow globe about to burst.

"They have horses. Shouldn't we have horses?" asked Morgan, breaking the silence between the four of them. He flinched at the bright camera bulbs. Each store emptied out and its patrons followed them. Union Market, Hafford's, the Cosmopolitan, the meat market. Several butchers, their aprons dripping with calf's blood, drifted into the streets, lured by the smell of bedlam. Saloon birds, too, their eyes lined in coal and gold tequila.

"If they try to make a running fight, kill the horses," said Wyatt coolly.

"Hate to down the mounts if it can be helped," responded Morgan.

Doc whistled and nodded to some of the reporters he recognized. There was Wentworth with his notepad out. He'd always seen Wentworth as a small man, but there was something more substantial about him now. His cheeks had grown fatter and redder. He looked healthy. His spindly legs now attained some girth, and he made direct eye contact with Doc, which he'd never really done before. Doc nodded to him. Wentworth almost smiled back, but then as if realizing for the first time what Doc truly was, lowered his nose and continued to scribble notes around his charcoal silhouettes. Doc's eyes were the hardest to draw. There was something ethereal about them. Something that was not meant to last, and they changed color with the fickle temper of the ash and sun.

Doc and the Earps turned off Fourth onto Fremont. Ned Bailey, who'd followed Behan all the way to the Corral, shouted excitedly, "Here they come!"

Just as they reached Fly's, around the corner from the O.K. Corral's entrance, Behan emerged, his face still smeared with shaving cream on one side. "Hold up, boys! Don't go down there or there will be trouble."

"Johnny, I'm gonna disarm them," said Virgil, knowing full well what that meant.

"I've just been down there to disarm them." Behan stood in front of the four men, but Wyatt shoved him away with his forearm as they passed. They began to pick up speed, their dusters and overcoats floating behind them like capes. The Earps closed in on Fly's, half a block from the Corral, and Doc separated slightly, drifting out to the street to the right of the brothers, cutting off escape. The Cowboys—Tom and Frank McLaury, Ike and Billy Clanton—all backed into a vacant lot between Fly's photography studio and the Harwoods' house, walking two horses with them.

"All this meandering and all I had to do was stay home for a scrape," said Doc. He searched Fly's studio windows for Kate. For a moment, he thought he saw a lithe shadow. He returned his focus to the action.

They wouldn't reach the O.K. Corral, Doc realized. If the fight was going to happen, it would happen in this strange and narrow space. To the Cowboys' backs was a jagged, unpainted wooden fence with a post missing. On their right, Fly's studio, and on the left, the house of Jane and Leopold Harwood, an elderly couple who'd mostly made their money whittling mail posts into squirrels.

Ike Clanton lingered in the middle of the lot, directly between the two buildings. The McLaury brothers readied themselves next to Old Harwood's house with Billy Clanton—in front of them were two horses packed with Winchesters. Doc held his ground on the road; he stepped back to the middle where he felt the dug-out water line at his heels. The Earps closed in, and Billy backed up against the wall next to the McLaurys. His gun belt clanked against the wood. He tensed. *Must be his first fight*, thought Doc. Billy's revolver gleamed in his trousers. Each Cowboy had a pistol and rifles in their saddle boots.

"Lying sonofabitch," growled Wyatt. "They're armed as ever."

The light from the sun extinguished and the camera flashes obscured because they were in too tight a space between the buildings. The reporters backed off. Virgil closed in on Ike in the lot so that the Earps nearly had their backs straight against Fly's. He raised Doc's cane in the air. "Throw up your hands, boys. I intend to disarm you one way or 'nother."

"Oh, we will!" Frank McLaury grabbed his Colt on his hip. Billy reached for his gun, too, his hand shaking. The air tasted like metal. Tom McLaury threw back his coattails, reaching for his revolver. Wyatt pulled his Smith & Wesson.

With Wyatt drawn, Doc knew the fight was on. He jerked the sawed-off ten-gauge from beneath his overcoat. He drew the hammers, ready to fire. All that could be heard were the clicks of hammers echoing off the dry walls in that lot.

"Hold! I don't mean that!" shouted Virgil. He still held Doc's cane but began backing up toward his brothers for a less-vulnerable position.

It was too late. Wyatt fired the first shot. The bullet tore into Frank McLaury's soft belly fat straight through his navel. The bullet shattered in his stomach, ripping through his kidney and leaving an exit wound three inches around. The blood spattered against the Harwoods' house in the shape of an eye. Returning fire, Billy Clanton blasted right of Wyatt. For a moment, no bullets flew as Virgil held the cane in his left and felt for his pistol with his right. Doc didn't have a clear shot at Tom McLaury, who was using the horses as cover. Frank staggered forward toward the street, cupping the blood pouring from his gut. There was so much, like a spilled barrel of wine.

Ike, panicking, had never drawn. He charged up at Wyatt with a terrifying despair in his eyes and lips. He grabbed onto Wyatt's coat, and they grappled for a moment.

"Fight's on. Go to fighting or get away!" Wyatt snapped, tossing him off. He gave an eye to shooting him right there on the ground, but a bullet whizzed over his head and when he ducked, Clanton kicked up dirt and ran through Fly's studio door. A couple of stray shots shattered the windows around him as he banged down tripods, smashing lenses and trampling fresh, wet photos of Kate with his muddy soles. He was running so hard and with such abandon that he didn't stop there. Clanton refused to die, and he knew if he just kept running, the dust would settle behind him. He ran through Fly's into another lot, through Kellogg's Saloon, continuing out on Toughnut Street, nearly six blocks away, before he finally stopped for breath.

Frank McLaury, realizing he was fading, took his hands from his open wound and began firing. He hit Virgil in the calf. Virgil kicked out his leg and hit the dirt hard, clasping at the wound and flinging Doc's cane toward the wounded Frank. Young Billy Clanton fired wildly from behind his brown horse. Billy, his eyes nearly shut and the smoke and dust painting the air black, shot over his horse's saddle, hitting Morgan in the back as he was reloading. The bullet seared a piece out of his vertebrae and immediately cauterized, hissing as it fused his skin together in fire.

"I'm hit!" cried Morgan. He stumbled back toward Doc, extending his fingers to his breakfast partner, but Doc could not spare his hand. The shotgun required both. Morgan tripped backward over a mound of dirt that had been dug out for water pipes in the center of the street. He went to the ground on numb legs.

Doc, fearing the worst for Morgan, closed in on Tom McLaury, hiding behind the other horse next to the Harwood's house. Tom reached over the saddle for the Winchester on Doc's side of the horse. With all the blasting, the horse went wild, kicking out and rearing on its hind legs. Tom pulled back his arm, and as the horse lifted its haunches, he was exposed for just a second. The horse's mane rippled, and its hooves shifted through the air; Tom must have combed its black hair because it was smooth and shining. Doc squeezed the ten-gauge's trigger. It kicked back, and flame spewed from its barrel. Twelve buckshot pellets entered Tom McLaury's body at close range. First, it tore away the skin of his right arm so that his bone snapped down to the marrow, and his veins hung down like cut wires. The rest of the buckshot ripped into his right side, cracking four ribs, severing his nipple, and splattering blood over the face and eyes of his horse, now returning its iron shoes to the earth. With no weapon drawn, he stumbled toward Doc, a look of godless fear in his brown eyes. He crumpled against a nearby telegraph pole next to Doc. His throat and deconstructed arm soaked in splinters as he slid down the length of the pole, trailing a blubbery, dark film behind him.

Doc tossed the empty shotgun and pulled his nickel-plated .38. The pearl handle felt cool in his hand after the wooden shotgun butt. From the seat of his pants, Virgil fired a shot into Billy Clanton's leg so that he limped out from behind the horse, throwing his head back, screaming into the salted, burning air. Wyatt stepped forward and landed a bullet in Billy's fleshy shoulder, above his heart. Falling backward against the Harwoods' unsanded exterior wall, Billy

Clanton reloaded, propped his pistol on his knee, and fired two more shots, missing Wyatt completely. With each squeeze of the trigger, he wailed with pain.

Frank McLaury, the last Cowboy standing, took the reins of Billy's horse, using it as cover, bleeding profusely through his ripped shirt. Again, he fired at Morgan, who was in the street, covered in dirt with a stunned look in his eyes. The horse, spooking, broke off and ran, leaving Frank exposed once again. With little left in him, he squatted in the street, close to Morgan, neither man able to lift his gun for the moment. Doc closed in on him, but McLaury recovered his feet and slowly raised his pistol to Doc's chest. The blood and salt and grime had turned him into a sopping monster, leaking at all ends. He'd shit himself from the sheer force of the blast to his belly. He had nothing left but the bullet in his chamber.

"I've got you now," wheezed McLaury.

"Blaze away." Doc was ice calm. "You're a daisy if you have."

Three shots fired at the exact same moment, five feet from one another. Doc nailed McLaury in the sternum and Morgan, from behind, blasted the side of his head, so the cradle of his skull lay broken in the mud like a milk bowl. Frank McLaury's final shot grazed Doc's hip, cleaving his favorite gray overcoat, spilling hot blood down his thigh.

"I'm shot right through," said Doc. He was incensed. The wound stung him. Frank's body convulsed on the ground, pumping blood and gunpowder into the scorched afternoon, and Doc charged in. "The sonofabitch has shot me, and I mean to kill him." But when Doc kicked over McLaury's body, it was clear there was not much left of him. He wore a grim expression on his corpse. Doc could hardly stand to look.

At this point, the smoke was clearing and some of the onlookers braved a closer glimpse. It was a grisly scene. Mr. Fly, finally bold enough to leave the photography studio, stepped over some broken glass. He'd seen Ike run through earlier and smash it up but had remained hidden. He stepped through the smashed window and went up to Billy Clanton, who was leaking all over himself, still propped up against the Harwoods'.

Fly searched his broken, young body with pity.

"Gimme some cartridges," whispered Billy with all the voice he could muster.

Fly never responded. He just took Billy's empty pistol from his limp hand.

Onlookers rushed the scene, trying to gather bloody dirt and bullet shells as souvenirs. One even scooped up Frank McLaury's spleen and slipped it into his pocket amid the confusion and dust. The flies descended, their wings beating heavy in the powdery air like smacking gums.

CHAPTER 36

Can't Pretend

Fly, Ned Bailey, and some other onlookers meandered through the gruesome scene. A miner from the next town over made off with Tom's pistol. It showed up three years later, pawned in a poker game. They hooked their arms under the injured Cowboys and dragged them onto Third and Fremont. The Harwoods, who'd been inside their house the entire time, finally poked out their withered heads, checking the bullet holes and glaring at the bodies propped up along their front lawn. Frank was already dead, and Tom was dying next to him silently. He was hardly breathing when they dragged him into the street.

Billy, clinging to his final breaths, glared at Mr. Fly, who was trying to wet his lips with a canteen. "I been murdered. Get and let me die." With the little strength he had left, he swatted his hand at Fly, who backed away. By the time the doctors arrived, Billy Clanton was dead.

Morgan, who Doc thought was paralyzed at the very least, got up as if nothing had happened. He went straight to Virgil, who'd been hit a little worse, but Virgil picked up Doc's cane and raised himself up on it. Only Wyatt remained unscathed.

Doc held his side where the bullet had grazed him. "Goddamn you, Wyatt. You are healthy as a milked cow. The rest of us bleed in gunfights." Doc figured Wyatt would never need the fountain. He was a man destined to live forever.

Virgil steadied himself and handed Doc his cane back. "You know that boy's never been shot his 'tire life. Not even by a BB gun."

Wyatt just shrugged. "Thought you had the worst of it, Morgan."

Morgan stretched out his back. The blood darkened his coat. "Musta just stunned me."

It was then that a rabble of armed men emerged from up Fremont. They carried hunting rifles and knives. The man leading them was the owner of the meat shop. He'd tied a blue bandana around his waist.

"What in the hell is all this?" said Wyatt to the group leader.

"Heard Indians was attackin'. Hell if I'm gonna let some leatherneck rape my wife and eat my soup."

"No one's eatin' your soup," said Virgil. "Go on home." He waved his arms. "Get."

After all the gunfire, rumors had swelled quickly. Anyone who hadn't witnessed the fight made up his own story. Some of the Hollideans concluded that Doc had finally decided to run the town and huddled a few miles away casting ballots to make him vice-mayor of Tombstone. But seeing that there was no Indian threat, the militiamen disbanded. As they scattered, Behan resurfaced. There was no telling where he'd been hiding or with whom he was colluding.

"I have to arrest you, Wyatt." Behan didn't have his gun drawn. There were no other deputies, and he spoke from ten feet away. A breeze whipped some ashen skin into the air. The scene was a grisly mess, blood clotting the dirt, fresh clouds balancing overhead. Fly, Bailey, and some other local businessmen flitted around the bodies as if their nervous footsteps could revive the boys' hearts.

"Won't be arrested," said Wyatt. Virgil, Morgan, and Doc stood by him, though each slumped with injury.

Doc's head went light. He desperately wanted to walk the fifty feet to Fly's, into his bed and Kate, but he stood his ground.

Wyatt was firm in his stance. He towered over Behan, even from a distance. "You deceived me, Johnny. Told me they weren't armed. I'll be here to answer what I done."

Some of the augmenting crowd spoke in Wyatt's favor. "Let him be!" They screamed. The journalists scribbled furiously, attempting to document the scene with some accuracy. Much of it had already been picked clean for souvenirs. "He done right by killin' them!" another yelled. "We will uphold them. I seen the whole thing." But their faces were obscured, only disembodied voices in the electric periphery like an unbathed Greek chorus.

Deputy Breakenridge showed up on the scene. He didn't know who to tell, so he spoke to Virgil, Wyatt, and Behan. "Ike's been found. We're holding him in jail, but there's a lynch mob forming."

"Bring me to him," said Behan, who left without another word to Wyatt.

"Don't know who's more crooked," said Morgan to Doc, but Doc was looking pale. "You okay?"

Doc nodded. "Didn't get to finish my breakfast is all."

Fat-bellied blowflies gathered around the bodies as the coroner measured the lengths of the corpses and inspected the width of the bullet holes. Doc made his way into Fly's. There was glass everywhere. The shards stuck in his bootheels. He climbed the stairs, out of breath. When he opened the door, there was Kate. He was glad to see her. She was sitting rigidly in the bed, the sheets taught over her balled-up knees. Doc let his cane clatter to the floor and eased himself into the bed. Kate took his head in her arms. His eyes welled up.

"Are you hurt?" Kate carefully removed his gray overcoat, discovering dried blood on his thigh. His shirt was ruined.

He slapped his face over and over with his palm until it was hard to tell how he felt under the blood and soil slashed all over his cheeks. He wrinkled his nose and shook his head violently so that his ashen hair swished back and forth, trying to get ahold of himself. He didn't ever want Kate to see him weak from another man's bullet. He thought of how one second, one inch more, and Morgan would be a cripple. In each eye, he saw a shard of Frank McLaury's brittle skull. "I am fit as a feather, darlin'."

"I've never seen you cry, I don't think. Maybe with fever, but that's different." She stroked his head. "He's got gray hairs," muttered Kate. "One for each bullet. You're an old man suddenly. When are we going to have babies, Doc?"

Doc wiggled his finger through the hole in his coat. "Children are just a man's way of correcting what he got wrong as a boy."

"And what if it's a girl?"

"Well, that's just God's way of punishing a man, isn't it?" Doc wiped his nose with his thumb and got up. He brushed the dust and powder off his pants.

"And just where in the hell do you think you're going?" Kate furrowed her brow with as much force as her forehead could bear.

"I've got to check on Virgil and Morgan. They're not safe, and they can't defend themselves right present."

"You're full of blood yourself! What about me?"

He ran his hand over the bullet hole in his overcoat. "I have never been so sure that you are safer the farther you are from me." He leaned in to kiss her, but she turned from him, and her red hairs wedged between his lips. He plucked them out, wet and wriggling.

Doc saddled his overcoat over his arm. He headed for the door.

"Are you even gonna tell me what happened out there?" Kate's frilly dress spread over the bed like petals.

"They all bit the ground, save that snake, Ike Clanton."

"Johnny Ringo?"

"Wasn't there."

"You do it? You kill them?" There were equal parts fear and arousal in her voice.

"I paid my share." Doc picked his cane off the floor and left. He locked the door behind him.

Doc knocked on the door of Virgil's house.

Wyatt opened it with his revolver pointed, without ever saying a word.

"For someone who has never been shot, you sure are jumpy, Wyatt," said Doc.

Wyatt ushered him in with the muzzle of his Smith & Wesson. Doc took stock of the scene: Morgan and Virgil lay in separate beds. Allie, Virgil's wife, and a doctor tended to their wounds. Allie reassured Morgan that his wife, Louisa, was on her way as she held a clean rag to Virgil's bloodied leg.

Wyatt whispered to Doc, the two of them still hovering in the doorframe. "You hear anything out there? Anything 'bout a raid?"

"Quiet before the 'cane I think."

"Behan'll charge us with murder."

"Can you be sure?"

Wyatt nudged Doc farther inside, still out of earshot of the others, locking the door behind him. "I can be sure enough he wants us away now. Better if we're in a crowbar castle than killin' his voting bloc."

"I guess I see your point. How are your brothers?"

"Tough sonsabitches. They'll be good, but right now it's up to us to fight if a fight's brought."

"You can count on it, Wyatt."

Wyatt, a little weary from the whole ordeal, placed his massive hand gently on Doc's chest. "I know I can."

As the doctor worked to pull the bullet from Virgil's leg, Allie couldn't bear to watch any longer, so she went to check on Morgan. He was grimacing, rolled onto his side.

"How's my young Earp?" asked Allie.

Morgan didn't respond. He had his back to her. She walked around to the other side of the bed. Morgan was holding his pistol.

"Oh my, what's that for?"

"Hold out your hands." Morgan placed the gun in Allie's palms. "If they come, Al, you'll know they got Wyatt. Take this six-shooter and kill me and Virge before they get us."

Allie stuffed the pistol in her bustle so Virgil wouldn't see it. She never said a word. A few minutes later, Louisa arrived and ran to Morgan.

That night, without Allie ever explaining it, Allie asked Louisa to help her stack mattresses and cushions in front of the windows. Allie stayed up all night with that pistol in her lap, and dark thoughts swam through her head. It was very quiet except for the sound of a song. The tinkling of an old funeral song. It gave Allie chills to hear it. They used to play it whenever someone died in the war and they couldn't find his body. Allie's mother had made her learn it as a child just in case. She remembered it in her fingers. She felt the notes in her bones. She gripped that pistol, but the Cowboys never came.

CHAPTER 37

The Funeral

One Day Later

Immediately following the Fremont Street Fiasco, as the morning papers had named it, the reaction was squarely in favor of Doc and the Earps. The businesses supported their bravery, the papers questioned why Behan had not acted himself, and it was a general consensus that the killings had been not only just but deserved celebration. The funeral for Billy Clanton, Frank McLaury, and young Tom McLaury took place the morning following their fatal shootings.

Their bodies, gussied up and displayed in lavish caskets, headed the procession through the Tombstone streets. Beneath their caskets, a sign read: MURDERED IN THE STREETS OF TOMBSTONE. Someone had carved it into the wood and painted the letters black so everyone could see. A huge crowd turned out for the funeral procession, shutting shops and saloons. Even the normally scheduled church service was held an hour earlier to accommodate parishioners who wished to attend.

The public outpouring seemed in direct opposition to their words. A brass band of five musicians led the procession: the corpses, dragged by two hearses; Ike and Finn Clanton, the lesser-known brother, in a wagon; over three hundred people on foot; twenty-two horse-drawn carriages; a stagecoach; and Cowboys on horses adorned with black bands and sashes. It was by far the largest of its kind in Tombstone's history.

The band played sad, mewing songs that carried through the streets. Its grandness was eclipsed only by its hypocrisy. Doc and the Earps did not attend. They heard the commotion from Virgil's house, however, and the wives strained to see the crowds from over the mattress edges. Curly Bill and Ringo also could not attend. They had gotten into a scrape in New Mexico and were in Lordsburg Jail.

It was a somber and fantastic sensation, closer to a strange, mournful holiday than an honest-to-God funeral. Townspeople drank in the streets, little boys running alongside the hearses, streaking their faces with rat's blood in the cool afternoon. Mrs. Harwood wept as the three young men passed her house. Somehow she felt responsible, in the way that a host who hadn't offered cake might.

Many of Tombstone's businessmen attended, perhaps fearful of what would happen did they not. They wore dark outfits with clouded spectacles and emerald-studded tiepins. They paraded out their wives, who modeled their finest linen finishes and silk plaid mixed with cotton, straw sailor hats plumed with ebony pheasant tails, and veils that obscured their turgid, beaten faces. And young girls, never sure whether to appear virginal or morose, unaware of the procession's grim undercurrent, wore their church whites with velvet lavender bonnets like flowering handmaidens.

The dead rumbled down Fremont, their cheeks rouged and bullet holes stuffed with sateen. In the crowd, Behan and Sadie Marcus looked on. He twisted his mustache hairs until they burned. It already felt like winter.

The following day, Behan issued warrants for Virgil, Wyatt, Morgan, and Doc. The *Tombstone Nugget*, in the pocket of the Cowboys and Behan, was the first to call for the charge of murder against Doc and the Earps. It cited the funeral attendance as clear support for such measures.

Due to their wounds, Morgan and Virgil were excused from jailing, but Wyatt and Doc turned themselves in. Business owners and friends in town raised the money to bail out Wyatt. Wyatt bailed out Doc. William McLaury, lawyer and brother of the deceased, would head the prosecution.

CHAPTER 38

Hide and Seek

While Doc was in jail, Ringo came to Fly's Boarding House to visit Kate. At first, Mr. Fly didn't want to let him in, but Kate said it was okay. Ringo grinned as he passed Fly and climbed the stairs to her room.

Kate opened the door and backed into the room. There wasn't as much light as there was back in the old hotel. The room smelled of boot leather and perfume.

Ringo shut the door behind him. He looked around the space at the lines of empty, overturned bottles on the floor. "Got anything to drink?"

"Some laudanum. You want a nip?"

Ringo picked up a bottle of Cyrus Noble, unscrewed the cap, and tilted it up to his mouth. A few drops splashed onto his tongue.

"It's still ten for an hour."

"Where's Doc?"

"You've come here asking 'bout my husband?"

"He's not your husband."

Kate loosened the lace on her cleavage. "Funny the things people remember and what they don't."

"What're you still doing here?" Ringo got up close to her and stopped her from undressing by grabbing ahold of her tiny wrists.

"I think this is the soberest I ever seen you."

"Go to Globe. It's not far from here."

"I like it here. It suits me."

Ringo laughed. He let go of her hands and pulled up a rickety chair covered in black lingerie from underneath the writing desk. "Ike Clanton and his brother are watching you. They're gonna kill Doc, and if you're here, they'll bed you down too. Likely worse."

"I'd be pretty low if I just took off then." She retied the lace over her breasts and crossed her arms in a huff. Her hair fell over her eyes, coloring the room.

"Outta cash?"

"Doc lost all my money in faro."

"Your money, eh? Dirty girls gotta make dirty coin."

"If you came here to insult me then get out. What's the matter? Your prick out of order? Have another drink, John."

Ringo made a swift move, kicking out his seat, and grabbed Kate by her bare shoulders.

"That's what makes you a man? You want it rough. It'll cost you extra if you want to slap me."

Ringo let go of her. He lowered his head and brushed his hair back. It was dark in the room, but her legs were always shined up. "Here." He tossed fifty dollars in wet bills on the bed.

"For what?"

"Somebody's gotta look after a soiled dove like you. Don't wanna see you again."

She ran her hands over the money on the bed, still staring up at him. "How'd it get so wet?"

"Dirty boys gotta make money too." Ringo smiled for a moment, but it quickly turned sour as if he recalled something he'd tried to forget. He scratched the hair on his neck for a little while and left without saying goodbye.

Kate hurriedly stuffed all the cash in her purse and began packing her bag. When she picked up a white negligee, she noticed there were red spots all over it. She looked on the bed, her purse, and then turned up her palms. They were smeared in warm blood.

When Doc got out of jail, Kate was gone. She hadn't left a note, only some of her less expensive clothes and blood on the bed sheets. He assumed it was her womanly time because there wasn't much of it and there was no sign of forced entry. Still, the whole scene gnawed at him.

The trial took place over the next few months. It was a lot like Doc's other trials. The Hollideans supported him with spirited reenactments of the shoot-out and drank and slung dung piles at the courthouse after dark. There were no reprisals as Wyatt had thought. McLaury dragged all of their names through the mud, but in the end, Judge Spicer acquitted them of any culpability. Foolhardy, but not murderers. Once the papers were through with them, the town—everyone but Wentworth—viewed them as more liability than law. The weather changed. The town soured on the Earps.

CHAPTER 39

Alcohol

December 3, 1881

Immediately following the trial, Doc decided to celebrate at the recently re-opened Oriental. It still smelled like a fireplace, but the chairs and the booze were fresh, and they'd made it up to look about the same—barroom, gambling parlor, and a nook for the hookers to turn their charms. Doc remembered Ringo and Curly Bill bucking the flames, and he wondered why they hadn't been around since the shooting. The only thing he didn't like about the Oriental was that old one-handed bartender.

In the corner of the room, above the full bar, Joyce had hung the photographs of the McLaurys and Billy Clanton in memoriam. Doc hung his weightless, skeletal chest over the bar counter. "Usually when you kill somebody you don't like to drink to their portraits."

"Maybe you shouldn't go killin' them then," said Joyce. "The hell you come back here for? You know I hate your lunger fucking guts."

"I believe you've answered your own question." Doc slid the glass forward for a refill. The bourbon swam around his head. He hadn't eaten since breakfast. Funds were low, and he had to choose. It was an easy choice. He thought about how disgusting it was back at Fly's without Kate to clean up—empty cans of beans and sticky bottles. A family of mice had moved in next to his bed, and he listened to them squeak at night, chattering along the floor, knocking into spare bullets.

Doc was about to finish the bottle when William McLaury and Frank Stilwell walked in. He caught their ugly faces in the mirror above the bar, which had somehow survived the fire but was now blackened and murky on its edges.

The floors were so freshly polished that people almost didn't want to spit on them anymore.

William McLaury was a notable lawyer, respected among those he worked for and hated by all else. He had a surly, crooked way of doing business, and he liked to attack character in his trials. The Fremont Fiasco trial was no exception. His beard was jet black, scraggly, and so dense it could have been housing various species of wild birds. His eyes were set low in his face so that his forehead appeared in command of his body. Stilwell was a miner, saloon man, up-and-coming young sport, and reputed Cowboy. He'd lain low until now, *perhaps noticing a vacuum in the Cowboy hierarchy*, thought Doc. He wore a short, round hat and chewed on an unlit cigar. His pants were too short and his bow tie too wide.

"Come to drown your sorrows after the trial, gentlemen?" Doc wasted no time antagonizing the losing side.

McLaury's face grew stern. He was an ill-bred man who'd found his niche in the diseased crevices of the law.

"'Scaped from jail already?" said Stilwell. "We got a criminal on our hands."

"Amen, brother," said Joyce.

"That is why I love the Oriental. Slanderous barkeeps. You just can't find that sort of vitriol anywhere else. Why don't we shake on it and make everything better?" Doc held out his hand.

Joyce trembled with rage as he stuffed his mangled palm in his apron and walked away, tending to another customer.

"That's a good lad. After all, this is a celebration." Doc raised his glass to McLaury's and Stilwell's faces, sloppily spilling most of the drink. "To justice."

"Ain't no justice in murder," said Stilwell.

"Which is why I believe the judge may have mentioned we did not murder a soul. He made that very clear in his decision. Did you not read it, McLaury? I thought you something of a lawyer. Or are you more of a dabbler? Sort of a jack of few trades and such."

William McLaury slammed his fist down on the bar and tossed aside one of the stools so that it slid along the polished floor, finally spinning to a halt on the other side of the Oriental next to a table of miners. A few of the other patrons took notice since Doc was involved.

"You've got a mouth on you," said McLaury, finally breaking his silence. His beard rumbled with the words: "Best hope you had was to escape that jail and disappear. Your bones will bleach on the mountains. I've tried to punish you all through the country's courts. That has failed me—"

"Oh," Doc gave a quick clap. "That was excellent. Was that *Richard the Third*? How wonderful. You remind me of the small boys of my youth. The very smallest."

"Why don't you get the hell out of my bar, Holliday?" said Joyce.

"Your bar? I believe Wyatt Earp owns a share here." Doc then fired his entire chamber into the ceiling, and Stilwell and McLaury leaped out of the saloon doors as if launched from a cannon. Doc sat back down and ordered another drink.

"Goddamn you, lunger," said Joyce.

A couple of minutes later, Deputy Breakenridge, who was nearby, arrested Doc and threw him in jail for the night. Wyatt bailed out Doc, and he was released with a twenty-dollar fine the next morning. Doc dreamt strange dreams of Mattie. He saw in her a nun's habit, naked, warming her hands by a lake of fire.

CHAPTER 40

The Gulag Orkestar

December 28, 1881

The gunfire at the Oriental seemed to galvanize the Cowboys. Over the next few weeks, they began to filter into the town—some from Dodge, some from Globe, Fort Worth, all over the West. They showed fraternal support by their sheer numbers. In direct response, the federal government appointed US Marshal Crawley P. Dake to oversee the Cowboy threat in Arizona and near the Mexican border. He would have authority over Virgil, but more importantly, over Behan. He was something of a war hero and made his name that way. He had not yet visited Tombstone but rather liked to communicate by telegraph.

It was cold, nearly in the thirties. A translucent frost built on the spines of the trees and clouded the town's windows. Virgil ate with Wyatt at the Oriental. It was early in the evening, but the sun hadn't shown all day, so it was gray, and there was a pattering of rain turned brown in the air because it mixed with the kicked-up dirt and the soot.

"I'll see ya tomorrow," said Virgil.

"Now that your leg's fixed up you always got somewhere to be," said Wyatt, his mouth full of beef.

Virgil put on his hat and left the Oriental. The drizzle slid off his brim like a dirty veil. He walked with a silver cane now. The injury from the gunfight was as healed as it would ever be. There was still a lot of construction in Tombstone proper. Many stores had lain vacant, still burned out from the fire, but the influx of Cowboys and new activity led to a rash of new buyers. Virgil turned east on Fifth, where a new framework rose—so far just a foundation and some angled pine. He heard some noise in the dark construction site and found it curious that anyone was working so late without any light. He stopped and peered into the darkness. Two figures stared back out. He made out the dull glint of their eyes.

Two shotgun blasts discharged in succession. A torrent of buckshot cut into Virgil, shattering his left arm, splitting his bone at the wrist. From the shadows, they reloaded and fired again. More buckshot tore through his upper thigh and penetrated his belly where it slit his liver and kidney. Two of the lead pellets reached his spine. Their sheer force flung him to the ground.

The figures in the construction site turned tail and ran. He never saw their faces, but as they fled, one of their hats drifted off. The copper rain beat the ground harder, mixing with his blood and forming small puddles like coffee springs. Virgil, stunned and bleeding out, forced himself back up on his feet and staggered down the street. His shirt soaked through and became heavy. He retraced his boot steps on the soft ground, never lifting his head, his hands covering the holes in his belly. Finally, he reached the Oriental, where he collapsed in Wyatt's lap at the dealer's table, to horrified gasps, leaving a drip trail in his wake.

"I been shot," was the only thing Virgil could say before the lights went black.

When Virgil woke, he lay in a bed, with Allie, Wyatt, Doc, Morgan, and two local doctors hovering above him. Wyatt had taken him to the room at the Cosmopolitan that he kept for Sadie. He hadn't even bothered to clear her things away, so Virgil lay atop a pair of used stockings. No one dared say a word.

"This ain't Heaven. I know 'cause yer here, Doc," said Virgil groggily.

Doc smiled, happy to see Virgil conscious again. Allie wiped away her tears before she knelt down at Virgil's side, holding his right hand. The left was wrapped tightly with a tourniquet. It was grisly with the bone jutting out and split in two.

"It's good you woke. We need to remove the arm, and we wanted your consent," said the short doctor. He was portly and had the look of a walrus too far from the ocean. He breathed strenuously through his egg-shaped mouth. The other doctor nodded in agreement. He had his arms crossed over his broad chest; his beard and hair were trimmed very neatly.

Virgil squeezed Allie's hand tighter. "You ain't taking my arm."

She started to cry harder and had to walk away from the bed. Morgan rubbed her back as she wept into his shoulder.

"Never mind," Virgil calmed Allie. "No matter what, I've still got one good arm to hold you with."

"Mr. Earp—" the short doctor started.

"No. You know what, Doctor," Virgil made a quick decision. "I don't give a goddamn what you do, when I go in my coffin, it's with both my arms."

"Okay," the tall doctor said, "let's get down to it then. There will be no amputation," he said as he prepared to operate against his own advice.

Over the next two hours, with Virgil going in and out of consciousness, the doctors removed five and a half inches of bone from his humerus and sewed him back together. A few hours later, Virgil woke with Wyatt by his bedside. He stretched his neck and found his arm still intact, bandaged up. "They ain't gonna stop now. It's begun."

Wyatt nodded. "Gonna telegraph Dake. Get a posse together. They've no idea what they started."

Doc, overhearing the conversation from the other room, walked in to where Virgil was resting. The room smelled of rotten flesh and piss. Virgil was pallid and weak. *He might not survive the night*, thought Doc. "Wyatt, if you're thinking of rounding up some men to fight, I've got a couple of names to throw atop your pile. Like the wolf said to the man: Blood for blood."

Virgil was shot by concealed assassins last night. His wounds are fatal. Telegraph me appointment with power to appoint deputies. Local authorities are doing nothing. The lives of other citizens are threatened.

—WYATT EARP

~

Spare no pains or expense in discovering the perpetrators of the deed. You have my authority.

—U. S. MARSHAL CRAWLEY P. DAKE

CHAPTER 41

Little Green Bag

The Earp Posse:

Dan G. "Big Tip" Tipton

Born in New York State, Tipton served on the USS *Malvern* in the Civil War. Sailor, miner, gambler, Wyatt's money handler at the Oriental. His hair was as lopsided as his sense of moral obligation. Beady-eyed and gaunt, he rivaled Doc for leanest of the group. He'd take any job that included gunplay or horseplay as long as he could attend Mass on Sundays. Ironically, he was only an average tipper.

Sherman McMaster

Born in Illinois with a silver spoon in his mouth, the curly-haired and bearded McMaster found leisure to his disliking, so he ventured to Texas, New Mexico, and the Arizona territories looking for action. Friend of Bat Masterson, Curly Bill, Ringo, and Wyatt's informant, McMaster's truest friend was menace. A pork packer, businessman, Wells Fargo undercover gunman, and mule thief. His baby face lulled you to sleep before he shot you down.

"Turkey Creek" Jack Johnson

Out of Missouri, Johnson was once a Cowboy raider but tired of the raping and monotony. Wyatt had helped free Johnson's brother from Yuma Prison; thereafter, he pledged his loyalty. Informant. Killer. Consumptive. All-around good guy. He always carried a full bandolier and a little green bag of knives over his washed-out denim shirts.

Origen Charlie "O.C." Smith

Born in Connecticut, a Dodge City associate of Wyatt's and Wells Fargo man, O.C. was shot and nearly killed twice before Tombstone. Lawman, gambler, and gunfighter, his cleft palate got him into more fights than his tongue. Every man who'd ever called him "Hairlip Charlie" was now dead or "missing."

Warren Earp

The youngest of the Earp brothers, Warren rejoined the group after hearing of the shooting. Tax collector, guard, faro dealer, lawman, and stagecoach driver, he was leaner and shorter than his other brothers. Often he found himself in the role of the bully back in California. He walked with a pronounced limp and parted his black hair to the left, unlike his brothers.

"Texas" Jack Vermillion

Out of Virginia, Texas Jack proudly served the Confederacy. Once the war was over, he came home and started a family, but they all died in the diphtheria epidemic of 1868. Drunk with grief and rye, he moved west. Wanted for murdering a man who cheated him at cards, Texas Jack was a prickly young man, crack-shot, drinker, gambler, and Doc's friend after Holliday saved his life in Montana as he was passing through years earlier.

Morgan Earp

Nearly Wyatt's spitting image and born in Iowa with his brothers, he abhorred farm life. Morgan usually followed Wyatt and Virgil wherever they went. He married Louisa in Montana and was a lawman most of his adult life as well as a shotgun messenger for Wells Fargo. Though he had a temper, he'd never killed a man until the Fremont Street Fiasco.

John Henry "Doc" Holliday

Dentist.

With the posse assembled, Wyatt left the Cosmopolitan Hotel to check on the shooting site and take a respite before they all started on their manhunt. Seeing Virgil so weak took a toll on him. Virgil was always the rock of the family. Now he was crippled at the very least, though the doctors were optimistic that his overall health would recover. *Strong sonofabitch*, thought Wyatt.

He walked a couple of blocks, but when he got to the corner of Allen and Grand, Ringo popped up in front of him. "Heard you're 'sembling a posse. Heard you don't like Cowboys no more." Ringo's eyes glowed red from basin liquor. He wore a sandy, stiff-crowned hat that sat high atop his head like a nest.

"Ain't you done enough?" said Wyatt, trying to get by.

Ringo held his ground and bumped shoulders with Wyatt. Wyatt growled at him, stopping.

"You must be crazier than a run-over 'coon you think you'll take us all down," said Ringo. "Lemme even the odds. How 'bout just you and me have at it?" He tapped his holster. A few passersby halted in their tracks, and a small audience began to form. A shockwave immediately wriggled through Tombstone.

"Maybe you oughta sober up before making dumb propositions. Yer as drunk as a fiddler's clerk."

"Then you should have me beat. Handkerchief draw. Right here."

A couple patrons from the nearby Alhambra stepped out of the saloon to watch. They licked their lips with anticipation of bloody rivalry.

Wyatt shrugged. "I've more important things to do than get tied up shooting you."

Ringo gnashed his molars together. They squealed like toes on chalkboard. Wyatt prepared in case he had to draw. They stared each other down like warring moose.

Doc's cold sweat punctured the ground.

Breaking the silence, he offered with a Southern drawl, "I'm your huckleberry." Doc stepped out from behind Wyatt. "That's just my game."

"Where'd you come from?" Ringo tightened up, but his hand lingered at his waist.

"Same place as you." His mustache pointed up neatly like the horns of a bull. "Ten paces out in the street?" Doc drew back his overcoat, revealing his pearl handle. The coat still had the hole from the Fremont Street Fiasco, and the dull winter sun slashed through it.

"Get 'em, Doc!" yelled a young Hollidean from the sideline crowd that had formed. He wore a gray overcoat, and he'd poked a hole in it, just like Doc's. "We're all rooting for you!"

Doc found his mimicry touching. As he smiled out into the crowd, a man with a badge wrapped his arms around Ringo's chest from behind and began dragging him away.

The crowd booed mercilessly. They threw horse dung patties and beer bottles at the officer. "Turn him loose!"

Ringo tried to wriggle out of his firm grasp. "Who in the hell're you?"

"Police Chief Flynn." He nodded to Wyatt, who out of courtesy nodded back. "I've taken over for Virgil."

"Where do you all come from? Is there a cupboard where they keep spare lawmen?" asked Doc. He was disappointed he could not shoot before his fans. He coughed loudly and spat green mucus into the dirt.

Wyatt snatched Doc by the arm and led him away. "Come on, I want to see about something anyways."

The crowd slowly dissipated. Wyatt brought Doc to the construction site where Virgil had been shot. The rain had washed away most of the blood, but there were still streaks of it and boot marks that had wrenched deep in the mud and crusted over in the morning sun. There wasn't much to see except for some brass shotgun casings and a couple of burnt-down cigarettes.

"They musta been waiting here for a while before Virgil came along," said Wyatt.

Doc wasn't listening. Something caught his attention. He stepped over some wood in the construction site and bent down, leaning on his cane. "Recognize it?" He held up a floppy, rain-soaked hat. It smelled like mold from being wet in the shade.

"No other sonbitch wears a bushwhacker hat like that one. No one but Ike Clanton."

CHAPTER 42

My Body Is a Cage

Wyatt had pulled everyone together. Each man in the posse made his final arrangements before they took off for the Arizona plains. They'd go off in search of Ike and Fin Clanton first, who'd jumped town. The posse, except for his brothers and Doc, didn't work for free, so Wyatt sold his shares in the Oriental to pay them a daily wage and buy any extra food and ammo they might need on the trail.

Since Wyatt didn't own a piece anymore, they'd forsaken the Oriental as their headquarters and now preferred to frequent Campbell and Hatch's Saloon and Billiard Parlor on Allen Street. It was fairly new, built after the fire, and Hatch let them play pool for free so long as they bought drinks, which was never a problem with Doc around.

Doc was on his way to meet Wyatt at Campbell and Hatch's when he ran into Allie Earp.

Doc didn't usually like to make small talk, but he stopped because Allie was a nice lady, and he felt bad for her. She wore a little blue bonnet over her hair because it was threatening rain. The clouds were black and bulging, about to burst any moment, and the birds grew quiet. The barbed trees surrounding Tombstone quivered with anticipation. A lukewarm wind picked up, funneling dirt from place to place. Horses racked up outside the saloons became restless, rattling their heads and braying at the bloated sky.

"How is he?" asked Doc, but Doc knew exactly how he was. He'd been to see Virgil every day since the shooting.

"Wish he'd get better so we can get from here. Tonight, if possible." She was carrying a basket of candy in her tiny arms.

Doc picked out a caramel and sniffed it. He placed it back in the basket. "Reminds me of Georgia. My mother used to let me pick out three confectionaries at the general store when we went into town. I remember how impossible it was to choose. I wanted them all."

"Well, not much changes. You all are little boys." Allie squeezed Doc's shoulder affectionately. "Virgil loves these things. I don't have a sweet tooth like he does."

Doc checked his chainless pocket watch. He would be late to meet with the others, but this somehow seemed more important. "Here," he said, cupping his hands under the basket. "Let me carry that for you."

"You needn't—" Allie started to protest, but Doc had already taken the basket and was walking her in the opposite direction back to the Cosmopolitan.

In the meantime, Morgan and Tipton made their way to the billiard parlor to meet Wyatt. The floors were black slate, and the tables were broad and heavy. Pyramid light fixtures hung down in triplets, providing a fork of dim table light, shaded in green by the glass surrounding them. One of the lamps was broken. Only one other table was in use: a couple of local miners who shared time between the game and the stove because it was cold, and Hatch allowed them to cook soup there sometimes. The sound of the ivory pool balls cracking head to head reverberated around the room.

The bar lay to the right of the room as well as a glass case housing cues, gloves, and chalk to borrow or buy. Hatch lingered behind the checkerboard bar, pouring half-drunk drinks mindlessly into a tin bucket—behind him was the game room, where Doc often spent his time. The front of the parlor was fairly wide open with large, clean windows on either side of the door so you could see who was playing at the time. A couple of stagnant ceiling fans hung over Wyatt as he waited by the corner table near the open back door. A breeze flowed in. It was damp. Rain approached.

Morgan and Tipton arrived. Morgan smiled as usual. "Saved a table for me, I see. You won't beat me today."

Wyatt nodded, unamused. He enjoyed beating his brothers at anything they could be beaten in.

Tipton slid to the bar to order a drink. He noticed Sherman McMaster at the bar and patted him on the back. "'Bout ready to hunt some Cowboys?"

McMaster didn't answer; he just breathed in deep and then breathed out and lit a cigar.

"Guess I got first then," said Morgan, swiping the pool cue from Wyatt and chalking up the stick. He lined up his shot, his hind side brushing the back wall next to the door. Tipton set a chair adjacent to their table to watch the break. He slurped his drink loudly. The clouds drifted languidly along the gray sky, plump and dark.

Morgan slid the cue against his chalky fingers. He leaned down to shoot, then straightened up, squinting with a dumb look on his face, peering out across the other tables at the entrance. With a double-shattering whipcrack from behind, Morgan clattered to the floor. It sounded like thunder, but no rain followed. The first bullet had landed in his back, left of his spine, almost straight through his scar from Fremont Street, but far deeper. His stomach convulsed. It pierced his liver and kidney and exited on the right side of his body near the gallbladder, and it then struck one of the miners warming his hands by the stove. The second shot missed just to the left of Wyatt's head, splitting the wood paneling on the wall. The blood ran from Morgan's back, gliding along the slate floor.

Tipton got up and yanked Morgan's body away from the back entrance. Wyatt slammed the door. Hatch ran out from behind the bar and through the card room on the other side, into the backyard, searching for a shooter. Without a word, McMaster rumbled out the front door and toward the office of the town doctor.

Wyatt knelt down and held Morgan's hand. Morgan looked broken. "Let's get him up on the table," said Wyatt. He and Tipton got under him, their hands soaking in hot blood.

They swiped aside the pool balls and laid him out on the green felt.

"You just wait till the doctors get here. They'll fix you right up just like Virge," said Tipton. But Morgan was only looking at Wyatt, in whose eyes flashed the lightning that had never come.

Twenty minutes later, Doc, Virgil, and the doctors arrived. McMaster sat in the corner with a glass. They were the same two doctors who had tended to Virgil. They stepped away from Morgan's makeshift deathbed.

"There's no point in operating. We'll only put him through unnecessary pain," whispered the shorter doctor to Wyatt.

Wyatt nodded absently and returned to Morgan's side. He'd been awake the entire time somehow. Virgil and Doc leaned down to pay their respects too. In the confusion, no one found Louisa.

"I've played my last game of pool." Morgan tried to smile a little.

"Save your strength, brother," said Virgil.

Morgan's hair spread out on the green felt, and the dark blood seeped into it. "Won't be long. Are my legs stretched out straight?" He was talking to Wyatt now. "Can't feel nothin'."

Wyatt nodded.

"My boots on?"

The words stung Doc especially hard, and he joined McMaster next to the warm stove by the dead miner.

Morgan motioned Wyatt to come closer, his hands stained, trembling. "You know who did it?" he whispered.

Wyatt lowered his lips to Morgan's pale face. "Yeah, and we'll get 'em."

"All I ask is don't let them get you, brother. Every bullet's missed you before."

Wyatt placed his hand in Morgan's and stood up straight. He looked directly at Doc, and they made an understanding between them. They never had to exchange a single word. It was clear in Wyatt's stare that together they would butcher every single Cowboy regardless of rank or law or moral code. They would ignore everything inside them that made them human until the deed was done. It was cold-blooded revenge he was after, and Doc would be by his side until the end of it.

The doctors took their leave with Wyatt's permission. There was another gunshot wound on the other side of town. Morgan lasted for another forty minutes. He did not speak for that time, but just before he passed, he murmured something. It wasn't clear if it was a last word or just a breath or if it was his body giving out, but in any case, no one got any satisfaction out of it. He died with his brothers and Doc by his side.

When Morgan had passed, Wyatt, Virgil, and Doc waited for the coroner. McMaster and Tipton tended to the women. Wyatt wanted to be the one to tell them, but he couldn't find his way to leaving his brother's side. In their grief, the wives even asked Sadie to join them, but she said she preferred to be alone until Wyatt could come and see her.

Wyatt hung his head down at his brother's limp, curled fingers. His nails were strangely clean. He noticed the dead miner in the corner of the room. "Who is that?"

"Name's Berry," said Virgil. "Nice guy. Just wanted to get warm."

"Ain't that the long and the short of it."

When Doc left Campbell and Hatch's and said goodnight to Wyatt, he headed back to Fly's. He dreaded walking into that place with the emptiness he felt in his belly. He wished they could ride out that night in the darkness and start the killing. Burn them down. He was a block away from Fly's when he saw Ringo standing in front of the entrance. He drew his pistol and walked up to him.

"Here so I can ease your conscience? I'll set you free right now," said Doc, his finger tightening on the trigger.

Ringo held up his hands. "Don't got my gun." His jacket pulled back with his hands in the air. His holster was empty. "Ain't you heard it's 'gainst the law to carry guns in Tombstone?"

"You come here without your steel? You are a peach, you know that."

"Just came to say I want nothing to do with this all. I look out for myself. I'm all I've got."

"You had nothing to do with it?" Doc eased his finger off the trigger.

"Never shot a man's back in my life. Not that I recall anyways." Ringo was flushed, but he wasn't too drunk. Not like Doc had seen him before. He had this despondent look on his face like he'd been cracked straight down the middle, and the pieces no longer fit. "You all'd better look out though. Storm's coming."

Doc looked up at the sky. It swirled the color of coffee, and Doc remembered the Indian in the desert and what he'd said. He remembered where he was going and where he'd been. The fountain and how far away salvation was now, crawling deeper into the sickness. A couple of drops hit his dry face. He snapped out, looking back down, but Ringo was already halfway down Fremont. Doc wondered where he had left to go.

CHAPTER 43

How You Like Me Now

The next day was Wyatt's thirty-fourth birthday. He, his brothers, Doc, Turkey Creek Johnson, and McMaster traveled the rail to Contention in order to get Morgan's body home to Colton, California. Virgil and Allie decided to leave as well, even though Virgil hadn't fully recovered. They all decided to see Virgil through to Tucson to make sure he'd be all right.

Wyatt and Doc got off at the Tucson station carrying ten-gauges. Everyone else remained on the train in case someone tried to come after Virgil. Doc walked toward the caboose. Wyatt headed for the engine. The platform was full of steam. To Wyatt's left was a long set of arched stone buildings, and to his right, the train. He could still see Virgil resting on Allie's shoulder in the window behind him.

As Wyatt neared the front of the train, he saw a couple of men ducking in the flatcar near the engine. He cocked his shotgun, looking back for Doc, but he was too far, and Wyatt didn't want to reveal his position. One of the men was clear as day: Frank Stilwell. He could make out his pudgy ratface. He'd grown whiskers while following them, which patched along his pockmarked skin. The steam that bubbled up around the train obscured the other figure. Wyatt was sure in his heart that it was Ike Clanton.

Wyatt vaulted into an all-out sprint at Stilwell, jumping into the space between the tracks. Both men took off. Stilwell ran onto the tracks in front of the train. The other figure bolted out of the flatcar and toward town. Wyatt still couldn't see his face. He concentrated on Stilwell, running as fast as he could with his shotgun aimed.

Wyatt ran with fury in his lungs. Stilwell's pistol dropped from his waist-band, and after a short sprint, Stilwell pulled up, knowing he was unable to escape. He just stopped and froze. Wyatt approached with quick breaths. They were about thirty feet from the engine, and the smoke obscured them from the train's view.

Stilwell began to tremble. He was shorter than Wyatt. He shook his head. "I didn't have nothin' to do with it. It was Ike."

Wyatt got in close. He clicked back the hammers on the shotgun. Stilwell grasped the barrels in his hands. They burned from the sun. It seared the flesh on his palms, but he didn't let go. Wyatt pointed it at his chest. Wyatt let loose with the double barrel. The pulse rattled his body. The buckshot ripped away Stilwell's abdomen, flinging his flesh along the boiling tracks and gravel. His ruined corpse crumpled at Wyatt's brown boots.

Doc, McMaster, Warren, and Turkey Creek all heard the shot and ran toward the sound. They arrived only to find Wyatt standing over the distorted, bony husk with his shotgun smoking. Doc clicked back the hammers on his ten-gauge, and the other men drew their weapons. Doc released into Stilwell's leg, severing it at the knee. Turkey Creek slugged the body under the armpit, and that traveled into the lung. Warren and McMaster shot him in each arm and once in the thigh.

The conductor pulled the whistle signaling departure. Wyatt kicked the body off the tracks. The five men returned to the platform, and as the train pulled away, he held up a single digit to Virgil. Virgil nodded grimly and was gone.

The cleansing had begun. Once Virgil, Louisa, and Allie were safe, the posse headed for Spence's wood camp off Chiricahua Road in the Dragoons—an expedition trail forged during manifest destiny. They'd nearly cleared the forest around the site. Log piles littered the ground. The camp consisted of a series of beige tents, saws, axes, and a few men in tight red shirts who looked as if all they'd ever done their whole lives was chop wood. Doc wondered how a life like that would feel. If it was better than his.

Wyatt approached one who was detached from the rest of his crew. "Any idea where we could find Spence?" Wyatt loomed above the lumberjack on his white-spotted horse, his face only a black shadow in the sun. Spence allowed just about anyone to stay overnight at the camp so long as they paid up. He was a Cowboy sympathizer, and if they could find him, they'd put him down like a broken steer.

"Hey, I know you," said the woodcutter. He pointed at Doc.

Doc's horse was a little shorter than the rest, and he liked it that way because he never enjoyed being too far off the ground. Doc smiled. "Pleased to meet you. Any ideas where we can find some Cowboys for the killing?"

"Ha! Just like in the papers!" The woodcutter stuck his hands on his hips. "You know, they do come up this way, but none lately. A couple passed through 'bout a week ago."

"Where do they usually come up from?" asked Wyatt.

"South Pass." The woodcutter searched around his pockets for a moment. He pulled out a knife.

Sherman McMaster quickly drew on him, and he flopped to the ground. "No! Nothin' like that." He rolled over, his back against sawdust, and he held up the knife to Doc. "Was just wondering for your John Hancock. My daughter would be real grateful."

Doc laughed, but the mulch caught in his lungs, and it evolved into a bubbly cough. He covered his mouth with his white handkerchief.

"You okay?" asked the man.

"Never better." Doc dismounted and selected a clean cut from a nearby woodpile. "Put your steel away, Sherman. Never had a fan before?"

"A fan? Fan a what?"

Doc helped the lumberjack, who was scared, to his feet. Really, the lumberjack helped himself up, but he smiled in appreciation at the gesture. Doc carved "JHH" into the wood.

With no luck finding any Cowboys, or Pete Spence, they camped for the evening and headed out in the morning. On their way back to Tombstone, they took the South Pass, but only a few minutes down the road, they spotted Florentino Cruz on horseback, heading toward Spence's. A middling Cowboy, he'd never really given them any trouble. They rode up alongside him, surrounding him. Warren shoved him off his horse, and he slammed to the ground, breaking his right arm.

As he squirmed with pain, Wyatt and O.C. dismounted; the others remained on their horses, weapons drawn. A couple of willowy trees bobbed alongside the dirt road. Their thistle skidded through the air and twisted and burnt in the sun as they sunk to the ground around Cruz like caterpillar bones. The trunks were thin and forked off in threes from the roots. The South Pass stretched out long, and even though it was in the distance, the woodcutters' silhouettes still appeared, watching.

"Hold him down," said Wyatt.

O.C. got down on his knees and pressed his fingers against the man's chest. It was easy to keep him down because he wasn't trying to get up.

"Who shot my brother?" Wyatt placed his boot heel on Cruz's neck.

He whimpered a little.

"Open your fucking eyes, you coward." O.C. forced open Florentino Cruz's eyes. He cringed at the sight of O.C.'s cleft palate, his gums black and rotten. "Now look at Mr. Earp."

Cruz squinted at Wyatt.

"You see, I mean to kill you. Not just you. All a you. But I need to know who to especially kill. That's where you come in."

"Mister—I never even seen you before."

"But you know who I am, don't you? Who was it?"

O.C. grabbed Cruz's wrist and forearm and wrenched backward.

Cruz squealed with pain as the dislodged bone fragments cracked against one another. "Please. Oh, God."

"Didn't you hear?' said O.C. "There ain't no God out here in the reeds. Ain't no Cowboys neither." He let go of Cruz's arm, took out his pistol, and shot him twice in the right shoulder.

Cruz hardly had enough left in him to scream. He writhed on the ground. The floating willow passed through the horses' legs, and one of them took a shit. He just started naming names. "Curly Bill, John Ringo, Hank Swilling, Stilwell. They just paid me twenty-five dollars to hold the horses. I swear it."

"Twenty-five dollars?" Wyatt lost any compassion he'd had left. "Twenty-five for my brother. All you put together ain't worth this pile a shit." Wyatt crushed his boot heel into Cruz's forehead. The sharp edge splayed his skin. "Stand him up. I want this sonbitch to draw on me."

From atop his horse, Doc fired two shots into Florentino Cruz's chest. In a way, he felt bad for the man. "Didn't even have an arm to draw with, Wyatt."

For a moment, Wyatt's fury transferred to Doc, but the feeling quickly dissipated, and he mounted his horse. He spat sloppily on Cruz's body, then drew twenty-five dollars from his pocket and let it sift slowly down. Some of it stuck to the blood, some tumbled farther away. The rest of the posse started down the road.

O.C. dragged the corpse under one of the willow trees. He left his eyes open. The flakes of filth and earth, the fur of animals and feather plumes soon encased his sticky pupils. Before O.C. headed to catch up, he picked up the notes Wyatt had left on the body and stuffed them into his pockets.

CHAPTER 44

Fire & Fast Bullets

The posse drew within a few miles out of Tombstone on the main road when a stocky rider approached. They all pulled their weapons, but Wyatt quickly realized it was Bob Paul, the Wells Fargo shotgun man from the robbery.

"Wyatt?" he called out. "That you?"

"I know him," Wyatt calmed the rest of the gang.

Paul rode up. Sweat beaded on his rippling forehead. "Came to warn you off Tombstone. Behan's got a posse of Cowboys assembled, ready to arrest y'all. 'Specially you and Doc."

"Especially us!" said Doc. "Isn't that darling of him to think of me at a time like this."

"Appreciate it," said Wyatt. "Know where they're headed?"

"You should read the papers though. They're killin' him. You all are just about heroes. Heard something 'bout San Pedro but can't be sure. They're lookin' for you, so I suppose wherever *you* are maybe?"

"Thank you, Bob," said Doc with a smirk. "You are a font of information." He took a swig from his canteen. It was nearly empty. They hadn't stopped anywhere civilized for days.

"Not to be countrified or nothing but we getting our share anytime soon?" said Texas Jack. "I ain't gotten a decent buzz since we left. Wouldn't mind hittin' a doggery, have a swig and some tail."

"You have to conserve, Texas," said Doc.

"All you goddamn packed was family disturbance. I'da brought more fire-water, too, if I'da known it'd be like this."

"I'll make it right," said Wyatt in a paternal tone. "O.C. and Big Tip, will you kindly go into town and find E.B. Gage?"

"The Jew?" said Tipton.

"That's the one. Tell him I need a thousand. Ride in with Bob here and bring it to Iron Springs. Be careful to stay out of Behan's way. If it's just the two of you he won't notice."

"Iron Springs? What's there?" asked McMaster.

"Booze, cunny, and breakfast."

"Ha! I like two a those things an' I hate breakfast!" said Texas Jack, perking up.

"After that, we're only a day's ride to San Pedro. That's where we'll find Curly Bill."

"I'm heading into town too," said Warren. "I'm sorry, brother. I'm not cut out for the road like this."

Wyatt shook his head with disappointment. "Fine. But, Warren, tell Sadie—I miss her. Tell her I'll be back for her soon as this is done." He said it in a low voice, but everyone heard.

Warren nodded. "Anything for Celia Ann?"

Wyatt remained awkwardly silent.

"Tell that blonde with the missing tooth at the Oriental I'll be back for her soon too," said Doc.

The group chuckled to themselves, and the tension dissipated.

With that, O.C., Warren, and Tipton handed Wyatt some extra ammo and provisions. They headed into town with Bob Paul. Wyatt, Doc, McMaster, Creek Johnson, and Texas Jack all about-faced and started for Iron Springs. Just hearing about the springs made Doc realize how far away he'd gotten. How far he was from Kate. He wondered if she were happy—or dead. Then he got to thinking about how many strangers' oily cocks had been inside her since he last saw her. How he couldn't help but love her and how he was sick for it. Part of him wanted to die, but revenge kept him alive. And Wyatt.

Doc ached for the springs. He felt his bones dissolving inside him and wondered if renewal would taste like the Indian's coffee. He hadn't tasted anything that good since. It was as if everything around him grew fainter every day; nothing tasted or smelled or grabbed the same way as it had before. The world beat around him like a flea circus trampoline.

The night at the Whetstone Mountain Inn was one of the most epic in Doc's impressively intoxicated history. The five men drank the joint out of just about every whiskey they had. Doc remembered the night in flashes.

A hooker named Rita-Lou.

Shooting empties in the tall grass.

Texas Jack punching a Mexican who was actually an over-sunned White man.

Broken barber's chair.

An old Georgian lullaby.

Tuxedo shirt.

Sandwiches.

Missing piano key.

A quiet moment for Morgan.

Fire.

Two teeth on the floor.

Turkey Creek's flaccid penis.

The smell of a blown-out candle.

Black hair.

Golden hair.

No hair.

Doc woke with one boot missing and no pants. He, Wyatt, Texas Jack, Creek Johnson, and McMaster ate breakfast in silence. The booze rose off their skin, forming pungent ribbons in the air. They waited for several hours, but O.C. and Big Tip never came, so they mounted up and, wildly hungover, headed toward Iron Springs where they'd cross. It was only a half-day's ride to San Pedro from there.

The scenery was quite beautiful on the ride, and Doc had not felt so close to God since his childhood, when his mother would hold his tiny hand in church and the smell of the Holy Ghost emanated from the pews, blazing the rose windows with firelight. He recalled the choir's honeyed voices, especially the young girls', fragile as glass.

Black mountains rose up around them with white rivers and moss spotting their backs. A strange orange stream flowed under the horse's steps. They clopped along jauntily as the water cooled their ankles, painting them like bellicose braves. The mountains reflected off the orange water that was stagnant with scum and had grown a fleshy film, broken apart by every step; the silence of the valley they traversed was sanctified. Doc could not believe that anyone else had trodden there in a hundred years. He loved thinking that he was the first to touch the land since God, so when he stepped down to take a break by the hot earth, he emptied the liquor from one of his three canteens and took in some of the tangerine marsh water. *Perhaps there is a fountain out here that could heal me,* he thought after feeling this connection to the land.

After a few hours of travel, Doc smoked several cigarettes in succession. The group grew worn out. They came across a small creek, on the other side of which was a log cabin. These were the Iron Springs, nothing close to the warm, milky land they'd passed through earlier. Everything on their side of the creek appeared strangely burnt as if a forest fire had ripped through it, and the smell of sulfur bubbled up from the springs. The other side, with the cabin, was lush greenery—tall trees through which almost nothing could be seen except at the very top of them, a cross, far in the distance. That was San Pedro.

The embankment was dark and muddy. The water didn't seem too deep, but there was no telling. The four men approached on horseback. Their side of the creek contained several fallen tree trunks and boulders that would be troubling for the horses.

"I feel like shit," said Texas Jack.

"Maybe if you hadn't drank all the liquor in the entire bar you'd feel something human," McMaster replied. "And why'd you sock that—"

Before McMaster could finish his thought, a bullet whizzed out of the trees on the other side of the creek and struck Texas Jack's horse in the throat. The horse crumpled down onto his own leg. He yelped in pain. Creek, Doc, and McMaster all rode in different directions for cover back into the charred forest. Shots rained from the other side of the creek, their origins impossible to decipher except for the initial blast and the glint of steel shadows. Wyatt dismounted but remained close to his horse, out in the open. He wrapped the reins around his forearm and grabbed his shotgun from the saddlebag.

"Wyatt, get over here!" Doc continued galloping in the opposite direction.

Wyatt's horse panicked and kicked and reared up on its hind legs. Several shots landed around Wyatt's feet, through his boot heel and saddlebag, but missed the horse; some splashed down in the creek. Others splintered the tree trunks alongside him, and the ashen bark settled in the air. That was when Wyatt recognized a face. There were around twelve of them in the woods, all too far to be very accurate, hiding behind their numbers, but one madman walked into the creek.

"Curly Bill!" Wyatt called out as a challenge.

Bill Brocius laughed and sent a shot beneath Wyatt's terrified horse. He wore a bright red shirt with his curly chest hair hanging out and a couple of leather strings holding it together at his belly. His hat was brown and so were his pants. He aimed his six-shooter at Wyatt, across the creek. "You ought to be careful with that mount. It'll be the death of you."

Wyatt tugged hard on his horse and cocked his shotgun. He trudged toward Curly Bill. The shots from the forest stopped because Curly Bill was in the way.

Bill let go of two more shots, again wide of Wyatt.

Wyatt drew closer, visibly biting down on his cheek. The creek water soaked in his boots. He aimed down the long barrel and fired. Curly Bill let out a vicious scream. The buckshot tore through his chest, and the blood snaked against the water and over the gray rocks.

Wyatt's gun belt had fallen and slipped over his legs. Now, the stunned Cowboys in the trees returned fire. Texas Jack fired back from underneath his horse as Wyatt tried to saddle up but struggled with his gun belt at his ankles. With one hand he attempted to pull up the gun belt, but two shots ripped it off, striking his saddle horn, exploding several of his own bullets. A puff of smoke wafted through the air. Another two shots ripped straight through his black overcoat. Eventually, he tugged himself up on the horse and went to help Texas Jack.

He got off the horse again quickly, shoved Texas Jack's dead horse aside with his shot-up boot heel, and remounted. Texas Jack limped back into the woods as Wyatt rode alongside him, Jack firing wildly behind them. Wyatt spotted Doc ducking behind a large, rotten tree trunk in the pine forest. The forest floor pulsed with black beetles and maggots shimmying their way under the leaves and toward the horse's flesh.

Doc poked his head out. He saw Wyatt's coattails had been shredded by gunpowder. "Are you shot all to hell?"

"About as much as you." Wyatt looked himself over as he steadied his horse. The gunshots behind him had stopped. Not a single bullet touched his skin.

"You are a miracle worker, Wyatt. Now's our chance to attack!"

Wyatt looked down at Doc sternly. "If you fellas are hungry for a fight, you can go and get your fill. I've had mine."

Doc got out from under the hollowed-out log. "Maybe that's enough fighting for one day. I prefer more gentlemanly scrapes."

"Wyatt killed Bill," said Texas Jack.

"That right?" Turkey Creek Johnson nodded approvingly. He remained atop his horse behind a tree. "That's fine work. We should get the body for the reward."

"Is there a reward?" asked Doc.

"There's always a reward." He thought about it for a moment. "There's usually a reward when I've killed someone."

They waited for over an hour. Gunpowder and blood lingered in the salty afternoon air. Every now and again they'd search the trees across the river. In the undergrowth, Doc passed around his flask with the last of his bourbon. They slurped it up and wiped their mustaches with their dirty sleeves. Eventually, the posse cautiously approached the Iron Springs in search of Curly Bill's body. There was nothing there. The blood had washed away, and the creek flowed lazily by as if it had all been some bleak dream. The only signs of a gunfight were some loose shotgun shells, Texas Jack's dead horse, and bullet casings. Curly Bill's body was gone forever.

CHAPTER 45

There Goes My Gun

The Earp posse never made its way to San Pedro as they had intended. Wyatt expressed concern over O.C. and Big Tip. He decided to send them a telegraph in Tombstone and backtrack, holing up at Hooker's ranch.

Hooker was a good cattleman and citizen who welcomed the posse. "Good to see you all well and alive," said Hooker. "The papers have made quite a row about you all." He was a broad man with large arms from his cattle work. He had some political connections, too, so he had worked with Virgil, Wyatt, and Behan on separate occasions.

The property stretched out over several acres. It was flat and dry, but the cattle seemed to like it there. They mooed intermittently. The rectangular barns sat to the right of the property—white structures with a couple of water towers above them in case of a fire.

"We appreciate the stay," said Wyatt, dismounting his horse slowly, his legs sore from riding.

"Any news to report?"

"Curly Bill's dead," said McMaster, rubbing the scruff on his face. "Wyatt shot him down." He liked to stay clean-shaven. He eyed some of the cattle, and they looked back at him with their big, wet eyes.

Turkey Creek Johnson's consumption was worsening, and he threw himself into a fit of coughing, nearly falling off his horse. It made Doc remember how mild his illness had been of late. It would not last that way forever, he knew. Hooker helped Creek Johnson down from his horse and had a cattle hand bring him toward the beds.

"Good work, Wyatt. Keep it up, and when you've finished I'll get you pardoned," said Hooker.

"'Preciate that, but what we really need is some fresh mounts. We can pay as soon as O.C. and Tipton get back."

"Nonsense. You all are my guests. In fact, I'd be happy to pay you the thousand reward for Curly Bill. Our Cattlegrower's 'Sociation put it up."

"Told you there's a reward!" said Creek Johnson from fifty yards away.

"Can't accept. It was my pleasure," said Wyatt.

"In any case, I hear most of 'em headed out to Mexico when they heard about you all rampaging the plains."

"We'll pick off who's left."

The group stayed and rested for a few days. Tipton and O.C. finally showed up, saying that Behan had imprisoned them briefly, but they got out and they had the money. After two days' rest, the posse headed out. Their plan was to check out some nearby watering holes where Cowboys sometimes passed through.

In the meantime, Behan and his posse of outlaws set out to Hooker's ranch as well. Doc, Wyatt, and the rest had only left a few hours before.

Atop his horse, Behan waved to Hooker. He looked ridiculous riding in a full city suit and loafers. Behind him rode Johnny Ringo, Ike Clanton, Fin Clanton, as well as seven others. "We're here looking for the outlaws Doc Holliday and Wyatt Earp, along with his posse."

Hooker approached the grouping of Cowboys. "Well, Sheriff, I don't have any idea where they are, and if I did I certainly wouldn't tell a pimp like you."

"You must be upholding murderers and outlaws then," said Behan.

"No sir, I am not." Hooker spat tobacco to his side, keeping his eyes on Johnny Ringo. Ringo appeared pale and disengaged, as if his body were somewhere else. "I know the Earps, and I know you, and they have always treated me like gentlemen; damn such laws, and damn you, and damn your posse; they're a set of horse thieves and outlaws."

"I ain't no horse thief," said Ike. He looked out into the ranch. "I enjoy me some cattle though."

"Son of a bitch knows where they are. Let me make him tell," said Fin Clanton.

With that, some of the farmhands, who'd been watching all along, stirred, and the foreman rumbled up from behind Hooker with a Winchester, pointing it at Clanton. "You can't come here an' call him a son of a bitch! Now you skin it back. Skin it back! If yer lookin' for a fight and come 'ere and talk that way you can get it 'fore you find the Earps; you can get it right here."

Hooker held his ground. "Pretty little set of horse thieves and cutthroats you have."

Behan cleared his throat, as if, for the first time, realizing the political implications. "They are not my associates. They are only here on this occasion."

"Well then, I'd be happy to host you at my table, Sheriff, and no one else. Not a one."

The foreman kept his gun aimed at Fin Clanton.

"We'd best move on. If they've not been here, then we're cold on the trail," said Behan. He waved his arm and turned his horse around. "There is something in it for you if you do happen to see them, Hooker. Remember that."

"Oh, I know exactly what you have to offer," said Hooker. "There's no mistaking it."

For over a week, Wyatt, Doc, and the rest scouted local watering holes and Cowboy frequents, but they found nothing, verifying that Hooker's information was accurate. Most had fled to Mexico, and the job was nearly done. Wyatt made plain that he still wanted Ike Clanton though.

A week of riding behind them, the posse needed rest and fresh horses again, so they headed toward Camp Grant, a lightly guarded military outpost offering respite for weary travelers on their way out of the Arizona Territories.

Riding in, the local colonel, Biddle, recognized him on sight.

"'Fraid I have to hold you here, Wyatt. They're looking for you, and there are warrants for arrest. But come and have something to eat first."

There was no sense in resisting because officers overran the camp, and Wyatt had never made it his business to kill lawmen anyway. The party dismounted and sat down, digging into the meal that Colonel Biddle had his men bring out for them in a nearby tent. The officers served as waiters, and it was a very strange scene. The banquet consisted of a large turkey with some uncooked vegetables, a jug of water, and a bottle of spoiled red wine in the center. The officers retreated and stood stoically at the tableside when they finished serving.

When they were about halfway through, Biddle pushed out his chair and got up. "You'll have to excuse me, gentlemen. It was nice to have met you. It's a shame you all didn't make your way to New Mexico. I hear it's easy to get along there." He left the tent.

"What an odd thing to say," said Doc. He waved to one of the nearby officers. "Don't have any whiskey do you?" The officer stood at attention, unresponsive. "I would settle for gin, honestly. No? Nothing?"

When they were finished eating, the other officers took their leave as well and, a bit confused, Doc poked his head outside the tent. Seven new horses packed with supplies waited for them. There wasn't another person in sight. "I think Colonel Biddle might be one of the good ones," said Doc, waving everyone else out of the tent. So, with fresh mounts and warrants behind them, the Earp posse headed for New Mexico, their job, if not complete, then close enough.

Doc felt somewhat unsatisfied, as if the journey had been cut short. They still hadn't found Ike, and he knew Wyatt would head back to Tombstone or send for Sadie wherever he ended up. He felt like he'd lost something. His journey wasn't over though, he knew. The fountain awaited him, and it both thrilled and terrified him.

"Don't you think we ought to finish what we've started?" Doc asked Wyatt, off to the side where the others couldn't hear.

"A minute ago we were about to be hanged. We killed Bill, thinned the herd, and somehow or other got Ringo to cut his own suspenders. I think we done all right."

Doc's mouth was so dry he could hardly get the words out. He hacked into his sleeve, leaving a salty wet patch of mucus on the cloth. "I've never known you to be one to cut losses."

"Losses is all we got left," said Wyatt. "Best hold on to them."

CHAPTER 46

All Tomorrow's Parties

May 1882
Albuquerque, New Mexico

O.C. said his goodbyes at Silver City. The rest traveled on to Albuquerque. They set up for a few nights of celebration before everyone went his separate way. The only problem was that Doc still had one quest left. He wondered if Wyatt would abandon him now that he'd done his bloody work. He wondered where Kate was now. If he'd ever see her again. He thought of the sickness of Georgia, of his cousin Mattie. Had she really gone through with it?

Doc and Wyatt sat at the bar in Fat Charlie's. Tipton gambled in the card room with Texas Jack and McMaster. Creek Johnson lay in bed with pneumonia. Doc had been drinking since they entered New Mexico, and he was half-seas over.

"So, what do we do now, General Earp?"

Wyatt had been drinking as well, and his thoughts seemed to be elsewhere. "Do you think she's waiting for me?"

"Who?"

"Sadie. That girl is something amazing." Wyatt's eyes sank. He was tired, unused to being so drunk.

"I'd watch out with her, Wyatt. You don't want to become like me do you?" Doc spilled some whiskey and covered it with his hand. The liquid cooled his skin. He was running a fever and his cheeks flushed.

"Can't you ever see anything good about anything? You're a real sonofabitch sometimes. No wonder yours left."

Doc's head swam. "How does it feel to know that Behan is sticking it to your Jew girl right now? Do you even recall having a wife?"

"Fucking lecture me about family values? Get gone with you. You'll quell in the morning with less liquor on you."

Doc couldn't stand to let Wyatt just walk off. "Why doesn't anything ever happen to you? Three wives and no bullet holes. You were my only friend, and now you're nothing. It is done between us because I said so, and nothing would make me happier than for you to go back to my old whore and call her your wife."

"You've served your purpose, Doc. Get on with it." Wyatt threw a few coins on the counter and left.

Doc never felt so abandoned in his whole life. He remembered the moment when his mother died—it was that empty sort of twist in the gut. The awareness that nothing could ever have the wholeness it once did. He poured some whiskey down his throat. He could feel the sickness coming back, the darkness of it. The way it sat on his breath like chalk and blood.

Trinidad, Colorado

Doc and Wyatt never said goodbye. Rumors flew around national papers that there had been a rift in the posse. The *Albuquerque Review* wrote that an unknown Cowboy shot Wyatt while he was returning from Colton, California. The *Tombstone Epitaph* reported that Dan Tipton and Texas Jack were both thrown from different trains and killed in different cities on the same day. The papers called them desperados, vigilantes, heroes, and outlaws, sometimes in the same article.

Doc's fame grew to epic proportions again. He took Big Tip along with him to Trinidad, where Bat Masterson reigned as marshal, and they immediately sought out the gambling halls. Trinidad was much the same as it had been five years back when Doc visited with Kate, except bigger. All the construction that had begun then made the town sprawling now. The air was crisp. The brown flattop mountains in the background now seemed proportionate to the colorful town—the hills receding and the green withering. The clop and clank of the town drowned out the sound of the water completely.

Trinidad had hardened into a corrupt amber. The elevation made it hard for Doc to breathe. He remembered how he'd almost died the last time he stepped foot in Trinidad and how his fallen angel had revived him. Doc walked down North Avenue with Big Tip, passing the newer buildings, many of which were tall and red; their windows were clean, and businessmen in fine cotton suits hurried along the paved streets. Modernity had struck Trinidad hard. Carriages flew by Doc, who walked along the right-hand side of the street. The Colorado Supply Company and other forward-thinking businesses popped up, preparing for the Steam Age. Industry had begun. But nothing civilized could ever exist without its counterpart. In an alleyway, a ring of fifteen men gathered around two dogs. They flapped bills in the air and shouted. One of the dog's ears lay by their feet. It was just a small black triangle with jagged lines of flesh at its end.

Miners, ranchers, and investors all gathered at the gambling houses, pouring drinks side by side, grabbing plump prostitutes in a line as if inspecting fruit. As Doc entered the saloon, a Hollidean popped up from behind the player piano and kissed Doc on the cheek. The man, dressed lavishly in silk, his face powdered, bowed to Doc and then burst off through the saloon doors like an uncaged squirrel.

"Don't see that every day," said Big Tip.

"I do, just about," said Doc smiling.

Big Tip broke off and went to order drinks. Every single patron in the saloon recognized Doc. They whispered loudly to one another.

"There he is."

"Do you think he'll shoot somebody?"

"If I was ever gonna be shot I'd like it to be by him."

"Heard he and the Earps are on the outs."

"He's littler than his pictures. Looks like a seabird could lift 'im."

A man around Doc's height with his black hair parted straight down the center approached. His greasy handlebar mustache stretched down to his chin. He had a few days' worth of stubble on his cheeks and wore a dirty white shirt under his blazer.

"I know you. Name's Perry Mallon." The man did not extend his hand, and Doc looked past him.

"Yes, that's very kind."

"You saved my life in Santa Fe."

Doc was confused. Had he forgotten a trip? "You must be mistaken. I've never been to Santa Fe."

Mallon was undeterred. "I just seen Josh Stilwell on the train over there."

"Frank Stilwell's brother?" The name caught Doc's attention. Doc watched him die at the O.K. Corral all over again. His body swarming with flies and sinking into the dirt.

"You say anything I'll kill you." Mallon then unbuckled his pants, dropped them, stripped off his shirt, and showed Doc a pair of circular scars. They looked like cigar burns. Patrons turned their heads in disgust. "They're gunshot wounds." He buckled up and walked away.

Doc remained confounded at Mallon's absurdity.

Big Tip walked over with two glasses of whiskey. "Who was that?"

"Just some Mary who likes to burn himself, I think."

"It takes all kinds."

Doc took the drink and downed it in one gulp, forgetting the crazy, scarred man. His throat burned again. The ulcers resurfaced. "Let's make some money, shall we?"

The gambling parlor was a small room filled with cigarette smoke. It seemed to stick against the paisley walls and hover as halos around the lightbulbs suspended from the ceiling. The whole place glowed incandescent yellow. There was a faro table and a blackjack felt along with roulette. Doc and Big Tip sat down, bucking the tiger for several hours.

After a while, Bat Masterson walked in with a distinguished-looking older gentleman. Gray hair grew on the sides of his head, matching Doc's newly grayed hair. Doc stood up immediately. "Bat, nice to see you again."

"I hear you and Wyatt have been doing good work out in Arizona."

"Yes . . . Wyatt." The sound of his name sent a sting into Doc. "It was some bloody work, but good, as you say."

Bat and Doc shook hands. "This is my friend, Governor Grant."

Doc shook his hand, too, introducing Tipton.

"Please, call me Jimmy," said Governor Grant. "I'm not one of those politicians who likes to separate himself."

"Yes, we met one of those in Arizona, didn't we, Tip?"

"Sure did," said Tipton, but he quickly returned to his faro hand.

"Listen, forgive my bluntness, but you've got quite a reputation, Doc." The governor's eyes shot down to Doc's pearl-handled .38.

"That business is done with. I'm retired."

"That's good, that's very good, because as you can see this state is on the grow. It's a modern state and all that gunslinging is behind us. It's the past."

"Couldn't agree more."

Governor Grant smiled. "Well, that's very good. All this is to say that—Bat here told me what a good man you are."

"Bat said that?" Doc was surprised. They'd never really gotten along, but he realized in that moment that he felt the same way about Masterson.

"Anyway," Grant continued, "what I wanted to say was that I've got a pardon for you—for what you've done. As long as you're in Colorado you'll be safe. That is, as long as you keep to your word. I'd hate to see you extradited to Arizona."

"There are more than a few who'd love my neck in a noose there."

"Exactly. Back scratching works both ways. You're a hero of the Old West. A celebrity. With this newfound notoriety—they call Trinidad the Pittsburgh of the West. It's going to be something really special, and I've got an election coming up."

"I've always been especially flexible," said Doc. It was strange to think of himself as some celebrity in repose. Only some months before, a politician would never have approached Doc Holliday in a bar. Now, he was talking quid pro quo with him.

"What's that?"

"For back scratching."

The governor chuckled, clearly feigning understanding. "So, it was a real pleasure. Bat?"

With that, they took their leave and exited the gambling hall.

"What you gonna do if you can't kill no one?" said Tipton, leaning back on his chair.

"Not sure. Take up some hobbies, I reckon. I hear there's a fountain worth seeing in this state."

"Fountain, who told you that?"

"An Indian. Just a regular old Indian."

CHAPTER 47

Shells of Silver

Denver, Colorado

Denver glowed with fresh money and the scent of silver. It exuded a bold affluence that extended into the multicolored fashion and buildings. It was a city built on unrelenting greed, and its forty thousand residents preferred silver coins and grinning with silver teeth.

The coal tar that coated the streets stuck to the bottom of Doc's soles as he walked down Larimer Street. He'd heard the Windsor Hotel was a good place to stay, so he telegraphed ahead, but he'd check in and announce himself to the authorities first. The train ride had been long, and he was feeling decrepit. He had not felt so sick in months. Black rings formed under his dry red eyes. His skin flaked off on his yellowing fingernails.

The gummy road fixed to horses' hooves and clogged up wagon spokes. It kicked up into Doc's throat and tasted like a cigar someone had been chewing on for days. The affluent city-goers wore fine, shiny bowlers—some square-crowned or conical, but nearly always with fur because it was more expensive than a leather sweatband. Some wore top hats, taller than their arms, with checkered pants and vests and topcoats that only covered a small portion of their shallow chests. There were so many buttons, bronze and silver and ivory. Their muttonchops ended where their fine mustaches began. Doc suddenly felt like a remnant of the past. He stuck his pearl-handled .38 in his small leather carrying luggage. The only thing he had in common with these men was that they all used canes, but theirs were accessories, delicate adornments that would break if they ever leaned on them.

The women wore fine silky bonnets and ribbons that he'd only seen on special occasions. There was a certain brutality to it all though. As Doc passed a grand tailor's shop selling elegant clothes on multiple floors, he saw a Chinaman being beaten in the street. The policeman nearby laughed alongside a stocky man in a Homburg hat smoking a cigarette through a white cigarette holder like a lady. The policeman placed his body between the Chinaman and the building as if not to sully its fresh white paint. Doc didn't understand these people. The man beating the Chinaman was a miner, and his blackened fingers left dark imprints all over the body, branding it with more than just bruises.

The Chinaman met eyes with Doc as he walked past. He said something in his language, but before he finished, the miner knocked out his front teeth, and when he began to bleed, the policeman told the miner to stop.

"He's had enough. You learned your lesson, yeah?" The policeman loomed over the broken man. His gun sparkled as if it had never been touched.

Doc lost view of the altercation. The sky was clear, and the spring weather made him think of Georgia warmth. The streets twittered with busy pedestrians and whizzing carriages pulled by great hulking beasts, leaving thousands of ashen trails in the tar like rattlesnake tails. Above, telegraph lines ran in myriad directions, contorting and crisscrossing in taut rectangles above the heavy beat of leather and hoof.

Doc walked into the sheriff's office a bit winded, his body betraying him once again. A portly man in a navy police uniform sat behind the desk in front of him.

"Hello, I'm Doc Holliday."

The man looked him up and down. "Yeah, and I'm President Arthur. Nice to meet you."

Doc furrowed his brow. He didn't understand. "I'd like to check in. I want to announce my presence."

"Buddy, first of all, I don't have time for this. Second of all, you're too old. You got gray hair and a cane. You look like a gun could hold *you*. What are you, about a hundred pounds?"

Doc pressed the sides of his ribcage. He didn't have much left to him. He felt the spaces between his bones. Behind the policeman lay a shiny metal rifle case, and even in the reflection he realized the sides of his hair had gone completely gray as if overnight. Even his mustache was turning. His face was sunken and sallow. His reflection distorted in the tin. He turned away.

"Be that as it may, either I *was* Doc Holliday or I still am, but now I'm here, so tell someone who might be of some use. I see the law work is about the same here as everywhere else." Doc turned and left.

He checked into the Windsor Hotel. It was a gargantuan spectacle of a building that took up an entire city block. An awning ruffled above nearly every entrance. The hotel was made of red stone, and one of the corners ended in a steeple. Atop it, in large letters, it read: "W-I-N-D-S-O-R." Even the air inside smelled luxurious, the halls well-lit, showcasing arches and jade plants. Doc began to worry that he could not afford the place, but at least for a while he would use the money that Wyatt gave him and some that he'd won in Trinidad. Silver chandeliers hung from silver chains, and the delicate masonry on the walls was like nothing he'd ever seen outside of a church.

A boy carried his bag up to his room. "Hotel'd like you to know your room's free for the week. Place has never been so filled as since you telegraphed."

"That's kind," said Doc wearily. The boy placed his bag down in front of the open door and scurried off before Doc could tip him.

A partition divided the enormous room down the middle, a chandelier hanging in each half. Gas ran through it with porcelain table lamps and seashell couches. A gilded mirror hung on the flower-printed walls, reflecting the Oriental rug. It was a lavish accommodation fit for someone far more discerning. Doc slept for several hours on the plush bed. He hadn't slept like that in weeks.

He woke up around nine at night and decided to find something to eat. He'd just left the hotel and was walking along Fifteenth Street when a short, familiar-looking man jumped out in front of him and pointed two revolvers at him.

"Throw up your hands, Doc Holliday. I've got you now!"

Doc looked around to see if there was some kind of acting troupe behind him. Passersby froze in the street to watch. The man quickly turned Doc around, at gunpoint, and shuttled him anxiously to the sheriff's office a few blocks away, where Doc had attempted to check in several hours before. Doc didn't resist because he didn't have his pistol on him and, anyway, he figured, it was best not to start any trouble after what the governor had said.

A couple of deputy sheriffs took Doc into custody there. As they turned Doc around, he recognized the figure apprehensively aiming the revolvers at him. "Aren't you that odd little burner fellow?" It was Mallon from Trinidad who'd loosed his trousers. Doc figured this would be simple to get out of since the man was clearly a loon. "Oh, you can drop that." He motioned toward the guns. "Nobody is trying to get away from you. I have no weapons."

A crowd had followed from the initial confrontation and now grew around the sheriff's office. Mallon proclaimed, "No, you won't get away from me again.

You killed my partner, you bloodthirsty coward, and I would have taken you in Trinidad if the men I had with me had stood by me."

"What men? Who are you? I'll not be abused by this bunko artist." He appealed to the deputies, but their attention was on the growing crowd. They were not used to it. Journalists materialized as if by spontaneous generation. "I refuse to take abuse from this tiny man any longer. May I make a statement?"

The crowd awaited his statement, but the deputies, fearing the mob, began to force Doc into the holding cell. That's when Doc recognized a familiar face with a notepad and glasses. "You!" It was Wentworth. "Just the man I want to see."

But the deputies wrenched Doc away from Wentworth and threw him into a cell.

Behind the scenes, Wentworth worked to get Doc's real story out, but truth always took longer than fiction. He was unable to reach Wyatt but managed to contact Bat Masterson, who could vouch for Doc. Unfortunately, it would take at least a day to get him to Denver.

Once again, Doc sat in a cold cell with a steel bottom. The deputies allowed reporters to observe him from a distance like a diseased chimp. A hard thirty-one now, his hair turned by the hour; he was barely one hundred thirty pounds, and his soft hands chafed against the tough metal. His cough had come back with a fury and so had the blood and the ulcers in his throat. They wouldn't give him any liquor in the cell, so the pain shot through his carved-out body like a railroad spike. It was a smooth kind of pain, constant and familiar. The Denver journalists wrote down the deputies' statements and interviewed Mallon.

> **Rocky Mountain News:** How would you describe Doc Holliday?
>
> **Mallon:** Perhaps he's the greatest villain that ever lived.
>
> **RMN:** They said that of Jesse James. Who was the greater scoundrel—James or Holliday?
>
> **M:** Doc Holliday, of course. He is vanity itself. His heart is a stone and has not one germ of true manhood. He's savage.
>
> **RMN:** How many men has he killed?
>
> **M:** Impossible to say. I'd say fifty. He was the Cowboy leader after all.
>
> **RMN:** Was he?
>
> **M:** Seems you Denver boys don't know much except what you hear from the Earp camp. He's wanted in Arizona for all sorts of murderous crimes. He'd kill your daughter just to take her dolly.

RMN: You were bold to take him down like that.

M: Some men are just born a certain kind. I like to think myself born to serve justice upon the unjust. I'll have him back in Arizona soon enough.

Mallon reveled in the attention. He could hardly conceal his sadistic glee. He accepted congratulations and took pictures with some of the locals.

The next day, Bat Masterson arrived just hours before the Denver authorities were set to release Doc back into Mallon's custody. Immediately, he brought Mallon's accusations into question. "Doc Holliday is no criminal at all," he told the sheriff. "The governor himself has pardoned him, and sending him back to Arizona would be a death sentence."

"You all are just about wearing me out," said the Denver sheriff. He wore a bowler and a badge, and his breath reeked of cabbage. "First this Mallon fella comes in and demands my deputies' assistance in apprehending Holliday. I heard a him, and I heard he done some pretty nasty things, so I don't think nothing of it, but now—now y'all are making me work." His accent was not of Colorado. He'd come from farther south.

Doc had hardly moved since they'd locked him up. Chills ran all over his body, and pneumonia came on him quick. He hacked blood and sputum all over the cell. A great darkness surrounded him, and he reached out for what seemed like the lip of something. The cusp. Water everywhere, burning long, jagged streaks like the stems of wings in his back. He was unable to touch them, unable to tell if it was a dream, but dampness soaked into him, and he wondered if dying felt like a wintertime bath.

Finally, on the third day of his incarceration, and with doctors now tending to Doc in his cell, Wentworth's article came out in a local paper. Bat Masterson, along with some detective work by the sheriff's office, had uncovered a telegraph from Tombstone:

Perry Mallon.

Five Hundred dollars delivered to me at Denver. Answer when arrested.

J.H Behan, Sheriff

When the Denver sheriff searched for an explanation from Mallon, he was nowhere to be found. He'd bought a ticket to New Mexico earlier that morning. The county released Doc, but his health quickly deteriorated. His body resembled a cicada shell in Georgia summer, brittle and loose. The lawyers' fees and bail cost him the last $500 he had to his name.

CHAPTER 48

Nothing Changes

July 14, 1882
Morse's Canyon, Arizona

Johnny Ringo sat behind the sunset with a bottle of Old Crow in his sweaty left palm. In his right, he gripped a loaded Colt .45 revolver. He thought about his father. He wondered if there was something he could have done. Ringo considered himself a coward. The warm remains of the sun beat his chest.

The sky was vanilla, and the oxblood rocks glowed around him. He leaned his head against the trunk of a small tree. It was the only one around, starved and spiky. The craggy earth seemed to swallow him up like an ancient hump-backed beast. The bark felt cool in the spots where it reached through to his scalp. His black hair curved around it.

Ringo tinked the bottle against the hard reeds and against his teeth. Nearly finished. He wondered if anyone knew he was out there. He realized that this was the best he would ever feel. For some reason, he thought of Doc Holliday pulling out one of his teeth, though he was sure that had never happened. His mother was a sweet lady. The clouds did not move. The earth moved beneath him. Worms dug deep holes, loosening the dirt against his thighs. He sliced one in half with his fingernail. Both parts wiggled away, encircling him, digging, reproducing. The earth moved. The clouds remained still.

Johnny Ringo picked up the revolver, placed it against his temple, and pulled the trigger.

CHAPTER 49

Fall to Pieces

December 1883
Leadville, Colorado

"PERSONS TROUBLED WITH WEAK LUNGS OR HEART DISEASE SHOULD GIVE THE NEW CAMP A WIDE BERTH. THE RARE ATMOSPHERE ACCELERATES THE ACTION OF BOTH THESE ORGANS AND UNLESS THEY ARE IN PERFECT CONDITION, SERIOUS RESULTS MAY FOLLOW."

—TOURIST'S GUIDE TO LEADVILLE AND THE CARBONATE FIELDS

Doc lay in his bed at the Star Block Hotel off Harrison Avenue in Leadville. He'd spent the better part of a year there after the incident in Denver. The wallpaper was light green and damp; the corners peeled a little off the wall each day so that they hung down like ivy. A photograph of a man with his horse adorned the otherwise bare wall. He rode alone in a high grassy field. The man was very small, and the horse was very big. The background was blown out, so there was no sky.

The headboard to the bed was curiously ornate, much more so than the rest of the room, which was dingy and smelled of unripe boysenberries. Several gelatinous stains marred the carpet, which did not cover most of the warped wooden floorboards. It was hard to tell anymore which stains he'd created and which had preceded him.

Doc held the eggshell blanket tight to his chest. He didn't want to look at the time, but he knew he was already late to work, and Mannie Hyman had been all over him lately. He'd taken a job dealing at Hyman's trying to build up enough bankroll to finally chase after the fountain. His pneumonia bouts had grown more severe, and it was hard to tell which days he would be able-bodied. Those seemed less and less frequent.

His heart sped as he slid up on the headboard, gasping for air. Nothing came through the tiny, fingerprinted window. It looked as if someone had been desperately trying to get out. He coughed lazily because there was so much liquid in his lungs that no amount of coughing could clear it. He knew this was one of the days when he would not be able to talk. He swigged some laudanum and chased it with Kessler whiskey to calm the ulcers growing in his throat. He liked the old man on the brown bottle. He reminded Doc of his grandfather a little. Doc remembered him as being mostly silent except on the matters of food and women. Usually, the two coincided. Doc didn't enjoy using the laudanum, but it eased his cough and the local druggist liked Doc or maybe he pitied him. Either way, he gave it to him on the house.

Suddenly, he felt a pain in his belly. He pushed up off the bed and scuttled down the hall to the bathroom. The floorboards chilled his delicate white feet, and a splinter pricked his heel. He got into the shared bathroom down the hall and released his bowels into the brown bowl. His toes squished against a coating of piss. Nothing came out solid anymore. The consumption had shredded his stomach, and he had to go constantly. It disgusted him. His shooting hand shook as he attempted to wipe himself.

Doc limped back to his room and under his covers. He glanced at his watch. Twenty past three. He was two hours late. It wasn't even worth going in to work. He was so tired. A fever came on. It did that sometimes. It would come on out of nowhere and then dissipate. Sometimes it would last through the night, and he would sweat and dream of Kate pouring water on his searing forehead, but no one was there. That was the worst of it, to wake up having soaked through the sheets, wet and cold and alone.

He picked up the letter he'd received from Mattie a few months back. He'd read it over thirty times, but he wanted to read it again. It smelled like ink, but he pretended it smelled like her. It seemed so long ago that he'd been so close to her. He tried to bury her in his thoughts, his memories of her small ankles, their florid conversations. He wasn't sure how she'd found him. Maybe he was in the papers again. He never checked anymore. They wrote all sorts of things about him, and it didn't matter what was right or true or good; his life no longer belonged to him. The newspapermen would decide who he was.

Sometimes his friend Pat Sweeney would tell him things out of the news. He told him that over the summer Doc had killed Johnny Ringo. Doc remembered just smiling and saying, "I wish someone had told me sooner. I would have celebrated."

He smiled now just thinking about it. Ringo was a sad character in his own mind. It was only fitting that he'd written his own ending.

Doc had never spent so much time in his own thoughts before, and he found the echoes of his past haunting. He fantasized about the fountain and how once he was better he'd find Kate, and they would make love like they used to, rough, his hand wrenching her long red hair, and she would howl with love. He remembered when they'd first met, and he knew she was different than the other women like that. It wasn't just her accent. There was something inside her that gave her the ability to fuck like he imagined a Mayan princess would fuck: Sex before the bloody sacrifice. He couldn't even imagine breathing a full breath right now. He coughed up blood onto the sheet and tossed it away, afraid to look at what else had spilled out of him. What else he'd lost.

The letter, as he read it again, only said that Mattie was now a Sister of Mercy in Savannah, and she'd taken the name Sister Mary Melanie. He didn't like that she'd taken a new name. He felt her past slowly washing away. Washing his filthy thoughts off her. "With Love" she'd written, but he figured she loved everyone now. She was so full of love and God, and he hated her for it. He refused to forgive her. He knew that if he forgave her she'd be lost. He hoped the years had been terrible to her, knowing that she grew absolution like strands of hair.

Doc closed his eyes but could not sleep. He wondered if it would be cloudy again tomorrow. He wondered if it would be cold.

The following day, Doc still felt the effects of the pneumonia, but he decided he was well enough to go to work. At one, he dressed himself very gingerly and exactly, wearing his gray overcoat. He combed his gray hair to the side. He picked up his cane, heading for Hyman's right next to Monarch's Saloon on Harrison Avenue. It wasn't far from his room, though it took him longer to get places now. The weather was turning. The wind ate at his lungs.

When he walked in, he saw a young man in a crisp black vest dealing at the faro table. He looked fresh and tidy. Doc didn't recognize him, which was strange because he could recognize just about every gambler and young sport in Leadville. He walked over to Hyman, who was counting the bottles behind the bar. "Have you replaced Scott?" Doc's voice was hoarse, and he couldn't raise it above more than a whisper.

Hyman tilted a bottle up to the light, inspecting the liquid. "I replaced you."

"Me? But I'm right here."

"Not usually. I'm very sorry for your condition, but I'm running a business, you understand. I half to replace you half the time as it is."

"I've been sick."

"Don't I know it." Hyman, who was a large man, adjusted his red suspenders, sliding them back over his moon-shaped belly. His peppered hair was thinning on top of his fat head. "It's not worth it to me to have an unreliable dealer just cause you're Doc Hallerday."

"Holliday."

"Exactly, see, if I don't even know yer name that's probably not a good sign. I'm sorry, Doc."

Doc's right hand began to tremble. He quickly gripped it with his left and squeezed hard until it hurt.

Johnny Tyler popped up behind Doc. He was a local thug with a big black beard and a scar running through it. Wyatt and Doc had gotten the best of him back in Tombstone. "You afraid, Holliday? Why you shakin'?"

"My condition."

"What? Speak up. You know, I know you. I know yer whole bunch from Tombstone. I know Earp, that sonofabitch."

"Well, good for you," said Doc. "We shall have a memory game sometime."

Tyler grabbed Doc's frail arm. A group of his friends stood behind him, cheering him on. "You know, suddenly you don't seem so tough. You got something wrong with you, lunger?" He laughed, and his cronies laughed along with him. He drove Doc up against the wall. Doc's shoulder crashed into the wood and his cane went flying. "You oughta be more careful. Next time you might die."

"Draw on him," said one of the group.

"I haven't got it," whispered Doc.

"Yeah, Holliday, draw on me. Aren't you some kinda famous outlaw?" Tyler guffawed, showing his steel. He kicked Doc in the ribs. Doc fell and tried to catch his breath but couldn't. His hand wouldn't stop shaking. It trembled against the floor.

"You yellow lunger coward."

"You Mary bag a shit. Fight!" called another crony.

The jeers continued. Doc tried to breathe. He went unconscious. He lay there for several minutes. No one helped him. Slowly, he came to. Tyler had turned to talk to his crowd. Doc got up and stumbled out of Hyman's. He made his way to the police station nearby.

It was a fairly large station on the corner of Harrison. Uniformed policemen hurried around him. It made Doc uncomfortable. He approached the officer at the front desk.

"I need your help."

"What with?" said the officer, glancing at some paperwork.

"Johnny Tyler is threatening to kill me. The governor told me not to fight back. If you can protect me, I can keep my promises."

The policeman picked up his head. "Uh-huh, and you are?"

"Doc Holliday!"

"Huh, just like the famous outlaw. That's a hoot. Okay, Doc, if you could just fill this out, we'll file your complaint." He slid a piece of paper over the desk.

"Goddamn you people. I'll handle this myself." Doc stormed out of the station and back to his hotel room. He rested for a bit, building his strength back up. After a few hours, he grabbed his pistol and headed back to Hyman's, wishing he still had his cane. He opened and closed his fist, trying to get the tremors out, but it was no use. *At least I've got my boots on*, he thought. As he headed around the corner to Hyman's, he noticed someone trailing him. He turned around deliberately.

"Not as quick as you used to be."

"Wentworth, you just follow me around the globe, don't you?"

"I wish it could be for a whole lot longer. You sure you want to do this?"

"It's as good a time as any. I've never been one to back down from a fight."

Wentworth glanced down at Doc's hand.

"All they are is mosquitoes. They've been waiting and waiting until you're nearly asleep."

"I can fire my pistol asleep or not."

"He doesn't deserve to be the one. Can't you sit out one gunfight your whole life?"

"But my dear Wentworth," said Doc, "what would they say about me in the papers?

Doc pushed open the saloon door and walked up to Tyler at the faro table. "A handkerchief duel. Ten paces. I've got my steel now."

Tyler paused. He looked around, but his friends had left. "Yer in no shape to fight. Wouldn't be fair."

Doc saw Wentworth in his peripheral vision, watching Doc's wiry figure through the window blurred.

"Fair? You goddamn coward. You kick me around without my pistol, with all your cohorts at your back, and you back down alone."

Tyler got up out of his seat. "Ain't no one backing down." He held up his hands. "This time I ain't got *my* gun."

Doc spotted a bulge in Tyler's jacket where his gun lay. "You're the kind of man who can only shoot a sport in his back. I've known men like you. I've killed men like you." A sudden pain shot down Doc's chest and into his belly. He keeled over, nearly falling to the ground.

Tyler exhaled. "See. Wouldn't be right. Consider yerself lucky yer 'bout to die anyhow."

Doc collected himself, picked up his cane by the wall, and walked back outside where he met Wentworth.

"How'd it go?" asked Wentworth.

"I reckon I'm still alive. Seems to be a daily victory." As they walked, Doc's eyes teared with fury. "If I should kill someone here, no matter if I were acquitted, the governor would turn me over to Arizona. I would stand no show for life there."

"It's funny, I guess I never thought I'd have to see you like this."

Doc nearly smiled. "Sorry I've disappointed you, old boy. I outlived myself."

"Is there something I can do?"

"Just keep writing what's true and right and leave the others to the fable. I haven't a cent, have few friends, and they will murder me yet before they are done." Doc thought of Wyatt, and he wished he were with him. Wyatt would always be strong. He was just that kind of man. He'd be rock solid even in his coffin.

"Where are you off to now?"

"To see how much I'm worth." Doc limped off down Harrison Avenue. He ducked into the first pawnshop he saw. Outside it said, "Watchmaker and Jeweler," and in the window there were seven clocks all with different times. Each one ticked just a fraction apart from the others so that the sound filled the room like the snapping of fresh grass. He felt almost overwhelmed by the weight of it. He thought briefly of William Leonard. Doc pretended the clocks showed times from all around the world: Hindustan and the Isles. He imagined what it would be like to sail. What real air tasted like.

Four men stood outside the entrance on either side, wearing fuzzy Russian hats. It was unclear whether or not they were part of the establishment. Inside there were all sorts of taxidermied mammals: foxes, armadillos, and pheasants. There was even a penguin, but Doc didn't stop to verify its authenticity. About ten pistols of different makes and models sat in the case below the owner, surrounded by gold and silver necklaces, bracelets, and a few watches.

"I've got the best silver around. Straight from the mines to your pocket," said the owner. Doc could tell he'd used the line many times before. He even bored himself. His white muttonchops extended down to his lips.

Doc gripped his pearl-handled .38. The owner flinched, but Doc set it on the table. "How much?"

The pawnshop owner felt its weight in his palms. He held the pearl up to the light. "I'll give you five dollars for it."

"Five dollars! Five dollars for Doc Holliday's gun?"

The pawnshop owner furrowed his brow. "Doc Holliday's gun. How'd you come by it?"

"Jesus, what is it with you Coloradoans? I *am* Doc Holliday." He pointed his finger at the J.H.H. carved into the pearl butt. He took out his flask and showed the same initials. He smiled wide as if posing for a picture and pointed to his mouth, but he coughed before the owner could get the full effect.

"You feelin' okay?"

"I'm peachy. How much for the gun?"

"Well, don't make sense for me to give you more in cash, but I can throw in another pistol on top. That'd come in handy being that you're a gunslinger an' all." He only sounded half sure of the story.

Doc sighed. He really just needed the cash, but he should have a gun on him just in case. He dangled his head over the case, trying not to notice his own pale reflection in the glass. "How about the .41?"

The pawnshop owner took out the Colt .41. He spun the chamber and placed it on the counter along with the five dollars. "Hope you never have to use it."

"You've got it all wrong," said Doc, collecting his new pistol. It felt light and flimsy in his hand. He ran his thumb over the tarnished barrel. "You must use it just a hair before they do."

Doc lost the five dollars that very same night in a poker game and then the ten dollars that he got from pawning his jewelry. Everything but his flask. His cough forced him deeper into opiates and whiskey. He teetered on the edge, and after winter was over, he was forced to borrow another five dollars from Billy Allen, a saloon man at the Monarch and former lawman.

Doc scraped by. It was now June. The warm weather usually suited Doc, but his condition only seemed to worsen, and he was farther from the fountain than ever. That Indian said it was in Colorado, but nothing seemed as godless as Leadville. Maybe it was all a myth. Every time he asked around it got farther and farther from his grasp. One man told him the fountain was just an idea created by a madam to attract customers. Another man told him the fountain was actually where they used to feed dying mules to newborn mules to make them stronger. Even a local preacher weighed in on the fountain, saying that its restorative powers were a sign that the Devil would reappear in one month, but that was a month ago.

It was like something was keeping him in this hellhole. Like they all tortured him for everything he'd done before. Tyler and his band continued to prod Doc from afar, and sometimes he would see Allen with them. Allen increasingly harassed him for the money he didn't have.

Allen approached him outside of Hyman's. He'd just emerged from another bout of pneumonia.

"Doc Holliday, you gonna pay me that money 'fore you're dead?" Allen wore a black, curve-brimmed hat. He was pale, and his skin pulled tight against his bony face. The only ruffle on his icy façade was his mustache, which was reddish-brown, lighter than his hair. "What happened to your friend?"

In their last conversation, Doc had mentioned that a young man in Sowbelly Gulch owed him money.

"He lost it in faro and the fights."

"That does sound like a friend of yours."

"Let me alone, Allen. I'll get you the money. My jewelry's in the soak. Is this about Tyler?"

"Holliday," his top lip quivered, "I'll give you till tomorrow at noon to pay this money, and if you don't pay it, I'll lick you, you sonofabitch." Allen marched off to his job providing protection at Monarch.

Doc stepped inside Hyman's where his friend Pat Sweeney played faro. "You look like someone just about stepped on your grave, Doc." Pat always smelled of cashews and had a very pleasant face for a gambler.

"He's pushing me."

"Who?"

"Allen. He's with those Slopers, with Tyler."

"Don't do nothing stupid," said Sweeney, half concentrating on his hand. "Go get some sleep, and you'll see clearer in the morning."

That night, Doc couldn't sleep. Not an hour, not a minute. He stared up into the cracked ceiling and saw that nothing was connected. He did not find God that night; he did not have any revelations. He lay awake with his Colt .41 on his chest and the scent of catfish in his nostrils. Someone was cooking it downstairs, and it smelled like sixty-year-old pussy. Nothing was his anymore. He imagined dying and no one even recognizing him. John Doe. Unmarked grave. Died in Leadville, Colorado to a gang of bullies a man like Doc Holliday would have carved up with his pistol like pieces of clay. But he was no Doc Holliday. He was no John Henry. He was the sickness.

The warm night bled in on him, pressing on his chest. He tasted his own insides. He tasted bile. Strings of blood dried over his lip. His eyes reddened. He loaded his pistol. It was six in the morning. He licked each bullet before placing it in the chamber. He wanted to taste anything but himself. Time passed slowly. It was 6:01, but he didn't know it. There was no time worth keeping anymore. He'd hocked his watch for three dollars. Doc couldn't remember the last time he ate. Every few minutes he'd take a swig of Freeport and a nip of laudanum.

He felt everything. The whiskey glugged down. A rat squeaked by his doorway. A woman outside called for her husband. "Jimmy," she said. "Jimmy? Jimmy." Doc wondered if Jimmy ever came. He wondered if Jimmy was even himself anymore. Maybe Jimmy was the greatest villain who ever lived, and now he'd traded places and Doc was supposed to go down there and tell that woman no one loved her—that no one really loved anyone in Leadville.

Around eleven, the church bells rang. Doc began the process of dressing. It took him almost an hour to look presentable, but he had to do it. It was part of him. He couldn't let it go. The Colt didn't fit as neatly into his old holster, but he forced it in.

Doc entered Hyman's at noon. He smiled at Hyman behind the bar. "Time's up," said Doc.

"For what?" asked Hyman. He turned around and started pouring Doc the usual—two shots, up.

To Hyman's left stood a tall glass cigar case. Hyman liked to leave it open to fill the air with the scent of tobacco. "No man can resist it after a warm bourbon," Hyman liked to say. With Hyman's back turned, Doc stuck his pistol in the cigar case between two boxes of cigars so that no one could see it. Hyman turned back, looking around as if he'd felt Doc's presence close on his back.

"You will see soon enough," said Doc.

CHAPTER 50

Hollywood Forever Cemetery Sings

Doc took down the whiskey. His head swam. He was delirious with laudanum and lack of sleep. "Look out for Allen, would you?" he said to Mannie Hyman. Doc sniffled, his eyes drooping. He lingered by the cigar case. His right hand trembled next to the smudged glass. Saliva and tobacco flowed freely into his gullet.

In the meantime, Allen had just had his boots shined. They glowed against the tar-soaked road. Leadville law allowed Allen to carry a gun in the Monarch, but not outside it. Something bulged in his coat, and Bradbury, a local cop, stopped him.

"Whatcha got there?" said Bradbury.

Allen licked a rash forming below his mustache. "Just my cock. Want a look-see?" He pushed by Bradbury, who grabbed him by the arm.

"A little warm for an overcoat. Where you headed?"

"To hunt my party. He owes me five dollars."

"I'd advise against it. I've seen you now."

Allen's lip twitched. "Relax. I just wanna talk to 'im. I used to be where you are. Show some solidarity, brother." Allen turned onto Harrison and stepped through the door to Hyman's with his hand in his pocket.

Doc recognized him immediately. He'd seen a hundred hands in a hundred pockets, and the scene never ended well. Doc stepped behind the counter, grabbing the Colt .41. He gripped it as tight as he could. It hurt to squeeze his fist tight. He leaned over the cigar case and fired. The bullet burst through the wooden door to Allen's right. In a panic, Allen turned to run, but as he did, his feet tangled and he crashed down onto his splayed palms. Doc squeezed off another round, his wrist pulsating and shaking. The bullet struck Allen's arm between the shoulder and elbow. It ripped open the artery, slicing through the muscle. Blood poured down onto the wood floor. Hyman wrapped his arms around Doc as Doc attempted to fire another shot.

At that moment, Bradbury swung the door open, hitting Allen on his left side. "Doc, I want your gun!"

Doc calmed down, slamming the Colt on the cigar case, cracking it. "My gun for your protection."

A scene of confusion took over Hyman's as some of Allen's friends from the Monarch carried him off to a doctor. One of them stashed the gun. Bradbury took Doc into custody. It all happened so fast that the reporters didn't even get there in time. Even Wentworth arrived after the fact.

Bradbury did protect Doc for the next year and a half as he awaited trial. Various appeals and proceedings delayed it, along with Doc's notoriety. To pay his lawyer, Doc even shot an advertisement for some extra cash. A man with a large telescopic lens prodded Doc, made him wear ridiculous outfits with feathers and leather so that he looked like some kind of outlaw pheasant. He took shot after shot and the flash ate at Doc's eyes, and Doc coughed and ruined pictures running by off to the toilet.

In the end, it was a print ad with Doc holding a giant bottle of Sunny Brook Whiskey. It read: "Sunny Brook Whiskey means PURE Whiskey. Properly used it's the Best and Most Healthful *tonic known.* Doc Holliday accepts no substitutes."

They gave him a toy gun to hold and caked so much makeup on him that Doc hardly recognized himself. He felt like a pimp.

The trial itself was fairly short, and the public stood firmly with Doc. He was acquitted on self-defense, and Allen lived, though his arm would give him trouble the rest of his life.

CHAPTER 51

Bang Bang

Denver, Colorado
May 1885

Doc headed back to Denver after the trial. He knew he had to head to the Glenwood Springs in search of the fountain soon. He'd asked people along his travels, but no one knew much about it. It was because of this mystery that Doc began to believe, for the first time, that something truly miraculous might lie there.

Doc checked back into the Windsor, and they agreed to put him up for free so long as once a week he'd stand outside the entrance with a blank-filled shotgun and reenact the 'Shootout at the O.K. Corral' as they'd decided to call it. It wasn't even accurate. They'd pinned up a banner for the hotel in the background, but Doc felt he'd debased himself enough that this final pitiful display wouldn't make a difference in the afterlife. He had become a caricature of himself. *Maybe I always was*, he thought.

After one of these farcical acts on a sunny day in May, Doc retired to Fashion, the hotel bar, where they gave him two drink vouchers after each show.

Doc liked to drink with the air on his cheeks. He stood as a silhouette in the barroom doorway. It was one of the only entrances that did not have an awning above it, and they'd installed swinging doors like back in Arizona. It was a tourist attraction, just like him. He propped himself up against the wood frame, his gaunt figure barely obscuring the stark indigo sunset. Doc's phlegmy cough shook his whole body, and his gray overcoat tails bristled in the dry breeze that arrived around dusk. He was always cold now, even in the spring.

The sun dipped under cloud cover, and for a moment Doc's bone-pallid figure became clear and grisly. The black rings surrounding his eyes made him seem ancient, sinister. He hadn't slept for days, dealing faro, and had only come out three dollars richer. It was all he had to his name, that and his Colt .41 and flask.

It was in this moment of despair that Doc recognized a familiar figure approaching the bar. He was with a woman. Doc had to be sure before he got invested. His insides couldn't take it unless it was real. Then, he was standing right in front of Doc with a great big smile, looking as fit as the day they parted.

"How are you, my friend?" said Wyatt Earp with his deep, booming baritone.

"How did you find me?"

Wyatt smiled. He hugged Doc tightly. It hurt a little, but it was a good kind of hurt, like when he thought of his mother sometimes. It was the kind of pain he always wanted to keep close. "Shit, I just asked the police where I could find the drunkest crack-shot in all of Colorado, and they pointed me to this fancy hotel. You must be doin' all right!"

Doc didn't have the heart to tell Wyatt how things really were. He was hoping Wyatt hadn't seen the show, or at least that he wouldn't mention it. "I am a model of health and well-being," he said with a lilt in his voice that had eluded him for some time. It was energizing to see Wyatt, and he missed his burly presence.

"I'm being rude," said Wyatt, nudging Sadie forward. "This is Mrs. Wyatt Earp."

Doc extended his bony fingers toward her. He tried to control the trembling, but Wyatt noticed. "A pleasure to see you again, Sadie. I'm very glad to see you two so happy. I'm a—"

"Never mind anything else," said Wyatt. "I'm starving. Can we eat?"

"Absolutely." Doc decided not to ask about Celia Ann. Perhaps she'd died or he'd left her in Tombstone, alone in a town they'd set aflame. None of it mattered anymore.

"I'll leave you two alone," said Sadie. "I've no stomach for old man reminiscence and gunfight tales." She took her leave to their room upstairs.

Doc and Wyatt sat down together at a small table. A waiter, wearing a black and white serving outfit, leaned over to take their order.

"I'll have the potato soup and some bread," said Wyatt, handing over the menu.

"Nothing for me," said Doc.

"You sure?"

The waiter walked away.

Doc pulled his silver flask from his coat pocket and put it to his blistering white lips. He poured the whiskey down his throat, burning his ulcers. "I am sustained, Wyatt." His voice echoed as a drawling whisper, unable to speak louder.

"Where's Kate?"

"The lovely and enigmatic Kate disappeared some time ago, though I don't think our reunion would help the matter. She never found you much of a . . ." he trailed off.

"You stickin' around?" asked Wyatt.

"I don't think this climate agrees with me much." Doc heaved violently into his stained handkerchief and swigged more whiskey. It dripped slowly from his ashen mustache.

"You know I could be there when it happens. If you come back."

"Don't think I don't appreciate the ironical nature of expiring in Tombstone, Wyatt. I really do." He realized then that his mind had betrayed him. He had suddenly fallen years into the past. He shook off the thought. "Or wherever you are now. California, right? That's what people tell me. In any case, no. I've got plans."

Wyatt hadn't grown much older or smaller or grayer. He looked like the same man Doc had ridden into battle with. The same man who'd led that ravenous band of outlaws exacting vigilante justice upon the damned. Vengeance treated him well. "You still talkin' 'bout that Indian fountain of yours?"

"I'll outlive you; you'll see. I'll be the oldest child in Colorado." Sweat dripped down his forehead and over his fading blue eyes. He'd lost the rosy color in his cheeks. There was a moment in time when neither one could say a word because it was too hard.

"Where're you looking to get?" asked Wyatt.

Doc lit a cigarette. The sun reappeared, beaming through the window. Smoke glimmered over his face. "You remember when that piss-faced Cowboy nearly stuck you from behind? Morrison, right?"

"I remember you saved me then."

"Saved you?" A trickle of blood spotted his lip.

"You helped me lots more than that, Doc." The potato soup arrived with an oversized spoon. They both chuckled over the lumpy gray meal. "Best hotel in Denver, huh?"

Doc couldn't even think about eating. He'd just shit it right out. He took a drag from his cigarette. "I never did a goddamn thing better than know you."

Wyatt tried to ignore it, but Doc's fragility was so apparent. He nearly excused himself but instead ladled some soup into his mouth.

"How long are you in town for?"

"Just the night," said Wyatt. "We're on our way to see my niece. Wanted to stop in and see you. Didn't like how we left off."

"It's nice to remember old things, isn't it?"

They sat like that for hours. Wyatt ate his soup, and Doc swigged some whiskey when the bartender wasn't looking. They recounted stories of their time on the Arizona plains, and Tombstone, how the newsmen had embellished everything, made them legends of the fading, fabled West. It seemed nothing existed as it had only a few years ago, and they talked about Morgan and how good he was and how funny. It got late, and though Wyatt would have stayed all night, Doc knew he had to leave.

"I think I'll head home now, Wyatt. I think I'm catching a cold or something."

By the bar, a miner with silver dust in his black hair ordered a shot. "Who's that duck lunger over there with Wyatt Earp?"

"Are you crazy? That's Doc Holliday. He'll shoot you straight dead," said the bartender.

"*That's* him? Doesn't look like much no more."

Doc got up out of his chair. He reached for his cane, but Wyatt was already handing it to him. He'd sold its silver handle, and it was more of a walking stick now. Wyatt stood up and shook Doc's hand tightly. "Goodbye, Doc. I hope you find that fountain of yours." Wyatt's eyes welled up with tears. He forced them away with his palm.

"Goodbye, old friend," said Doc. "It will be a long time before we meet again."

CHAPTER 52

How Low

Glenwood Springs, Colorado
May 1887

After a good amount of searching, Doc found a ride to the Glenwood Springs on the Carson stage. He had to share the coach with three other passengers. They all looked just about as sick as he was. Nobody really knew what was on the other side. The stagecoach driver was a tightlipped man, and it was never really good to rattle the shotgunner before a long trip.

The four horses started to tug, and the big golden wheels got rolling. The back wheels were much larger than the front. Doc glared across at a thin man who seemed to fall asleep almost immediately. Doc wished for that kind of illness. He couldn't sleep anymore.

"Excuse me, sleepy gentleman," said Doc, rustling the man's arm.

"What?"

"Do you know what we're in for? Have you been there?"

"Naw, nobody who's gone there has ever come back. Not that I know of anyhow."

"Does it—does it work?" asked Doc. He plucked a cigarette from his coat pocket.

"Could you not?"

Doc nodded.

"It's the land a the Utes." The man's eyes began to close against his will.

"Utes?"

"Indians. They call it 'the cure.'" His head bobbed, trying to stay awake.

"Is there a fountain?"

The man was already asleep. The wagon bumped along the road, and the hot dust and rock spat against the carriage windows. Doc's skin felt scaly and cool. He imagined bathing in the hot springs, the fountain pouring over him, flushing the color back into his chest, his veins, his cock. He imagined being powerful again. He closed his eyes and listened to the sound of rock and wheel. The cabin reeked of death. Doc gasped for breath but found none. His vision radiated white. He tried to call for help, but nothing came out of his swollen throat. He lurched forward and went unconscious.

When he woke, he was alone in the carriage. He stretched his tired arms and unfolded his legs to stand on the soft ground. The horses chewed raw oats from buckets wrapped around their faces, their eyes darting nervously. A warm mist emanated from a nearby lagoon. Doc felt warm for the first time in months. It was dusk, and the sky melted red. Layers of yellow and orange clouds sunk underneath, passing through his clothes. They hung so low to the lagoon that Doc could touch them, but as soon as he did, they dissipated in his hands and turned to dew. He blew the orange flakes off his moist palms and approached the spring. In the middle of it, he saw a fountain.

Doc dropped to his knees. It was not what he'd imagined, but there it was. It had formed out of the earth, dirt and rock and mud and silt all uprooting as a single volcanic force, pushing water up from the spring and misting into the air as a salty powder.

A small, lush valley surrounded him, swallowing everything. It was quiet except for the sounds of the fountain.

Doc crawled closer to the spring, but as he approached, the smell of eggs entered his nostrils. His stomach turned, and he vomited to his side. Still, he crawled forward. The mud clung to his hands, and fat-gutted mosquitoes smacked against his face and sucked on his neck and eyelids. He swatted them off, streaking his cheeks in soil. The closer he got the harder it was to breathe, but he crept forth. His whole life had amounted to this moment, releasing every regret, absolving every sin. He could begin again as a child, as a god, the days of blood and thunder behind him. His chest grew dense. He heaved out blood. It was the cleansing he had sought. He reached the lip of the water. He dipped his hands in. Finally, he would taste the fountain of youth. He thought of Kate, her voice; he could almost hear it. He cupped his hands, allowing the steaming water to fill his palms, caked in the skin of the earth. He lifted the spring water to his mouth, but just as he was about to take a sip, a figure came running in from out of nowhere and smacked the liquid from his fingers. It dribbled slowly through, disappearing back into the spring bed.

Doc snapped out of his trance. He rolled over on his back, the scalding mud spreading over his clothes.

"My boy, what are you doing out here all alone?"

"I'm taking the cure." Doc grew lightheaded. The world seemed thin as wings. He saw himself holding a bottle of whiskey to a flash of lightning; only he was behind the camera. The sky turned black.

"Yes, we'll take care of you here." The man looked back at the carriage. "Careless people," he said, shaking his white-haired head. "Only thinking of themselves." He took Doc's filthy hands in his. "Are you a man of God?"

Doc squinted, his vision blurred. He saw the collar of a Catholic priest. He saw the cross. He remembered his mother's hands. How long her fingers were. He wondered what she really believed.

The priest took a different approach. "Do you know what Ute means? The people who used to live here? The people who found these springs blessed them in their homegrown rituals."

"Indians?" Doc could hardly speak. He held onto the priest as if about to fall. The water soaked into his hair. The sulfur permeated his lungs.

"Land of the sun. Isn't that pretty?"

Doc nodded.

"Let's get you home now, okay?"

"I would like that very much," said Doc. He breathed in the sweet tang of Georgia, knowing nothing would smell like that ever again.

The priest lifted Doc like a newborn into his arms. His feet sunk into the mud, but he seemed adept at extricating himself and soon began to trudge toward a tremendously long building. It was red on top and white on the bottom with hundreds of windows overlooking the spring. Doc had not seen it through all the mist. It loomed above him and he squinted to see the sign ahead. The priest beat forth. Doc could just about make it out. A chill of terror raked his chest. The sign read: Glenwood Springs Sanatorium.

The priest who'd carried him to the sanatorium was Edward Downey. They became quick friends, and every day Downey would accompany Doc to the Glenwood Springs. Upon arrival, his fellow travelers had thought it best to leave Doc where he was until they could find a doctor. He was used to being alone anyway, so he forgave them.

Doc bathed in the pale green water with his shirt off. Small sores sprouted on his shriveling body. His cough deepened. "This is some cure you all have found."

"Has it made you worse?" asked Downey. "I can't quite understand it."

Doc breathed in the sulfuric fumes. They clung to his insides. "Smells more like Hell than Heaven here."

"Have you talked to God a day in your life, John Henry?"

Doc found it funny that the priest called him that. John Henry had been dead for years, a victim of consumption and the bottle and the bullet. Doc waded out of the warm water and into Father Downey's arms, which wrapped him in a soft white towel. They walked together back to the sanatorium. Doc's legs wobbled, and he gripped Father Downey's shoulder, his toes squishing into the black mud.

The sanatorium halls were white and gray and long. There were hundreds of rooms with hundreds of sickbeds, identical and sterile. Each sickness made a different sound. It got so that Doc could walk down the hall and know who was coughing or retching just by the melody of it. A deathly signature. Doc kept up his visits to the spring as long as he could. He found it hard to admit to himself that perhaps there was no miracle fountain. Maybe it was all some lurid dream.

Doc's room was small and white. A window with short blue curtains overlooked the springs. He'd sometimes watch other patients bathe there. Sometimes they would not return the next day. Doc didn't wonder where they went. Every day, even as the months went on, Father Downey visited him, and they spoke of belief and vision.

After everything he'd gone through to get there, the springs only expedited his disease. Galloping consumption began, and the doctors stopped visiting him. They told him they would pray for him, and with what he could muster, Doc laughed. Large, puss-filled sores raked his body. His shoulders slumped down, and he could not take the walks he enjoyed so much any longer. Winter was coming. His knees and ankles swelled up to the size of grapefruits, and his knuckles no longer bent dexterously enough to play cards. He could not eat. His face became vacant; his eyes descended into the black of his cheeks, and his body atrophied under the clean, stiff sheets.

He constantly filled his bedpan as he sweated; breathing became a tedious, vulgar task as graveyard coughs ravaged his body. Some nights, he felt like he was suffocating. He could not sleep or dream, he could only choke, and then as if by some cruel joke, air throbbed through his ulcer-ridden throat, and he would survive the night.

Still, his mind was clear. He sat with Father Downey one November morning. It was bright outside.

"Could you let me see the light?" asked Doc.

Father Downey walked over to the window and opened the drapes a little.

Doc covered his eyes. He was so used to darkness.

"I'm sorry. Would you like me to close them?"

"No," said Doc. His face had taken on a different shape. He no longer resembled his legend. "Please. That's just how I want it to be. It has been far too dark for too long."

Father Downey sat on the bed, his thigh touching the little that remained of Doc Holliday. He held Doc's cold hands in his. "I don't believe a word of it. You have been nothing but light here."

Doc nearly smiled. Then, as if by some miracle, there she was. It was Kate. She'd come just in time. Her hair was long and untamed. She kissed his lips wet.

"I guess it worked," she said. Her voice sounded like melted glass. "You're new again."

Her arms squeezed tightly around his delicate body. He had so many questions for her. They had so much catching up to do. Her hair turned to sand in his fingers, and her lips melted into the sun. The wind lashed through the drapes, and it became night. She was the last thing he saw.

His eyes were closed when he passed. A small sigh released from his lungs. It was all they could hold.

Father Downey remained with Doc for several minutes after his death. A chill ran down his body as he looked around the empty room. All these people he'd talked about—characters in his life, loves, villains, friends. No one had come. He hoped he, at least, had been of some small comfort. Eventually, he brought the nurse in for an official record. "I'm sorry, you'll have to excuse me," said Downey. He left because he couldn't take any more.

The nurse took out a small notepad. She perused the body and the bed. He was so slight, she thought. She reflected for a moment about what she would say and then wrote: "Doc Holliday died in Glenwood Springs, on the 8th of November, with his boots off."

EPILOGUE

Bonus Track: No Bold Villain

John Wentworth

When Wentworth heard of Doc's passing, he followed a group of reporters and Hollideans up to Glenwood Springs to pay their final respects and take pictures of the body. Before most of the other reporters could snap any shots, Wentworth lifted the sheets and put Doc's boots back on his feet. He went on to write the "true" history of Doc Holliday. It became his life's work.

Ike Clanton

Ike And Fin Clanton were charged with cattle rustling and followed by a detective to a ranch south of Arizona. Fin surrendered, but Ike Clanton finally drew his gun. He was shot dead on June 1, 1887.

Perry Mallon

After his brush with Doc Holliday, Mallon moved around a lot. He impersonated a California marshal in Ohio and then severely beat his wife. He served four months in jail because he could not pay the $65 disturbance fee.

Celia Ann Blaylock Earp

Celia Ann returned to Colton, California shortly after Morgan's death. She waited for word from Wyatt, but the two never spoke again. Out of money, she fell back on sex work in Globe, Arizona. On July 3, 1888, Celia Ann overdosed on laudanum and died. Her friend, S.E. Damon, was convinced that it was not an accident. Wyatt Earp did not attend her funeral.

Mary Katherine Horony Cummings

Kate maintained, until her death, that she visited Doc at Glenwood Springs, though no one ever saw her. After Doc's passing, she married George Cummings, a blacksmith. He was a violent alcoholic, and it ended after just one year. She died in Arizona on November 2, 1940. She was 90.

Wyatt Earp

Wyatt Earp worked in saloons, chased the gold rush in Alaska, and finally settled in Los Angeles. Years later, when asked about Doc for the *San Francisco Examiner*, Wyatt said he was a "mad merry scamp with a heart of gold and nerves of steel who . . . stood at my elbow in many a battle to the death. . . . He was a philosopher, but he preferred to be a wag. He was long, lean, and ash-blond and the quickest man with a six-shooter I ever knew." Wyatt remained married to Sadie his entire life and died in 1929 of old age. He was never shot. Not even a scratch.

About the Author

Matthew Di Paoli has been nominated for the Pushcart Prize three times, including 2020. He has won the Wilbur & Niso Smith Adventure Writing Prize for *Holliday*, the Prism Review, 2 Elizabeth's, and Momaya Review Short Story Contests. Matthew earned his BA at Boston College where he won the Cardinal Cushing award and the Dever Fellowship. He received his MFA in Fiction at Columbia University. He has been published in Boulevard, Fjords, Post Road, and Cleaver, among others. He is the author of *Killstanbul* with El Balazo Press and teaches writing in New York City. You can find more at matthewdipaoli.com.

Made in the USA
Columbia, SC
12 April 2024